T0128550

"The lamps are going out all over Europe, we shall not see them lit again in our life-time."

Sir Edward Grey

OTHER NOVELS BY GENE COYLE

The Dream Merchant of Lisbon
The Game of Espionage

No Game for Amateurs
The Search for a Mole on the Eve of WW II

Diamonds and Deceit
The Search for the Missing Romanov Dynasty Jewels

A Spy's Lonely Path

**Nazi Gold, Portuguese Wine, and a
Lovely Russian Spy**

If You Can't Trust a Fellow Spy
A Story of Friendships, Betrayal and Revenge

Everybody Lies in Wartime
A Tale of WW II Espionage in Moscow

LAST VOYAGE ON *THE* DANUBE

A TALE OF PRE-WW II ESPIONAGE AND LOVE

GENE COYLE

authorHOUSE®

AuthorHouse™
1663 Liberty Drive
Bloomington, IN 47403
www.authorhouse.com
Phone: 1 (800) 839-8640

Published by AuthorHouse 01/20/2020

ISBN: 978-1-7283-4358-7 (sc)
ISBN: 978-1-7283-4365-5 (e)

Library of Congress Control Number: 2020901271

Print information available on the last page.

AUTHOR'S NOTE

Several of the characters briefly mentioned in the story, such as British Prime Minister Neville Chamberlain, German Fuhrer Adolf Hitler, famed musician Hoagy Carmichael and former I.U. President Herman Wells are true historical individuals. The other characters and events within this novel are fictional and any resemblance to real people and facts is purely coincidental and unintended.

My thanks to Erica Moore for her editing assistance.

PRINCIPAL CHARACTERS
(In order of appearance)

Arthur Smith – Chicago banker, Indiana University class of 1924 and organizer of the alumni river cruise. Known as an old-fashioned, steady sort of fellow. He wishes to change that life style on this cruise to being more adventurous.

Jan Smith – Arthur's wife. They'd lost their only child, a daughter, to a drunk driver years earlier. She is suffering from a serious illness. The cruise is to celebrate their fifteenth wedding anniversary.

General Fritz von Breithaupt – Commandant of the Wehrmacht regiment posted at Munich, Germany. He comes from a long line of German military generals, is married and has two sons in the Army. He considers himself a true patriot, secretly doubts if Hitler is good for the nation and wonders what he can do to stop Hitler's rise to power.

Tom and Lenora Bishop – He is an insurance executive in Cincinnati, Ohio, I.U. class of 1924. Lenora is his extravagant-spending wife, a widow whom he married a few years after graduation.

Hanna Bishop – She is the beautiful daughter of Lenora from her first marriage. She is seventeen years old, flirtatious and an exhibitionist.

Simone Chevrolet – She is a French chanteuse, class of 1924 and had dated Tom Bishop back in their senior year of college. She is recently divorced and principal owner of a successful Parisian nightclub.

Bob Hall – He is a minor screen writer in Hollywood, currently on location in England, shooting a movie. He attended college with all the others, but didn't graduate in 1924. He is longtime divorced and waiting for his big break.

Mike and Candy Taffe – He is a financial man in New York City, working mostly with Broadway productions, class of 1924. He is of Irish descent out of Boston. Candy is his third and much younger wife.

Fred Hendricks – He is a graduate of the class of 1924 and recently forced out of the Navy as a Lieutenant Commander because of his heavy drinking. The drinking began after the death of his wife in a car accident two years prior to the cruise. He currently makes his living as a stock broker. He has been in London on business just prior to the cruise.

"C" – He is the head of the British Foreign Intelligence Service, MI-6.

Karen Conner – She is a middle-aged American who had met and married her German professor in the 1920s while studying in Munich. He has died and she makes a living by serving as a tour guide when Americans or British are sailing on various cruise lines in Europe. She knows all the best shopping spots in all the tourist locations.

Gestapo Colonel Werner Blickensdorfer – He is a former Munich Police homicide detective who joined the Gestapo upon its creation in 1934. He speaks English, is very competent in his work, well-educated and a loyal Nazi, but career ambitions are his main motivation.

Gestapo Lt. Holger Heinz – He comes from a working class background who had a very difficult time during the hyper-inflation years of the 1920s in Germany. He is a loyal Nazi, but mostly because the Gestapo has given him a good, steady job. He is single and speaks good English.

Mary Beth Jones – She had been a rather dull "plain Jane" during college, the class of 1924, but by her late thirties has blossomed into a charming and very attractive woman. She is a successful author of children's books. She'd been married to an Englishman, but lost him to an illness several years earlier. She's maintained close ties with her father-in-law.

Ivan Bogatyr – He is a handsome, well-off Russian emigre who resides in Paris and is a regular at Simone's nightclub. Peter is single, but is allegedly seeking a wealthy woman to marry. He has a reputation of being willing to do most anything for money.

Captain Johan Ornsdorfer – He is the middle-aged, Austrian captain of the *Danube Princessa*. He is a charming host, but drinks too much. His philosophy is to generally agree with everyone. He is a widower and his fifteen year old daughter, **Hanna**, lives on the ship with him. She is lovely, smart and speaks several languages.

Mikaela LeBlanc – She is a Cajun beauty from New Orleans who does Tarot card readings for a living. She's been in Germany doing predictions for various high-level Nazi officials. She does card readings for five passengers on the ship, which seem strange predictions, but then they do seem to be coming true as the cruise continues.

Maurice Garnier – He is a French national who'd studied at Indiana University for two years in the early twenties and came to know many of the other American passengers. He is the Socialist mayor of a small French city and a firm believer in communism. He is a bachelor.

Inga Snelson – She is the lovely, thirty year old Swedish masseuse on the ship. As she and Kinley are the only two female staff on the ship, they are good friends.

Miles Pembroke – He is a delightful, sixty year old Englishman and the second son of a minor English nobleman, who mostly just travels around the world enjoying life. His lovely female traveling companion of half his age, **Elizabeth**, is allegedly his daughter.

Professor Timothy Langweilig – He is an elderly professor at the University of Munich and occasionally sails on the *Danube Princessa*, to give lectures to the passengers on the history of the areas in which they are passing.

Joe Jefferson – He is an African-American piano player, who has been living and working for several years in Paris. He is booked to provide entertainment on the cruise and is a big hit with Mr. and Mrs. Smith, as well as with Mary Beth Long.

Princess Caroline Landschknecht – She is a young, German widow from a small principality near Leipzig. This is the third time she has taken this cruise over the holidays and allegedly is greatly interested in sex. She is listed in the Gestapo files as being anti-Nazi.

Captain Brunner, the Chief of the Homicide Department of the Bratislava City Police – He comes aboard the Danube Princessa to investigate a murder. He considers detaining the ship at Bratislava for several days to continue his investigation.

Mr. Tristan Kensington-Smyth of the Passport Control Office, British Embassy Athens – He is the MI-6 officer in Athens, operating undercover.

Mr. Winslow – The British MI-6 officer posted in Lisbon, Portugal.

CHAPTER 1
September 1, 1938 Chicago

The highly polished, black Duesenberg pulled smoothly to the curb in front of the First National Bank in downtown Chicago. Mr. Arthur Smith, one of its younger vice presidents stepped out of the backseat of the expensive vehicle and headed for the door, with no further words for his chauffeur. He wore a dark-gray fedora, which matched nicely his gray, three-piece suit, and he carried a small, executive-sized Italian leather briefcase. It had his first and last initial stamped in gold on the top of the case. Tradition was that a person with such a quality briefcase would have all three initials on it, but as his middle name was Samuel, he'd decided that that wasn't a good idea for him.

Smith looked to be in his early forties with just a few extra pounds around the middle of his five foot ten inch frame. He had a few streaks of gray showing below the brim of his hat, but he had a "youngish face" as his wife called it. His face did have several permanent wrinkles across his forehead, giving him the look of a man always in deep concentration. He walked gracefully and athletically, even though he'd never played on any organized sports team, even back in high school. Smith gave a cheerful smile and said "Good morning" to Mark, the elderly doorman for the bank in his dark-red uniform as he opened the door for Vice-President Smith. Arthur had been saying things to Mark ever since he'd been a teenager and would come occasionally to the bank to visit his father. His dad had also risen to the rank of vice-president there in 1926. The police had kindly listed his father's death as a "misadventure", not a suicide, as they'd found no note near the open window that sad "Black Tuesday" in October 1929.

While Smith always spoke to his doorman, he was oblivious to an elderly lady thirty feet from the bank entrance, selling apples from a battered wooden tray hung from her neck with a piece of rope. The recovery of FDR's New Deal hadn't reached everyone by 1938. He also paid little notice to the hundreds of Chicagoans on the sidewalk hurrying to get to work in nearby office buildings. Smith could spot the smallest anomaly in a corporate spread sheet, but he was fairly blind to things that didn't directly concern him. He'd inherited his father's philosophy on life – good things came to those who worked hard and minded their own business. That philosophy had brought him a very good career in banking, a good wife and a circle of friends whose company he enjoyed. His life was orderly. That was a word he would have used had he been asked to choose one single word to describe his world on that fine, sunny first day of September, 1938. His personal world, however, was about to dramatically change and in twelve months, the world for millions of people would also turn disorderly. Everyone thought the Great War had ended in November,

1918, but it had really just had a twenty-year pause until part II started.

Smith had arrived at ten minutes till nine, as he did every work day. Even though he rarely ever personally met with a bank customer, he believed it a good example for others that he be at his desk before the bank opened to the public at 9:00 a.m. Arthur and his wife, Jan, lived only ten minutes away on fashionable Astor Street, near the intersection with North Lakeshore Drive, so it was easy to time his arrival. Other bankers, captains of industry and also just plain, lazy rich people who'd inherited their wealth and had managed not to lose it all during the Depression were his neighbors.

As he came to his secretary's desk in the outer office to his own on the fifth floor of the bank building, he again smiled and said, "Good morning, Kelsey."

She quickly handed him several telephone messages that had already come in that morning from outside the building, or internal calls from more junior bank officials who wanted to speak with him. Kelsey suspected that at least a few of the latter phoned so early in the morning simply to show Mr. Smith they were at their desks before he was. Kelsey's day started at 8:00 a.m. so that she could have papers, memos and reports that Mr. Smith would need each morning neatly arranged on his desk before his arrival. She was tall, slender and blonde, twenty-seven years old and very efficient. She almost never wore earrings or necklaces, which Smith at first had thought odd of any woman, but he'd finally realized that with such a beautiful face, jewelry simply wasn't needed. He had no thoughts of anything improper happening with her outside of the workplace, but he admitted, at least to himself, that it was pleasant having such an attractive woman around the office. She always had a single flower stem in a glass vase on the corner of her desk. It was her one indulgence to herself, replaced every two or three days as the previous flower faded. Today she had a bright red rose in her vase. Some days he'd comment on what flower she had. That morning he did not, which told her that he already had important things on his mind.

"Good morning, sir. Your first appointment is not until ten. Details are in the folder on your desk. And then your wife will be picking you up at eleven to accompany her to her doctor's appointment. Would you like a cup of coffee this morning?"

"Yes, thank you." He didn't have to tell her how he liked his coffee. She'd been bringing him a cup just about every work morning since he'd been promoted to his vice-president's position fifteen months earlier. He was only one of seven vice-presidents, still it was a senior position in the bank. According to the water cooler rumor mill, he would be rising even higher in the coming years, particularly as it appeared that the Great Depression was finally nearing its end.

An objective assessment of Arthur Smith by anyone who knew him well would be that he was quite efficient and productive, not overly cheerful, but always pleasant. In sum, he was the epitome of a successful banker and one who loved his wife dearly. He never forgot her birthday or their anniversary. He was the type of man that upper management would choose to send to represent the bank at difficult negotiations, but not necessarily the best choice to organize the office Christmas party.

Once he'd returned a few phone calls and finished his coffee, he took from his briefcase a folder and then buzzed for Kelsey to come into his office. He handed her the folder. "Here is a list of thirty-five people that I went to college with at Indiana University back in the early twenties with their current home or business address. Please send each of them a telegram this morning. The text of the message to be sent is also in the folder. Take a quick look at that page, just to make sure you can read my bad handwriting."

She opened the folder. His last comment was a joke between them, as he actually had the most precise and beautiful handwriting she'd ever seen. She quickly read through it and commented, "Oh, how wonderful. You and Mrs. Smith are going to take a holiday cruise in Europe, down the Danube River!"

"Yes, and hopefully with some old friends from our college days. So, get those sent out today please and here is a stack of the cruise brochures that you can mail out to those who respond positively back to you by phone or telegram."

A somber look came to her face. "I trust none of the political problems going on over in Europe between Germany and England will interfere with your cruise."

"I'm sure they won't. None of that posturing by Hitler has anything to do with America."

"That isn't what my grandfather who was born in Hamburg, Germany says concerning Hitler. He says there will eventually be another great war."

Arthur smiled. "Well, normally I wouldn't doubt your grandfather, but President Roosevelt just gave a speech last week in New York City where he said that he expected that the major powers of Europe will peacefully work out their differences. In any case, America won't get involved in any more foreign wars."

She gave him a shrug of the shoulders, which he knew meant that she still knew her grandfather was right, but Mr. Smith could believe whatever he wanted. She returned to her desk to start work on the telegrams. Kelsey noted that several people were in England and France. Smith began reviewing the materials for his 10:00 a.m. appointment. Kelsey returned a bit later and showed him the typed draft of his telegram, to see if he had any last minute changes to add. He read it aloud:

Dear Friends. Please join me and Jan for a European holiday reunion cruise this December as we retrace our honeymoon cruise of 1919. We will gather in Paris on the 20th, then on to Munich for Christmas. We board the *Danube Princessa* on the evening of the 25th at Regensburg and we'll celebrate New Year's Eve in Vienna to welcome in 1939. The cruise will end in Budapest. We will then fly to Athens and sail home from there. We're sailing from NYC on the 13th for Le Havre on the *SS Normandie*, but make whatever plans you wish to reach Paris and after Budapest. Hope to get as many of our old friends together for this journey as possible. Please contact my secretary, Miss Kelsey Biers, at the phone number or address listed below and she will immediately mail you a brochure from the travel company about the cruise.

Sincerely, Arthur and Jan.

He looked up at his secretary, "Well, does it need to say anything else?"

"Not a thing, sir. I'll get these right out." She gave him one of her lovely smiles. "Mrs. Smith must be very excited." She took a step toward the door, but then turned back, smiled again and added, "And don't worry, I won't let anyone here at the bank know what an old romantic you really are – retracing your honeymoon cruise." She didn't wait for a response from him and closed his door as she exited the room.

He laughed at the thought of anybody thinking of him as "romantic." He reached for his phone and dialed his wife. They had a live-in maid in their three-story mansion, but Jan often answered the phone herself as she did that morning.

"Hello," she answered.

"How are you feeling this morning, dear?"

"Just fine. I was up a bit in the night with a headache, but I'm better now after a little breakfast." They'd slept in separate rooms for the last six months, as her headaches and sleeplessness had increased, so there'd be no danger of him awakening her when she did finally get to sleep.

"Well, hopefully after all those recent tests, this specialist today will be able to tell you just what it is you're suffering from – and then you can start the treatment to make you well."

Jan wasn't as optimistic as her husband about getting better, but conceded that after feeling poorly for six months, she wasn't in an optimistic mood about many things. "We'll see."

He could hear her depression over the phone line. "Well, I'm so confident you're about to have a real change that I had Kelsey go ahead and send out the river cruise invitations this morning. In just over three months, we'll be floating down the Danube River, drinking champagne with old friends and dancing late into the night as we did in 1919!"

She laughed. "Artie, we only danced one time on our entire honeymoon trip and I had to physically threaten you to get even that dance, so don't go talking about dancing the night away as we did back then." They both laughed.

"We can discuss that topic later," he replied. "You're going to pick me up at the front of the bank at eleven?"

"Yes, we'll be there at eleven sharp. Now, go make some money. Bye, dear."

"Bye, sweetheart." He leaned back in his expensive leather chair and hoped that his optimism would be proven in a few hours. He reminisced about how he'd met Jan at an Army dance in spring 1917 and how he'd been madly in love with her since the end of that first night. She was going to enter the University with him, but then their daughter came along and Jan opted to be a fulltime mom. Further thoughts about the love of his life were interrupted by

Kelsey knocking on his door and entering without waiting for a reply.

"Research just dropped off a few more papers for you to read before your 10:00 a.m. meeting with that consortium wanting to build new apartment buildings down on the south side."

"Ah, thank you Kelsey. I assume you've already read through them. Anything really worth my bothering?"

"Why, Mr. Smith, I would never take the liberty of reading anything sent here marked 'private' for you."

He smiled. "You better go look in a mirror when you leave here. Your nose is getting longer. Talk young lady!"

She smiled back and then gave him a quick oral summary of the papers from Research.

"In other words, I don't really need to read them."

"No, sir." She started to leave and once again, stopped. "Don't worry, I'll get you out of the meeting in plenty of time for you to be down on the street at five of eleven to meet your wife. And I hope you'll be getting good news today."

He hadn't shared all the details with her, but they were close enough that he'd made her aware that some mysterious illness was afflicting his wife in recent months. Kelsey had been instructed that any time his wife phoned he was to be interrupted, regardless of with whom he was meeting.

Dr. Henke was in his late forties, but prematurely and completely white-headed. Worrying about his patients had left his face quite creased and wrinkled. A Harvard Medical School graduate, he was considered one of the premier doctors in the Chicago area. He began with a few minutes of typical patient chat-chat about the unusually nice weather they'd been having and whether Mr. Smith had managed to get out to any Chicago Cubs games as the season had been winding down. "I'm telling you, the Cubs are going to catch the Pirates in these closing days and take the championship."

"Let's hope so," Mr. Smith politely replied.

The doctor gave a smile, then opened the medical file on the desk in front of him. "Well, let's get down to business. We had a number of tests done on you Jan about two weeks back. I received yesterday morning the test results and analysis from the specialist I had sent you to see, to try to see if we could figure out what's been causing these constant headaches and the other symptoms you've described to me." He looked up from the file at the two anxious faces before him. There were times when he hated being a doctor. This was one of them. His face tightened. "Actually, I received the results last Friday and I then asked that the specialist have all the samples retested just to make sure no error had been committed at the laboratory." There was a long silence.

Mr. Smith spoke, "And the results are?"

"Jan, you're suffering from glioblastoma – that's the

fancy medical term for a brain tumor. I'll come back to more of a description of that ailment in a minute, but I don't want to prolong this any more than necessary." He closed the file and turned his face directly to her. "The medical community doesn't really know what causes this condition and therefore has no real treatment for it." He paused for several long seconds. "And don't start wondering whether coming to me sooner would have made a difference – it wouldn't. Our experience is that once you have this malady, you have it, and there is no corrective treatment."

Jan spoke. "So, what exactly does 'no treatment' mean, doctor?"

"Predicting the future is never easy or certain, but I'd say that you have four to six months to live. Maybe you'll have a few more months than that, and there are on record a few unexplainable cases of a person living another four or five years, but I'd be lying to you if I told you that you realistically had beyond six months."

"And how will I feel in the coming months? Will these headaches continue or even worsen?"

"Experience has shown that in the coming months you'll feel about as you do now. Perhaps you'll feel more tired towards the end, and I can prescribe you a drug which will lessen any pain that you might feel... in the final stages."

The doctor had not had to deliver such bad news to too many patients in his career – usually a prognosis came with at least a slight hope for recovery – but he was impressed with how stoically the couple was taking this dark news. He picked up the file. "Excuse me for just a few minutes, I want to get you a fact sheet on what we do know about your condition." He actually just wanted to give the couple time alone to absorb what he'd just told them.

For the first minute, they just sat in silence while Arthur held her hand. A few tears started down both their faces. "This just doesn't seem fair does it, dear?"

"No, it doesn't," replied Jan. "We lost Jane in that silly automobile accident. And now…" She was crying harder and couldn't say anything further. He handed her his handkerchief.

Finally, he spoke. "What you say? Shall we go ahead with the cruise? I don't see any point in simply sitting around on Astor Street these final months. Let's be adventurous."

"Yes, let's go," she responded without any hesitation. "No sense just watching it snow in Chicago in my final weeks. I know you've never liked snow," she teased the born and bred Chicagoan. They both managed a little laugh.

"Yes, let's go ahead with our second honeymoon. We'll check with the doctor, but if he sees no problem, we'll go. We could even go sooner."

She shook her head, negatively. "No, you've just sent out all those telegrams and the plans for that cruise ship have all been worked out for late December. I think New Year's Eve in Vienna sounds very romantic. But let's just keep my condition our secret, alright? I don't want everyone on the ship telling me every hour how sorry they are."

"Of course. We'll just keep this to ourselves. And you can have all the dances you want on the cruise!"

"Can I get that in writing?" she jokingly asked.

"Certainly, but seriously, we both should look at

these coming months as a time to be adventurous, to try new things."

The doctor knocked on the door and slowly opened it. "Any further questions come to mind?"

"Just one," replied Jan. "Is there any reason I can't sail to Europe and then take a Danube River cruise in late December?"

He was taken aback slightly with the question. It wasn't one that he'd expected. "I'll check with the specialist for his thoughts, but I can't think of any medical reason not to go. Show some good sense about overly exerting yourself on the journey, but sitting in the lounge of a ship, drinking a little champagne and indulging in whatever food you like… well, that sounds like a wonderful way to, uh, spend Christmas. Do you have a specific trip in mind?"

"Yes," replied Arthur. "We've been planning a journey with some old college friends that will start in Paris and finish in Budapest."

"That sounds lovely."

"I have one more question, a typical one I suspect," began Mr. Smith. "I don't mean to insult you or this specialist, but are there any other specialists around the country that we should consult, just to be certain? I hate to say it, but money is no object."

"No insult at all. That's a natural question. Unfortunately, this man I used is the expert on this medical condition. He's the doctor that other doctors around the country come to for a second opinion."

Jan rose from her chair. "Well, thank you doctor. I'll

check in with you before we start the cruise, but if there is nothing else to discuss at the moment, we'll be on our way."

"I'm going to prescribe a medication that might help you sleep better at night and deal with the headaches, but otherwise I'll just see you in early December before you start that trip. But do call immediately if you have any real change in how you feel." He didn't express how sorry he was. He'd been practicing medicine long enough to know that patients very quickly got tired of hearing that line.

Once back in the outer office, Mr. Smith asked to use the receptionist's phone.

"Kelsey, it's Arthur. I'm taking the afternoon off. I'll see you in the morning."

"Of course, Mr. Smith. I'll take care of anything that might come up yet today. I'll see you in the morning." She knew immediately it had to have been bad news at the doctor's. In fifteen months, he'd never once before referred to himself as "Arthur."

As the two rode the elevator down to the street level, Arthur spoke, "How about we go have a nice lunch somewhere?"

She smiled, "Well, I suppose I could clear my calendar for lunch with such a handsome man – as long as my husband doesn't find out." They both laughed. She thought for a moment about which restaurant. "How about that Irish place, down on the south side, that we used to go to when we first moved to Chicago?" "Good lord, you mean The Dubliner? What brought that place to mind? I'm not sure it's even still in business."

"Oh, I was just feeling nostalgic. We can ask Charles

when we get down to the car. He'll know if it's still open, or of another good Irish restaurant near there."

Ten days later, Smith was reading an article in the Chicago Tribune about the big Nazi Party rallies and speeches that had been going on for several days in Nuremberg, Germany. He didn't normally pay much attention to foreign affairs, unless they were events that might affect the U.S. stock market or his bank's business affairs. The paper extensively described the massive and well-organized Nazi rallies, the fanaticism of the speakers and the thousands of attendees. Arthur always took descriptions of anything in the Trib with a grain of salt. He thought to himself that one could say about the same things of the people at the 1932 Republican Party Convention in Chicago, which he himself had attended. Most of the speakers there spoke in hyperbole and tried to stir the crowd to a frenzy – such were political rallies. He didn't think much of Hitler, but doubted the petty territorial disagreements would turn into a war. Surely, all nationalities of Europe could still remember the horrific results of the Great War. A miserable war, of which Smith himself had been an unhappy participant in 1918. Besides, there was now a League of Nations, or some such organization, that was supposed to peacefully settle international disputes. No, he couldn't see any reason for the Indiana group not to take their trip down the Danube River in late December.

September 30, 1938 London

British Prime Minister Neville Chamberlain came down the stairway from his plane at Heston Airfield, just west of London, on a gray and rainy afternoon and stepped over to a bank of microphones. He'd just returned from meeting with German leader, Adolf Hitler, in Munich. Hitler had demanded that the German populated areas of Czechoslovakia, the Sudetenland, be given over to Germany. Chamberlain pulled from his inner coat pocket a document, held it high and said to a vast radio audience anxiously awaiting news of the negotiations: "I believe it is peace for our time!"

At MI-6 headquarters, the Chief of the Service, known as C, nodded to an aide to switch off the radio. He and a few of his senior officials had been listening to the Prime Ministers' speech from the aerodrome. Not that the result was completely unexpected, but still, it was disheartening. C was the first to speak. "Disgraceful. We've just sold the Czechs down the river, and for what, the delusion that this will avoid war with Germany?" He took a large sip from his cut crystal glass, filled with first-rate single malt Scotch whisky.

"Well, it wasn't just Chamberlain," added his deputy. "The French Prime Minister, Daladier, had already told the Czech government that they wouldn't live up to the treaty between the two countries and take any military action if Hitler did invade the Sudetenland."

"And the Poles and Hungarians are both angling

for Czech territory as well," commented the head of the European Department.

C nodded in agreement, but verbally replied, "It's just damn cowardly on the part of Chamberlain. He foolishly thinks that you can negotiate with a street thug like Hitler. He and his fellow Nazis are pure evil. Had our PM shown courage, the French might have done the right thing as well. Couldn't have been a clearer case of good vs evil than if it had been a Sunday school exercise!"

One junior fellow in the room, hesitatingly remarked, "I'm not sure he really could have decided otherwise. The public simply has no stomach for another war. We won the last war against Germany, but no one wants another one. And the state of the British Army is deplorable."

C gave him a withering look and didn't even bother responding to him. Speaking to all, he stated solemnly that "We have avoided a war today, but one is coming. All departments of MI-6 must start preparing first thing tomorrow for a war against the Nazis. We must begin developing good sources within the German government and military."

CHAPTER 2
October 1, 1938 Munich, Germany

At a German Army base on the edge of Munich, a general, several colonels and various junior officers of the Wehrmacht had gathered that Saturday evening in the officer's club. The club had been in that same building since before the Franco-Prussian war of 1870. The dark, wood-paneled walls were full of paintings, swords and military memorabilia celebrating victories or bravery in losses over a seventy-five year period. The officers were toasting Hitler's great victory in obtaining the Sudetenland without having to fire a shot. A few of the younger officers were saddened that they had lost a chance for glory on the battlefield, but the older officers, especially ones who'd fought in the trenches during the Great War, were happy that no one had to die that week in battle.

"General Breithaupt, how soon do you think a war against France and England will begin?" asked a young lieutenant, who'd been drinking heavily.

"Well, it won't start until you're sober again Karl, so it won't be this week," he tactfully replied with a smile. Many of the others laughed at the General's remark. General Fritz von Breithaupt was the most senior officer present and looked as if he'd come straight off one of the oil paintings on the wall. He was tall with a fencing scar on his left check and was still at the same weight as when he'd made captain. His hair was mostly gray and cropped short. He had blue-gray eyes and a very typical North German face. His appearance alone commanded respect and when he spoke, an audience of ten or a hundred men knew he was a leader.

He was actually rather saddened by the whole Sudetenland affair, as he thought it showed how reckless Hitler was willing to be. Had France and England called Hitler's bluff over the province and the German Army had had to militarily conquer the Czech territory, he believed it would have been a bitter and close battle. He knew better than most how limited were the resources available to the Wehrmacht at that time. Sometimes a brilliant strategy won a war, but it also required bullets, artillery shells and rations, as well as trucks to move them and men to fire the rifles. He was too smart to express such pessimistic thoughts in front of the other officers, but he didn't share their enthusiasm for a possible war against other major European powers — a war which he feared that Hitler was knowingly leading the nation towards. His family had been providing generals going back to Frederick the Great; he was a well-educated, wealthy member of the Junker class of Prussians. There was no question of his bravery or his loyalty to Germany, but having fought in the Great War, he knew well the human sacrifices that came with modern warfare. He appreciated the Nazis rebuilding the German Army over the previous five years, but he'd hoped that once

Hitler had come to power in 1933 that he would transition into a more traditional politician compared to his fanatical rantings in the late twenties and the start of the thirties. So far, that had not happened.

On Sunday morning, General Breithaupt slept late, as he often did on that one day of the week, even if he hadn't been out drinking the previous night. He finally sat down at the breakfast table around ten and his wife immediately had breakfast on the table. Monday through Saturday there were two corporals in their house to cook and serve, but on Sundays, they preferred some privacy. Leila was in fact an excellent cook and she enjoyed Sundays when she had her kitchen all to herself. She'd been the ideal officer's wife for many years. She'd happily stayed home to raise their two sons, knew how to be gracious to his superiors and their wives and since he'd become a general, she was kind and helpful to his junior officers' wives.

Midway through the meal, his wife inquired as to how the celebrations had gone the night before. "I suppose everyone was quite pleased with Herr Hitler's success?"

"A few junior officers were disappointed that in the end there had been no battles, but yes, everyone was quite impressed that Hitler had outmaneuvered France and England to get the Sudetenland. I fear that the Wehrmacht will soon have no control over the "Little Corporal" and he will become ever more adventurous. Such is the hand that Fate has dealt to Germany." He shook his head from side to side to express his pessimistic view of what was coming.

Leila sighed heavily as she finished her coffee. "Well,

there's nothing that the Wehrmacht or you can do. You're a general, but he is the elected leader of our country."

He remained silent for several long seconds before enigmatically replying. "Maybe there isn't, but maybe there is."

A car then pulled up near their front door. She rose from the table, looked out a window and waved. "Jurgen has arrived."

Jurgen was the older of their two sons, both of whom were junior officers in the Wehrmacht. Ironically, both were fanatical supporters of Hitler, so the parents had to be careful what they said, even in front of their own children. His arrival thus brought to a close any further discussion of Hitler and the Nazi Party.

With the Munich Pact, Hitler had promised British Prime Minister Chamberlain that the Sudetenland would be Germany's last territorial demand for expansion. Approximately ten days later, Hitler summoned General von Breithaupt and a small group of other senior officers to a conference at Army Headquarters in Berlin. Fuhrer Hitler personally addressed this secret meeting and gave them the date of March 15 as the day that the German Army would move in and take control of the rest of Czechoslovakia – so as to provide the German people "lebensraum" – "living space." Hitler often spoke in his speeches about this need and the right of the great Teutonic people to expand Germany's current borders. General Breithaupt and his Bavarian Corps were assigned a key role in the planned attack.

Upon General Breithaupt's return to Munich two days later, he did not share this military plan with his wife, but she could see that he was quite agitated about something, and he remained so over the next several weeks. Having been married for several decades she knew when it was best to just leave him to his own thoughts. He would spend hours alone every evening in his den, taking various books from his massive collection which covered two whole walls. Mostly, he was reading about past, great leaders of Germany, like Frederick the Great and Bismarck. After reading, he would then sit, smoking his pipe and staring into the flames of the wood fire while he thought. The General was considered one of the best strategists and planners in the German Army. The corps under his command would lead the March invasion of Czechoslovakia.

At first, he actually felt guilty that he was even contemplating disloyalty to his beloved Wehrmacht, of which he'd been a member since he was seventeen years old. His father had been a general and his father before him. The Breithaupts had served the German state with honor for many generations, but as he continued to contemplate his dilemma over several days, he finally decided that Hitler's Germany was no longer his Germany. He'd always given his loyalty to the state, and always would, but Hitler was another matter. As a matter of principle, he finally decided that he could act – but bringing himself to actually commit an act of treason was another matter. As a mental exercise, he went ahead and contemplated how he would do it, if he did actually act.

Chicago

By mid-October, Smith had received positive replies from ten of his old college classmates, which with spouses had the number of travelers up to seventeen. He and Jan brought the total to nineteen and he still expected positive responses from a few other old friends. The ship had room for sixty passengers, so the Indiana alumni group would perhaps make up almost half of the ship.

After dinner one evening at their home, Arthur and Jan went and sat on the sofa by the fireplace to have coffee. He opened a leather folder and together they looked over the list of those who to date had committed to the journey. They discussed who they remembered and what had happened to various old college friends over the past 15 years.

"Oh, this is marvelous," she said. "Our Danube River cruise reunion is shaping up very nicely. I see that Tom and Lenora Bishop are coming, and they're bringing their daughter, Hanna. How old do you think she is now?"

"Hmm. Let's see, she was maybe four when Tom married Lenora, so Hanna must be seventeen or so now. When he was up to Chicago on business six months back and we had lunch, he showed me a picture of her. She's turned into quite a lovely young lady." He didn't tell Jan that Tom had also shared with him his comment about how every man in Cincinnati also found her very attractive and this had caused a few problems. Tom hadn't gone in to any details, so he wasn't quite sure exactly what "problems" there had been.

"You know, Tom's never talked about it and always referred to her back when they'd first met as the Widow Lenora, but I still remember that cousin of hers getting very intoxicated at their wedding reception and talking about Lenora's first husband as if he was still alive somewhere. I've always wondered if he really just ran off and abandoned her and the child," speculated Jan.

"I have no idea and I don't care. That was long ago and none of our business."

"I suppose you're right, but I'm glad her marriage to Tom has worked out."

Arthur didn't respond. From a few other comments Tom had made to him that day, he wasn't sure that things between Tom and Lenora were in fact all that great, but saw no reason to burden his wife with such speculation about the other couple. They spent a half hour exchanging comments about who all was making the journey with them.

"I'm having trouble placing a few of these folks," she commented. Who is Simone Chevrolet?"

"She was that attractive French girl, studying in the Music School. A singer as I recall, though I can't quite put a face to her."

Jan gave him a dubious look. "You're telling me you can't remember the face, or any other parts, of a beautiful, young French woman!"

He gave her a smile. "It's sort of coming back to me now. I recall that she was often going out with Tom Bishop in his senior year."

"And what has become of her in these intervening years?"

"She went back to France, married and I read somewhere that she has become quite a well-known chanteuse on the Parisian nightclub scene."

"Oh, look," Jan exclaimed. "Bob Hall is coming. Is he still writing or whatever he does out in Hollywood?"

"It may be more 'whatever', but yes, he's still making a living out in Los Angeles."

"What do you mean by that statement?"

"I mean, in his Christmas card of two years back, he said he was still doing screen writing for movies, but have you ever seen his name in the credits of any movie?" You go to the Roxie two or three times per month and you sit there for some reason till the very end of the credits. Have you ever once seen his name listed?"

"Well, no, but maybe he writes under a different name than Bob Hall. Maybe that isn't exotic-sounding enough for Hollywood," she optimistically replied. "I see that he cabled his response from England. I wonder what he's doing over there."

"I presume that if they're shooting a movie over in England, they take along a writer in case last minute changes are needed."

"That must be quite exciting, getting to travel around the world making movies."

Arthur pointed further down the list. "How's this for exotic? Candy. Mr. Michael and Mrs. Candy Taffe of New York."

"Candy? That wasn't his wife's name the last time

we were in New York City and had dinner with Michael and his wife, was it?"

He smiled. "No, apparently he has a new one."

"Is this Candy his second or his third?"

"Must be at least his third. Good thing he makes lots of money, since he shares it with so many people," he added with a big smile.

She slapped his arm. "Behave yourself." She turned back to studying the list. "Oh, look, Freddy Hendricks is coming. Is he still in the Navy, dear?"

"No, he left the Navy a year or so after his wife died in that car wreck. And from what I heard at the Club one day recently, he hasn't been sober since her death and that's why the Navy finally 'suggested' he retire. They gave him a medical retirement, so they could quietly ease him out the door, and he wouldn't be an embarrassment anymore."

"That's such a shame. He was always such a delightful fellow. I see that it's just him listed. Sad that he's traveling alone, since his wife…" Her voice trailed off. She realized she was heading into an awkward topic, given that in another four or five months, her Arthur would also be traveling alone. "Any idea what he's doing now?"

"Not in the least, but it will be good to see him. This trip will be such fun to catch up with all these people from our youthful days back in college." He reached over and gave her right hand a squeeze and then they both remained silent as they stared at each other, until a tear started to form in one of his eyes, so he immediately stood up. "I'm feeling sleepy. Let's make it an early night." He'd promised her immediately after the last visit to the doctor's that there would be no tears over her final months.

"Yes, I'm feeling sleepy myself. Let's go to bed." They headed up to their bed in the Master Bedroom. Ever since her diagnosis back at the beginning of September, they'd returned to sleeping together, whether it affected her sleep or not.

Munich, Germany

On the morning of November 11, General Breithaupt was reading the Volkischer Beobachter over breakfast. The entire front page carried stories of "spontaneous uprisings" by loyal Germans against Jewish stores and homes throughout Germany over the previous two days. According to the article, the police in various cities had stood by and let the "will of the people" be expressed against the disloyal Jews. Hundreds of the "Untermensch" had been killed and thousands had been arrested because of their betrayal of the Fatherland. The General remembered many Jews who had served around him in the trenches of the Great War – and that they had bravely shed their blood and died for Germany. How were they now "disloyal" citizens? "I saw many Jews die in the trenches," he said to his wife. "Their blood looked red and German to me in 1918!" And how did all of these riots happen to spontaneously break out on the same day around the country, he wondered?

He showed the front page to his wife and softly

uttered "ganz quatsch", utter nonsense, to her, so that his staff in the kitchen could not hear him.

"The paper says that the riots were spontaneously triggered when a young Jew in Paris went to our Embassy and shot one of our diplomats two days ago," commented his wife.

"Oh, the shooting of von Rath? I heard at the office yesterday that he was a fairy, as was the young Jew, and that the shooting was nothing more than some lover's quarrel. Did the newspaper mention they were both homosexuals? No, I expect not!"

His wife shifted her eyes toward the kitchen, reminding him to keep his voice down. He did lower his voice as he added, "I will not sit by and watch this man ruin my country."

She nodded in agreement with him, but then shrugged her shoulders, indicating that she didn't see what they could do.

This outrage against perfectly loyal Germans was the final straw for General Fritz von Breithaupt. "I have been giving this some thought since my return from Berlin. Tell the cook that we're going out tonight for dinner. We shall talk on the way to the restaurant." He then stood, came over to her side of the table and kissed her on the cheek as he had every morning for several decades of their marriage, at least when he was at home and not out with his beloved soldiers.

She was confused, but knew it was best to wait till that night to hear what was on his mind. "Alright, dear. You have a good day at the base and watch what you say around the office." In recent weeks, the General had become less guarded in his critical remarks about Hitler and his political decisions.

She was beautifully dressed when he returned home at seven. He changed into civilian clothing and then they were out the door. Normally, he had a chauffeured staff car at his disposal, but he was known to enjoy driving and often went out on nonofficial drives with himself behind the wheel. He did so that evening.

Once they were well on their way to the center of Munich, he restarted his conversation from the morning. "I cannot sit by and allow that maniac destroy my country. And that circle of fanatics around him are even crazier than he is!"

"But what can you do, darling? I know you're a general, but he is head of the nation and the Gestapo is everywhere. You'd never get near him with a gun."

He looked at his wife as if she was crazy. "You are correct about that, but I'm not planning on shooting him! I'm just going to make sure that he loses his first battle and then hopefully the German people and the Army will see what a failure he is."

She again looked puzzled.

"If Hitler has his way, he'll plunge Germany into a massive war against all the other major European countries – a war that Germany cannot win. But if his planned invasion of Czechoslovakia is a failure, then his reign will soon end. It will cost many German lives, but it's the only way to avoid a massive disaster later for the German people." He paused for many long seconds. "I intend to warn the British

Government of Hitler's plans and timetable for the invasion of Czechoslovakia. The British, French and Czech armies can thus be ready for him in March."

She stared at her husband in silence. How could he be contemplating insuring a defeat of his beloved German Army? And what if their two sons would be in such a battle?

"I have prepared a letter to be sent to a well-known British General I once met – General Strickland. He's retired now, but I'm sure he'll know the right people to pass my letter along to once he reads it. We must find an Englishman we can trust to carry my letter to England and see that it's delivered to Strickland. I did not put my actual name in the letter, as that is too risky. I have simply said that I am a senior officer in the Wehrmacht, and I have proposed that they send someone to secretly meet with me one night in late December here in Munich."

"And how do we find an Englishman who will do this for you?"

"We're going tonight to a restaurant that I know is frequented by foreigners, in particular by the English. Perhaps someone will speak German. Otherwise, my dear, you will have to use your English to translate for me. We'll start out by simply being sociable with him or a couple, until I have a feel for them. If my impression is good, then I'll give them my letter to take to England."

She remained skeptical of such a risky plan, but she knew that once Fritz had made up his mind, it was pointless to try to change it.

Her silence told him of her disapproval. Finally, he spoke again. "Do you think I am a good man?"

"Well, of course you are, dear. What a ridiculous question."

"And should a 'good' man just stand by and watch bad things happen?"

She didn't like where his argument was headed, but after a long silence, softly replied, "No, I suppose he should not." They both sat in silence for the rest of the drive to the restaurant.

The first two nights out were unsuccessful. He wore civilian clothing, as he usually did when it was just he and Leila out for dinner. He thought this would draw less attention to them, than if he wore his general's uniform. There appeared to have been a few foreigners in the first restaurants they visited, but he couldn't control where he was seated and he didn't feel like he could simply walk clear across the restaurant to start up a conversation with some foreigner. The third dinner out, however, the General's luck turned. The restaurant was not overly crowded, and they were seated next to an elderly couple who were speaking English.

As both couples were nearing the end of their meals, the General had Leila make a comment in English to the woman at the next table about how lovely her dress was. She quickly confirmed that they were indeed English tourists. After a few further casual comments, General Breithaupt stood, and using his wife as translator, invited the couple to join he and Leila at their table for an after dinner drink.

The couple accepted. The General ordered four glasses of kirshwasser and first name introductions were made.

"How long have you been in Munich?" asked Leila?

"This is our third night, here, but we've been in Bavaria for almost two weeks. We return to London tomorrow morning on the nine o'clock train," replied Malcom.

Leila gave Fritz a quick, short translation of the man's reply.

"You've been making a holiday tour of beautiful Bavaria?" asked Fritz.

"In a way, yes. I retired from teaching a year ago at a school near Bath. I have always been interested in the architecture of churches of the 15th through the 18th centuries – that's when the most beautiful churches were built in Europe. I've slowly been writing a book, you see, and so Mildred and I have been photographing many of the churches I intend to cover in my book."

"How lovely," Leila replied.

Over the next half hour, and a second-round of drinks, each couple discussed their children, their favorite vacation spots and how they'd met their respective spouses. Fritz just vaguely referred to himself as a retiree. He continued to glance around the restaurant to see if anyone appeared to be paying any particular attention to their foursome. So far, nothing had caught his eye.

Finally, the General gave Leila a nod and he began his planned approach to the topic of the letter he needed delivered to England, using his spouse to translate.

"As you've no doubt seen from the newspapers

in recent months, these are dangerous time in European politics. I need to ask you for a favor that is very important for both our countries. I'd like for you to take a letter for me and mail it once you're back in England. It is to a retired British General, Sir Strickland, who lives in London. I met him once several years ago and I know that he'll know what to do with my letter once he receives it."

He could see by their facial expressions that they were quite taken aback by his request and were afraid of getting involved in whatever it was that this letter might mean. Malcolm didn't really know anything about spying, but this sounded suspiciously like something that was connected to spying.

He began a polite rebuff to the request, but had only gotten out, "Well, you see..." when the General interrupted him.

"I know that you are a devoutly religious man and I assure you that the safe delivery of my letter to England is a Christian act of the most importance for the people of England as well as Germany. Please take my letter."

Malcolm's interest in churches was not in fact simply architectural and the General's plea that the delivery of this letter was a Christian act had a great impact on both Malcolm and Mildred. They looked at each other, then they nodded positively. Leila took from her purse a small envelope and slipped it under the table to Mildred. Fritz continued talking about the beauty of the Bavarian woods and smiling, while discreetly looking around to see if anybody else might have observed the passage of the letter.

After a few more minutes of conversation, the two

couples bid each other goodnight. The English couple left first, as the General stayed to settle his bill. He was relieved to see that no one came rushing up to arrest the nice old couple, nor himself!

London

Three days later, the couple was back in London and rather than trust the public mail system, Malcolm put on his best clothes that he had with him on the trip and personally called at the Naval and Military Club, at 94 Piccadilly Road, which was the address that was on the envelope. It was apparently the only address the German had for General Peter Strickland.

Malcom explained concisely to the doorman that he had a private letter "from abroad" for General Strickland and inquired if he happened to be at the Club that day, as he'd been entrusted to deliver it personally to the General.

"Yes, he is dining here today, but it's most irregular for non-members to seek an audience with a member, especially while he's dining."

"Yes, I'm sure it is, but these are most unusual times in which we are living." Malcom remained calm, but assured the doorman in a lowered voice that as he had personally carried the letter, with some risk, from Germany, he had to personally see that it reached the hands of General Strickland. "I have no need to speak a word with him, but I must give it to him directly."

The doorman remained silent for several long

seconds. It was of course against all Club rules, but the gentleman was properly dressed, did seem of sound mind, and he'd read enough articles in day-old copies of The Times left lying in the Club in recent months to know that they were indeed living in "most unusual times." He knew no more about real espionage than Malcom did, but he'd read a couple of spy novels by John Buchan. He could believe that the elderly man before him might be part of British Intelligence and on a secret mission.

After staring at the elderly gentleman for several long seconds, he decided that he was after all the head doorman and made a decision on his own. "Come in, sir, and let me see what can be done."

He led Malcom off to a small library and told him to wait there, and then headed off to the main dining room.

Wearing his most serious face, he leaned over closely to Sir Peter's ear and said, "Sir, there is a gentleman waiting to see you in the small library. He said he has a secret missive for your hands only, from Germany. Do you wish to see him?"

General Strickland pushed back his chair, laughed and said to his luncheon companions, "Something about my gambling debts. I'll be right back." He then followed the doorman in silence to the library.

After entering, he dismissed the doorman and closed the door. "I'm General Strickland. I understand that you've brought me a letter or something from Germany and it can only be delivered directly to me."

Malcom produced the letter and handed it to the retired General without saying a word.

Sir Peter put his monocle in place and opened the envelope. "The bloody thing is in German. What's this all about?"

Malcom proceeded to give him a very concise recounting of being approached at dinner in Munich by a well-dressed, German gentleman, who'd said it was of great importance for the letter to get to General Strickland. "He said that you would know what to do with it. He looked to be in his mid-fifties and while he was in civilian clothing, I had the distinct impression from his bearing and mannerisms that he was a military man."

"Don't suppose you can read German?"

"Not a word, sir."

"And you have no idea what it's about?"

"I know nothing about the contents, sir. I can only tell you that the gentleman was with his wife and she translated for him; he seemed quite sincere in the importance of this letter reaching England and of it being given directly to you."

"Hmmm." Suddenly, a smile came to his face. "Did old Colonel Worthington put you up to this? This smells like one of his foolish pranks. Go ahead, man, confess. He's had his good joke on me." Sir Peter continued to smile.

Malcom looked offended at the suggestion. "I can assure you, sir, I know no Colonel Worthington and this is no prank. I discreetly carried this letter from Munich, probably at risk to myself and my wife. I promised the

German that I would deliver it personally to you. As a Christian act, I have done so, and I bid you good day." He then made the slightest bow and left the room with no further words uttered.

Strickland stood there in silence, scratching the back of his neck and looking at the handwritten letter, which he believed to be in German. "Blast it, I suppose I better take this around to somebody," he stated to no one except the hundred year old wood paneling, for he was quite alone in the library.

After he'd finished his lunch, he caught a taxi to the War Office and called on a former aide of his, who was now a full colonel. Fortunately, he was in his office and not at some meeting. He gave him the letter and told the peculiar story of a little man personally delivering it to him at his Club.

"Did the man tell you the name of the German?" asked the Colonel.

"He only knew the German's first name. It was Fritz. This English fellow thought the man was a military officer, given his behavior."

"Very odd," replied the Colonel as he pulled thoughtfully on one ear lobe. He sent immediately for someone who could read German. Sir Peter declined to stay to see what it said. "None of my business. I'm retired and intend to stay retired." He then headed for home for a well-deserved nap.

After hearing a verbal translation of the letter fifteen minutes later, the Colonel concluded that if the letter wasn't simply from some nutter, it was clearly some sort of espionage matter, which didn't concern the Army. He therefore had it hand-carried over to the MI-6 chaps for them to sort out. He then went back to consideration of who should play for the Army side in the upcoming annual cricket match against the Admiralty.

CHAPTER 3
London

C, the head of MI-6, was a man of average height and build and an unremarkable face. His hair was mostly gray, but he was still of an indeterminate age. He had the perfect non-descript appearance to be the head of a secret intelligence service. While his appearance was average, his mind certainly was not. He was well-read, knowledgeable and could easily retain facts once presented to him. However, what truly qualified him to head MI-6 was his cunning and crafty mind – to call him "devious" was an understatement. He was a master manipulator of men and nations.

When C came into his office the morning following the arrival of the German's letter, his aide presented him with the original version as delivered by General Strickland to the War Office and a polished English translation. "We have quite an interesting offer, sir."

C read it quickly and then once more, slowly as his eyebrows arched and danced. He smiled and looked at his watch. "Best call a meeting of all the appropriate senior staff who are available at 1100 hours, and we'll see what everyone thinks of this."

"Yes, sir. I've already sent a copy to the head of

European Operations and Counterintelligence. I'll check and see who else might be around this morning."

Precisely at 1100 hours, C cleared his throat and the other seven men seated around the highly polished, but slightly battered table in the conference room became silent. According to legend, the table dated back to the time of England's first formal spymaster, Francis Walsingham, who had served Elizabeth I some three hundred and fifty years earlier.

"David, why don't you read out the English translation, so we're all starting from the same page."

C leaned back and lit his pipe. David picked up the translated letter and began to read:

"Dear General Strickland,

Forgive me for contacting you in such an unusual manner, but I could not trust the German postal system. I'm sure you will know to whom to forward my offer. I am a senior Wehrmacht officer who believes that Fuhrer Hitler is leading my beloved country down a path that can only lead to ruin and I have limited options before me on how to stop him. Despite his promise at Munich to your Prime Minister, Herr Hitler has already set a date for the full invasion of the rest of Czechoslovakia. Despite what may seem an act of treason, I am a man of honor who wishes to protect his country. I have not included my name here only because I was not certain whether my letter would get to you, or wind up in the hands of the Gestapo.

If you will send a representative of yours to a meeting

with me at 2000 hours on the night of December 24th, in the old Maria Therese Courtyard, here in Munich, I shall meet with your man. He must be able to speak German. I will provide to him my identity and the full plans for the German military campaign, which is scheduled for the coming year. With this information, you, the French and the Czechs should be able to soundly defeat Hitler's troops and then perhaps the German people will lose faith in him.

Have your man carry a book with the title on the cover clearly in English. I will also be carrying a book. Your man should ask me for directions to the Hauptbahnhof. I will simply reply that the Hauptbahnhof is a long way to travel by foot.

With respect,
Officer X"

David then added, "Our native translator said that given the vocabulary and grammar used in this letter it was written by a well-educated, upper-class German male, probably at least forty years of age. So, if it was written by a confidence man, at least it was written by an elderly, well-educated one."

Several of the men around the table laughed.

"And, yes, there is a Maria Therese courtyard in Munich – nothing special about it, but it is on the map of the city."

C looked around the table while smoke rose from his pipe bowl and drifted towards the ceiling. "Well, what does everyone think? Is this the gift from God that all intelligence services dream of receiving, a confidence man who is simply looking for money, or worst, an entrapment by the Germans?"

The head of the Counterintelligence Department spoke first. "Well, I'm paid to be suspicious and paranoid, so I'll have to vote for option number three. This is just too good to be true."

Charles, head of the European Department, spoke next. "We're in the business of gathering information and taking risks. I haven't believed in Santa Claus for a long time either, but if this fellow can deliver even half of what he's promising, I don't see how we cannot take the chance."

All seven men around the table eventually spoke, saying more or less what the first two had said. When the steam had run out of the conversation thirty minutes later, C, who had so far only been listening and nodding, tapped out his pipe in a large glass ash tray and spoke.

"Good points all around gentlemen. We can either conclude that by not giving his true name or any real details about his position, that he's simply a cautious person, or that this a trap. Although, if it's an entrapment ploy against us, why not give us the genuine name of some colonel, or even a general, that we could confirm existed within the Wehrmacht? Anyway, while there is indeed a significant risk that this is a trap, we are charged with gathering intelligence of value to our government. And the potential value here is tremendous. Therefore, if it comes down to the risk of one of our officers getting arrested, versus the ability to win a war, or perhaps even prevent one – well, we aren't running a kindergarten here." He looked around the table and no one was disagreeing with him. While he sought subordinates' views, his was the only vote that counted at the finish.

He turned to Albert, the head of the German section. "You have one week to draw up a plan for someone to make the meeting on Christmas Eve in Munich." Albert scribbled himself a quick note and then looked up as he commented, "Who to send will not be an easy choice. I'd say that the Gestapo has a pretty good idea of who all our officers stationed anywhere around Germany are, so we may have to send in someone from another country. He'll need to have fluent German and be experienced enough to make some snap decisions on the spot, depending on what this mystery German has to say, or demands. And not to be overly pessimistic, but I'd prefer not to send a married man – just in case."

C nodded in agreement with what had been said, then added, "I'm not doubting your own judgment Albert, but I'd suggest that you also immediately cable Nigel in Washington and bring him up to speed. He'd been our Station Commander in Berlin until just six months ago. See if he has any thoughts on this offer, and also, whether he has any ideas on who might be a good choice to send to make the meeting."

"Yes, sir. I'll get a message off to him within the hour."

The wheels of British espionage were starting to turn.

Chicago

Kelsey buzzed Mr. Smith on the intercom. "It's Mr. Bennett from the travel bureau, asking to speak with you, sir."

"Yes, put him through."

His phone rang and he picked up the receiver. "Good morning, Mr. Bennett. How are you today?"

"Just fine Mr. Smith. We're about a month away from your sailing date and I wanted to give you an update on the cruise."

"Excellent. Everything going to plan?"

"Yes, everything looks good. As of this morning, we have twenty-five people signed up as part of your university alumni group. The ship can take sixty. We've been advertising in London, Paris and Munich as well, with a current total of fifty-four. So, if you get a few last minute travelers, we should be able to accommodate them as well. We have a number of Brits, a few Frenchmen, and even a half dozen Germans signed up. We may get a couple of last-minute decisions over in Europe, so we'll probably have a full ship when she sails."

"That's good. Anything else that our group needs to do?"

"No, I think everything is in order. I'll send over to you today the final list we have of your alumni group, just to make sure we haven't somehow missed anyone. There are also another ten Americans who have signed up for the cruise, and I'll send you their names as well."

"Good. My wife and I are certainly looking forward to the trip."

"Since we have such a good-sized group, I'm arranging for a woman who often works with us out of Munich to come over to Paris to assist you. She'll make sure that everything goes smoothly in getting all of you and your luggage from the hotel to the train station on the 22nd. She'll accompany the group on the train to Munich and then on over to Regensburg where you'll board the ship on the afternoon of the 25th."

"That's excellent that we'll have someone to shepherd us along. Is she French or German?

"Actually, she's an American woman, but she'd married a German many years back and has been living in Munich for more than a decade. She also speaks French. I believe she's a widow now. She's worked with us on many previous trips and we've always gotten rave reviews about her. Her name is Karen Connor. I would guess she's about forty-five years old and quite delightful. Most importantly, she seems to know all the best shops in all the cities you'll be stopping at along the Danube."

"That should make my wife very happy!" They both laughed.

"Well, that's about all the news. I'll have a courier bring you that list of all the American travelers later this morning. Let me know if you see any discrepancies between my list and anyone who has told you that they were planning on going on the cruise."

"I'll do that. Thank you, Mr. Bennett."

Just before lunch, Kelsey brought in to Mr. Smith the

list of passengers that had arrived from the travel company. "It looks like you're going to have a pretty good turnout for your cruise, Mr. Smith."

He took the document from her and glanced down the list at the names. "Yes, we have some wonderful old friends who will be joining Jan and me on our cruise."

"Ah, how romantic, sailing down the Danube River with good friends and spending New Year's Eve in Vienna," said Kelsey with a wistful sigh.

"You're going to meet the man of your dreams one day and soon you'll be cruising in the moonlight down some romantic river," replied Smith.

As Smith was looking over the list of river cruise passengers, he noticed several names of former college friends he hadn't seen since they'd all left Bloomington back in 1924 – Alex Wilson and Mary Beth Long among several others. Alex lived in Virginia, had married a wealthy widow and had one or two children. As for Mary Beth, he'd heard second hand about her success as a writer of children's books and that she'd married some Brit several years back, but nothing more. There'd been Christmas cards between them the first few years after graduation, but then many of them who'd been so close in school just drifted apart as their lives got busy. He was as guilty as anybody else. It was hard holding on to friends of the past as everyone scattered around the country and pursued their own lives and careers. New acquaintances and new friends took up one's spare time.

Arthur spun round in his chair and put his feet up on the window. He looked out at the Chicago skyline and began to reflect on his own life. He'd done well in his banking career, but he honestly assessed that he'd led a rather dull and predictable life. He smiled to himself as he remembered the first time that an acquaintance noted that he wore both a belt and suspenders! Yes, well, he admitted to himself that he was a cautious man who generally played by the rules – that was the safe way to go through life. But maybe it was time to be more adventurous in the coming months. He made a mental note to stop the next day at his tailor's and buy some new shirts and ties to take on the cruise – items with a little flash. He began thinking about how did one assess whether one was living a "successful" life? What was the yardstick for such a measurement?

A buzz on his intercom from Kelsey brought him back to the present.

"Yes Kelsey."

"You have an international phone call from London. It's a Mr. Charles Weatherby. He said it's about a loan that our bank is contemplating involving his firm."

"Hmm, Weatherby you say. Doesn't ring a bell with me. Does it with you?"

"No, sir. Shall I put him through to you?"

"Sure, why not, it's his nickel. Must be something I've simply forgotten about."

Kelsey stifled a laugh, as she'd yet to see Mr. Smith forget anything in over a year of working together. About ten minutes later, Smith came out of his office. "I'm going out for lunch." He started out the door when he turned and said, "Remind me when I return to call Peterson down in the International Department – about that call from London."

"Yes, sir. And don't forget that you have a meeting at 1:30 with the lawyers for Smith and Smith Construction."

He gave her a quick smile. "Right. Must be relatives of mine, there being so few Smiths here in Chicago!"

She smiled back. "Will you be giving them the family discount rate on their loan?"

"Ha" was the last word she heard as he closed the door.

Munich, Germany
Gestapo Headquarters

A medium-sized man with blonde hair and very Germanic features in his mid-forties, dressed in the uniform of a full colonel of the Gestapo, stubbed out his cigarette in a small ashtray and called the Monday morning staff meeting to order. Werner Blickensdorfer had been in the secret political police ever since it had been formed in 1933. Previously, he'd been a policeman since turning eighteen years old and had risen to being a successful homicide detective with the Munich City Police. In his five years with the Gestapo, he'd risen from the rank of captain to colonel. He'd only been in his current position for three months and his staff was still getting to know him.

"Well, Johan, what is the first order of business today?"

His deputy opened a folder. "It's the question of the loyalty of General Fritz von Breithaupt, the commandant of the Wehrmacht base here in Munich. We've been getting more and more reports from our informants within his military command of his questioning of the Fuhrer's decisions. He never quite comes out and directly criticizes Herr Hitler, but he's made a number of joking comments, which could be taken as insults. I suggest that we look closer at the General, beginning with full-time surveillance of him over the next month, at least coverage of him once he leaves the Army base." Given poor relations between the Gestapo and the Wehrmacht, the Gestapo was not allowed to come onto the base itself.

"Yes, I've met von Breithaupt several times at official receptions," responded Blickensdorfer. "He's quite insufferable, with his perpetual arrogant look and his smug, aristocratic comments. Start surveillance coverage of him tomorrow, but make sure it's discreet. He is after all a general and we don't want any complaints from Berlin." He turned to Lt. Holger Hinz, one of his more experienced officers. "Lieutenant, I want you in charge of this surveillance coverage, to make sure things go right. Bring me a report at the end of the first week."

"Yes, Commandant."

Surveillance began the next morning, December 10th, on General von Breithaupt when he was out and about the city. The General was easy to cover, as other than the occasional dinner out with his wife or a classical music concert, the man rarely left the base, or his nearby home. The best information on him continued to come from a young Army lieutenant on the General's staff, who, though married, was having an extramarital affair. The affair itself wasn't much of a transgression, but unfortunately for him, and luckily for the Gestapo, the affair was with a young Jewish woman. When presented with photos one evening of such a transgression against the new Aryan Laws, he immediately agreed to cooperate in informing on General Breithaupt, in order to save his own career and from having the young lady sent to prison.

After one week, Lt. Hinz met with Colonel Blickensdorfer as directed, to give him the results of the coverage on the General. The Colonel was in a friendly mood and even offered Holger coffee while they met in his office.

"So, what have we learned in our first week of coverage of von Breithaupt?"

Holger opened a leather folder and began to read from it, describing his daily movements for the last seven days and also the latest informant reports about him.

Blickensdorfer lit another cigarette. "A rather dull man, it appears. He goes to the base, does his work and goes home. One evening a week he goes out with his wife for dinner. Is that about it?"

"Yes, sir. And most of what the General has said about Hitler has continued to be only joking comments, no out-and-out criticisms of the Fuhrer personally, or of his plans."

The Colonel blew a large and perfectly round smoke ring towards the ceiling. "So, nothing which could be used in sedition charges against him. I believe he's very well-connected and liked by all the other senior Wehrmacht officers, who would come to his defense involving any charges for which we did not have solid evidence. And I presume that given his family background, there are no Jewish ancestors or relatives?"

"Not that we have discovered and as you said, given his family history, it wouldn't seem likely," responded Holger.

Blickensdorfer then just sat there in silence, smoking his cigarette. Holger also remained silent. He didn't know Blickensdorfer well and felt it best not to offer his own ideas unless he was asked to do so. Finally, to break the silence, he simply offered an optimistic, "Perhaps something more interesting will turn up in the coming week."

At that moment, the deputy knocked on the office door and entered. "You said that you wanted to be informed when the current interrogation session of Becker had ended."

"And how did it go?" asked the Colonel.

"He's still just cursing at the Gestapo, his interrogator and you in particular. I was told that he had a number of choice adjectives for you." Johan smiled.

"Alright. Tell them that I will be there in twenty minutes."

"Yes, Colonel," replied Johan and closed the door.

"Normally, I leave the actual interrogating of prisoners to that staff, but I like to keep my hand in now and then." Blickensdorfer smiled and lighted yet another cigarette. "I'll share with you a little secret, Holger. This Becker is a huge man, over two meters tall and he's been loudly cursing ever since his arrest yesterday for stealing Party funds. He'll break within the first hour when I get down there. The big and noisy ones always do. Now, it's the small, quiet men who are difficult. It's as if they have internalized all their unhappiness and hatred, and it has made them stronger. You really have to work to psychologically break that sort of man."

"Yes, Colonel, I'll remember that."

"Alright, Holger, I'll see you tomorrow." The Colonel returned to reading papers on his desk.

On Holger's way out, he stopped to talk with Johan, Blickensdorfer's deputy, whom Holger had known for several years. "The Colonel seems a very serious fellow, doesn't he?" began Holger.

"Most of the time, yes, but he has a good sense of humor, when subordinates aren't around. He's very driven to get ahead and he thinks he should be all business during the work day. And did you notice all the poetry books on the top shelf in the small book case behind his desk?"

"Just vaguely. I could read on a couple of spines the names of Heine and Goethe. Does he actually read them, or are they there simply for show?"

"No, he actually reads them. I've come in several times during the lunch hour and found him eating and one of them open in front of him on his desk." Johan shrugged his shoulders. "Strange guy."

"Where did he come from?" asked Holger.

"He'd been in the Homicide Bureau of the Munich City Police for many years, but then transferred to the Gestapo in 1933. Make no mistake, he's a dedicated Nazi, but he's also a talented policeman, and he really wants to make general."

Holger shrugged his shoulders. Well, we'd all like to

be promoted. Does he have the right friends in high places, so that his desire of becoming a general might actually come true?"

"Hard to say for sure, but he works hard at it. Whenever there have been senior Gestapo officers down from Berlin, it's amusing watching him kiss their asses. He's mentioned to me a few times about how he just needs to find one high profile case to solve, so he'd get noticed in Berlin. That's where he wants to be transferred to when he makes general."

Holger grinned. "Well, it's good to have a plan. Will he take you with him if he gets promoted?"

"He's hinted at it, but verbal promises come cheap!"

Holger nodded in agreement with that statement and went on his way. Holger had been naïve in his early years and thought that working hard and doing a good job would get one ahead in the Nazi organizations. He too had been vaguely promised by several early superiors that "they would take care of him" and reward him for his hard work, only to watch them move upward and forget him totally. If he was to play a part in any future success of Colonel Blickensdorfer, he was going to make sure that everybody knew of his contribution. Still, he thought, when he'd joined the S.A. a decade back, he hadn't known where his next meal was coming from and now he ate well, was well respected and had risen to the rank of lieutenant within the Gestapo.

London

Andrew, the Chief of Counterintelligence for MI-6, was waiting in a comfortable chair in C's outer office, reading a magazine on trout fishing. Normally, C was a very punctual man, but today for whatever reason, he was running late and his secretary had never been one for sharing information about with whom the Chief was currently meeting. Finally, the door opened and out came young Albert, the head of the German Section. C was finishing a joke he'd been telling him, shook his hand, and then waved over at Andrew to come in.

C greeted Andrew with a smile. "Come on in, sorry to have kept you waiting."

"Good-day, sir. Has Albert come up with a plan yet for making a meeting with that German Army volunteer?"

"Yes, it looks like a pretty good plan, with minimum risk to our people. He thinks he's found an outsider who will act on our behalf in making an initial meeting with this volunteer in Munich, but he'll have one of our men standing by as a back-up just in case. Once we know better what we're really dealing with here, we can then have one of our officers take over the regular handling of the fellow, if it looks worthwhile."

"Let's hope for the best. As we both know, one well-placed agent can be the equivalent of a whole infantry regiment," replied Andrew.

C snorted cynically and laughed. "Yes, and in our case, a regiment we don't even have!"

Since the signing of the Munich Pact, C had made Germany the number one priority for almost every department at MI-6. He'd also had a meeting with Vernon Kell, the longtime chief of MI-5, the internal, counterespionage service, in order to encourage that service to focus more attention on Germany as well. Kell was inclined to agree with C, but pointed out that as he only had thirty-six officers assigned to MI-5 at the time, the capabilities of his service were quite limited. They'd both agreed that such short-sighted frugality would come back to haunt the country. They'd also agreed that it wasn't a question of whether there would eventually be a war with Germany, only a question of how soon it would start.

CHAPTER 4
December 1938

Mr. Smith left early for the bank the cold, but sunny morning of their planned departure day for New York City and the beginning of their European journey. He told his wife that he had several projects he had to wrap up on his last day at work. Their train didn't leave Chicago till six o'clock that evening, so there really was plenty of time. Their trunks were packed and Charles would see that all their luggage would get to the train station that afternoon, with most to be placed in the baggage car. Their two small, overnight bags would be waiting for them in their first class sleeping compartment. Charles and Jan would arrive at the bank at five o'clock to pick him up and they would go together to the train station. The Chicago Limited would arrive in New York City the following day and they would then immediately go to the pier to board their ship. The *SS Normandie*, with its beautiful art deco design, was considered one of the premier cruise ships of the day. Many of their old college friends were also sailing on the same ship.

What Arthur didn't tell his wife was that his first

stop that morning was a pre-arranged meeting with Dr. Henke.

"Thank you for seeing me this morning, Doctor. We're leaving this evening on the train for New York in order to catch our ship for Europe."

"Yes, Mr. Smith, your wife told me a few days back of your impending trip when we had our last appointment together. I believe she'll be fine to make the journey, if that's your concern."

"No, I'm sure she'll be fine for the sailing to France. What worries me is how she'll be feeling by the end of this trip. Given your initial description of her illness and likely timeline of how her tumor will probably progress, it sounded as if it might be quite painful... towards the end."

"It could be, yes."

"Well, I'm not sure just how good the medical care is off in the part of Europe where we're headed, and I'd feel much more comfortable if I simply took along with me whatever medicine she might need at the finish, to bring her pain to an end."

Dr. Henke stared in silence at Smith for several long seconds. "If I understand you correctly, Mr. Smith, you're getting into a very ethically questionable area for me."

"It isn't a question of anything for you Doctor. You'll be several thousand miles away. I simply see no reason for my dear wife to suffer pain in her final days – and she'll tell me when it's time to give her such pills."

Henke didn't respond.

"You're married, aren't you Doctor?"

"Yes, I am."

"For how long?"

"Almost twenty years."

"Would you want your wife to needlessly suffer pain, just to continue breathing for another few days?"

Dr. Henke nodded, then silently rose and went over to a medicine cabinet. He returned with a small paper pill envelope. "These two tablets contain a morphine-based drug. They should make her drowsy in about fifteen minutes and within a half hour, it will be over, though some people react differently."

"I guess it's the banker in me, but perhaps then you should send me with four tablets, just to be sure."

"I understand," replied the doctor as he stared hard at Smith for several long seconds, then he returned to the cabinet and added two more tablets to the envelope.

By mid-afternoon, Vice-President Smith had wrapped up all his outstanding work at the bank and gone around and said good-bye to many of his colleagues. All were quite envious of his holiday cruise and wished him well. He spent several hours with Nick, the young man he'd chosen to fill in for him while away. Arthur had surprised some and annoyed a few others with his choice, as he'd reached down several bureaucratic layers to make his selection. Smith did so, first of all, because Nick was quite talented, but he'd also seen the way the young fellow looked at Kelsey whenever he'd come to his office. Smith had never tried playing "Cupid" before, but he really liked Kelsey and thought she ought to have something more in her life besides work at the bank. He just thought he'd put the two of them in close proximity for a few weeks and see what happened. He'd set the wheels of romance in motion. The rest was up to them.

At 4:00 p.m. Smith went up to see the President of First National for a quick farewell chat. "So, you're going to go cruising down the Danube – sounds lovely."

Arthur took a seat in front of the President's desk. "Should be good food and wine, beautiful scenery and days spent with old friends. Can't ask for much more than that for a vacation," replied Smith with a wide smile.

"No, I guess not. You've been working hard and certainly deserve a break, though I must say I was a little surprised when I heard about your planned trip."

"Why is that?"

"Oh, it just sounded a little too adventurous for an old-fashioned fellow like you, Arthur. Last year you took the train down to Florida for two weeks and now you're going clear across the Atlantic Ocean. Next year, you'll tell me you're going to Australia!" They both laughed.

"Well, I've been promising Jan ever since I married her that I was going to show her the world. Figured I'd better get started on that plan."

"No doubt both our wives deserve such trips – putting up with guys like you and me all year long." He gave a big smile. "I won't even ask whether all is ship shape in your department before you leave as I know it will be. You're our steady rock around here Arthur." The President stood and walked around his desk to shake Smith's hand. "You and Jan have a great trip and I'll see you in 1939. Bring me a little trinket from one of those exotic places you'll be visiting."

"I'll do that JP."

They shook hands and then Arthur was gone.

While waiting for the elevator to go back down to his floor, he started thinking about the comment that he was too old-fashioned for such a vacation. Indeed, he had always thought of himself as a conservative, old-fashioned kind of guy, but he considered that a positive virtue. And in any case, hadn't JP noticed his new, flashy tie that he'd specifically worn that day to reflect the new and adventurous Arthur Smith as he started his European journey! Kelsey had noticed and commented on it as soon as he'd come in the door that morning. Maybe she ought to be running the bank, since she was much more observant than its current president!

The elevator door opened and Arthur had a wide grin on his face, from the thought of promoting Kelsey from an executive secretary position to that of president of the bank.

As he exited the elevator at his floor, the operator said to him, "Have a great trip over there in Europe, Mr. Smith."

He smiled and said, "thank you." The comment confirmed for Smith his opinion that if ever you wanted to know what was going on in the building, ask one of the elevator operators. Amazing what they learned every day just from sixty second snippets of conversation in their cars as the employees rode up and down and chatted. He returned to his office and a few last small tasks. His mind again drifted back to the subject of his being an "old-fashioned, steady rock." Not a bad image to have, but perhaps in the coming weeks he should show a more daring and exciting streak to his personality!

"As five o'clock approached, he buzzed for Kelsey to come in to his office.

"Have I completed everything I needed to do before I take off?"

"You have. You can run away to Europe with a clear conscience, though I do expect post cards from every city you visit!"

He smiled. "I promise, postcards from everywhere. And you take good care of young Nick while I'm away."

"I will. You and Mrs. Smith have a wonderful journey and take lots of photos to show me when you return."

"Of course."

Smith handed her a large, sealed envelope. "My will is in here and a few personal letters. Put this in your office safe please."

Kelsey didn't like the sound of that and her face must have shown it as well.

"Just a precautionary step. I am sailing across the Atlantic Ocean in winter time. You remember what happened to the Titanic," he added with a grin.

She took the envelope and laid it on her desk. He took both her hands, then pulled her close and gave her a long hug.

"Farewell Kelsey. A very Merry Christmas and a Happy New Year!"

"And to you and Mrs. Smith."

Then he was gone. In the year she'd known him, he'd never done more than occasionally pat her on the shoulder.

He'd said nothing further about his wife's medical condition since he'd accompanied her to her doctor's appointment back in early September. Kelsey had concluded that they'd gotten bad news that day. She'd briefly seen Mrs. Smith when she'd stopped by her husband's office the day before Thanksgiving. She'd looked tired and frail.

Kelsey had a premonition that cold December evening that she might never see Mrs. Smith again, and she hated to even imagine what a wreck her death would make of Mr. Smith.

London

Albert had just sat down at his desk in the German Section of MI-6 when his phone rang. "Albert here."

"This is Sister Thompson at St. Mary's Hospital. A gentleman named Reggie Danvers has been admitted to hospital after being hit by a bus and he asked that I inform a Mr. Albert Cromley at this number of this fact. Are you Mr. Cromley?"

"Yes, I'm Mr. Cromley and Danvers works for me. Is he hurt badly?"

"Well, he'll live, but he has a very badly broken leg and the doctor is checking him over now to see if he has any internal injuries."

"Thank you Sister. I'll be right down to see him, if he can have visitors?"

"Within about an hour, he should be able to have a

visitor. Does he have any family members or relatives that need to be notified?"

"He's unmarried and his parents live up near Bath. I'll take care of notifying them once I've seen Danvers myself. Thank you for your call."

He'd barely gotten the phone back in the cradle when he uttered a "damn!" He still had several days before there was to be an agent briefing in Paris, but it was damned inconvenient having to find another officer to take on the task at this late date. He rose from his desk and was headed for the Director's Office to give C the bad news when he bumped in to Kim Philby in the hallway.

"Albert, how are you old chap?"

"Fine, Kim, fine. "You're about to head off to Lisbon aren't you?"

"Yes, in just a couple of weeks I'll be headed south."

"Ah, you lucky devil. Wonderful country I've been told."

"Yes, I'll get a couple of months of sunshine anyway before I'm to return to Headquarters at the end of March," he replied with a smile and a slight stutter.

Albert had a sudden thought. "Say, Kim, don't suppose you could handle a simple one-day job in Paris on your way to Lisbon?"

"Possibly, what's afoot?"

He led Kim over to the side of the hallway and lowered his voice. "We've got an offer from a fellow claiming to be a Wehrmacht officer, probably a fairly senior one. He volunteered via a hand-carried letter delivered to a retired British general in London and he wants to be met in Munich on Christmas Eve. We've got a civilian who will be in Munich at that time as part of a tour group and is willing to do the initial meet for us. However, our traveller needs a final briefing on the 22nd in Paris – just in case there are any last minute changes or further instructions. Think you might be able to handle that? Would give you a nice day or two in Paris."

"Would I have to hang around Paris and wait for this agent to come back from Munich?"

"No, you could go on to Lisbon soon as the briefing is done. This tour group is jumping on a Danube river cruise at Regensburg on Christmas night and going all the way to Budapest. Someone else will handle the debriefing at the other end and receive the promised letter from the German."

"It would delay my arrival in Portugal by a few days, but if that's fine with C, I'm willing to do it."

"I'm on my way right now to discuss this with him. Can you meet me in my office in an hour and we can work out the fine details and get you read-in on the operation."

"Fine, I'll see you in an hour."

Ten minutes later, Albert managed to get in to see C.

C looked up from his desk. "Yes, what is it?"

"I've just had a call from St. Mary's. Danvers was hit by a bus this morning. He's supposed to go to Paris next week and brief our agent for that Munich volunteer operation"

"Good god! Is he alright?"

"I'm told that he'll live, but he'll be in hospital for at least a week, and probably in a wheel chair for several weeks after he's released. We'll have to quickly find a replacement for Danvers to go to Paris."

"Of course, of course. Who do you have in mind?"

"Kim Philby has a few weeks free before he's to arrive in Lisbon. He's a good dependable chap and we could get him read-in on the operation in less than a day. I'd feel comfortable having him do the briefing of this person we've selected."

C buzzed his secretary.

"Yes, sir."

"Have B1 come in here immediately, if he's around."

Two minutes later, B1, better known as Charles, the Chief of the European Department came in and sat down. Albert repeated for him what he'd just told C.

"So, what do you think of delaying Philby for a few days and sending him to Lisbon via Paris?"

"Can't do it, sir. Philby has to be in Lisbon by the 18th for a turnover of an agent there, who he's to handle for the next three months. He knows that. I'm surprised he even tentatively agreed to help you out."

"So, Philby is out. Who else is just sitting around HQS and won't mind a free trip to Paris to do his Christmas shopping?" asked C.

Charles responded, "Al McIvor is just back from his training trip to Canada and he doesn't really have anything to do until he heads off to Tripoli as Station Commander there in early March."

C responded first, "Yes, I think he'll do fine. He's a bright young fellow, definitely on his way up in the organization."

Albert nodded in agreement.

C looked back at Albert. "Then we're decided. Go make it happen. Tell him I personally chose him, etc. You know, the usual fluff and stroking."

Albert smiled. "Yes, sir. I'll make him feel truly loved by you and the King."

An hour later, Kim Philby came to Albert's office in anticipation of being briefed on the German military volunteer and his upcoming trip to Paris.

"Sorry, old boy, Charles said you have to be in Lisbon for a turn over of an agent there to you on the 18th. Had you forgotten about that?"

"Sorry, I must have been so dazzled by the thought of a free trip to Paris that the Lisbon operation slipped my mind." They both laughed. "Does this German volunteer look like anything worthwhile?"

Philby knew that looked like he was fishing for information, but he couldn't resist trying.

"Oh, hard to say yet. Might turn out to be nothing," was Charles' subtle rebuff. "Do stop in and say farewell before you leave for Lisbon."

"Yes, absolutely."

Philby then exited and headed off for lunch.

At 5:00 a.m. the following morning in his bachelor flat, Philby took from behind a false wall in a bedroom closet a secret shortwave radio by which he could send coded radio messages to the Soviet Embassy in Brussels, which would then relay his message to the NKVD Headquarters building in Moscow. He had arisen at 4:00 a.m. in order to have time to encode the message which would simply be a string of numbers.

His message told the Soviet Intelligence Service all he knew about the alleged senior German military officer who'd volunteered to provide secret information to the British Army. Relations between Germany and the U.S.S.R. went up and down, but Soviet Intelligence was definitely trying to learn all it could about the capabilities and intentions of the Wehrmacht. If there was some way for the NKVD to "hijack" this volunteer and make him their own, they would. As they didn't know exactly where or at what time in Munich this initial meeting was to take place on Christmas Eve, probably the best the NKVD could do would be to somehow figure out who'd met the German officer and then to be on that Danube River boat cruise – and steal the report from him, or if necessary, kidnap the British agent and "convince" him to talk. Once the message had reached Moscow, instructions were immediately sent via radio to an NKVD agent in Munich to find out what cruises would be departing from Regensburg on Christmas night. The NKVD could then arrange to have one of their officers or agents, perhaps someone out of Paris, on board the same cruise.

Russian espionage wheels were turning.

SS Normandie

The voyage across the Atlantic Ocean was a bit rough, given the time of the year, but several other couples from the Smiths' college days were also on board, which made it a fun journey. The six days at sea allowed the Smiths time to get reacquainted with Tom and Lenora Bishop of Cincinnati. Tom was still a handsome man, who'd done a better job at controlling his waist line than Arthur. The bit of gray creeping into his hair gave him a distinguished look. They'd only known Tom at school, but had met Lenora six or seven times since their marriage in 1925. Lenora, likewise, had remained a very attractive woman in her late-thirties and she dressed very stylishly. Their seventeen year old daughter, Hanna, had also come with them. Hanna had blonde hair, a beautiful face with dark eyes and the body of an adult woman. A number of the crewmen noticed her immediately, especially her body.

Arthur whispered to Jan one evening at the dinner table, "We'll never lack for our water glasses being full as long as Hanna is at our table." She gave him a stern, disapproving look for such commentary.

Hanna excused herself from the table as soon as dinner ended, which gave Arthur the chance to comment to the Bishops, "The last time we saw Hanna, she was only nine or ten. She's certainly turned into a lovely young woman."

Lenora smiled. "Yes, she's quite popular at her high school."

Tom, who was on his fourth martini, added, "Maybe a little too popular!"

Lenora gave him a frown. "She gets invited to a number of dances around the city. She came in second this past summer in the Young Miss Cincinnati contest and she's doing quite well in school."

The ladies excused themselves to go find the "powder room", which gave Arthur and Tom the chance to talk of the economy. "How's the insurance business going for you down there in Cincinnati, Tom?"

"Pretty good, these days. Like everyone else, the early and mid-thirties were tough. When companies and people are going broke, they can't worry much about the future, nor have money to spend on insurance. They're just trying to survive the present. But it looks like we're finally pulling out of this recession, and we're expecting a good, strong 1939," was his reply. "It better be," he added, "given what my wife just spent on all the clothes for her and Hanna for this trip!" They both laughed.

"Ah, here come the gals," commented Arthur. The orchestra had started playing again. "How about a dance, my dear?"

"That's right, you did promise me unlimited dances on this trip, didn't you?" She and Arthur headed off to the dance floor.

Tom turned to Lenora. "Jan looks awfully tired to me. How does she seem to you??"

"I asked her about that while we were fixing our make-up. She said she was just getting over a bad cold and then all the preparations for this journey had exhausted her. She said she just needs a few good days of rest."

"Ah, good, glad to hear it's nothing serious. By the way, where has Hanna gone off to?"

"I suspect she's in the bar. Apparently, there's no age

restriction on drinking alcohol out on the high seas, and I suspect there are a number of men on board happy to buy a pretty young girl a drink," she added with a proud smile.

Tom wisely said nothing out loud, but thought to himself that as Lenora aged, she seemed more and more to live vicariously through their daughter's beauty and popularity.

"Perhaps you'd best go check on her."

"Oh, I'm sure she's just having a good time in the bar. A young girl likes a little attention," she replied.

"Her getting 'a little attention', as you call it, is what has us on this cruise!"

"Well, you're her father. You go check on her."

"I will. I'll see you down in the cabin."

The following day, Jan and Arthur were heading into the dining room just as their old college friend Mary Beth Long arrived for lunch. Jan recognized her first, even though they hadn't seen each other since 1924 and she had changed.

"Oh my god, it's you Mary Beth! I almost didn't recognize you." She wasn't quite sure how to phrase her comment about the change in Mary Beth. At college, she'd been a rather plain girl in her features and dress. She was now absolutely stunning in both regards. She now had her brown hair cropped fairly short in the current fashionable style and wore just enough make-up to accentuate her good facial features and dark brown eyes.

"Arthur and Jan. You two haven't changed a bit – young as ever."

They all hugged and then headed for a table to dine together and catch up.

"The last we heard of you was that after Bloomington you'd moved to New York City to write children's books and within a few years, you'd married some Englishman. Correct?" asked Arthur.

"Correct on both accounts, but my husband, Winston, died in 1935 from a burst appendix, and so I moved back up to my home town of Portsmouth, New Hampshire. I'm still writing."

"And you've gone back to your maiden name? I saw that you were listed as Long on the roster."

Mary Beth laughed. "Actually, I continued to go by Long after our marriage. I'd had some success by 1927 when we married and I was going to keep publishing as Long anyway. Winston said he didn't care what I called myself as long as I came home to him every night."

All three of them laughed. "Besides, he had an absolutely awful family name. He even admitted it was terrible – Higginbotham-Bromley! Said he could never inflict that on any woman."

"Do you travel much?" asked Jan.

"No, I'm afraid I've become a bit of a recluse since I moved back to New Hampshire. I have this wonderful cottage on a hill that gives me a lovely view of the coastline. I write and take walks, but I stay pretty close to home. I suppose I should be a little more adventurous. In fact, that was the deciding factor of why I finally signed up for this journey. I figured I better get out and see some of the world while I can – I'm not getting any younger!"

"None of us are "replied Arthur. They all laughed.

"Well, I've bought several of your children's books about the adventures of your adorable rabbit character, Mr. Riley. I even gave Arthur one this past summer for his birthday and he loved it!"

"We hadn't seen you on board the first two days, so I was beginning to wonder if you'd made the trip after all," interjected Arthur. "I saw that you were a last minute sign-up for the river cruise."

She laughed. "I'm on the cruise, but I still need to finish the book I'm currently working on by early-January, so I've been spending most of my time in my cabin, writing. Now that I know you are a fan, Arthur, of Mr. Riley, I'll send you an autographed copy when the new one is published this coming summer."

They continued to swap stories of their college days and the following years all through lunch, until Mary Beth excused herself, to get back to her room and her writing. "I'm trying to get this finished on the sailing to France, so I can mail it back to New York from Paris, and then truly enjoy the Danube cruise."

"An excellent plan, but hopefully, we'll see you at least for a few dinners while we're at sea."

The ship arrived at Le Havre, France only a few hours late of the scheduled docking time. Clearing French Customs was a mere formality, at least for the Americans. The French officials seemed to have the attitude of "what could an American have worth smuggling into France?" Within three hours of stepping onto French soil, they were all on the train to Paris. When checking into the Hotel Vernet late that same afternoon, they all found a brief note from Karen Connor, the representative of the Chicago travel bureau. She invited everyone to join her for a "Welcome" drink in the Blue Room at six o'clock, so as to get acquainted with her and their fellow passengers for the upcoming cruise. She also wanted to explain to them the schedule for the next few days. After the reception, most of the forty travelers present opted for dinner upstairs in the main dining room. Above them was a beautiful iron and glass cupola that covered the entire room, which had been installed when the hotel had been built in 1913. It had been designed by Gustav Eiffel; the same fellow who'd done the Eiffel Tower. The lights sparkled off the crystal glassware and fine silverware, all placed precisely in the correct positions on the white linen table cloths. Most all of the gentlemen were in black tuxedos and the ladies elegantly attired in evening gowns. More of Tom Bishop's money was on display in the gowns worn by his wife and daughter that evening.

Arthur and Jan Smith stood by an empty table for six and thought they'd just take their chances of meeting someone new and interesting – or at least someone who hadn't been on the ocean liner with them. Arthur looked elegant in his custom-made black tuxedo and Jan equally so in her floor-length blue gown. Fortunately, Karen had passed out name tags for everyone to wear, so as to help everyone recognize each other. Some people hadn't changed in the least, but several were totally unrecognizable from their college days.

Bob Hall came to the Smiths. "Arthur, how are you? You look exactly the same as you did in 1924!"

Arthur patted his stomach, which extended an inch or two beyond his belt. "Well, I might be a little rounder than when we last saw each other."

Bob laughed. "I thought you bankers called that 'prosperity' and just bought a new belt. But at least you still have all your hair," he commented as he rubbed his hand over his thinning crown.

Jan joined in. "You still have plenty of hair, Bob, and it's still that lovely shade of auburn. And your tuxedo is spectacular." She ran her hand over the material of the sleeve.

Bob laughed and leaned in a little to Jan. "I know one of the tailors at the studio. He occasionally sells stuff out the backdoor. He claimed that this had been worn by William Powell in one of the Thin Man mystery movies."

"Well, he couldn't have looked as nice in it as you do tonight."

"You're still writing for the movies, right?" asked Arthur.

"Oh, yes, tell us about the glamorous stars of Hollywood you've met," chimed in Jan.

"Yes, I'm still writing for the movies. In fact, I've been in England for the past month working on a script about a posh English boarding school for boys and their relationships with one of the teachers over the years. They've already started shooting some of the scenes, but nobody likes the current ending and that's what I've been assigned to do over this break – think of a better finish."

"I saw that you were a last minute sign-up for the trip. I'm glad you were able to fit the cruise in with your filming."

"Well, none of the actors wanted to work over the holidays, so they've shut down production until January 10th, and I wasn't having any brilliant new ideas while looking at the damp and dreary stone walls of a boys' school. I thought that maybe cruising along the Danube and drinking good wine with old friends might be just the stimulus I needed to give me some inspirational thoughts."

They all laughed. Jan took his arm and said, "Well, I'll try to be your muse tonight. Did you bring anyone with you on the trip?" Jan's none too subtle way of inquiring if there was anyone currently in his love life.

"No, just me. I couldn't afford such a trip for two people on my meager salary."

At that moment, a beautiful woman came up to them, showing a big smile and wearing a gorgeous green, silk dress with just one strap over her left shoulder. Her shoulder-length brown hair was fixed perfectly and she had large, brown eyes. One could tell immediately from her demeanor and attire that she was a European. Her sparkling pendant earrings were definitely real diamonds and each one at least a full caret in size.

"Bon soir, Arthur," she said softly with a sensuous French accent. "You're looking as handsome as when I last saw you in 1924!" She leaned in to kiss him on both cheeks. "And Jan, of course, how are you?"

Arthur, Jan and Bob all stole a quick glance at her name tag. "Simone, how good to see you after all these years," mumbled Arthur. There were cheek kisses all around and then Bob suggested that she join them for dinner.

"Yes, do join us," said Jan. "We only met a few times in Bloomington, but I certainly remember your name. You're back living in Paris, I believe?"

"Yes, after I finished at the university, I decided to return to France and have been making a living singing ever since. I've had a little success in recent years."

"You're being much too modest," commented Arthur. I believe you're one of the most well-known chanteuses in France and run a very successful night club here in Paris."

She smiled, "Oui, I am part-owner of a small club and make enough money to keep the wolf from the door. That is the correct American slang expression, non?"

"Very good," said Bob, as he pulled a chair back for her, so that she could sit next to him. Bob had only casually known her at school, but definitely remembered her beautiful smile. No one else came to join them, so the four had lots of opportunity to chat and find out what was new in each other's lives over the last fifteen years. By the time dessert arrived, they'd learned that Simone had married in 1930, but about a year ago, her husband, a professional gambler, had been arrested and sent to prison for being a house burglar and jewel thief.

None of the others quite knew how to respond to that unusual bit of news, so Simone asked of Bob, "And have you ever been married?"

"Yes I was, within a year of moving out to California.

She was a young aspiring actress that I met around the studio. Like hundreds of others, she'd come to Hollywood wanting to get into the movies and was always looking for her big break."

"And did she get it?" asked Jan.

"Yes, about one year into our marriage she discovered that sleeping with a director was the way to get ahead in the movie business. So, she got a break and I got a divorce."

"Oh, that's terrible," replied Jan.

"It did rather put me off on romance!"

"And what has become of her? Did she become a star?"

Bob laughed. "No, there is justice in the world. She was doing well and moving up the ranks and then sound pictures arrived in 1928, and guess what?" Bob switched into a heavy hillbilly accent. "Well, the little girl from the hills of Tennessee sounded like a girl from the hills of Tennessee! And within a few months, she and hundreds of other 'silent' actors were history. Suddenly, you not only had to look good, but sound good as well."

The other three all laughed hard.

Turning to a more pleasant theme, Bob told some amusing stories about Clark Cable, Mae West and Mickey Rooney. Arthur thought to himself that his life seemed rather dull in comparison – all he'd done since college was make money.

"Seems like your dream of becoming a screen writer has worked out well for you," commented Jan.

Bob shook his head. "Well, the jury is still out on that one. I've been doing a lot of script writing, but mostly I'm always a behind-the-scenes guy – fixing up other people's work or adding dialog as the movie is being made. I'm still waiting for my break to be the head writer for a serious movie. This current production is about a lonely British teacher at an exclusive private boy's school in England, who finally gets to become its head master. The producer of this current project has intimated to me, that if all goes well on this movie he's going to give me a chance with a major production in the coming year."

"That sounds very exciting, and perhaps your big break," replied Simone. "Any idea what this next project will be? And, is there a role for a lonely French girl, who can sing a little?" She giggled as she drank more champagne.

"It's to be a spy story, to be set somewhere in Europe and it involves a foreign correspondent for an American newspaper. Supposedly, the studio is trying to line up Alfred Hitchcock to direct it. At this point, I don't think much more than that has been settled on for the plot. It would be fun to work on a script, while the plot is still open for discussion. Of course, in Hollywood, verbal promises are as common as cocktail shakers!"

"Still, that sounds quite exciting, but do you know anything about espionage, Bob?" teased Arthur.

"You don't have to know anything about a topic to be able to write about it in Hollywood!" replied Bob, and they all laughed.

Jan tugged at Arthur's arm. "It's getting late and I'm ready for bed." They all agreed to call it a night.

Once back to their room, he asked his wife, "Did I keep you up too late?"

She laughed. "It's nothing to do with the tumor, dear, we're just not nineteen anymore! And if we're to go out and see gay Paree tomorrow, we need to get some sleep."

The following morning, everyone was out of the hotel straight after their *petit déjeuner,* so as to see the sights and hit some of the fashionable stores on the Avenue des Champs Elysees. Many of the passengers spent money quite freely, especially Mrs. Bishop, who'd left her husband at the hotel so she wouldn't have to hear him complain about how much she was spending.

The morning outing did tire Jan out, so she decided to stay at the hotel in the afternoon. She was having tea in a side lobby around three o'clock when Mary Beth came in, taking a break from writing. Jan waved to her.

"Come over and join me, Mary Beth."

"Yes, I'd love to. I thought you'd all gone out to make a day of it in Paris!"

"Oh, I was out this morning, but decided I'd have a relaxing afternoon here at the hotel. Arthur wanted to go to the top of the Eiffel Tower, so I told him to go right ahead and I'd be in the lounge having a nice cup of hot tea!" They both laughed.

"I'm still trying to get as many pages done on the new book as I can, so that I can then just forget about it while we're on the Danube."

The two ladies chatted and drank tea for almost an hour, when Jan raised a delicate subject. "Mary Beth, I hope you don't mind my asking such a personal question, but how have you dealt with life, since your husband died several years back? I don't know quite how to phrase it, but are you lonely? Have you considered remarrying?"

"Well, the first few months were horrible. I'd half wake up at night and reach across the bed, getting ready to snuggle up against him, and find him not there. For a second or two, I'd wonder where he was, then my brain would kick in and I'd remember, he was dead. Finally, I had to move into a different bedroom. Things were better by the end of the first year without him, though there were still times when some sight or sound would suddenly bring him vividly back to my mind and the tears would flow – and still do."

"I'm so sorry, and sorry that I asked the question, which has clearly brought back very sad memories for you."

"It's OK, I can deal with it much better now. It's been four years since his death. My publisher couldn't believe the rate at which I was turning out new books in the first two years. He'd even suggested that I take a break from writing shortly after Winston's death. What he didn't understand was that my keeping busy with my writing was the only thing that kept me from going insane."

"That's quite interesting. Thank you so much for sharing that with me."

A darkness came across Mary Beth's face. "Oh god, is there something wrong with Arthur?"

Jan laughed. "Arthur? Good god, no. He's healthy as a horse. I was just curious. You seem so happy and satisfied. Do you think you might remarry some day?"

"Oh, I don't rule it out, but I'm not out searching daily to find the second man of my dreams. I figure, if it happens, it happens, but I'm quite satisfied right now with my life."

"That's good to hear, but you're still quite a young woman – maybe 35 – you have many years ahead of you yet. I'm sure you'll stumble across some charming gentleman one day when you least expect it!"

Mary Beth smiled. "Maybe, but Arthur's already taken and there are so few good men like him around these days."

Now Jan smiled. "Listen, there are days when you could have Arthur for five cents." She paused and then said, "But on other days, he is quite wonderful." She had to fight to keep back a tear. She checked her watch. "Listen, the shops are still open for another two hours. How about we go out together and you can help me find something wonderful to wear on Christmas Eve in Munich. Karen told me that she has arranged a marvelous ball that evening."

"Alright, that sounds like fun. I'll have the emotional thrill of shopping, but get to spend someone else's money! Give me ten minutes to go up to my room to change, then we can hit the streets of Paris."

"Perfect. I'll meet you here by the door in ten minutes. I'll talk to the concierge and get the names of a few shops to explore. This should be a great outing. And if I find a new dress, can you hide it for me, so Arthur doesn't even know I have it until Christmas Eve?"

"Of course, I'll be back in a flash."

As Mary Beth was riding up the elevator, she felt envious of Jan and the wonderful marriage she and Arthur had going. She recalled the rather indifferent answer she'd given Jan about possibly remarrying someday. That wasn't quite true. She had by most definitions, a good life going, but Riley the Rabbit was no substitute for a nice firm chest to lay her head upon in bed at night.

CHAPTER 5
April, 1924 Bloomington, Indiana

Simone Chevrolet and Mary Beth Long sat in the cafeteria of the Student Union Building, drinking coffee and killing time until their next classes started in about an hour. Others were studying, though as the spring weather brought more warm and sunny days that activity was getting harder and harder to do. This was especially true for the seniors, who knew that in less than two months their studying days would be over for good.

Life at Indiana University had been quite a change for Mary Beth. More people lived in her dormitory than had attended her entire high school back home in her small town in New Hampshire. Her father ran the local hardware store and fortunately for him, she'd won a scholarship that covered most of her college expenses. She was not an unattractive girl, but there was little money to spare for fancy clothes or make-up products. However, her biggest problem probably came from the fact that her mother had died when she was quite young and she'd grown up in a household of only brothers and her father. In short, nobody had ever really taught her how to dress and act like a woman, especially a flirtatious one. She was smart with a good sense of humor, but even by her senior year, she was still a diamond in the rough.

"What are your immediate plans after the graduation ceremonies?" asked Simone.

"I'll go back home to New Hampshire for a week to visit my family and then I'm off for New York City."

"That will be very exciting. Do you already have a place to live lined up for when you arrive?"

"No, finding an apartment will be my first task and after that I'll start making the rounds of publishing firms."

"Do you know anybody in the publishing business?"

"No, I'm just going to go office to office and drop off examples of my writing, especially of my children's stories. That's what I really enjoy writing."

"I expect that's going to be tough – breaking into the business as a totally unknown person."

"Well, I've saved up enough money to last me six months or so, and if I can find a part-time job, even a little longer. If I haven't gotten my foot in some door by then, I guess I'll head back to New Hampshire and maybe find a teaching job. What are your plans? Will you go back to France or stay in America?"

"Oh, to tell you the truth, all I'm thinking about today is the Spring Dance on Saturday night and what dress I should wear for Tom."

Mary Beth smiled. "You look good in everything, so don't worry too much about it."

"What about you? What are you wearing to the dance?"

There was an awkward silence. "I don't think I'm

going, so at least I don't have to worry about that question. I mean, well, it's Thursday and no one has asked me yet."

Simone realized she'd put her foot in her mouth, as they said in France and wanted to quickly change the subject."

"No matter. It's just a silly dance. As for your question about my plans after graduation, my mother always thought I would become a famous opera singer. The problem is, to be honest, I'm not that talented and it isn't really the type of music I enjoy the most."

"What type do you like?" asked Mary Beth.

"I like torch songs and jazz. I'd like to become a nightclub singer in Paris – that's what I'd really like to do and I'm going to give that a try. I don't want to go back to my small, rural village. It's the fast and glamorous life of Paris for me."

"I suspect that's a hard business to break into as well."

"No doubt, but I've got a lead on a manager at one of the better clubs in Paris, who if a singer will sleep with him, he'll give her a one week try-out in his club."

Mary Beth was shocked at this and her face showed it. "You'd have sex with that man just to get a chance at performing?"

Simone shrugged her shoulders. "It goes on all the time in France, but I'd make him sign the contract first! You probably can't trust some of those managers."

Mary Beth was still in shock.

"You don't think such things happen in America in the publishing world?" asked Simone. "What would you do if some publisher says he'll publish one of your manuscripts if you'll sleep with him?"

"I'd tell him no, of course. I've heard of such stories, but I don't know if they are even true. In any case, women of little talent might have to resort to that, but not talented people like myself."

Simone just smiled. "Well, I look forward to reading your first published book!"

At that moment, a mutual friend of theirs, Bob Hall, came by and sat down with them. Bob was also interested in writing, but not books. He'd been talking ever since he arrived at the University of going out to Hollywood and becoming a screen writer for the movies. He came from Indianapolis, but never talked much about his family or background.

"Bob, you look like you've had a hard day. Anything wrong?" asked Mary Beth.

"I just had a tough exam in my Philosophy 301 class. My brain is fried."

"I thought you were an English major. Why are you taking an advanced level Philosophy course?"

"I'm an English major, but with a minor in Philosophy. I thought such classes might help me someday with my writing."

"What did the test cover today?" asked Simone.

"It was on concepts of good and evil from Ancient Greece up till 1900."

Simone shuddered. "It's much easier to just sing about people doing good and evil in operas." They all laughed.

Another of their friends, Mike Taffe, stopped at the table. "What's all the laughter about?" he asked.

"Bob just had a Philosophy exam on right and wrong. How do you decide, Mike?" asked Mary Beth.

"Oh, that's easy for us Irish," he replied with his obvious Bostonian accent. "I'm always right and anybody who disagrees with me is wrong." Again, laughter around the table.

"You're an Accounting major, right Mike?" asked Bob. "What are your plans for after graduation, or is it still up in the air for you?"

"My Uncle Seamus figures he can get me a job with some firm back there in Boston."

"What does your uncle do? Does he have a company that might need an accountant?" asked Mary Beth.

"Well, he has his hands in a number of enterprises, so he might have influence with some company that could use a good accountant."

Bob was smiling as he listened to the answer. Mike had told him once how his Uncle Seamus was fairly high up in the Irish Mob of Boston. He was particularly active in bootlegging during Prohibition, but also active in the protection racket, so he probably did know some company that would be willing to hire Mike.

Finally, the foursome broke up and headed off to their next classes. Simone started thinking about any guy she knew who hadn't yet made plans for the dance and perhaps she could "encourage" him to ask Mary Beth, but no one came to mind.

Saturday brought clear skies and warm air to campus, so the Spring Dance would be a pleasant affair, despite it being just the first weekend of April. A number of daffodils and crocus were in bloom around the lovely, wooded campus, dotted with buildings made of Indiana limestone quarried from nearby. Hoagy Carmichael, IU law student and budding piano player, had arranged for Bix Beiderbecke and the Wolverines to come down from Indianapolis to provide the musical entertainment for the evening. With the warm weather, the dance could spread out onto the outdoor patio area from the large Alumni Hall within the Student Union Building, which was also built of imposing limestone. From there, the students had a lovely view of Dunn Meadow down below, particularly with an almost full moon shining.

Arthur and Jan Smith had managed to get a babysitter for the evening for their very young daughter and thus were able to enjoy one of their few nights out. They sat at a table with Tom Bishop of Cincinnati, who'd brought Simone. The third couple consisted of Mike Taffe and a young lady named Alyssa Kelly, also from Cincinnati and also of Irish ancestry. The three men looked elegant in their black tuxedos and the ladies in colorful evening gowns. To no one's surprise, Mike had a large flask on his hip with which to "improve" the taste of the ginger ale punch.

All of the students at the table would be graduating in only a few weeks and this might be the last time that all six of them would be together before they went their separate ways. This led to much discussion of how they would all stay in touch and even manage to gather together every few years. Numerous toasts to their friendship and the successes that would be coming their way in the coming years punctuated their conversation. Those were optimistic years in America.

"These are going to be great years ahead for all of us and all of America," predicted Tom Bishop. "My economics professor was just talking in our last class about how the rest of the 1920s would be nothing but growth and expansion for the entire country."

"And where will you be in five years, Tom, with all that growth?" asked Arthur.

"Oh, I suspect that I'll own several banks back in Cincinnati, and maybe one over in Paris – then I'd have an excuse to sail over and visit Simone," he joked as he squeezed her hand.

"What makes you think I'll be in Paris? In five years, I might be singing in New York or London. You'd best send me a cable before showing up in Paris and expecting to find me at home." They all laughed.

"What about you, Arthur? By 1929 will you be president up there at your father's bank in Chicago?"

Arthur put on a grave face. "No, in five years, I'll only be vice-president. My father would be very upset if I outranked him in only five years." Again, laughter around the table. At that point in time, Arthur was in fact the only one who knew exactly where he was going to work after graduation. He was headed for the First National Bank of Chicago, where his father was a department head and clearly moving up within the organization in the years ahead.

Late in the evening, Mike and Tom headed off to the Men's Room and while standing next to each other at the urinals, their conversation shifted from the expanding economy to the frequent topic among college males of whether either expected to get "lucky" that night.

"You and Miss Cincinnati seem to be hitting it off pretty well. You think you might have a chance with her tonight?" asked Tom with a grin.

Mike grinned back. "You just never know. This might be her lucky night to learn something amazing at college! How about you and Miss Paris?"

"Well, she might discover just how big is the back seat of my Model T."

"She might discover how big is your what?" replied Mike as he started to laugh.

As they walked back to their dates, Mike thought to himself that it was a shame Alyssa's father was known as the toughest SOB in Cincinnati and if he even lifted his little girl's skirt above her knees, he knew he'd be singing soprano within a week.

Tom was thinking that as much as he'd like to put the moves on Simone and see if the rumors about French girls in bed were true, he didn't want to risk angering a girl he just might be falling in love with in those closing days of college.

As the two neared their table, Alyssa was wondering whether Mike would soon suggest that they head off somewhere to be alone. She certainly hoped so. She'd worn her brand new, French lace underwear that night in anticipation.

Simone was wondering if she might find out that night if the rumors about what an American was like in bed were true. She'd heard some amazing stories from her much older sister about the American "doughboys" back during the war. She didn't want Tom to think she was "easy", but she was wondering what she might do to let him know that she was ready and willing. Singing about love was fine. Experiencing it in person would be even better.

Once all six were back at the table, Arthur announced that "I think it's about time for us old married folks to head for home. I have to get our baby sitter back home by eleven o'clock."

Even though Arthur and Jan were only two or three years older than their friends, Arthur definitely came across as the steady, dependable guy of the group. Perhaps having been to war and killed other men had matured him sooner than was normal. Mike had observed that all the young veterans who'd fought in France were that way, compared to the typical college guys simply enjoying the Roaring Twenties to the fullest – like himself. Of course, arriving at college already with a wife and soon thereafter, having a child, changed a guy's perspective on life. Arthur was by nature a quiet sort of fellow, but when he spoke, he generally had something to say that was worth hearing.

Arthur raised his glass, full of "ginger ale punch", and the others joined him. "To my classmates and friends. We'll only be classmates for a few more weeks, but we shall always be friends. To the future." They all emptied their glasses and then placed them upside down on the white table cloth. Arthur and Jan rose, as did the others and there were long goodbye hugs among them. Bix Beiderbecke was playing a soulful, solo version of *That Old Gang of Mine* on his coronet. It was the perfect ending to a perfect evening and left all with good memories that would last forever – for they were young and invincible and only great things awaited them in the future.

CHAPTER 6
Paris

Arthur Smith and Bob Hall were both early risers and were the only two people waiting to enter the hotel restaurant when it opened at 7:00 a.m. on their second day in Paris.

Both ignored the menu in French they'd been handed when they were seated.

"A croissant, scrambled eggs, ham, and coffee, please," stated Arthur.

"The same for me, please," added Bob. After the waiter had nodded and walked away, he leaned over to Arthur and commented, "You know, when your hotel is eighty percent full of Americans and Brits, would it kill them to have a few menus printed in English?'

"I don't care so much about the menus, but it would be nice to have a waiter who knew how to smile. They all look at every meal like they've just come from a funeral." They both laughed.

"By the way, I saw you lunching yesterday with Fred Hendricks. How's he doing?" asked Bob.

"I'm not really sure. He's out of the Navy and he's still grieving pretty hard over the death of his wife in that automobile accident from two years back. Even for a sailor, he was drinking a lot during lunch. I'd heard second hand a while back that's why he was politely invited to leave the Navy."

Bob nodded. "Well, there are other things to do in life besides float around on the ocean. By the way, what was his specialty in the Navy?"

"He was in Naval Intelligence, whatever that exactly means. Now, he sells stocks and bonds. Apparently, he focuses particularly on current or former military personnel for clients, so I guess he's getting some mileage out of having been in the Navy."

"Was he on the ship with you on the way over?"

"No, he said he'd been in London for the past week on business and just came across the channel, so as to arrive in Paris when we did. He did share with me at least one reason for his heavy drinking."

"What's that?" asked Bob.

"Please keep this just to yourself, but the night that his wife had the fatal car accident, he'd been out seeing another woman. That's why the hospital hadn't been able to get hold of him for several hours after she'd been admitted, and not until after she'd died. He feels pretty bad over that," explained Arthur.

"God good, that sounds like some Hollywood melodrama! I guess that would drive me to drink as well. That's quite a load of guilt for him to carry around. What did you say to him when he told you that?"

"Just that it helps no one for him to regret forever a past error. At some point, he has to get on with his life."

"Sound advice."

"Yes, except I suspect that's a lot easier said than done."

"True. Was the woman he was out with a serious thing, or just some one-off affair?"

"Apparently just a one-evening affair with some woman he'd only met that afternoon while out shopping. He said he never saw her again after that night."

"Well, hopefully, all will turn out OK for him. By the way, have you ever been to Paris before?"

"Just briefly, back in early 1919. Me and ten thousand other American doughboys marched down the Champs Elysees as part of a victory parade, just shortly before we sailed home to America. There must have been a hundred thousand Frenchmen lined up along the boulevard that day, cheering."

"That's right, I'd forgotten you'd been in the war before starting college. Must have been a pretty exciting day."

"For some I suppose it was. As I was marching along, I started thinking about all the guys I'd gone through training with who weren't going home, ever."

"Yeah, when the fighting's over, we tend to forget those who gave everything. We celebrate the victory and then most everyone simply gets on with their lives."

"Living up in those trenches was horrible. It was cold and wet, the food was terrible, lice in your uniform and the smell of dead men and horses everywhere. I began to wonder which was worse, living or dying. I can understand why there's no enthusiasm in France or England for standing up to Hitler and risk starting another major war."

"I know, or at least secondhand I do. My family had gotten a number of letters from my older brother who was in France, before he was killed."

Smith stared down at the table cloth, with a grim look on his face. "Well, if you ever write a screen play about war, please show people how horrible it really is. War at times may be necessary, but there's very little that's glorious about it. We hand out medals afterwards, but when it's happening, a soldier is just trying to stay alive. The worst thing about being up in those trenches was when there had been one of those mindless charges of thousands of men across No Man's Land and then we would retreat because of the enemy's artillery and machine gun fire. We'd drag back with us the wounded that we could, but for hours afterwards we would hear the cries of badly wounded men still out there on the battlefield. Crying out for their mothers, or just crying out in pain. You put that in a Hollywood movie someday."

Bob decided that the conversation had turned much too somber and it was time to change the subject. "You and Jan going on the organized tour today?"

"No, we might just go out later and stroll about for a little while, if the sun comes out."

"Going to go anywhere in particular?"

"No, we're just going to wander up and down along the Seine River, like a couple of tourists, staring at all the beautiful buildings. Then we'll find a little bistro, where they don't speak anything but French for lunch."

"Sounds like a nice, romantic plan, particularly for a banker."

"Yes, and then I'm going to take an afternoon nap. All this culture has been wearing me out!"

Bob laughed, but then his face turned serious. "Forgive me for asking, but is Jan feeling well? She's looked rather tired and has had headaches the last two days."

"Oh, she's fine. She's just getting over a lousy cold and there were all the preparations, plus she doesn't really do well out on the ocean. Now that we're on stable ground, she told me she's already feeling better, but thanks for inquiring."

"That's good," replied Bob.

"What about you? You taking the tour?" No, I'm feeling mildly creative, so I'm going to work a bit on this script. I still have to come up with a couple of better ideas for an ending for the director to consider." Bob waved to a waiter for the check. "I'll see you and Jan later."

Arthur stayed a little longer, drinking coffee and thinking back to the war, even though it had been twenty years. As he'd told Bob, one of the worse things was the sound of dying men in pain, crying out for help. What he hadn't told Bob, nor had he ever told anyone, not even Jan, was that on one occasion he'd actually shot one of those poor devils. The fellow had been moaning in pain for almost an hour and there was no way to send anybody out to rescue him, so in the end, Arthur shot him to bring his misery to an end. He knew it had been the right thing to do, but he still occasionally had nightmares about that day. He couldn't tell from his position in the trench if the dying man was someone he personally knew. It didn't matter. He'd left it to God to decide whether it was the ethical or Christian thing to do. It was simply something that needed doing that day and he did it. He pondered if JP would consider him taking that shot the action of an old-fashioned, steady sort of guy.

When Mary Beth entered the restaurant at 9:00 a.m., the only other guest present was Karen, who was just having a café au lait as she went over the group's schedule for the coming day.

Mary Beth walked over to her table. "May I join you, Karen?"

"Of course, dear. Sit down and let's see if we can catch the eye of one of the sleeping waiters."

"Just some strong coffee and toast will do me. It'll be lunchtime in only a few hours, but I do need some coffee."

"Were you out late?" the middle-aged woman enviously asked.

Mary Beth smiled. "I wish that was it. No, I was up late working on my manuscript and didn't lay down till almost five this morning."

"Oh, that's right, someone told me that you're a writer, of children's books, correct?"

"Yes, and I'd hoped to be able to mail back to New York from Paris a finished version for my publisher, so I could then totally relax on the river cruise, but I'm afraid that was wishful thinking."

"Well, perhaps drifting peacefully along the Danube will make it easier for you to write."

"Hopefully. May I ask how you wound up living in Munich? I heard that you're originally from Pennsylvania."

"I came to Germany as an undergraduate student in

the fall of 1913 to spend a year at the University of Munich. Of course, I had to go home by early summer 1914 when it was starting to look like war might be coming."

"That must have been pretty exciting, to be in Germany in 1914."

"Oh, I didn't really understand what was going on at the time, but I finally got back to Munich in 1921 to work on my doctorate, concerning German fairy tales of the eighteenth century. But then I got interrupted again."

Mary Beth gave her a puzzled look.

"I fell in love with one of my German professors. He was tall, handsome and charming – just like in a fairy tale!" They both giggled like school girls. "So, I got married instead of finishing my studies and we were living happily ever after, but then he feel ill and died in 1936. I decided to just stay on in Munich and stumbled into the tour business, which helps pay the rent."

"I'm so sorry about your husband, but it sounds like you've had a pretty exciting life."

"I heard that you also lost your husband a few years ago."

"Yes, and it was very hard the first year, but I really threw myself back into my writing, which helped a lot. Maybe that's why I enjoy writing children's books so much – only good things happen in them."

They exchanged stories about their dead husbands.

"Have you stayed in touch with your husband's relatives around Munich since his death?"

"No, sadly not. He had two brothers and a sister, but none of them had been very happy that he'd married a 'foreigner' and after a few months of mandatory Germanic politeness following his death, that was the last I heard from any of them."

"That is very cold. I've been very fortunate. My father-in-law has made a great effort at staying in touch with me since my husband's death. Whenever he is over from England, he's made a point of coming and visiting me, and I spent a month last summer over in England with him."

"You probably help him keep the memory of his son alive."

"I suppose so. Listen, totally different topic, but might I ask you what's going on in Germany these days with the Nazis and this Hitler fellow. From what I read in the newspapers, he sounds like quite a bully."

"Oh, I don't follow politics very much, but I suspect that much of what you read in the major American newspapers about Herr Hitler is rather exaggerated. They're all owned by Jews and they have a rather biased view of Germany. I spend my time keeping track of where are the best shops at the various ports along the Danube River – a much more pleasant task than paying attention to world politics. Speaking of which, are you looking to buy anything in particular on this trip – dresses, dishware, a cuckoo clock, perhaps?"

Mary Beth laughed. "No, mostly I just came along to see old friends from my college days, but… you never know… if I see a bargain along the way!"

"Well, we'll keep an eye out together for you on the cruise for a bargain! But for now, it's a lovely, sunny day outside, and you should be out on the boulevards, seeing the sights of Paris – and letting the men of Paris see you!"

After Karen left the table, Mary Beth stayed for one more cup of coffee and started thinking about what Karen had said about how Jews owned all the American newspapers, and all that implied. Karen wouldn't be the first anti-Semite she'd ever encountered, but it was a bit surprising, given what a sweet, pleasant image she otherwise projected. Perhaps Mary Beth was reading more into Karen's comment than she'd meant by it. After all, she had an uncle who referred to FDR as that "god-damned communist in the White House." Mary Beth decided she'd contemplated politics for long enough. It was time to get back to the next chapter of Reilly the Rabbit and his latest adventures.

Everyone returned from their city excursions to the hotel for dinner, which was superb. After dinner, Arthur and Tom Bishop went out on a glass-enclosed balcony to enjoy cigars and brandies and a spectacular view of the city. It was a bit chilly, but not too bad. From their chairs they could see the Eiffel Tower, lighted and standing out against the dark skyline.

"I can see why many American painters and writers have come to live in Paris. It must be quite inspirational," offered Tom.

"Did you ever have the urge to run off to Paris and become a writer," jokingly asked Arthur.

He gave him a sad look. "Really Arthur, how many insurance men do you know who ran off to Paris in their youth?" They both laughed. "And just what would I do in Paris?"

"Grow a goatee and become an artist."

"Could I paint beautiful, nude French women?"

Arthur smiled. "Well, it's been done before."

"I don't see myself as a painter, but it is a beautiful and vibrant city. I can see why artistic types come here, or maybe it's just because of all the beautiful women!"

"You might have hit on something there, Tom. And speaking of beautiful French women, Simone has certainly maintained her beauty, hasn't she?"

"Yes, she has. In fact, if it's possible, she's even more beautiful now than when we knew her in college. Must be the Parisian water," Tom joked.

"Well, if that's the case, remind me to take a case back to America! As I recall, you and she were dating back in Bloomington your senior year, weren't you?"

Tom smiled off into the distance across the skyline, like a man suddenly recalling fond reminiscences out of his past. "Yes, we went out a few times, but that was a long time ago… back when I was young and foolish, and didn't have to think about a mortgage, car payments, college expenses and all those other little things that come with being a responsible adult."

They both sighed. "Maturity is overrated," added Arthur. "Tomorrow, why don't you go buy a straw hat and a walking stick, and just go strolling along the boulevards, pretending that you don't have a care in the world. If a French woman comes up to you, tell her that you're Bing Crosby!"

"And if it's an American woman?"

"Then, tell her you're Maurice Chevalier." They both

laughed as they continued smoking and looking out at the snow-covered rooftops below them.

"We were all so optimistic back in 1924 when graduation came around, weren't we?" asked Arthur.

"Indeed we were," replied Tom. "We were all so sure that we were invincible and that life would go exactly as we planned."

Arthur blew a big cloud of smoke. "Well, for the first few years, I think that for most of us, it did. Then the stock market crashed in 1929, followed by the Great Depression, and millions of Americans had tough years, not just our graduating class."

"Tough times for sure," replied Tom.

"And now that business is picking up, well, life still has its ups and downs." A sadness came to Arthur's face, but he said nothing about Jan's illness.

Like others, Tom had noticed that Jan hadn't looked well, but he didn't want to raise the topic of her health. Since they were having such a philosophical discussion, he did raise one of his own problems. "Yeah, my business has started to turn around, but Lenora and I have been having difficulties over the last year or two. It doesn't seem to be any one particular issue. I guess sometimes, people just change as the years roll by."

"That certainly must be the case for a lot of couples. I hope things work out for you two, but if not, well... you're still a relatively young man. Sometimes, you just have to bite the bullet and make changes, even though that might be a hard thing to do in the initial months."

The two then just lapsed into silence, staring out at

the beautiful Parisian skyline. Arthur thinking about his wife's illness. Tom thinking about his financial and marital problems, and of wonderful evenings with Simone long ago in Bloomington.

MUNICH

Colonel Blickensdorfer read through the weekly report on General Breithaupt, then dropped it down on his desk.

"So, Holger, still nothing of real interest on him is there?"

"No, sir. He continues to make his occasional disrespectful remark about the Fuhrer, but they're always in a joking manner, which one can interpret in various ways. He rarely leaves the base, but when he does, it's generally with his wife simply to go to dinner. Occasionally, he's with another Wehrmacht officer and his wife, or with one of their sons."

"Anything interesting on the two sons?"

"They are both junior-grade officers, but frankly they both seem more fanatically loyal to Herr Hitler and the Nazi Party than their father."

The Colonel laughed. "Well, a father can never be held responsible for his children. My son ran off to Rome, married an Italian girl and sits around all day painting pictures of old buildings."

"Is he any good, sir?"

"I think he's fairly mediocre, but he manages to sell

enough of them to rich tourists passing through the city to make some sort of living. At least he chose a nice, warm, sunny place in which to be a failure!"

Holger wasn't sure whether he was supposed to laugh along with the Colonel at that remark or not, so he just mildly smiled.

"Shall we continue the coverage of General Breithaupt?"

"Oh, absolutely, my instincts of an old policeman tell me that the good General is hiding something and if we're patient, we'll eventually find out what it is. Catching a spy, or a disloyal Army general, in the coming months would help me very nicely. There will soon be an opening for a very desirable job at Gestapo Headquarters in Berlin. Colonel Koch thinks he has a lock on that job, but we'll see. Unfortunately for me, he has the job now of ferreting out disloyal Jews and other Untermensch here in Bavaria, which brings him lots of publicity in Berlin. But, if I could uncover a traitorous senior Army officer, well..." Blickensdorfer just smiled. "So, keep at it, Holger, and there might be promotions for both of us in the coming year."

As Holger was leaving the building after his meeting with the Colonel, he was rather depressed. He hated to think that what to him was hard, but patriotic work for the good of the Fatherland apparently was seen by Blickensdorfer mostly as simply a stepping stone to promotion.

CHAPTER 7
Paris

On the group's last morning in Paris, Tom Bishop and Simone found themselves alone at a table in the restaurant. Everyone else had finished breakfast and gone out to do their last sightseeing or shopping in the City of Light. The waiters had retreated to the kitchen to smoke and drink coffee before they would eventually venture out to clear the dishes and reset the tables for lunch.

They were seated next to each other and after they'd finished eating, Simone reached over and placed her hand on his. "Oh, Tom, you don't know how good it is to see you after all these years. I've missed you so, mon chère." Her soft voice, with its French accent was mesmerizing. Tom stared deeply into her beautiful brown eyes.

He squeezed her hand and smiled. "And it's great to see you. I still think about you from time to time. The oddest little thing will trigger a memory of us doing something together back in Bloomington and of how happy I was when with you."

"And I have continued thinking about you as well. A few years after returning to France, I thought about writing you, but then I learned that you were married and decided it was too late for me and you."

He looked at her sadly. "For of all sad words of tongue or pen, the saddest are these: It might have been!"

"That's lovely, but very sad."

"It's from an old American poem. Well, you have a wonderful singing career going. Having your husband go to prison wasn't so nice, but I hear that your night club is doing well. So life hasn't turned out too badly for you."

"No, I suppose not and now my divorce is final, so I can get on with my life. It sounds like you have a successful career going back in Ohio, and a lovely family."

He laughed. "Well, nothing is ever as it outwardly appears. There are days when my daughter drives me crazy."

She smiled. "Yes, I have noticed that your daughter dresses and acts like a Parisian street-walker... but at least like an expensive one." She smiled. "I'm amazed your wife allows such behavior."

"Allows! She encourages it. I won't spoil our day by going into the details, but her looks and behavior have been a big problem. But never mind Hanna, it's so nice just being with you again. And we'll have the next ten days together to create new memories."

She smiled like she used to when she'd been a young girl at the University.

"Ah, I was so in love with you back then," she whispered.

"And I was with you. Why didn't you say something?" he asked.

She smiled and shrugged her shoulders. "Why didn't you?"

He shrugged his shoulders. "I guess I was afraid that you'd laugh at me. I mean, I knew that you enjoyed spending time with me, but I never imagined that such a beautiful girl from France could love me – a simple boy from southern Ohio, with no real prospects."

She laughed. "That was about the same reason for me. I couldn't imagine that an American could fall in love with a simple French girl.

There was a long silent pause as they just stared at each other.

Finally, Simone spoke. "Do you remember where we were the last time we saw each other in Bloomington?"

"Of course I do."

"So, where was it?" She grinned as she was skeptical that he did."

"It was in the old Well House in the middle of campus. You wore a blue dress and I was wearing a dark blue blazer. We kissed right in the center under the bright light. It was only three days before graduation."

"Ah, so you do remember. I'm impressed." She didn't have the heart to tell him that her dress had been yellow. She started to say more, but then paused and looked down at the table.

"What? Go on and tell me what you were about to say."

She blushed. "During the night before that last meeting, I had dreamed that on that last date that you would ask me to marry you. I didn't believe that you really would, but then you led me over to the Well House on the way back to my dorm – and well, you know the tradition of fellows asking their girls for their hands in marriage on that spot." She again stared down at the table.

Tom remained silent for several long seconds, before lifting her chin up. "Well, we must make up for all those lost years on this cruise," he replied while staring into her beautiful eyes.

"Yes, we must chat more, but now I must go over to my night club to make sure all is under control while I'm away."

"OK, but I was wondering why you've been staying here at the hotel, when you live in Paris?"

"I live almost out of the city and I didn't want to be traveling back and forth. Plus, this way I can spend more time with my old friends."

"I'm so glad you were able to join us. I'll see you tonight on the train for Munich."

"A bientot, my love." She kissed him on the check, then stood and left.

He sat back down and mumbled to himself, "Indeed, what might have been."

The travel group ate an early dinner at the hotel on December 22nd, while the luggage was being taken by several trucks to the train station. At 8:30 pm, two buses took all of the river cruise passengers to the Gare de l'Est train station for their 9:00 p.m. scheduled departure. Organized chaos was the best description of their arrival at the station and boarding of the train, but to Karen's credit, everyone was on board when it pulled from the station. Steam billowed from its massive engine and its wheels began to turn – starting them on their great adventure. Soon the lights of the magical city disappeared behind them as the train entered the dark, surrounding countryside of rural France.

MUNICH

The French train arrived an hour late the following morning in Munich, but the transfer of luggage and people to the Hotel Beethoven was accomplished in a much more orderly fashion than had been their departure from Paris. Several people joked about being able to see that they were now in efficient Germany. By noon, everyone was checked into their rooms and had had their luggage delivered. They had the afternoon free to do as they pleased, either wander about the city, or simply rest up from the train journey. They were scheduled to dine as a group at 7:00 p.m. Most of the European travelers of the planned cruise were only joining the group there in Munich, so there would be new people to meet.

Arthur was sitting in the elegant hotel bar in the afternoon, when in came Ivan Bogatyr. Arthur had seen him on the train with the tour group the previous evening, but he'd not had a chance to speak with him.

He likewise recognized Smith and came over to him. "I believe we're both on the Danube River cruise," he said in heavily accented English. He smiled broadly and extended his hand. "I am Ivan Bogatyr of Paris," he said with an unusual accent to his English. He was nearly six feet tall, with a full head of wavy brown hair and a sculptured chin. Jan would have definitely called him handsome.

Arthur rose from his chair. "I'm Arthur Smith of Chicago and yes, my wife and I are on the river cruise. Please, join me."

"Thank you. As you can tell from my name and my accent, I am not French." He smiled. "My family came from St. Petersburg and I am Russian."

"A pleasure to meet you. When did your family leave Russia?"

"We left in early 1917. My father saw what was coming and managed to leave with most of his money while he still could, as opposed to the hundreds of thousands of Russians who fled in subsequent years with nothing, and are now taxi drivers and waiters all over Paris. My father owns and runs several hotels around Europe." He smiled again.

"And do you work with your father in the hotel business?"

"Technically, yes, but mostly I work hard at spending my father's money." They both laughed.

"Well, I am one of those capitalist bankers that Mr. Lenin was always talking about getting rid of, for the good of somebody."

Ivan laughed.

"Are you married Ivan?"

"No, though I am more seriously looking around for a wife these days, than in years past. I'm soon turning forty and my parents have been strongly hinting that they would like a grandchild! Plus, my father thinks I would spend less money if I was home nights with a wife rather than out with different women many nights in various clubs and gambling casinos. That by the way, is how I know Madame Chevrolet. I have often been at her Parisian night club and it was she who mentioned to me about this holiday cruise."

"I'm glad that you were able to join us. At least this way, you'll be able to spend some of your father's money in several different countries."

"I like the way you think, Arthur." He raised his glass in a toast. "So, are there any beautiful women in this group?"

"There is one exceptionally beautiful woman, but unfortunately for you, she's already married to me."

"You know Arthur, you can't really be a banker – you have too much of a sense of humor! This is going to be an excellent cruise."

They toasted once again.

"You live in Paris, but you're only joining us here in Munich?"

Ivan laughed. "I almost missed the entire trip. I had been down in Marseilles, on business, well, let's call it business." Ivan smiled broadly. "And then my train up to Paris arrived late. I barely caught last night's train here to Munich."

"Well, you're here now and from here on, I believe we are all supposed to relax and simply enjoy the culture, the scenery and the good food."

"And the beautiful women of the Danube?"

"I don't believe that was mentioned in the tour brochure, but you are free to search on your own."

Ivan laughed and slapped Arthur on the shoulder. "I need to make you my banker. I shall see you tonight at the dinner."

"Until tonight," replied Arthur. As he walked away, Arthur was quite pleased with himself – not once had

Bogatyr described him as being "solid" or "dependable." Perhaps the new Arthur he was striving for was coming through.

Towards the end of the official welcoming dinner that night, Arthur went over to the table where Simone was seated, took an empty chair next to her.

"So, what did you do on your first day in Munich," he asked.

"Not too much. I wandered around a little near the hotel in the early afternoon and then I indulged in a long hot bath and a nap."

He was also curious to ask her about his new Russian friend. "By the way, I met one of your steady night club customers this afternoon – Ivan Bogatyr. He said you had recommended this cruise to him."

She gave him a curious smile. "Did he offer you an opportunity to invest in one of his businesses, or inquire if you knew any rich and beautiful women?"

"As a matter of fact, he did inquire if there were any beautiful women on our cruise, but didn't raise the question of their bank accounts."

"He will eventually."

"Do you know him well?"

"Not really. He and my ex-husband used to go to horse races and casinos together. He's been quite the international playboy for the last decade. However, rumor has it that he's now looking for a rich wife. Probably so that he can continue his luxurious lifestyle, without depending totally on his father's money."

"He has quite an interesting story. Anything else I

should know about him, before I get into any card games with him?"

She leaned over close to Arthur. "The White Russian emigres think he spies on them on behalf of the Soviet Union. The Communist Government in Moscow probably thinks he's working to overthrow them, so he can get his minor palace back. An official of the French *Deuxieme Bureau* told me one night after much wine that they think he does spying for the British."

"What do you think?"

"I think he'd probably take money from anybody willing to pay him, to do most anything."

Arthur laughed loudly. "So, he's an equal opportunity espionage agent. By the way, for whom do you work?"

"Moi?" she smiled. "I work for Simone!"

"Probably a wise policy in these troubled times," Arthur leaned over and kissed her on the cheek and then rose to leave. "Good night."

"Bonne nuit, Arthur."

Simone remained seated. She had no recollection of mentioning the cruise to Ivan, though it was possible — perhaps she'd been drinking one night and she just didn't remember. She wondered what Bogatyr was up to on the trip. She was curious because the Ivan she knew never did anything or went anywhere without there being some angle or plot for him to make money. The idea that Ivan was simply taking a river cruise for pleasure was inconceivable.

On the morning of the 24th, some slept late, some hit the streets with Karen to shop for handmade, Christmas ornaments and some just wandered about the lovely city on their own. Most came back to the hotel to have a hardy lunch that would tide them over until late that night when there was scheduled at 10:00 p.m. a Christmas Eve party for the group in the hotel ballroom. People were coming and going all day long from the hotel.

That evening, a number of the churches around the city were holding Christmas Eve services. Many of the passengers headed off to various churches to attend the religious services, or some to simply listen to the music. That was why the party at the hotel was set for so late. It was lightly snowing and not too cold that evening. A number of church bells were ringing around the city as large, fluffy flakes floated gently in the air. It was a beautiful night when one expected to see an angel appear at any moment.

Aside from the church goers, other passengers decided to just go out and walk about in the snow and see all the lovely Christmas decorations, especially down in the ancient part of the city. In the town square, a number of stands were set up to sell mulled wine, called gluwein. They had also set up a skating rink by the large Christmas tree, complete with a small brass band. Dozens of teenagers and young adults were skating.

Mike and Candy Taffe had decided to simply sit in the lounge area just off from the main lobby and drink a little wine after a light dinner, until it was time for the Christmas party upstairs. They watched the Bishops, Bob Hall, Fred Hendricks and Mary Beth Long all head out into the night between seven and seven-fifteen. Several of them stopped by and chatted briefly with the Taffes. Ivan

Bogatyr went rapidly through the lobby at seven-thirty, clearly in a hurry.

Just after Bogatyr left, Arthur Smith came over to them, carrying his fedora and gray wool coat.

"Good evening, Mike, Candy. How's the wine?"

"Excellent. Where are you off to?" asked Mike.

"Oh, Jan is upstairs taking a nap and I'm feeling a bit restless, so I thought I'd take a little stroll out in the snow. Funny how back home in Chicago I never like it when it snows, but this stuff is just floating down in such big, soft flakes, it's almost like a movie."

"Is Jan feeling alright?" asked Candy. "Does she need an aspirin or anything?"

"She's fine. She just wanted a little rest, so she'd be good to stay up late tonight for the Christmas party."

"Well, enjoy your stroll. Give my best to Santa Claus if you bump into him out there," joked Mike.

"I'll do that," Arthur replied as he put on his coat and hat and headed out into the wintry night.

At the German military base located just a couple of miles from the Hotel Beethoven, General Breithaupt finished an early dinner in the mess hall and then returned to his deserted office. Everyone had gone for the day. At seven, he put on a captain's coat and hat, picked up his book and quietly slipped away from the base to make his scheduled 8:00 p.m. clandestine meeting – he hoped. Gestapo Lt. Hinz was sitting alone in a car across from the main gate of the military compound. He'd given the six men of the surveillance detail the evening off for Christmas Eve, and he, a bachelor, had taken the evening watch. Frankly, he hadn't expected the General to go anywhere on Christmas Eve, except straight to his home, but he did just manage to see him leaving the base on foot. He hadn't recognized him at first, expecting him to go home in his chauffeur-driven staff car. The coat of a captain coming out the gate had fooled him at first, but the man looked much too old to be a captain. Hinz found this all very suspicious and followed him on foot. As there was only he, it was hard to follow and not be obvious.

The General seemed to be in no hurry and simply wandered about the streets of Munich in the falling snow. About forty minutes into the stroll, the General suddenly disappeared on Hinz, in a maze of narrow, twisted streets.

At ten o'clock, the guests started drifting into the ballroom of the Hotel Beethoven for their Christmas Eve party, which included music provided by a ten-piece orchestra. Karen had told people there was no need for formal attire that night, but most of the men did show up in tuxedos and the ladies in cocktail dresses. Jan looked gorgeous in her new lavender cocktail dress she'd purchased in Paris.

Karen had arranged for a children's choir from a nearby Catholic Church to come and sing. Some of their songs were even performed in English. Hearing their beautiful voices and seeing their cherubic faces got the evening off to a wonderful start. The nun who accompanied the fifteen children to the hotel also announced that the

Church was in the middle of a fundraising drive to assist the children at the orphanage run by her Order. Even the atheists in the room donated generously.

There was not a formal dinner per se, but rather all sorts of serious appetizers and wonderful desserts had been placed at all the tables, and bottles of vintage French champagne were in plentiful supply. Many of the guests freely moved around to different tables to chat with various people. Jan learned from Fred that he'd gone to a Catholic Christmas service earlier in the evening. He'd greatly enjoyed it, even though he was a Baptist. He hadn't understood much of the sermon as it was in Latin, not German! Mary Beth told Jan that she'd wandered around a bit in the center of the old city, admiring the decorations and enjoying some spiced cider on the town square. Once back at the hotel, she took a little nap before it was time to dress for the gala event. Lenora and her daughter, Hanna, had rented skates and gone skating at the town square. Tom said he'd skipped the skating as he'd developed a bit of a headache and had come back early to the hotel for a rest before that night's party.

Simone mentioned to Arthur that she too had been suffering from a headache in the afternoon and had taken two aspirins and then just slept until time to come down to the party in the ball room. Bob Hall told Arthur he too had wandered about in the beautiful snow, hoping to get some inspirational thoughts for his movie script. Arthur mentally noted that he never did see Ivan at the party that night, but thought that he might just have been at a table on the far side of the room.

The orchestra was very good and Arthur was living up to his promise that Jan could have as many dances as she wanted. She did notice at one point in the evening that he was looking rather tired from all the dancing, so she invited Mike Taffe to join her for a foxtrot. He graciously obliged. As they were headed for the dance floor, Arthur smiled and silently mouthed to Mike, "Thank you."

At the stroke of midnight, Karen mounted the small band stand and led the group in a singing of O Holy Night. Everyone had had enough wine and spirits by then that they thought they sounded good. She then reminded them that their buses would be leaving "punktlich" at one o'clock the next day for the train station and their 2:00 p.m. departure for Regensburg. From that ancient port city, they would then board the *Danube Princessa* to begin the river portion of their journey.

Late in the evening, Mary Beth spotted Arthur and Jan sitting off in a quiet corner, with champagne glasses in one hand and holding hands with the other. They looked very contented. She hoped that she might someday meet a second man in her life, with whom she could spend her older years in such contentment.

By 1:00 a.m., most all of the travel group had had their last glass of champagne and called it a night. Jan was in a wonderful mood. Christmas had always been her favorite holiday. This one was extra special since she was having it with many old friends and because it would likely be her last. It had been a great evening. She'd danced many tunes with her beloved Arthur in her beautiful new dress. What more could any woman ask for as a Christmas present.

At 10:00 a.m. Christmas morning, Lt. Hinz had the unenviable task of calling upon his superior, Colonel Blickensdorfer, at his home to brief him upon the previous night's "odd behavior" by the General. He'd also recalled his men to duty and put full surveillance back on Breithaupt.

Holger knocked on the Colonel's door and then stood at attention until it was opened by Blickensdorfer. "I'm guessing Lieutenant that you're coming to my home on Christmas morning is not a good thing?"

"No, sir, it's not."

"Well, come in and let's have some coffee while you explain the situation to me."

They settled in the den. Only after Mrs. Blickensdorfer had brought them coffee and then disappeared, did the Colonel nod for Holger to begin.

"I was on duty last evening, keeping an eye on the front gate of the military base. I presumed that all General Breithaupt would do would be to have his driver take him directly home, where he and his wife would remain on Christmas Eve. Therefore, I gave all the men in my surveillance detail the evening off, so as to be with their families."

"A reasonable assumption and a kindly gesture on your part to your men, but obviously a bad decision I take it."

"I followed the General on foot after he left the base wearing a captain's coat and hat, which I thought strange. He mostly just slowly strolled through the old part of the city. I thought perhaps he was simply enjoying a little walk in the lovely snowfall, reminiscing of his youth or something like that. As there was only me, I had to stay fairly close, so as not to lose him. He seemed to be making no effort at checking for surveillance, or of trying to lose surveillance, if he did have it. I kept thinking that any moment, he would turn around and head back to the base, but he just kept wandering. About forty minutes into his walk, I suddenly lost sight of him in an area of small, twisted old streets, near the well-known Marienplatz. I checked to see if he'd gone there, but it was almost thirty minutes later when I saw him leaving a small square nearby, which had five or six streets running into it. I also caught just a glimpse of the back of another person, going out another small street of this square. It was probably a man, but not a very large one – and could even have been a woman in a man's coat and hat. I wasn't sure if that person was particularly significant, so I decided that I should keep following the General. From this square, the General went directly back to the base. He walked much more purposefully, compared to his earlier wandering style. Within minutes of returning to the base, his driver took him directly home, where he stayed the rest of the evening. Approximately two hours later, the lights went out in the house and I presumed they'd gone to bed."

"So, you think 'something' happened during that half hour when you had no sight of him?"

"Yes, I do. His whole demeanor changed after I caught up with him at that square. Later that same night, I went back to that small square, not knowing exactly what I was looking for, but I wanted to check around there. That square would have made a very good place to have quietly met with someone. I saw nothing special, except I found a cocktail napkin from the Hotel Beethoven on top of the snow. It looked as though it had only been laying there a short time; it was clean and still fairly dry. It wasn't much, but I decided to go to that hotel to check it out."

"And did you find anything interesting there?"

"I talked with the desk clerk and he told me there was a party of some sixty foreigners staying there, mostly wealthy Americans and Brits and a few Frenchmen. And worse, the group is departing today at 2:00 p.m., to travel by train to Regensburg, where they will board the river cruise ship, *Danube Princessa*. They are traveling to Budapest, with several stops along the way."

Blickensdorfer stood up and strolled around the room with his hands clasped behind him and staring intently at the floor. "Hmmm. I fear your instincts might be right on this. First, it was a holiday night when the General went off and he might rightfully have assumed that most of the Gestapo would be off duty, and thus a good night to schedule a clandestine meeting. Second, your impression that his demeanor was different on his way back to the base compared to earlier in the evening was a very good observation and I think tells us something. Third, you saw someone walking out of the opposite side of that square, as the General was also exiting. Fourth, the cocktail napkin you found on top of the snow in that square was from a hotel where a lot of foreigners are staying, including British citizens. But the question is, what can we do in reaction to our suspicions?"

"Could we not just detain the entire tour group,

until we've had time to search their rooms and check their backgrounds?"

The Colonel smiled at Holger's naiveté. "No, we could never get such permission to detain a large group of Americans, on such short notice and thin evidence, especially on Christmas day!" He strolled once more around his living room. "The only practical option I see is that you and me, and perhaps two other men, will travel with them on this ship. This will give us, what, a week or more, to talk with the passengers and discretely check their cabins?"

"I believe it's nine days to Budapest, but will there be cabins available at this last minute?"

"Are there any Germans traveling on that ship?

"A few, I believe."

The Colonel smiled. "Well, they will simply 'voluntarily' give us their cabins. So, go home and pack and we will meet at the train station at 1:30 p.m. I know you only saw that person from the back in coat and hat, but perhaps you'll recognize someone on the ship. It will be good to have you go along with me in any case. I'll arrange for two others to join us. And while we're on the ship, I'll have my deputy back here pursue with Gestapo Headquarters in Berlin the question of whether we have enough to pull in Breithaupt, at least for some polite questioning, if not an out-and-out arrest."

"Very good, Colonel. I'll meet you at the train station."

The wheels of German counterespionage were set in motion. That small ship was going to be full of spies.

At 1:30 p.m. two trucks full of luggage and numerous

taxi cabs arrived at the Munich Hauptbahnhof. Traffic was fairly light on the streets of the city, given that it was Christmas Day, but the train station itself was quite busy. There were Germans arriving in the city to gather with relatives and residents of the city who were taking off on holiday journeys. A number of the American passengers commented about the difference at a German train station, compared to their boarding back in Paris. Karen was once again a master of management in getting her people and their baggage efficiently into the correct train cars. Former Naval Officer Fred leaned over to Arthur and quietly whispered to him, "I can see why no one wants to go to war against Germany."

Arthur just laughed, but in his mind he certainly agreed with what Fred had implied. He knew that military victories were a matter of logistical efficiency, not brilliant war plans.

The sky was still overcast, but the snow had stopped and everyone was in a cheerful, holiday spirit. The station porters were happy to work on Christmas day as they knew that the passengers, in the holiday spirit, would be tipping generously that day. At exactly 2:00 p.m. the train pulled smoothly from the station. Not that any of the American passengers had noticed, but four Germans who'd not previously been part of the cruise group also boarded the train in Munich that afternoon. There were indeed suddenly four spaces available for the river cruise once it had been explained to four German nationals booked on the cruise that they were "voluntarily" canceling their bookings and going home – or going to prison.

CHAPTER 8
Regensburg

The transfer of passengers and luggage from the small Regensburg train station to the *Danube Princessa* was once again a model of German efficiency, or at least it was under the direction of Karen! Arthur Smith found himself smiling as he watched the sweet, middle-aged shopping guide in action. Once she'd started speaking in German and giving orders to the ship's crew who'd come to the station to deal with the luggage and passengers, she turned into a totally different person.

The group arrived at the port only ten minutes later. Everyone got a good look at their ship, once they were all out of the buses. The luxury river cruiser had been built in Austria in 1913, but then it simply sat tied up to its mooring all through the Great War. Though it was twenty-five years old by 1938, it had been well-cared for both inside and out and looked as good as the publicity brochure about her had advertised. All the passengers were smiling as they walked up the boarding ramp onto the three-decker ship. It had been overcast when they'd arrived in Regensburg, but as they were boarding the ship the clouds broke up and the sun started to shine. Clearly, a good omen for the coming days on the river.

Before getting their cabin keys, all the passengers gathered in the Main Lounge area on the uppermost inside deck. The leather couches looked comfortable, the brass fixtures were well-polished and there was an elegant, mahogany-wood bar at one end. Captain Johan Ornsdorfer stood at the center of the crowd to officially welcome them on board. He looked like a sea captain straight out of a nineteenth-century oil painting. He had broad shoulders, a stern, weathered-face and keen eyes that darted around the room. All the brass buttons on his well-pressed coat were shining brightly. The neatly trimmed, mostly gray beard accented his face perfectly. His deep baritone voice had a heavy German accent, but his English was quite good.

"Welcome aboard the *Princessa*. I will see that your journey down this old river will be smooth and sure. My crew will ensure that you are comfortable and well-fed, and will respond to any needs that you may have. If, however, a crew member gives you an order, move smartly, because it will be in connection with your safety."

Waiters in white jackets were passing through the lounge handing out crystal flutes of good champagne while the Captain spoke.

"Also, be aware that pick pockets and card cheats will immediately be thrown overboard in mid-river. Beautiful women are of course exempt from such punishment." A wide grin then appeared on his face, turning him magically from a gruff mariner into everyone's favorite grandfather."

The passengers laughed. The Captain raised his

champagne flute. "To a smooth and pleasant journey – our last voyage of 1938!" They all raised their glasses and toasted one another. "When you are ready, please step over to this table and the Purser will give you the keys to your cabins. Your luggage has already been placed in your cabins. We will set sail in exactly thirty minutes."

Bob Hall wondered if the Captain would like to be in the movies. This real-life man looked and sounded better as an ancient mariner than any Hollywood actor in make-up and costume ever had.

Jan Smith was off talking with several other ladies and Arthur had found a space at the bar to wait until the line for the cabin keys had shortened. He nodded to the early-forties looking gentleman next to him and extended his hand. "I'm Arthur Smith, of Chicago."

"I am Werner Blickensdorfer, of Munich," replied the stranger in good English, but with a thick German accent. "A pleasure to meet you. You are part of this group of Americans?"

"Yes, my wife and I are traveling with many of our old friends from our college days. It's a reunion for twenty-five of us who were all together at Indiana University in the early twenties."

Werner smiled. "Ah, how marvelous – to be able to get together with old classmates in such a..." He pointed around the ship lounge. He was searching for the correct word. "Gemutlich" is the German word, but I'm afraid I don't know the correct English equivalent."

Arthur smiled. "You mean the setting here on the ship?"

Werner nodded.

"An American would probably say 'pleasant' or 'cozy' setting."

"Ah, thank you. So, all of you have been planning this trip for many months?"

"Most of us yes, but we have a few friends who signed up only ten days or so ago, once they knew they could get away from work or family obligations over the holidays. And what brings you on this cruise? Is it just you, or are you with your wife?"

"It's only me. I've been working very hard these last six months and I decided that I needed a vacation. My wife preferred to stay near her elderly mother and all her relatives for Christmas, so here I am alone." He then lowered his voice slightly and added with a smile, "And I don't really like her relatives anyway. I heard that there was still a cabin available at the last minute on this voyage and I signed up."

"Excellent. What is your profession?"

"I'm a banker in Munich." Blickensdorfer had decided to make that his cover story, instead of admitting to being with the Gestapo.

"A small world. I'm with the First National Bank in Chicago." He pulled out one of his business cards and gave it to Werner."

"I'm sorry. I don't have one of my cards on me. I'll give you one when I see you later."

"No problem. Ah, my wife is waving at me. I'm sure I'll see you later. Nice to have met you."

"Yes, nice to have met you." They shook hands once again and Arthur departed.

Blickensdorfer cursed himself for not having come up with a better story, but he'd only had a few hours back in Munich to even make the train. There'd been no time to obtain business cards and back stopping for his "cover story", but then he hadn't planned on such bad luck as meeting a real banker in the first hour on the ship! Holger Hinz was simply traveling as a junior Gestapo officer, who'd been sent along to make sure there were no security incidents on a cruise with so many foreigners present. The two enlisted Gestapo men that Colonel Blickensdorfer had chosen at the last moment to accompany him didn't speak but a few words of English and just vaguely told whomever inquired that they were "businessmen" on the way to Budapest. The Colonel had brought them along for "muscle" if needed, and for searching all the cabins.

As the Main Lounge emptied, Werner and Holger had a chance to speak together. "I learned from Mr. Arthur Smith of Chicago that most all of the Indiana University group, of which he is part, have been planning for this trip for several months. That doesn't mean that one of them couldn't have made a meeting with General Breithaupt last night, but for the moment I think we should consider them less likely suspects. Though Smith did tell me that there were a few of his group who only signed up for the trip in the last week or two. If we could find out who those are, they might merit a closer look."

"That's logical," replied Holger, "though I'd be more

suspicious of the British or French citizens on this cruise, rather than an American."

Werner nodded vaguely in agreement. "You and I should mingle separately, so as to meet as many people as possible and to learn as much as we can about the backgrounds of these foreigners. And most importantly, find out who was doing what on Christmas Eve in Munich." The two then headed over to get their cabin keys and then went to unpack. They were in rooms on different decks.

At seven o'clock, all sixty passengers gathered in the dining room for a Christmas dinner, which was a spectacular fare and gave all the guests a good idea of how well they would be dining in the coming days. There was also a trio of black jazz musicians from Chicago, called Joe Jefferson and the Jeffersonians. Karen stopped by Mr. Smith's table for a moment during dinner and so he asked her, "Where on earth did you find three musicians from Chicago?"

She laughed. "Well, they are from Chicago, but they've been playing in Paris for the last couple of years. I thought since half of the passengers on board this trip are Americans, you'd probably enjoy having American music. I hope you like jazz?"

"We do, this is a real treat for my wife and me, and for many others as well, I'm sure."

She leaned down close to his ear. "There was a little difficulty about having 'schwarzers' on the ship, but I ..." She saw that he didn't understand the German slang term. "I mean, there was trouble about having 'blacks' on board, so I listed them as being Algerians."

Smith was astounded. "And that made them acceptable?"

She smiled broadly, "Well, that and the envelope of German marks that I gave Captain Ornsdorfer. He's a very practical man."

It was Smith's turn to smile. "Interesting to see that money 'talks' in all languages."

Karen moved on and Smith's attention turned to watching a lovely woman enter the dining room after all the other guests had been seated. He'd not seen her at the welcoming reception earlier in the day. She was elegantly dressed and wearing an impressive diamond necklace with matching earrings that he guessed were the real thing. She appeared to be in her mid-thirties, with a slim build and her lovely face had Germanic features. Captain Ornsdorfer immediately came over to her, leaned over to kiss her extended hand and personally led her over to sit at his table. She moved with grace, as if she had once been a dancer, or at least had attended some finishing school which taught young ladies how to properly walk. Whomever she was, she clearly wasn't one of the average passengers on the cruise.

Blickensdorfer managed to insert himself at a table with seven Americans. As Mary Beth Long was a "single", he took the chair on her right to fill the table for eight. He was very polite and charming, though Mary Beth noticed that during dinner he asked a lot of questions about the background of the American passengers, but offered few details about himself. On his right was Fred Hendricks. After it came out in conversation that prior to Fred's current stock broker career that he'd been in the U.S. Navy, the German seemed particularly interested in him.

"You were an officer?"

"Yes, I was a Lieutenant Commander when I resigned with a medical discharge."

"Oh, how unfortunate. And what had been your specialty with the Navy?"

"I was in Intelligence."

Fred finally managed to start talking with the couple on his other side and end the questioning about a part of his life he'd just as soon forget.

However, a few minutes later, Werner got back in to conversation with Fred. "Did you come over on the same ocean liner as Mr. and Mrs. Smith and many of the others of your former classmates?"

"No, I had some business to conduct in England, so I'd sailed to London about ten days earlier, and then came over to France to meet up with the others in Paris on the 22nd."

"Oh, how fortunate for you. I've never been to London. At some point on our cruise, I'd like to speak with you and get some ideas on what I should see when I do finally get there for a visit."

"Certainly, I'd be glad to give you a few suggestions."

"And how did you enjoy my home city of Munich?"

"Very lovely, especially so when we had the snowfall on Christmas Eve."

"Oh, yes, that certainly put everyone in the Christmas mood, didn't it? Did you have a chance to get out that evening and walk in the snow?"

"Yes, for a short while. I'd gone to attend a Christmas service at one of the beautiful Catholic Churches near where we were staying. Afterwards, I strolled slowly back to the hotel enjoying the big, beautiful snowflakes coming gently down."

"Ah, so you understand German?"

Fred laughed. "Well, I know some, but not being a Catholic, I didn't know that the service would be in Latin." They both laughed.

Blickensdorfer turned to Mary Beth. "And what did you do on Christmas Eve in Munich?"

"I also went out that evening in the lovely snow to wander around a bit in the old part of the city. I drank some hot gluwein at the town square, then came back to get dressed for the party." She lowered her voice and leaned in towards Werner. "It takes some of us longer than others to get beautiful you know."

He laughed. "But you are beautiful to begin with my dear. You shouldn't need more than five minutes to get ready for any event."

"Why, thank you kind sir." She was flattered by his comment, but had found it interesting that Werner had spent more time during dinner speaking with Fred than her. His inattention to her had been a little insulting to her feminine ego, and she'd almost begun to wonder if despite his claim of having a wife back in Munich whether he might be a homosexual, but then he started reciting a love poem to her.

Du bist wie eine Blume,
So hold und schön und rein;
Ich schau' dich an, und Wehmut

Schleicht mir ins Herz hinein.
Mir ist, als ob ich die Hände
Aufs Haupt dir legen sollt',
Betend, dass Gott dich erhalte
So rein und schön und hold.

"That's lovely, Werner, though I couldn't understand all of it, but thank you very much."

"Ah, so you understand German?"

"I remember a little from my college days. Who wrote that charming poem?"

"Heinrich Heine wrote that little piece almost a hundred years ago about a woman's beauty. It seemed quite appropriate for you."

At the end of the evening, when alone back in his cabin, Blickensdorfer made notes about what he'd learned about the activities of all seven Americans on Christmas Eve in Munich. They'd all gone out from the hotel, but five of them had been out as a group. Only Fred and Mary Beth had ventured out by themselves. Fred's background in Naval Intelligence, his ability to speak German and having just been in London before the cruise definitely earned him a place towards the top of the Gestapo man's suspect list. However, his investigation was only beginning and so he remained open to suspect anyone at that early stage. He also needed to learn more about several British and French gentlemen who apparently had also only signed up for the tour quite recently.

On the following morning, the Smiths had a late breakfast in the dining room, while the ship was still docked in Regensburg.

"By the way, dear, I meant to ask you earlier, but got distracted, do you know why Mike is carrying a gun on him?"

A surprised look came to his face. "Are you sure?"

"Well, when I danced with him at the party on Christmas Eve, he certainly was. I was up quite close to him and I certainly know the feel of a gun pressed against me. Remember, we went to a lot of dances back in the twenties after we'd moved up to Chicago after college – when a number of gentlemen during the Prohibition Era always wore guns under their coats."

Arthur smiled. "Yes, a lot of fellows carried guns in Chicago in those years. No, I have no idea why Mike would be wearing one on this trip."

"Doesn't really matter. Just thought I'd mention it to you."

"Well, if a proper moment presents itself, I'll ask him."

The sunshine of the previous day had been short lived and more typical for Central Europe in December, dark and ominous clouds had rolled in during the night. Despite the threatening weather, many of the other travelers went off promptly at 9:00 a.m. on a city tour led by Karen. She took them to the 13th century Cathedral of St. Ivan and several other historical sites in the old part of the city. The city itself had started as a Roman settlement. The Christmas dinner the night before had been great fun, but had left Jan quite tired in the morning, so they had passed on the tour and risen late. They were the only people present in the dining room and had just received their coffee when Holger Hinz arrived.

"Good morning. May I join you?"

"Certainly, we were just about to order. Since you're arriving so late for breakfast, I'll ask if you were you up late last night?" jokingly inquired Arthur.

"A little bit," replied the German with a smile. "I am Holger Hinz," he added in his German-accented English."

"And you are German, I presume?"

"Yes, I am a security officer of the German government. Since there are so many foreigners on this trip, I've been sent along to make sure that there are no problems for you."

"Oh, I see," replied Jan. "And are you expecting problems?"

He smiled. "Not that I am aware of, but it would look bad for my country if foreigners were robbed or bothered in any way." He shrugged his shoulders, "but what do I know, I am only a lieutenant. They tell me to go on the ship, I go on the ship." He gave them a cheerful smile.

Having once been a lowly Army corporal in the Great War, Arthur understood about carrying out orders when they were given, even if there seemed to be no real logic to them. "Let's see if we can get the attention of the waiter. I'm starving."

Holger caught the eye of a waiter and raised his right hand in the air to snap his fingers. The waiter immediately came over to the table. Arthur was impressed.

After they'd placed their orders, there began the usual exchange of questions and answers about where they'd been born, lived now, etc. As Holger was not in a uniform, there was no way of knowing exactly which "security" service he was with and Arthur decided it was probably best not to inquire.

"Your English is quite good, Holger. Did you start learning it as a young boy in school?" inquired Jan.

"I started studying English when I was fourteen, but I don't have many opportunities to practice it in Munich. I do go to all of the American movies that come to my city, which are shown in their original English, with subtitles. That gives me some practice, but your American gangsters are difficult to understand." They all laughed. Arthur was about to do his imitation of Jimmy Cagney, but Jan touched him on the arm, indicating he should not. She knew he loved to show off his Cagney imitation, but only when others were drunk did anyone think he was funny.

Bob Hall suddenly appeared, which stopped Arthur's idea of imitating any actor. "Bob, do come join us."

As he introduced Bob to Holger, Arthur added, "I hate to say this to you old friend, but you look terrible! How much champagne did you drink last night?"

Bob shook his head in a sign of regret. "It wasn't the champagne. It was that Russian fellow, Ivan, and his suggestion that we should drink vodka towards the end of dinner."

The other three laughed. "You should never try drinking vodka with a Russian," cautioned Holger.

As they ate their breakfast, Bob repeated for Holger's benefit as to how he'd been in England working on a movie script and decided at the last minute that he could get away for a few weeks over the holidays with his old college friends. Holger was very impressed that Bob was involved in the making of movies in Hollywood. He also mentally noted that Bob spoke German with their waiter.

"I was just telling the Smiths how much I enjoy going to American movies, especially your cowboy movies. Are there really many Indians still in America?" asked Holger, quite seriously.

"Well, I'm sure that there are out in Arizona and Texas, but most of the Indians you see in the movies are just white men in make-up and costumes." Once he saw the crestfallen look on Holger's face, he realized what a mistake he'd made and tried to make amends. "But the gangster movies, now those people, except for the top stars like Cagney or George Raft, are all real gangsters. The studios have a deal with Alcatraz prison to borrow prisoners to play the secondary roles. That's why they're so realistic." Holger looked much happier. Jan hid a small smile behind her napkin.

The foursome chatted for almost an hour, then all went their separate ways. Jan decided to go back to their cabin to rest just a bit more before she and Arthur were going to venture out for a walk in the city. Arthur remained in the dining room to drink more coffee and have a cigar. Bob also went back to his cabin to return to bed, in hopes of speeding his recovery from the vodka. Holger went to Colonel Blickensdorfer's cabin to report to him as to what he'd learned about the various passengers at last night's dinner and that morning.

Smith moved over to a small table near a window,

from which he could watch activity on the dock. No sooner had he sat down than the clouds opened up and a steady drizzle of cold rain began to fall. There was no wind, so it came directly down. Arthur was now glad they'd skipped the walking tour that morning! A few minutes later, he saw the arrival of two large, black limousines flying Nazi swastikas on the front corners of the vehicles. They pulled up right next to the ship's gang plank. He presumed that some German VIP was about to disembark, and he saw a uniformed officer jump from the front passenger seat. He put up a large, black umbrella, then moved to open a back door of the car. Out stepped an attractive and rather exotic looking woman in her mid-thirties from the car. She definitely didn't look Germanic; she was much too dark-skinned and her eyes reminded him of women he'd once seen in New Orleans while there at a banker's convention. Her black hair was cut fairly short. She was dressed well, but not in anything one would call glamorous attire. Several suitcases were retrieved from the second vehicle and the entire entourage moved smartly up the gangplank of the *Danube Princessa* so as to get out of the rain as quickly as possible. The uniforms of the men escorting her were black, not the usual gray of the Wehrmacht, so he didn't know what branch of the German military they came from. He saw that Captain Ornsdorfer himself was waiting at the top of the gangplank to meet his new passenger, so Smith guessed she was someone important.

A few minutes later the Captain escorted the woman into the dining room and to Smith's surprise, he heard them speaking English. There was a slight accent to her speech, but she spoke English fluently. She had high cheek bones, very dark eyes and jet black hair. It made for a lovely combination. Arthur wondered if she was a famous model. It appeared as though Captain Ornsdorfer was about to sit down at the table with her, when she rather abruptly dismissed him and told him that she wished to have her breakfast alone. The Captain bowed slightly and turned away to leave her. On his way out of the dining room, he stopped briefly to say hello to Smith and inquire if he was well.

Smith continued his cigar and coffee, while staring out the window as the rain continued. Fifteen minutes or so had passed since the woman's arrival in the dining room when suddenly she was near his side and spoke to him.

"Would you have a match?" she asked. She was holding a cigarette.

He pulled a lighter from his pocket and clicked the flame on. She leaned forward and lighted her cigarette.

"Thank you. I heard the Captain speak English with you. Are you English?"

He smiled. "No, I'm an American." He stood and extended a hand. "My name is Arthur Smith, of Chicago."

She shook his hand. "Oh, I hadn't expected any Americans on a ship in Germany at this time of year. I'm Mikaela LeBlanc of New Orleans."

He smiled. "I'm pleased to meet you." She seemed to be in no hurry to return to her table and so he asked, "Would you care to join me?"

"A pleasure. Are there many Americans on this ship?"

"About thirty-five I believe. I'm part of a group who all went to college together. We're having a reunion while we cruise down the Danube to Budapest over the holidays."

"How very charming. I'm on my way to Greece and this seemed like a delightful way to travel, instead of on one of those smelly trains and I absolutely refuse to fly in an airplane."

"Well, I've been up in a few planes, but I agree with you that ship travel is much more pleasant if you're not in a hurry to get somewhere. By the way, that was an impressive arrival you made earlier this morning. Are you someone very important?" He gave her a pleasant smile.

She smiled back. "Oh, you mean the cars and the escorts? I'm not particularly important, but I know a few Germans who are. I've found in life that having well-placed friends is often useful. Is that not true in your business Arthur?"

"I'm in banking, so yes, it is."

The steady rain continued outside. "I hope I didn't bring the rain with me – that could be a bad sign for our journey!"

"Do you believe in 'signs' and such things?" asked Arthur.

She gave him a nice smile. "Yes, actually I do." She blew a perfect smoke ring into the air. "If you're wondering, I'm an Acadian, or a Cajun as they often call us down in Louisiana."

"I've heard the term Cajun, of course, but never Acadian."

"When the British took control of Canada from the

French in 1763, several thousands of us moved from Acadia down to the New Orleans area and to some of the Caribbean islands. I'm thus a mixture of French, Spanish and a little Choctaw Indian. I can trace my family back almost 150 years.

"And English is your native tongue?"

"I speak English, but also French, or a version of French anyway, although Frenchmen cringe when they hear me speak our Cajun version."

"They cringe when they hear me speak my high school French as well," replied Smith with a smile and she laughed.

She'd finished her cigarette. "It was very nice meeting you Mr. Smith. I'm sure we'll be seeing more of each other during our cruise."

"A pleasure meeting you, Miss Le Blanc."

He'd wanted to ask her what she'd been doing in Germany and why she was traveling to Greece, but he didn't wish to appear too inquisitive at a first encounter. He put out his cigar and headed down to his cabin to see if Jan still wanted to go for a little stroll on shore despite the rain.

While Smith was getting acquainted with Miss LeBlanc, Lt. Hinz and Col. Blickensdorfer were having their meeting in the latter's cabin. The Colonel had already put to paper what things he'd learned and simply let Holger read his report about the seven Americans and one British couple with whom he'd chatted the previous night. "As you can see from my notes, so far, the former American Naval Intelligence officer, Fred Hendricks, looks the most interesting."

While hating to disagree with his superior, Holger replied, "I still think we're most likely looking for an Englishman. You don't think the husband of the English couple you met is worth further investigation?"

"I'm having Hans and Manfred search all the cabins, including theirs, but if you'd met Mr. Porter last night, I don't think he'd be on your suspect's list. He's in his sixties and could barely decide what food or drink to order without first checking with his wife!" They both laughed. "What do you have to report?"

"Well, I spoke with several Americans last night, but none of them would seem to fit the profile of a secret agent working for the British or French. At my table was the Bishop family. Tom Bishop sells insurance in Cincinnati, Ohio and from the clothing on his wife and teenage daughter, it doesn't look like he needs to earn any extra money. His wife spent most of the evening bragging about herself or her daughter. And I'm glad I met the daughter, Hanna, with her parents. Otherwise, given the way she dressed and flirted, I might have thought she was a young prostitute working the ship!" The Colonel started laughing so hard he almost slipped out of his chair.

"I learned that on Christmas Eve, all three had gone to the city square. Mrs. Bishop and Hanna went skating, but Tom said that he'd felt a headache coming on and came back to the hotel before the other two, so that he could take a nap before the Christmas party that night."

"So he was on his own for an hour or more that evening?"

"Yes, and we have no way of confirming his story

of coming directly back to the hotel. This morning I met another American. His name is Bob Hall. He has been in England for the past six or seven weeks. He claimed he's been working on the making of a movie. His decision to come on the cruise was a last minute one and though he claimed he only knows a few words, when he spoke several times with the waiter, his German sounded very good and very colloquial. I asked him where he'd studied German and he claimed he'd only had a few semesters while at the university, but it didn't sound like school boy German."

"What about Christmas Eve in Munich, for this Bob?"

"He said that he attended one of the Christmas church services, got lost for a while trying to find his way back to the hotel and reached there about nine."

"So, he was also out and unaccounted for when the General might have been having a meeting."

"It looks that way. He didn't mention whether he was with any other passengers at the church and it would have been awkward to have specifically asked him about that this morning. He'd been drinking vodka last night at the party with the Russian, Ivan something, and he looked pretty hungover at breakfast."

"We'll keep an eye on him and make a point of searching his room very thoroughly. Then there's this Russian, Ivan Bogatyr." Blickensdorfer looked at his note book. "Apparently, he was also out for several hours by himself that night."

"So, another name for our list."

"We should learn more about Bogatyr. And what about Mr. and Mrs. Smith?"

"They're a very charming couple. He's a vice-president at some bank in Chicago. I can't see any reason for his helping British Intelligence, but apparently he went out alone for a stroll in the evening as well. It wasn't clear exactly when he went out or returned."

"Yes, I met him briefly yesterday at the bar. He seems a pleasant man, but if he was out alone during the evening when you lost track of Breithaupt, we'd best put him on our suspect's list as well."

Blickensdorfer looked once more at his notes and then his watch. "Very well for now. Let's get to the Main Lounge and chat with more passengers. You go ahead. I'll follow in five minutes, so we don't come in together."

The Dining Room was filling up quickly at lunchtime. Walking about Regensburg in the cold, wet weather had clearly worked up an appetite among many of the passengers. Standing at the main entrance in a traditional Austrian dirndl dress with white apron was a tall and lovely young lady of perhaps fifteen years. She had blonde hair and a broad smile. She was welcoming the passengers in excellent English to lunch. Once everyone was seated and orders were being taken by the waiters, Captain Ornsdorfer started visiting the different tables to inquire of how his guests had enjoyed their morning. He was quite cheerful and was drinking a clear liquid from a large glass. He had barely arrived at the table which included Mr. and Mrs. Smith when the young lady in the dirndl came up to the Captain, whispered something to him and took the glass from him.

He turned back to the table. "So, how was your

morning tour of Regensburg? It's a beautiful old city isn't it?"

Several of the guests agreed with his statement and mentioned St. Ivan's Cathedral and the tomb of St. Erhard in a former abbey in particular.

Arthur Smith was curious about the young lady who'd come over and briefly spoken to the Captain. "Who is the lovely teenager who just spoke with you Captain?"

He smiled proudly. "Ah, that is Kinley, my daughter."

"We spoke briefly with her when we entered the dining room. Her English is excellent," added Jan. "She travels with you?"

"Yes, her mother died when she was only nine. I left her to live with my sister and her husband for the next two years, when I was off sailing, but the past four years, she comes with me. She missed her papa."

"She makes a perfect hostess."

"Oh, not only that, but she can navigate by the stars, steer the ship and even knows how to repair the engines. The entire crew treats her as their little sister. She is spoiled rotten!" he said with a laugh. "And don't let that angelic smile fool you. Some of my crew has also taught her how to swear like a drunken sailor."

The whole table laughed. "Well, it's nice that she is able to travel with you," commented Jan with a hint of envy.

"That's why her English is so good. She has Americans and British to practice with all the time during cruises, and her French is quite good as well."

Captain Ornsdorfer moved on to the next table. Maurice Garnier, a Frenchmen who had come to study at

Indiana University in 1922, was seated with the Smiths. He'd only stayed two years and then went back to France. Rumor at the time was that his wealthy father had sent him off to America to get him away from the Socialists. His father had thought he'd been spending too much time around them and they were having a bad influence on his son. Maurice was a smallish man, perhaps five foot two with a thin build. He looked and dressed like a typical Frenchman.

It was the first time that he and Arthur had had a chance to talk as he'd only arrived in Munich barely in time for the Christmas Eve party. "Maurice, what's become of you since you returned to France back in 1924?"

"Against my father's wishes, I got involved in politics and am now the Socialist mayor of a small city just south of Paris. And what of you, Arthur?"

"Congratulations on getting elected. I returned to Chicago and followed in my father's footsteps into banking after college. Things were a little tough in the early 1930s, but now we're doing well. You remember Jan, don't you?"

He smiled. "Mais oui, who could forget such a beautiful woman!"

Jan almost blushed. "And what about you Maurice, are you married now?"

"Sadly, no. I claim that I am simply too busy with politics to find a wife, but the truth is, I enjoy too much being single!" He gave a mischievous smile.

"Did you ever finish a university degree, back in France?" asked Arthur.

"No, I realized that for what I wanted to do, namely,

go into politics, having a degree would be of no real help. In fact, it might even be seen as a negative thing by the people I want to vote for me." They both laughed.

"Have you made other river cruises, Maurice?" asked Jan.

"No, this is my first one. Though last year I went via train to Spain for two weeks, and the previous year, I visited Moscow to see how the Worker's Paradise was progressing."

"And how is it progressing?" asked Arthur.

"Very well, very well indeed. You know, all this talk of the danger of another European-wide war is nonsense. It will never happen. The workers of all the nations are growing closer and closer, and will simply pay no attention to any leader who orders them to attack workers of another nation."

"Well, let's hope you're correct, Maurice, about there not being another major war coming, for whatever reason. But in any case, whatever happens in Europe, it won't involve America like last time."

"America would just sit at home and watch Hitler and the evil Nazis take over all of Europe?"

"Perhaps the European countries should do something about a problem in Europe, if there is one. I didn't notice France offering to support Czechoslovakia back in September. Besides, you just told me that the workers of the various countries would never go to war against each other."

Arthur decided it was time to change the subject to something less serious. "I didn't see you at our Christmas

Eve party in Munich, Maurice. Were you out celebrating elsewhere, or did I just miss you?"

"I'd gone out to wander around in the old part of the city in the early evening and found a quaint little restaurant where I had dinner. The party at the hotel was well under way by the time I returned. I only stayed a brief while at the hotel Christmas Fete. By the way, did you and Jan get out to see something of Munich in the lovely snow fall before the party?"

"Arthur went out for a stroll, but I'm getting on in age and needed a little rest that afternoon, so that I could stay up past my usual bedtime for the party," replied Jan.

Everyone laughed.

"Well, it looked like everyone was having a great time at the party," commented Maurice.

"Yes, we did. It's a shame you missed hearing the children singing Christmas songs at the start of the party. They were wonderful."

Towards the end of lunch, Maurice brought the conversation back around to politics. "Arthur, you must know the mood of Americans pretty well. Do you think the socialist movement is growing as fast in America as it is here in Europe?"

"Oh, I don't follow politics as closely as you do, but I'd say it's actually the opposite. With the Great Depression coming to an end and people finding it easier to get good jobs, I think interest in socialist or communist ideas is actually fading in America."

Maurice nodded. "Well, we shall see in the years ahead how it goes, but I think a worker's state is the only real solution in the end for everyone to be happy. One day there will be a worldwide revolution of the proletariat, led by the Soviet Union."

"Perhaps, but do you think we have time for dessert and coffee now, before the workers all rise up?" asked Arthur with a perfectly straight face.

Maurice could tell he was being kidded. "Yes, I think we have just enough time, if we order quickly."

"Good, because I've heard that dessert today is seven-layer chocolate cake, and I don't want to miss that!"

"Absolutely not," agreed Maurice. "We shall postpone the revolution until after dessert." Everyone at the table had a good laugh.

Conversation was getting a bit heated at a nearby table where the two residents of Paris, Simone Chevrolet and Ivan Bogatyr, were exchanging insults. Holger Hinz found it all quite interesting.

"All I was asking, dear Simone, was whether the Parisian Police still considered you a suspect as being a part of your husband's jewel theft activities?"

"Ivan, it was my husband who went to jail earlier this year, not me. You two were such friends. I thought the police might still be investigating you in connection with those thefts. Or have you been too busy seducing other men's wives to be part of robberies of wealthy homes?"

"I only asked because it is quite interesting that several of the people who had their homes robbed were at your night club when it happened. One might almost think that you tipped off your husband about which rich people planned to be out on certain nights."

"Let's move on, Ivan, to a more pleasant topic," suggested Simone. "How is your effort at finding a rich woman to marry coming along? Any good prospects here on the ship?"

Ivan took out his pocket watch. "Oh, look at the time. I should get downtown to finish a little shopping yet today. I'll see you all later." He rose, bowed slightly and left. Simone refused to even look up at him. Several couples at the table also excused themselves and finally it was only Holger and Simone left, drinking coffee.

"I see that being from the nobility does not ensure that one has manners or politeness," snidely observed Holger.

Simone smiled. "Ivan's family was of such minor Russian nobility I don't think the Bolsheviks even thought them worth shooting."

"I gather from the luncheon conversation that you now own and sing at a famous night club in Paris, and that you had studied at this Indiana University with many of the other passengers. Correct?"

"Yes, I was born near Paris and was sent to study music at that American university. My mother hoped I would become a famous opera star, but such was not my dream, nor was I that talented."

"I suspect that you're being overly-modest, Madame. By the way, I was born in Munich. Tell me please whether you enjoyed your time in my home city?"

"It's a lovely city. I went to several beautiful churches and walked around on Christmas morning in the old part of the city."

"Did you get outside on Christmas Eve, when we had the spectacular snow fall, like in a fairy tale?"

"No, sadly I had a terrible headache come over me late that afternoon, so I just stayed at the hotel all afternoon and evening. I took several aspirins and was in bed until it was time for our party that night."

"What a pity. Mr. Bishop told me that he too came down with a headache that afternoon and came back early to the hotel to sleep. I hope you're feeling better now."

"Yes, I've felt fine since Christmas morning and I'm so looking forward to this cruise down the Danube. I've had beautiful fantasies of what the Danube River must look like ever since I was a little girl, and now I shall finally get to see it."

"I hope that it's everything that you've been expecting. Well, I should get up and do some walking around – create the illusion that I'm really protecting you."

"Protecting us?"

"Oh, most everyone else has heard, so I assumed that you had as well. I'm a security officer and have been sent along on the cruise to make sure that all of you foreign tourists remain safe."

Simone's face took on a serious look. "I see, and what German security organization are you from?"

"I am a lieutenant in the Gestapo."

"Naturally, I have heard of the Gestapo, but not always in the context of protecting foreigners."

"We carry out a number of duties for Germany." He could tell that Simone was not particularly pleased to hear that there was a Gestapo officer on board, so he bid her a good afternoon. "It was a pleasure to meet you. I hope you have no more difficulties with the Russian fellow."

"Good afternoon, Herr Hinz."

Holger knew that Jews and various other "Untermensch" did not like the Gestapo, but he was disappointed to see that such an educated and refined woman as Simone likewise had such a negative opinion of his organization.

Simone was a little worried that Lt. Hinz had been making a point in his comments that both she and Tom Bishop had been back at the hotel with headaches on the afternoon of Christmas Eve in Munich. She wondered if he suspected something was going on between her and Tom. No, she decided, she was just being paranoid. Why would Hinz even care, much less know that Tom had been in her room that day? A smile came across her face as she remembered the pleasure of making love with him that afternoon. She'd told him that it was the nicest Christmas gift she'd ever received.

CHAPTER 9
On the Danube River

The ship departed from Regensburg mid-morning the following day, the 27th of December. It had turned colder, but it was a bright and sunny day as the elegant 220-foot *Danube Princessa* moved smoothly from the dock. The engines generated a barely detectable vibration throughout the ship. The river was calm and the ship sailed southward in the direction of their next stop, Passau. After breakfast, many of the passengers had gone back to their cabins or were spread about in the lounge, reading or chatting. Jan had a massage after breakfast from Inga Snelson, who looked just like a thirty-year old Swedish masseuse should – tall, blonde, broad-shouldered and quite lovely. Jan had found back in Chicago that massages helped relieve her headaches and she'd scheduled one with Inga on the first day of the cruise. She'd found that first one quite relaxing and decided she'd indulge herself with one every day.

After the massage, Jan was having tea in the Main Lounge when she saw young Kinley walking by and called her over to her table. No dirndl dress today, but she still looked quite pretty in just everyday clothes and she had an infectious smile.

"Hello, my dear, I'm Jan Smith."

"Good morning, Mrs. Smith, I'm Kinley. How was your massage today?"

"Wonderful. Inga does an excellent job and is very cheerful and it was fun to talk with her."

"Yes, she's the only other female crewman on the ship so she and I have become good friends."

"Have a seat, Kinley, if you have a few minutes free."

"I do. I have no duties until lunch is served."

"My husband and I were talking to your father last evening at dinner. It sounded to me like you have a full-time job on this ship – taking care of him!"

They both laughed. "Yes, he requires much attention."

They spent a pleasant half-hour drinking tea and chatting. Kinley was very mature in her speech and behavior for a fifteen year old girl. She had short blonde hair, a pale, clear complexion and a round face, which was usually graced with a wide smile. She was nearly as tall as Jan. She clearly adored her father and enjoyed being on the ship with him, but she also enjoyed having a chance to chat with another woman about clothes and make-up. All the men of the crew were kind and helpful to her, but didn't know much about "women's subjects."

"Do you and Mr. Smith have children?"

Jan cleared her throat. "We did, but unfortunately, she died. We had a daughter, who would have been just about your age now. She was outside playing one afternoon and was hit by a drunk driver back in Chicago." Jan sat in silence, staring down into her tea cup.

Kinley was trying to think of something appropriate

to say. "I guess you feel about the same way as I do about my mother who died when I was young." They were both silent for several long seconds. "Well, I better go get ready for lunch today. I'm helping with the serving."

Jan smiled and squeezed the young girl's hand. "It was very nice meeting you today. I hope we can chat again one day soon." At least Kinley had her back turned and was walking away before the first tear rolled down Jan's cheek, as she thought about her dead daughter.

At the other end of the lounge, Blickensdorfer had trapped Fred Hendricks at a table, ostensibly getting tourist tips about London, but also again asking a number of questions about Fred's Navy background.

At another table, Holger Hinz was seated with Arthur Smith and another alumnus, Mike Taffe. His wife, Candy, who looked about half his age, had just excused herself to go for a massage before lunch. An elegantly-dressed, white-haired British gentleman of about sixty, named Miles Pembroke, was the fourth man at the table.

"Mike, you and Candy seem to be very happy. How long have you two been married?" asked Arthur.

"About eighteen months. I met her at a Broadway after-show party two Christmases past. She was a dancer in the chorus line. Soon as I saw her legs, I fell in love!" exclaimed Mike and laughed.

Having just seen the very attractive brunette walk gracefully away, it was easy for all to believe that she'd been a dancer in a Broadway chorus line.

"She's wife number three, correct?"

"Yes, I'm always falling in love, getting divorced

and then getting married again. It's a good thing that I'm making good money – given the alimony payments I make each month!" Even the German understood that bit of humor and they all laughed. "We were just in England before meeting up with the gang in Munich to start the trip. I had to get Candy out of the London shops while I still had any money left at all."

"Are you still mostly working in the financial world there in New York City?"

"Finances, yes, but for the last several years, I've focused almost exclusively on the show business world. Somebody has to put together the investment money and handle all the financial dealings involved with putting on a new Broadway show."

"I say, that must be very interesting work," commented Miles in his upper-class, English accent. Practically his first words since sitting down with them. "I trust you get free tickets to all the shows and get invited to lots of parties given by show people."

"Well, they're usually a cheerful and fun group, except when I'm having to explain to them that the show is already over the planned budget and no, they can't have an advance on their salaries."

Everyone laughed. Miles twirled the end of his fine handlebar mustache and commented, "Yes, well, people do tend to lose their sense of humor when it comes to money," he said in his very refined voice. He offered a thin smile and a slight nod of his head.

His mannerisms and his soft spoken voice reminded Mike of a famous British movie actor. "Forgive my odd question, Miles, but you aren't possibly related to the British actor, Ronald Coleman, are you?"

Miles laughed. "No, but you aren't the first person to ask that and I certainly wish I was, given the money he must make from all those wonderful movies he's made!"

Everyone laughed.

"No, I'm simply the second son of a minor English nobleman. If you're not acquainted with how the English aristocracy works, the first son inherits all the land and the money. The second and third sons are supposed to go into the military or the church and be poor, but respectable. My problem was that I'm a coward and I don't believe in God, and thus my older brother has always given me a modest pension to simply stay out of the country, so as not to embarrass the family."

Mike laughed loudly. "I wish someone would pay me to just stay out of New York!"

At that moment, an attractive woman, who looked perhaps thirty and had the typical pale-white, English complexion came up to Miles and leaned over to give him a kiss on his white hair. She had short brown hair and green eyes that sparkled. She also spoke with a well-educated, upper-class British accent. "I trust you gentlemen know better than to believe a single word my father has told you about anything. He has never shot a tiger in Ranchipur, nor found a gold mine in the Transvaal." She gave everyone a big smile.

Miles stood. "Gentlemen, this lovely, but totally unfaithful woman is my daughter. Her name is Elizabeth.

And if she wasn't such a good bridge partner, I wouldn't keep her around me at all!"

Holger hadn't said a word at the table up to that point. He'd simply been listening and making mental notes about his fellow passengers to write down later, but he did stand up to introduce himself to Elizabeth. He thought her the loveliest woman he'd ever met in his life.

Mike had found Holger's presence at their table annoying the whole time. By then, everyone knew that despite his civilian clothing, he was the Gestapo officer on board, allegedly there to protect them, but it was never clear from what exactly. Many thought he was there spying on them, but again, nobody had a good guess as to why any of them merited being spied upon.

Mike decided he'd had enough of Hinz' uninvited company and turned to him. "Shouldn't you be off somewhere beating up an old Jew or a Gypsy?" said Mike, loud enough for even people at surrounding tables to hear.

Holger turned to Mike. "I beg your pardon. What did you say?"

"I think you heard me well enough." Mike just sat perfectly still and stared at him. Even sitting down, it was obvious that Mike had six inches and fifty pounds on the German, and he struck people as a man who often spoke his mind, whether it might offend the listener or not.

"I'm afraid, Mr. Taffe, you have been misinformed about what goes on within Germany, probably by Communist and Jewish anti-German propaganda."

"I don't think I've been misinformed at all. My

friends in New York are quite well informed about what's been going on within Germany."

"Perhaps your friends in New York are Jewish. I've heard the Jews control that city."

"Yeah, my Jewish buddies and I secretly run America. Good thing I'm Jewish too." His last comment brought a smile to a number of faces, as Mike was the most Irish-looking Catholic on the ship.

Holger turned to Miss Elizabeth. "I hope you and your father have a pleasant day." He then turned and walked away.

"Good show, Mr. Taffe," said Miles to nobody in particular. "Too bad you're not the British Prime Minister instead of that mouse Chamberlain!"

The exchange between Taffe and Lt. Hinz served to break up the group and all went their separate ways except for Miles and Elizabeth. She settled in next to her "father" and they had a private conversation. "So, my dear, have you been having nice chats with the various wives on board, while admiring their lovely jewelry?"

"Yes, I have. I've seen a few worthwhile pieces and there are several show-offs on board, especially a Mrs. Bishop, who's even invited me to come to her cabin some afternoon to see her 'nice pieces' she's brought on the cruise."

"Well done, daughter. I think this cruise idea is going to work out quite well. Everything went smoothly in Munich and now we're safely floating on this ship. We have a week or so yet before we reach the final port and disembark, so we have plenty of time yet in deciding what is worth going after on the ship. And of course, we have work to do on shore in Vienna and Bratislava. By the way, you look particularly beautiful today, my dear."

She smiled. "Why thank you, 'daddy'. Perhaps when we go to our cabin after lunch for your mid-day nap, you can see if I look even better naked?"

He squeezed her hand. "What an excellent suggestion. Now run along and make friends with more of the other ladies on board ship. I'll see you at lunch time."

She stood, then leaned over and kissed him sweetly on the top of his head. He smiled, again rolled the end of his perfectly groomed mustache and admired her perfectly shaped ass as she walked away. He thought about what a brilliant idea he'd had a year back when he'd decided to pass his accomplice off as his daughter while they traveled together, rather than his much too young girlfriend. Rich, older women at hotels and resorts loved to show off their jewels to a younger, impressionable young lady.

Down at the other end of the Main Lounge, at the well-stocked bar, Ivan and Bob were having a pre-luncheon drink. Bob was introducing the Russian to American bourbon.

"I heard that our vodka drinking the other night had a bad effect on you. I'm very sorry."

"No problem. I've survived." They both laughed. "Though I didn't get much writing done the next morning."

"Oh, that's right, you write for Hollywood movies, yes?"

"I'm a screen writer. That's what I've been doing

recently in England. They're making a movie near London and I'm there to add additional dialog if needed."

"It's so nice that you could get away to take this trip with your old university friends. Did you join them in Paris or in Munich?"

"I met up with them in Paris."

"Ah, I just barely made the train to come to Munich. I much enjoyed that city. It's the first time I'd ever been there. Did you get out and see much of the lovely, old parts of the city, especially when it was snowing on Christmas Eve?"

"Yes, I went out early that night and walked around in the area near our hotel. I also stopped in to observe part of a Christmas service in one of the beautiful old churches."

"That must have been nice. Do you remember which one?"

"Hmm. I guess not. It was one saint or the other. I guess the champagne I drank that night at the Christmas party has wiped my memory." They both laughed.

"This American bourbon is quite nice. Shall we have another?"

Bob put up his hands in a defensive position and smiled. "Not me. I want to remember what I will have for lunch today."

Ivan smiled. "Very well. He emptied his glass in one shot and bid Bob farewell.

By noon, they'd moved into an area which had received a heavy snowfall. Lovely white snow, sparkling in the daylight covered the surrounding trees and the banks right down to the water, which gave a fairy tale look to the countryside. Arthur was seated in the Lounge, reading, when Captain Ornsdorfer came ambling by.

Smith flagged him over. "Captain, a question for you if you have a moment?"

"Certainly, Mr. Smith. What can I do for you?"

"Yesterday, I happened to notice the arrival of a fellow American to the ship, Miss Mikaela LeBlanc. You know anything about her background? She made an impressive entrance in two limousines and the fellows in the black uniforms."

Ornsdorfer sat down next to Smith and looked around to see if anyone else was within hearing distance of him. "Those fellows in black as you called them are members of the SS, the elite soldiers of the Nazi regime. Miss LeBlanc is a clairvoyant, a Tarot card reader. She had just been up at Nuremberg to visit Herr Heinrich Himmler, the head of the SS and Chief of all police in Germany. He and Hitler are both very much into the occult. I think that is the proper word in English, yes? She apparently had been telling Himmler his future."

"And is she any good at her card readings?"

The Captain shrugged his shoulders, indicating who could tell if such things really existed, or if she was simply an excellent con artist.

"Himmler seems to think she is good. She comes from some culture around your New Orleans, which is much into such things and voodoo."

Smith was smiling at all this. He was thinking to himself that it seemed hard to realistically fear a regime, wherein several of its top leaders believed in Tarot card readings!

"Anyway, when the head of the German SS sent a message to my company telling it to make available an excellent cabin and not to sail until she had arrived… well, we waited until she arrived and she has a very nice cabin! The German passenger who had been assigned to that cabin wasn't too happy to be told he was exiting the ship before we had even sailed, but once I explained who had made the request for a cabin, he happily volunteered his. It isn't only Jews who fear the Nazis Mr. Smith."

"No, I suppose not. Well, thank you for the information on Miss LeBlanc. Is she herself a believer in all this superior Aryan race babble the Nazis put out?"

Ornsdorfer smiled. I suspect she mostly believes in the large envelopes of money the Nazis give her for her predictions." The Captain rose and moved on.

After the tasty lunch, the passengers attended a lecture about the region of Bavaria from Regensburg down to Passau by Herr Professor Timothy Langweilig of the University of Munich's History Faculty. He gave lectures on five or six cruises each year, as a way to make a little extra money and he thus got free cruises with the excellent food as well. He particularly liked the good food! He spoke English with a heavy German accent and he looked exactly what everyone thought an elderly German professor should look like. He had thinning white hair, a round face and he wore round, wire-rim spectacles, which usually sat well down on his nose. His body was equally round. He probably hadn't been able to see his own feet without leaning forward for several decades. But despite his rather comical appearance, he gave a very interesting lecture about the region, from the Roman days till the last century. He told several humorous anecdotes about some of the ancient rulers of that part of Germany. Arthur noted that the Professor said nothing about the 20th century in his talk, which thus avoided a number of possibly unpleasant issues, such as the Great War or Hitler and the Nazis.

After the talk finished and the Lounge had emptied out, Holger came up to Dr. Langweilig. "Herr Professor, I greatly enjoyed your lecture. You never told me that you gave talks on ship cruises."

Holger Hinz was the last person Professor Langweilig had expected, nor wanted, to encounter on the ship. He worked as an informant for Holger around the University, but nothing else had ever been asked of him by the Gestapo. He didn't like even doing that, but Holger had learned somehow that the Professor's daughter-in-law was one-quarter Jewish, and was thus subject to the anti-Jewish laws. Holger had promised to keep that "little fact" to himself, if the Professor was willing to work as an informant against students and other faculty at the University of Munich.

"Ah, Herr Hinz, what a pleasant surprise. Are you taking a little vacation?"

"No, I'm working and now, so are you. The passengers seem to like you. I want you to chat with them and report to me every afternoon what you have learned about their backgrounds, especially of the British and the Americans."

"Of course, Herr Hinz, it will be an honor to assist you." Not only could Professor Langweilig be academic and funny, but when needed, he could be quite obsequious as well.

"Good, let's meet in my room, number 104, at 3:00 p.m. tomorrow afternoon.

"Of course, gladly."

"And how is your daughter-in-law these days?" The question served as a none too subtle reminder of why the Professor was cooperating with the Gestapo.

"She is fine. Thank you for inquiring." The smile went off the Professor's face after Holger had walked away.

Later in the afternoon, Blickensdorfer and Hinz had another consultation in the former's cabin about what new details had been gathered about the passengers.

"I still have this Fred Hendricks at the top of my list," began the Colonel. "It's clear he doesn't like to speak about his time in the US Navy, as though he's hiding something. Who did you meet today?"

"I met Mike Taffe, another American with this alumni group. He was in London just before coming to join the tour group, and I heard him speaking German with one of the waiters."

"Hmmm, he could be a possibility. What sort of a fellow is he?"

"Claims he works on financial matters in New York City and he's currently on his third wife. He also made it very clear that he is anti-German, with many Jewish friends."

"Interesting. See if you can get him one-on-one in the next day or two and get a feeling for his attitude towards the English."

"I shall try, but he's made it clear he doesn't like me. More importantly, I found out today that one of my informants in Munich is on the ship, and I've tasked him to get information on all the English and Americans on board."

"Who's your informant?"

"It's Professor Langweilig; the nice old man who gave the historical lecture after lunch today. He reports on students and faculty at the University of Munich for me. I had no idea he'd be on this cruise, but there he was, so I went up to him after his talk and gave him instructions."

"Excellent, a lucky break for us. Oh, and I saw you at a table this morning with some white-haired Englishman. Who is he?"

"His name is Miles Pembroke. He's traveling with his daughter, Elizabeth. He claimed that he's some minor aristocrat, who mostly just travels around enjoying life. He seems too old to be our suspect, but I'll see if I can learn a little more about him, perhaps through his daughter."

"Very well. We must keep working diligently. We only have a week before the ship reaches Budapest and the passengers will go in many directions. Hans and Manfred have managed to search about a third of the passenger cabins so far, but nothing of interest has turned up yet. Captain Ornsdorfer gave me a pass key yesterday, so that has helped."

"What's the Captain like? He's Austrian isn't he?"

"Yes, and he seems a typical Austrian. He agrees with everyone and will do anything to avoid an unpleasant situation. He also clearly likes his schnapps. Every time I see him, he has a glass in his hand. I trust that he doesn't actually steer the ship at night!" They both laughed.

Having finished their business discussion, Blickensdorfer opened two bottles of beer and invited Hinz to join him. "I saw in your file Holger that you were born in Munich, correct?"

"Yes, my family has lived in the city for many generations. I have a younger sister who married a farmer and moved out to the countryside five years ago."

The Colonel smiled. "The way you said 'farmer' makes me believe that you don't think too highly of the bucolic life of farming?"

"If that's what makes him and her happy, good for them, but I enjoy the city."

"And what were you doing before joining the Gestapo?"

"I was a printer's apprentice, but the whole shop went broke, and so then I just did the odd job that I could get so as to eat for a year or so before joining the S.A. a decade back."

"No wife yet?"

"No, no family yet. It takes money to start a family and I'm kept very busy with my duties for the Gestapo."

"Yes, well, we are doing very important, patriotic work for the Fatherland. Once we get rid of all the Jews and Communists, Germany can return to being the glorious country that it was before the Great War – and then perhaps you can start a family."

Holger raised his beer in a toast. "To the Fuhrer!"

"Yes, to the Fuhrer!"

Around ten o'clock that night, Arthur and Jan came up to the bar in the Main Lounge. Jan had discovered that a couple of glasses of good red wine at night helped her as much as Dr. Henke's pills to get to sleep.

Stefan, the young Romanian, who spoke four or five languages, was behind the bar, wearing his usual pleasant smile and white bartender's jacket. He was tall and thin, perhaps twenty-five years old, with a handsome face. Young Hannah was seated at the bar, drinking wine and flirting with Stefan. The piano player, Joe Jefferson, was over at the keyboard, working on some sheet music. The Smiths had met him the first night of the cruise and learned that he too was from Chicago. The couple took a table near the piano.

Arthur nodded towards Stefan. "A glass of red wine and a French 75, please."

Hannah nodded with a smile at them, then immediately left the bar.

"If I was that young girl's mother, she and I would have a serious conversation about those scandalous blouses she wears. They're unbuttoned almost down to her you-know-what!"

"Yes, but she's not our daughter, so don't let it concern you. And as for her drinking wine, apparently the drinking age in Europe is about twelve, so don't worry about that either."

"Good evening, Mrs. Smith, what would you like to hear tonight?" solicitously asked Joe. He had the whitest teeth and widest smile she'd ever seen.

She smiled back. "Oh, I like everything that you play. Whatever you're in the mood for."

"Well, let's see. How about Stardust? You told me last night that you and your husband had gone to college down there in Bloomington, so let's get started with a little of Hoagy Carmichael's music. I think he wrote this while he was in Bloomington."

"A perfect piece. You sound like you've met Mr. Carmichael, have you?"

He smiled again as he started to play. "Oh yeah, I'd met Hoagy a number of times when he was in and out of Chicago in the late twenties. We'd both be at late night jam sessions. Amazing how that boy's brain and fingers could work together."

Arthur chimed into the conversation. "Yours don't work together too badly either, Joe."

"That's very kind of you Mr. Smith", he replied as he let his fingers wander magically up and down the keyboard.

"We were lucky enough when we lived in Bloomington to have heard Hoagy play a number of times over at the Book Nook. Rumor had it that he was always cutting his law school classes to just go play the piano," added Jan.

"What brought you to Paris, Joe," asked Arthur.

"Oh, just some better playing opportunities. I came over with a jazz group in 1936 and decided to stay."

Stefan delivered the wine and in excellent English inquired, "How are you tonight, Mrs. Smith?"

"I'm good, thank you. Tell me Stefan, where did you learn your English? You speak very well."

"Multumesc, Doamna Smith", he replied in Romanian. "Oh, was I speaking English?" he jokingly asked. "I've just practiced with the customers in the bars where I've worked in Paris over the years. I've picked up a little English, French and German."

Jan smiled. "Over the years! You talk like you're forty years old. How old are you?"

"Tonight, I am twenty-five, and you look like you might be twenty-eight or twenty-nine?"

Joe chimed in. "Mr. Smith, don't go letting your wife come up here by herself some night... you can't trust these Romanians!"

They all laughed. Jan couldn't resist commenting about Hannah. "Hannah seems to have become a steady customer of yours, Stefan."

Stefan frowned. "Hannah's mother should tell her to go put on more clothes!"

"Stefan, I heard secondhand that last summer you won the Best Bartender of Paris Award for 1938. Is that true?" asked Arthur.

Stefan gave a big smile. "Yes, I did and that's what got me this job on the *Danube Princessa*."

"Well, you certainly make an excellent cocktail."

"Thank you. Some night you must let me make for you one of my specialty drinks." He then turned and returned to his bar. Joe returned to playing and Arthur held tightly his wife's hand. A melancholy smile came to his face as he thought of all the good times they'd had together. He kept telling himself that it was the quality, not the quantity of time together that really counted.

At breakfast the following morning, Mary Beth was eating with Fred and Bob.

"Say, have either of you had a chance to talk with the Captain's daughter, Kinley?" inquired Bob.

"Nothing more than to say hello," replied Fred. "About the same for me," added Mary Beth. "Her English is very good and she's certainly a pretty young girl. Why do you ask?"

"Oh, I chatted a bit yesterday with her while I was having a coffee in the Main Lounge. You're right about her English and she's quite a worldly young lady for only being fifteen years old. She'd heard someone say that I was a writer in Hollywood and she wanted to know whether I got my ideas for plots from books I'd read, or from my imagination."

"That was a rather sophisticated question," replied Mary Beth.

"Sophisticated! I'd say so. God, we have producers in Hollywood who don't even know where plots come from."

The other two laughed. "So where and how do you get your ideas, Bob?" asked Fred.

"Usually, after about my third large scotch", he replied and winked at Mary Beth.

"Hey, a different topic. Have either of you felt like someone has gone through your things in your cabin?" asked Mary Beth.

"I haven't," replied Fred.

"Me neither, but then my cabin is in such a mess, it would be hard for me to notice whether anybody had been rummaging about or not," jokingly replied Bob. "You think somebody has been searching about in your room?"

"When I went back to my cabin yesterday afternoon,

it just seemed like several things on the top of my dresser were in a different position and in one of the drawers, my…" She stopped for a moment and almost blushed. "My unmentionables weren't in the same order as I remembered them being in that morning."

"Perhaps it's just the cabin boy who has moved things around while in there cleaning," suggested Bob. "And as a writer, I can't resist asking, in what 'order' do you keep your unmentionables?" he teased.

She gave him a suggestive look. "If you must know, I rotate my colored panties and I would've sworn that the next pair on top yesterday had been blue, but this morning when I got dressed, the …, well, the blue ones weren't on top."

Bob winked at Fred. "If you like, Fred and I can come down after breakfast and verify what color is on top now for tomorrow and then when you come to breakfast tomorrow, we could, uh…could check for you."

"Enough, Detective Bob!" She gave him a feigned dirty look and then they all had a good laugh.

Just then, Simone and Tom Bishop walked up to the table. "What's so funny that we just missed?" asked Tom.

"Oh, we were just discussing what color the area rugs were in our cabins," replied Bob with a straight face.

"Mine is blue," stated Simone and the three at the table burst out laughing. "Where have you two been so early?" quickly asked Mary Beth, to change the topic.

"We were out walking around the top, outer deck, to get a little exercise," replied Tom. "If they're going to keep feeding me like this three times a day, I need some exercise." The two ladies subconsciously sucked in their stomachs.

The two latecomers took seats and there began a conversation of "do you remember so and so" at the University.

Tom and Bob had both been in the Sigma Nu fraternity. "Hey, Bob, do you remember that slightly round and funny guy who played tuba in the Marching Band, Herman Wells?"

"Yeah, he was a year or two behind us I think. A very pleasant guy, as I recall, enterprising as well. You remember how he loaned out money and held your tuxedo as collateral?"

"What?" exclaimed Mary Beth.

"Yeah, if a fraternity brother was a little short of cash one week, Herman would loan him $5 or $10 for the week, at a small interest. But to guarantee repayment, he'd take your tux and lock it in a closet, and you couldn't get it back till the loan was repaid. There was some social event almost every weekend, so you'd need your tux – pretty clever ploy by Herman."

"Is this the Herman Wells who was just made Acting President of our University?" asked Mary Beth.

"The one and the same," replied Tom.

"I hope he's as enterprising about raising money for the University now as he was for himself back in the early twenties!" They all laughed.

"You know Bob, with an old fraternity brother running the University these days, perhaps he could arrange for you to finally get your degree," teased Tom.

"You didn't finish your degree?" asked Simone in a surprised tone.

"No, I'd gotten a job offer from a motion picture studio to work as a junior script writer, but they needed me there by April 15th, or no job. So, I packed up and caught the next train to Los Angeles. I've never finished those last four courses I needed to graduate. Fortunately, nobody out in Hollywood gives a damn about such things, so it doesn't matter. Although, it's a little galling that while I don't have a diploma, I still get solicitation letters from the University asking me for donations!"

"Wait till you become a famous screen writer with an Academy Award, then you'll get twice as many letters asking for a donation."

"Well, if I'm going to become rich and famous, I better go get to work on that script. I still need to come up with a good ending. I'll see you guys later."

"And I better go find my family," added Tom and he departed as well, leaving just Mary Beth, Simone and Fred at the table.

"That Tom is such a nice guy," stated Mary Beth to Simone in an attempt to find out what was going on between her and Tom. "I've seen you two spending a lot of time together."

"Oh, we had known each other pretty well back in Bloomington, so it's good to be able to catch up and spend some time together while we're on this cruise."

Mary Beth let the matter drop, but wasn't totally convinced that the couple were only talking about times past when they were together on the ship.

A few minutes later, the attractive woman who Arthur had noticed at dinner the first night on the ship entered the dining room and the head waiter immediately rushed over to lead her to a table by herself. She wore no jewelry, but her clothing clearly showed that she had money.

Fred nodded at the unknown beauty and asked, "Don't suppose either of you know who that woman is who just came in for breakfast?"

Simone replied. "I asked one of the ship's officers last night. She is Princess Caroline Landschknecht, from some tiny little principality near Leipzig. She is a widow and this is the third year in a row she has taken this cruise over the New Year."

"My, aren't you a wealth of information," replied Fred, without taking his eyes off of the woman. "Tell me again how do you pronounce that mouth full of her last name?"

The two ladies laughed. "I wouldn't get your hopes up Fred," replied Simone. "I think she's a little above your social standing."

"I'm just admiring from afar," he replied with a smile.

Just then, in walked the distinguished, elderly Englishman, Miles Pembroke. The Princess gave him a big smile and waved for him to come join her at her table for breakfast. The debonair gentleman returned her smile and headed directly for her table.

"It looks as though the British aristocracy has already laid claim to the German princess," stated Mary Beth softly and with a smile to her table companions. Eventually, they all went their separate ways. Some passengers spent the day reading, others just sitting around in small groups chatting. Different members of the Indiana University group were still catching up with one another.

As the gong sounded for dinner at 7:00 p.m., everyone started heading into the Dining Room. There was no assigned seating and most people moved to different tables each evening.

The beautiful and exotic-looking Mikaela LeBlanc entered the dining room and seeing Arthur, headed over to his table. There was nothing exceptional about her clothing, but she had a physique upon which everything looked good.

"Good evening, Mr. Smith. If that seat is unoccupied, would you mind if I joined your group?"

Smith stood, as did Fred, to greet her. "Good evening, Miss LeBlanc. We would be honored if you joined us."

Introductions were made around the table and Mikaela took her seat and ordered a glass of champagne.

"Are you all part of this college alumni reunion?" asked LeBlanc, looking around the table. "Arthur briefly told me yesterday, he was traveling with old college classmates."

"Indeed, we all knew each other back in college," explained Fred. "Arthur and Jan were kind enough to invite us to come along as they relive their honeymoon journey on the Danube back in nineteen…"

Jan interrupted him. "Never mind the rest of that date, Fred," she said and gave him a stern look. They all laughed.

The reunion crowd gave Mikaela a quick update on

what all of them had been doing since their college days. Miss LeBlanc remained silent on her profession or travels, so Fred simply asked.

"And what about you, Miss LeBlanc? Where is home and what has brought you on this cruise?"

"I was born and continue to live most of the time near New Orleans. As for this cruise, well, it seemed like the most pleasant manner to make my way south to Greece from Germany."

The other dinner companions found that answer a bit short on specifics, so Jan gave it a try. "I think Fred was subtly trying to inquire as to whether you have a particular profession, or are you simply independently wealthy and you just travel around the world for pleasure, as one of the other passengers does."

Mikaela laughed. "I wish I was so rich as to be able to just travel the world." She paused for a moment. "I read Tarot cards. I tell people their futures, as did my mother and her mother."

No one spoke for several seconds. Arthur broke the silence, since he'd already learned something about the woman from Captain Ornsdorfer. "And can you foretell whether my steak will be cooked properly tonight?" he asked.

Mikaela smiled. "Well, I am without my cards, but..." She closed her eyes and raised her hands to her forehead with great ceremony. "Yes, Arthur, I see a well-done steak coming your way very shortly."

They all laughed.

"I'd also like to know if my stock portfolio will be

going up in 1939, but I suppose that's a little harder to foresee," commented Arthur.

"Well, naturally the portfolio of a banker as wise and charming as you are Mr. Smith will go up. One doesn't have to be a clairvoyant to make that prediction."

Smith could see why Nazi leaders enjoyed her predictions. She was very charming. Their soups arrived and conversation of LeBlanc's skills ceased until the main course arrived. As predicted, Arthur's steak was well-done, which led the table back to conversation about Mikaela's skills.

"I'll tell you what, after dinner, why don't we six meet up in the Lounge and I'll bring my cards and give all of you a prediction." They all nodded in agreement.

"But there will be a price. I'll do predictions if then Simone will sing a song or two for us."

The others sat in silence looking at Mikaela, wondering how she could know that Simone was a singer, as nothing related to that fact had been mentioned all evening at the table.

Mikaela then laughed. "I've been to Paris several times and I've been in her nightclub. Everyone in Paris knows that she's a wonderful singer!"

Arthur wasn't sure how much of a clairvoyant Mikaela really was, but she was certainly charming and knew how to work her audience, whether it was fifty or only five.

After dinner, Mikaela went to go get her Tarot cards and they all reassembled in the Lounge. Arthur ordered a bottle of champagne for the group as they sat at a round table at the quiet end of the Lounge.

"Do we need the lights turned down or anything?" asked Simone.

"Of course not," she replied. "How could I see the cards?" Again, they all laughed. "Who shall be first?"

Simone raised her hand. Mikaela had her take a seat directly across from her and began to deal out cards on the round table.

After looking at the cards for some twenty seconds, she said, "Death will soon be very near you. I recommend you be very careful."

That prediction certainly sobered up her audience, which had grown with other people already in the Lounge, who'd come over to see what was going on. Colonel Blickensdorfer was particularly interested in her predictions.

"Nothing about a tall, dark stranger coming into my life?" responded Simone with a laugh.

"I only said that death will be very near you, not necessarily that you will die."

LeBlanc turned over more cards. "Ah, better news. The cards say that love is coming your way, but it is forbidden love, so you must be very careful in whether you accept it or not."

Simone cast a quick glance up at Tom, who had joined the crowd around the table, then she said, "Can you see if he has hair or if he's bald?" Everyone laughed.

"That's all I see for your future. Who wants to be next?

Fred raised his hand quickly. "I need all the predictions and advice about my future that I can get."

"Very well. Please sit directly across from me." She then started shuffling her cards and placed five of them in a row in front of her. She made several soft utterances while laying out the cards, beginning with a "hmm", then an "ah ha" and finally a broad smile came to her face.

"First, I must tell you that the sound effects have nothing to do with my readings, but I've learned over the years that people expect me to make sounds while turning over the cards." She smiled as she stared directly into Fred's eyes.

She then became quite serious as she turned over another five cards.

"Well, it's usually better when I do this in private so as not to embarrass the person for whom I doing a reading, but I have seen that you are all good friends."

They all nodded in agreement. "Go ahead," said Fred. "I have nothing to hide from these people."

She pointed at the first card. "I see Fred that you've had a great tragedy in your life in the past."

Arthur thought that perhaps she was referring to Fred's dead wife, but then most people by his age had had something occur they considered to have been a tragedy.

LeBlanc pointed at two more cards. "I do see that you shall soon be seeing great love."

Again, Arthur thought to himself, what single person doesn't want to hear that he shall soon have great love.

"Money from unanticipated people will also soon come your way."

"I'm liking my future so far," said Fred with a laugh. "I have love and money coming my way!"

She turned over a few more cards. "Ah, I see that you have confidentially met with someone recently who will be very important for your life."

LeBlanc's face then turned very somber for a moment before she said. "Well, I think that's enough about Mr. Hendricks."

Blickensdorfer wondered if she had been referring to Fred and General Breithaupt as having recently met confidentially.

Smith decided that she was sounding more and more like a typical fortune teller at a carnival.

Mikaela turned to Arthur and Jan, who were seated next to her. "I shall read you as a couple, as I feel very strong emanations coming from you as a pair, not as two individuals."

They nodded in agreement.

She turned over cards for Arthur and Jan. The first one was the card of Death, followed by the card of Love and then one with stars and one of a stylized beach.

Even amateur followers of Tarot knew that the card of Death was not a good sign and everyone had become very still, particularly those who'd noticed Jan's headaches and tiredness in recent days.

Mikaela looked up at the surrounding crowd. "Do not be afraid of the card of Death my friends." Turning back to Jan and Arthur, she said, "In this combination, the cards simply tell me that your strong love for each other will last until your deaths on earth and will then continue on throughout the ages up in the stars."

Mikaela then looked directly at Jan and Jan asked, "Can you predict where death will occur, on water or land?"

"It's not perfectly clear, but the last card seems to indicate that it will be on land. Is it important to you where you die?"

"Not really, just curious," she replied as she squeezed Arthur's hand.

"And what is my future?" asked Mary Beth.

LeBlanc started to lay cards upon the table, but then she stopped and looked hard directly at Mary Beth's face. The medium felt a chill run up her spine. "You are not all that you appear."

Mary Beth was searching for a clever, light-hearted response, but remained silent.

LeBlanc continued. "I see that a rabbit is important in your life. I can't see exactly what it has to do with your future, but this rabbit plays an important role. Do you perhaps have a pet rabbit?" asked LeBlanc.

Mary Beth relaxed and smiled, as did several people who'd read some of her children's books. "As a matter of fact, there is a rabbit who plays an important role in my life. He's a character in the children's books that I write."

"Ah, that must explain it," replied Mikaela with a smile. "Well, I think that is enough for this evening. I'm growing tired."

The Colonel stepped forward. "Just one more Miss LeBlanc, if you please. I am Werner Blickensdorfer from Munich. What do you see in my future?"

She turned over a few cards, then dramatically announced. "I see you in a general's uniform in the future."

Everyone laughed and applauded as Mikaela stood and departed from the circle. As most of the passengers who'd spoken with Blickensdorfer during the cruise had concluded he wasn't really a banker, they thought it impressive and humorous that LeBlanc had spotted him right off as some sort of German military man.

As Blickensdorfer walked away, smiling, he was quite happy. He'd been impressed with her skills and also found it very positive that she saw him making the rank of general in the future.

CHAPTER 10
Passau

The ship slowed the following afternoon as it neared the confluence of the Danube, Inn and Ilz rivers, at which the town of Passau had sat for almost two thousand years, beginning as a Roman outpost. A massive fortress, the Veste Oberhaus, overlooked the ancient town. Karen would be leading a tour around Passau for anyone interested, or people could simply wander the cobblestoned streets of the ancient town on their own for a couple of hours.

Blickensdorfer planned on keeping a careful account of who went on the tour and who wandered about on their own in the town. Hinz was a bit mystified as why the Colonel cared so much about what the passengers' activities would be in the quaint little tourist town.

"Do you think our suspect could be up to something in Passau?" asked Holger.

"The local Gestapo commander brought me a telegram when we first docked. The authorities brought General Breithaupt in for questioning yesterday in Munich and are holding him."

"You mean they've arrested him?"

"No, not arrested, he's only being held for questioning.

So far, he has confessed to nothing. He claimed that he'd simply decided to take a nice long walk on Christmas Eve, in the lovely snowfall, and has denied meeting with anyone that night."

"Well, let's hope that they can break him and get him to confess."

"That would be nice, but I'll be surprised if a man like General Breithaupt can be broken – at least not verbally – and the leadership of the Wehrmacht is already pressing for his release."

"It would certainly make our task easier here if he could be made to talk." Changing topics, "Why are you so interested in what our passengers are doing this afternoon here in Passau?"

"There is a good-sized Wehrmacht base near here. I'm not supposed to share this with you, so keep it strictly to yourself, but Breithaupt attended last month a top-level Army meeting in Berlin. They discussed upcoming military plans. There is thus great concern at Gestapo Headquarters in Berlin whether Breithaupt might have passed information about those planned actions to a foreign agent on the night of the 24th. That's why he was brought in for questioning, despite the protests of the Wehrmacht. If he did pass such information, we must make sure that that agent doesn't get out of our area of control, or have a chance to get the information to a British, French or American embassy."

"Yes, but still, what has any of that to do with what a British spy might be up to in quaint little Passau? There are no foreign missions in Passau."

"My thinking is this – what if General Breithaupt is

not the only traitor? What if this foreign agent is picking up information during this trip from a number of traitors in our Army?"

"Ah, I see what you mean," replied Holger.

"Catching one spy would certainly be good, but to be able to wrap up two – well, that wouldn't hurt either of our careers!"

Hinz smiled. "No, it probably wouldn't, 'General' Blickensdorfer."

"I, along with Hans, will accompany the group tour and make sure that all of our suspects stay with the group. You will stay down on the docks and keep watch to see if any of the others leave the ship and go off on their own. I've arranged with the local Gestapo chief to have a dozen of his men in plain clothes available. You will give a signal if you see one of our main suspects coming down the gangplank and three surveillants will then follow that person."

"Very good, Colonel. I'll be ready."

By five o'clock, the tour group had arrived back to the ship. Six passengers had gone off by themselves and of them, only Ivan Bogatyr, the Russian, was on their possible suspects list. He returned to the ship in about thirty minutes. The local Gestapo team reported that he'd gone into a tobacconist's shop to purchase cigarettes and then he'd gone briefly into two tourist gift shops, but had bought nothing. They planned on watching the tobacconist and his store all night, in case he was being used as a relay courier to yet another agent. Whether they observed anything suspicious that night or not, the local Gestapo would then bring him in for questioning at noon the next day. The local Gestapo sergeant doubted anything would turn up, as he'd known the man for many years and he was not known to have any political views at all. He was nearly fifty and with his wife, simply ran his shop and minded his own business, but the local Gestapo commandant wanted to appear thorough. He also hoped that Colonel Blickensdorfer would report his efficiency to Gestapo Headquarters in Berlin.

All four Gestapo men met briefly in Blickensdorfer's cabin before dinner that evening. "Everyone on the walking tour simply stayed with the tour," reported the Colonel. "The highlight of which was that we learned that Adolf Hitler and his family had lived here from 1892-94."

Holger started to laugh, but then thought the better of doing so in front of Hans and Manfred. He reported about the brief sojourn of the Russian.

"Oh well, at least it was worth a try," commented Blickensdorfer. "During the dinner hour, you two can finish searching the rest of the cabins. Holger and I will continue chatting with the passengers. I don't see anything else for us to do at the moment." They all nodded in agreement.

Holger looked at his watch. "I'll meet with Professor Langweilig in a few minutes and see what information he may have learned today for me."

"Good," said the Colonel. Let's meet back here at 10:00 p.m. and I'll hear what you two may have found in any of the cabins, or what Holger might have gotten from Dr. Langweilig."

The ship would spend the night docked at Passau and would then cross in the morning into Austrian territory and reach the ancient town of Melk in time for lunch.

After another delicious dinner, a number of people gathered around Bob in the Main Lounge and he began telling stories about some of the rich and famous of Hollywood.

"You know the old joke about how rich people are just like you and me, except they have money. Well, it's almost the same for Hollywood celebrities – there are many who are just the nicest, down-to-earth folks you'd want to meet and others who are egotistical maniacs, but they all live in very nice mansions!"

"Who's the nicest actor?" asked one of the crowd around him.

"Now, you need to understand that as a lowly writer, I'm not exactly close personal friends with all those stars, but from what I hear, Jimmy Stewart is really as nice a guy as he appears in his movies."

"And who isn't a nice guy?" jokingly asked another person.

"Well, a number of those folks drink quite a lot of alcohol and unfortunately, they then turn into very different people when drunk, but I'd rather not go into those stories. There's a lot of people not in Hollywood who also drink too much." He smiled.

Fred held up his hand and said, "Like me!" Everyone laughed.

"Come on, Bob, give us some real inside gossip."

"Hmmm. Let's see. There's the story that when Joan Crawford first came out to Hollywood, she appeared naked in this low-budget production called *Velvet Lips*, an 'art film', as they call them out in California. Then when she started to become a star, MGM learned about that little film and had to run around and buy up all the prints and the negative. Supposedly, the guy who owned *Velvet Lips* was paid $25,000 for the negative.

"Is that true?" asked Mary Beth.

Bob smiled. "I'm just passing along what I hear."

"Who's the easiest actor to work with?" shouted out someone from the back of the circle around Bob.

"Oh, that's an easy one – Rin Tin Tin, the dog! The original dog appeared in 29 films until his death in 1932 and never once showed up late on the set or argued with his director."

Again, laughter from his growing audience. Another drink arrived for Bob, so he'd keep telling his stories. Mary Beth started thinking that perhaps Bob himself should be out in front of a camera, not just writing scripts for actors.

Thirty minutes later, he said, "One last story. Who do you think is the most talented actor in Hollywood?"

Various names were shouted out from his circle of friends, ranging from Lionel Barrymore to Mickey Rooney.

Bob kept shaking his head no, before requesting their silence. "The most talented actor is Warner Oland."

Everyone stared at him; most of them wondering who the devil was Warner Oland.

"Warner Oland, who was born in Sweden, played that clever Chinese detective from Honolulu, Charlie Chan, in sixteen movies. However in the first 'talkie', back in 1927, the Jazz Singer, he played Al Jolson's Jewish father from the old country, Cantor Rabinowitz. A Swede who can play a Chinese detective and a Jewish rabbi. Now, that takes real acting ability!" Again, everybody laughed.

"Enough, I'm going to bed."

The following morning, many of the passengers listened to another lecture by Professor Langweilig on the history of the region, as the ship sailed smoothly towards the ancient town of Melk. By the time they had docked, the blue skies had returned and the sun was shining, which helped put everyone in a good mood. They enjoyed a nice lunch, then headed off for a tour of the massive and beautiful Benedictine Abbey, which overlooked the small town of Melk. The monastery had been established in the 11th century and featured a library with one of the finest collections of medieval books and velum scrolls in Europe. Hannah was bored out of her mind, but her father insisted that she stay for the entire tour. Holger had gone along with the group, mostly to keep an eye on everyone, but found the library quite impressive. He hoped that no senior Nazi official back in Berlin or in Vienna would have the idea of doing a symbolic book burning at Melk, as had occurred in Berlin in 1933, and other German cities in subsequent years.

Holger and Mary Beth talked a good deal during the tour through the ancient monastery.

"Perhaps, someday, Frau Mary Beth, some of your books will be in this library."

She first thought that he was making fun of her children's books, but then realized that he was trying to be complimentary. "Thank you, but I doubt if any of my books will ever merit being part of a monastery's collection."

"Your books teach young children valuable lessons about how to behave and how to treat one another, do they not? I've never had a chance to read one, but I've heard a few of your fellow Americans talking about them. And is that not what the bible and many of the manuscripts in this library also teach?"

She smiled. "When you put it like that, yes, there is a similarity between my books and this magnificent library, but I still doubt whether what I write will ever merit being in such a place as this."

"Have you ever written anything other than children's books?"

A worried look came to her face. She wondered if he was hinting at her secret writing activity. Ever since she'd discovered that someone had searched her room, she'd been concerned at what they might have found.

"No, I've never written anything except children's books," she finally managed to reply in as calm a voice as she could manage.

Holger said nothing more about writing and the two walked on mostly in silence through the rest of the monastery.

Once back on the ship, many of the passengers sat around the Main Lounge area, chatting, while waiting for dinner. Bob was talking with Mary Beth and two retired high school teachers from the Chicago suburbs, named Rick and Patty. They'd both taught English for almost forty years in the Chicago area and Rick had doubled as the director of the school's marching band. Sadly, according to

Patty, the band almost every year had been better than the school's football or basketball teams!

This was their grand retirement trip. Bob started talking about the movie he was involved with in England, about the life of an instructor at a prestigious boys' school.

"The problem is the ending," he was explaining. "That's what I'm supposed to improve upon before we start filming again in mid-January. It's an interesting story of this elderly fellow's teaching career in England over the decades and how sadly, he'd lost his wife and baby in childbirth, but how does it end is the problem? He's not really accomplished much in his life."

"Oh, I would heartily disagree with your view on that," commented Rick. "You said that he's been teaching there for thirty or forty years, correct?"

"Yes, he's quite elderly and maybe he dies at the end, or maybe he just continues on as the headmaster. The director hasn't decided yet."

"Well, over those forty years, he's probably taught thousands of young boys. He's not only taught them history or mathematics or whatever he teaches, but he's taught them about life."

Patty agreed with her husband. "He's helped prepare them for manhood. If that's not an accomplishment, I don't know what is."

Mary Beth added her view as well. "I've never taught, but I'd agree that preparing thousands of boys to become good men should be considered a very successful life."

"An interesting view. I'll give that some thought, thank you," replied Bob.

Mary Beth glanced over at Blickensdorfer, who was sitting at the bar talking with Stefan. It seemed as though every time she'd looked in his direction, he was staring at her. She wondered if she was just getting paranoid. After all, men do look at women, or had it been Blickensdorfer who'd searched her room? Nobody, including her, had believed his story of being a banker, especially since the two younger German "businessman" who'd joined the journey at the same time as he did practically stood up at attention whenever he walked into the Lounge. His curiosity about every passenger's background had also been a topic of conversation among the non-German passengers. Maurice Garnier had quite pointedly gotten up and left a table the previous day when the German "banker" had sat down at his table.

The funny thing was that Ivan and Maurice had both also been quite inquisitive about all the Americans – at least that was the general impression that many of the Americans shared when it was just them at a dining table or in the Lounge in the evenings. Fred concluded that Maurice was simply hard up for anyone to talk with him, given his leftist politics, and thus he opted for asking about people's backgrounds as a nice neutral topic. Ivan on the other hand struck several people as being up to something – what exactly they didn't know, but he was certainly very nosy. And what was with all those questions about whether they'd liked Munich and what had they done while there?

Late that evening, Hanna found Bob alone in the Main Lounge and came over to chat with him. Like many a teenage girl in America, she dreamed of going to Hollywood and being "discovered", and he was the first person she'd ever met who actually worked in the movie industry.

"May I join you, Mr. Hall?"

"Of course. Hannah, isn't it?"

"Yes." She was flattered that he knew her name. "I've never met anyone from Hollywood before and I loved your stories earlier about Clark Gable and some of the other stars out in Los Angeles. Tell me some more please." She gave him her most seductive smile.

He was flattered that a pretty young girl thought of him as being part of "Hollywood", but he mostly thought of her of as being "very young" and of no romantic or sexual interest to him. If anyone had caught his imagination in the latter regard, it was Inga, the masseuse – along with half the male passengers on the ship!

"Well, I was about to call it a night, but I guess I could tell you one more story as I finish my drink and then go to bed."

After his phrase of "then go to bed", she gave him a big smile.

He'd been drinking Scotch all through dinner and after. "Let's see, what story would interest a young girl?"

Again the seductive smile. "I'm not so young."

"OK, well, you remember Jean Harlow, who died last year?"

"Oh, of course, she was one of my idols."

He leaned towards her and lowered his voice. "The rumors were that when filming all those sex kitten roles, she'd put ice on her nipples just before shooting so that they'd be good and hard, and easily show through her blouse. She of course never wore a bra."

"Really!"

It was his turn to smile as he stood up. "That's what I heard. Good night, Hannah. I'll see you tomorrow."

On his way out, he stopped at the bar and obtained a bottle of good French champagne and two glasses. He'd decided that the direct approach was sometimes the best approach — at least in the movies. What's the worst that Inga could say when he knocked on her door with champagne? No thank you, perhaps, but he was feeling optimistic that night and headed for her cabin.

After Bob left, Hanna headed up to Stefan at the bar and asked for a glass of ice to take with her to her room.

She smiled and said, "I'll be up late, reading."

At 10 p.m., the four Gestapo men met in Blickensdorfer's cabin to again assess where their investigation stood. They only had a few more days before the ship reached the end of the cruise in Budapest and whoever was the foreign agent could scatter to the four winds. They'd convinced at least themselves that there truly was an agent on board.

Colonel Blickensdorfer spoke first. "As of this moment, Fred Hendricks is my number one choice. He'd not only been a U.S. Naval officer, but he'd been in Naval Intelligence and it sounds as if he needs money. He was just in England for some unexplained reason before joining this American tour group and then there's my gut feeling. Back when I was a police detective, I often relied on my instincts about a suspect and there's just something odd about this guy. Whenever I've brought up about his time in the Navy, he acts very uncomfortable. We'll have to come to some decision on what to do before we get out of German or Austrian territory. We're quickly running out of time." He looked at the other three for their reaction.

"I certainly agree with you about Hendricks looking suspicious, but I don't want to forget about the Russian either," replied Lt. Hinz. "It appears as though Bogatyr also loves money and would do most anything to obtain it. If the British offered him enough money, I suspect he'd be willing to take such a risk as meeting with a German officer in Germany."

Blickensdorfer nodded in agreement. "Everything you say is true and I'd also like to bring up a new name for discussion. Have any of you observed that the elderly British fellow, Pembroke, has been spending quite a bit of time with Princess Landschknecht?"

"I've seen them eating together twice so far," replied Holger.

"Captain Ornsdorfer told me this morning that he believed that she'd been in Munich just a short time before the cruise began. Holger, could she perhaps be who you saw meeting with General Breithaupt on Christmas Eve? My idea is that maybe Pembroke is the MI-6 man to whom she is now reporting here on the ship? You said it might have been a woman you saw just leaving the courtyard when you'd caught up with the General. Anyway, take a good look at her from the back in the next day or so."

"It could have been her. I'll try to get a look at her from the back tomorrow."

"At our next stop, I'll send off a telegram from the local Gestapo office inquiring about what is known about Princess Caroline," added Blickensdorfer. He turned to Manfred. "How many more cabins do you need to search?"

"Only five more, sir."

"And still nothing of real interest has turned up?"

The two enlisted men shook their heads negatively and named the passengers who'd not yet had their cabins searched.

"Very well, search very discreetly Princess Caroline's cabin, but stay away from the cabin of Fraulein LeBlanc."

Hans and Manfred gave him a puzzled look as to why they were not to search the cabin of an American.

"She has very important friends in Berlin is all you need to know," explained the Colonel. He'd spoken that morning with the Captain and had learned of her connection to SS Chief Himmler – not a man whose friends you'd want to risk annoying.

After Hans and Manfred left the room, Holger asked the Colonel, "What will we do if we find no evidence in any of the cabins?"

"There may not be anything to find. I was hoping that General Breithaupt might have passed documents to the foreign agent, but he may have simply orally reported to this man – and thus there will be nothing to find in a cabin."

"I see, but still my question. What do we do if we find no evidence?"

"I'm working on that," was Blickensdorfer's vague reply.

At the same time as the Gestapo meeting, Arthur,

Jan and Mary Beth were having a drink and listening to Joe play in the Lounge. "Arthur, now that we don't have the four German Marx Brothers around, may I ask you a serious question," began Mary Beth.

He smiled at her reference to Blickensdorfer and pals. "What is your question?"

"This whole mess in Europe with Hitler and the Nazis. Do you think that Munich Pact is really going to settle things for the long run, or is there a war coming?"

"I hate to be a pessimist, but I think things are going to get a whole lot worse. The Munich Pact probably just pushed back by six or twelve months what is inevitably coming – and by that I mean a European-wide war. If Blickensdorfer and his boys are any indication of the new Nazi man, there's an ugly side to all of Hitler's National Socialism. Though, on the other side, the British and French leaders want to avoid war at all cost. Those men, like me, experienced trench warfare of the Great War during which several million people died. War is a horrible thing, to be avoided if at all possible – and maybe it can be, but I'm doubtful. I was a young man in Chicago during Prohibition and for some of those gang leaders, like Capone, no amount was ever enough. Capone couldn't spend all the money he was already making, yet he always wanted to control more parts of the city and he'd fight with other gangs. Hitler reminds me of that mentality. The Sudetenland will never be 'enough' – next year Hitler will want something more, and then even more the following year."

"And will America get dragged into such a major war, if it happens?" asked Mary Beth.

"Well, I know a lot of folks, including me, say we should just stay home and let the Old World fight it out, but I'm beginning to think that may not be possible. Once Hitler controls all of Europe, in a few more years will he want America as well? And there's a matter of principle involved here as well. Perhaps we should firmly come out on the side of democracies, but to tell you the truth, I change my mind about every other day. We got involved in the last European squabble twenty-five years ago, and what did it get us?

"Yes, but even if America should get involved, what can any single individual do?" asked Jan.

"True," sighed Mary Beth. "I had a conversation like this one, a few months back with my father-in-law, who is of course British."

Just then, up walked Fred, with a glass of Scotch in his hand. His usual appearance. He'd been listening to their conversation. "Well, we could threaten to sink the German fleet. Oh wait, we haven't commissioned a new ship in over a decade. We could bomb them, but the Army Air Corps is still flying planes from the Great War. And our Army? We don't really have one, so we better not go writing any checks we don't want people to try cashing."

He then wandered back over to the bar to refresh his drink.

"Well, we've heard from the U.S. Navy!" mocked Arthur.

DURNSTEIN

The following day, the ship docked at Durnstein, another ancient town, which time had passed by since the Middle Ages. It was a cold, gray and windy day. The thermometer was barely above freezing and only about a dozen of the heartier men opted to take the fairly steep walk up to the old castle ruins, which sat high above the town. The castle dated back to the 12th century. Duke Leopold V of Austria had held Richard the Lionheart there from December 1192 until the following March when the ransom was finally paid. Richard had been on his way back from the Third Crusade when he'd been taken prisoner. Dr. Langweilig imparted that knowledge on the ship during his lecture. However, the jovial, but overweight professor had no intention himself of trying to climb the narrow, rocky path to reach the castle. Besides the dozen heading up to the castle ruins, a few more passengers opted for a quick stroll in the ancient town right by the river. However, most people decided to simply spend the morning in the warm and dry Lounge, drinking hot chocolate with a large dollop of whipped cream on the top. Herr Blickensdorfer opted to go up to the castle.

About two hours later, the first of the adventurous passengers returned breathless to the ship to announce that there had been a terrible accident – Fred Hendricks had fallen from a narrow part of the trail and had been killed. The dozen men taking the walk had all been spread out at the time, some still looking around the castle ruins and others on the way back down. No one had actually seen Fred fall, but that was the conclusion of all as to what must have happened.

The local police recovered his broken and battered body from a rocky precipice an hour later. After a quick consultation with Captain Ornsdorfer, it was decided to place the body back on the ship for transport to Vienna, where there were proper facilities for dealing with corpses — should some relative wish to have the body sent back to America for burial. The local police chief held a quick group interview with all who'd been up to the castle that morning. After hearing that Fred had been at the ship's bar before he'd started the walk up the mountain, he declared it an accidental death.

It was a very somber lunch that day on the ship, particularly knowing that Fred's body was packed in ice in a crate, up on the top deck. Arthur Smith took it upon himself to call everyone together at the start of the meal to say a few words about Fred – remembering the fun and cheerful Fred of their college days together. The group of Hoosiers gathered separately after lunch and Arthur raised the question of what to do with Fred's body once they reached Vienna. His parents were dead, as well as his wife and he had no siblings as far as Smith remembered. No one could recall him ever mentioning any relatives, nor even what was his religious faith, if he had one. And no one even knew in what town the wife had been buried two years earlier.

"Perhaps we should just arrange for a nice burial in Vienna," suggested Arthur. "A couple of us can go with the Captain and look through his belongings in his cabin and see if something is found there that would change our minds about this, but otherwise..." He found himself unable to speak any further.

Bob picked up in Arthur's place. "We can report his death to the American Embassy in Vienna and perhaps there's some rule we're not aware of, but I think Fred would be just as happy being buried in Vienna as anywhere."

There was a slow nodding of heads in general agreement.

Mike Taffe spoke up. "And I don't want to see Fred just dumped in some pauper's grave, so let's arrange for some sort of head stone and a nice burial. "I'm good for $200 towards that."

All of the others expressed similar sentiments and willingness to contribute.

"Alright, Mike, why don't you and I go to the American Embassy soon as we reach Vienna? I'm sure someone there can give us an approximate cost and we can leave money with that person, who will make the necessary arrangements. If nothing else, we can alert the Military Attaché at the Embassy about the death of a former Naval Officer. I'm afraid we won't be in Vienna long enough for us to be present for the burial, especially with it almost being New Year's."

Bob Hall stood up. "Herr Blickensdorfer was at my luncheon table today and he raised the idea that perhaps Fred had committed suicide. He said Fred had sounded quite depressed yesterday when he'd been talking with him.

Anybody else have that impression of Fred's mood in the last day or two?"

"He didn't sound suicidal or anything to me since we started this trip, but it did come up the other day at the bar that we're within a week or so of the second anniversary of when his wife died in the automobile accident," contributed Tom.

"Well, I'm not sure speculating on accident or suicide really gets us anywhere, unless we find a note or something in his room. Mike, let's find the Captain and go to his room now and take a look, and we should secure any valuables or personal items, in case a relative does turn up somewhere, or there's a will."

The group split up and went their separate ways. By dinner time, everyone had heard the rumor, started by Blickensdorfer, that Fred might have committed suicide. Arthur, Mike and Captain Ornsdorfer found no note in Fred's cabin. The Captain, per law, took possession of what money had been on Fred and a gold pocket watch Fred's father had given him when he'd become an Ensign. All of which would be turned over to the Viennese Police, and probably then to the American Embassy.

By late that night, it was down to only six people sitting near the bar and the piano. During dinner and until about nine o'clock, the trio played on that deck. After that, it was just Joe at the piano up in the Main Lounge. They had all been avoiding the topic of Fred's death, until Arthur raised it in an odd way.

"Perhaps Miss LeBlanc isn't quite the charlatan I'd suspected her of being. Remember what she said that night about Fred. First, that he'd soon be seeing great love and that money from unanticipated people will soon come his way."

"Say, that's right," responded Bob. "He's seen the outpouring of kind thoughts for him by his old friends, and if you believe in a hereafter, he's now been reunited with his great love, his dead wife. And with the donations from everybody towards his headstone and funeral, he's received unanticipated money."

Everyone was silent for several long seconds. "And the death of his wife in that car accident had certainly been a great tragedy in his life. Like I said, maybe there's more to her skill than I had first given her credit for."

Jan felt a chill go down her spine. Whatever their individual conclusions on LeBlanc's talents, discussion of Fred cast a certain pall over them and soon all had gone to their cabins except Mary Beth. Bob had been the first to depart. He'd been looking at his watch every ten minutes or so and had eventually announced to one and all that he was calling it a night. Mary Beth had a funny feeling that Bob wasn't headed for his own cabin. Even Stefan, after having served her a last brandy, called it a night.

"Go to bed Joe whenever you feel like it. I'm just not sleepy, given what happened this morning."

"No problem, I'm a night owl myself. Comes from playing in those night clubs till three or four in the morning for so many years I guess. And I can understand how everyone's pretty shaken up over your friend's death. Were you particularly close to him?"

"We had been back in college, but I hadn't seen him for many years. Sad how friends sometimes drift apart as the years go by. I'm usually sound asleep by midnight, but not tonight," she sighed.

"Forgive me for saying so, Miss Mary Beth, but you look kind of worried. Something bothering you tonight, besides your friend's death?"

Joe had diagnosed her right on the money. Ever since she'd discovered that someone had been searching her room, she'd been concerned over what they might have found. And then there were the strange comments about her by Mikaela LeBlanc. The fact of the matter was that while she did indeed write children's books, and quite good ones which had even won awards, they didn't really pay the rent. Three years earlier, when complaining to her publisher about her financial problems, he suggested to her that she could make more money writing mildly pornographic novels than children's books. He said that having one written from a woman's perspective might be a novelty and be very popular, and thus lucrative for her. Initially, she'd told him he was crazy, but a week later she'd gone back to him to discuss it further. She'd now written four such novels under the pseudonym of Lusty LaRue and had indeed made money – that's how she could afford to go on this cruise. During the daytime, she was writing a new Reilly the Rabbit story, but at night, she was working on her next porno novel. She kept that notebook hidden in her empty suitcase up on a shelf in her closet, so not even the cleaning staff would stumble across it. But if someone had been searching through her clothes drawers, they could have easily looked in her suitcase as well. If it came out that she wrote such novels, it would be damned embarrassing and certainly mean the end of her publishing children's books!

Finally, she replied to Joe, "I guess I'm a little nervous about walking around on my own in such big cities as Vienna and Bratislava."

Joe leaned over and pulled out of his musical bag a small gun, an FN Baby Browning semi-automatic. "Here's a nice little gun that would easily fit in your purse. It only has six shots, but it will get the job done if you run into trouble some night when you're out on your own. Why don't you keep it until we get to Budapest?"

She looked a bit surprised that Joe carried around a gun. "Why do you have a gun?"

"Well, Paris at night, when I'm usually going home in the wee hours of the morning can get a little dangerous, especially in the neighborhood where I live." He gave her a smile. "I just brought it along on this trip out of habit."

"OK, I guess I would feel more comfortable – when out alone at night – if I had this in my purse."

He showed her how it worked.

"It does fit nicely in my hand and in my purse. Thank you very much."

"See, you look less worried already," he kidded her. "Now why don't you go to bed and get some sleep.

The ship remained docked over night at Durnstein and would only depart for Vienna at mid-morning the following day. Professor Langweilig was to give another lecture that morning about Vienna, but it was cancelled, as everyone was still in a somber mood over the death of

Lieutenant Commander Hendricks, as people had taken to referring to him as a sign of respect.

Arthur was an early riser and was the only person having breakfast when Captain Ornsdorfer passed through the Dining Room.

"May I join you Mr. Smith?"

"Certainly." He indicated at a chair next to his.

The Captain waved to a waiter to bring him a cup of coffee. They all knew he took his black, no sugar. Once he received his coffee, he looked around to make sure no one else was in the room, then said to Arthur, "There's something I wish to make you aware of."

Smith wasn't sure where this conversation was headed, but he responded, "Yes."

"I presume you've met Werner Blickensdorfer?"

Smith simply slowly nodded his head up and down twice as a "yes", but otherwise remained silent.

"He's not a banker, but rather a colonel in the Gestapo, the secret political police of Germany."

"It was rather obvious he wasn't a banker, as he claimed, but why are you telling me this?"

"Blickensdorfer is here investigating the loyalty of a general in the German Army. He believes that someone now on this ship secretly met with that officer on Christmas Eve, back in Munich, and is now carrying highly secret information to pass to a foreign government, probably the British."

"All very fascinating Captain, but again I ask, why are you telling me this? Do you mistakenly think I am a secret British agent?" Arthur was secretly flattered if that was the case, but couldn't believe anyone would think that of him.

The Captain smiled. "If you are a British agent Mr. Smith, I wouldn't expect you to admit it to me. And I don't even necessarily think you are, but you are clearly a very intelligent man. The kind of man who would probably make an excellent secret agent. But in any case, you are the leader of this large group of Americans and thus you might know or at least have your own suspicions of who in your group might be this man carrying out secret tasks on behalf of the British Secret Service."

"And if I did know or suspect such a man, do you expect me to tell you who he is?"

"Of course not, but I would ask that you warn him about Blickensdorfer."

Arthur was surprised by that response. "And why are you passing along this warning?"

The Captain smiled. "I am no Nazi, nor a fan of what they are doing. That crazy little fool in Berlin is going to start a war that Germany cannot win and one that will draw my Austria into it as well. I cannot risk openly taking any actions to help him, but I hope this British agent succeeds in getting his secret information safely back to England. Passing along this warning to you is all that I can do."

Smith stared in silence at Ornsdorfer for several long seconds before replying. "I do not know or suspect who among the passengers is this secret agent, but thank you for the warning. If I do run across such a person in the near future, I shall pass it along to him, without mentioning your name."

"Tell him he should be very careful. Colonel Blickensdorfer will stop at nothing to prevent that information from getting out to the West."

"The timing of your coming to me just after the fall and death of Fred Hendricks seems more than a coincidence. Are you possibly hinting that Fred's fall was in fact no accident?"

The Captain simply shrugged his shoulders. "Nothing can be excluded as a possibility," was his cryptic response.

The Captain reached over and shook Smith's hand. "I thank you for discreetly listening to me and I wish you good luck." He drank down the last of his coffee, stood and moved on.

Arthur continued to sit in his chair for several more minutes, his brow furrowed as he wondered just what to make of the conversation and what to do with the warning. Eventually, he finished his breakfast and returned to his cabin. Jan was still sleeping and so he undressed as quietly as possible and crawled back into bed with her and put his arm around her. She gave out a small little sound of contentment, almost like a cat purring, but didn't wake. He debated whether to even tell his wife of his odd conversation with the Captain. He decided not to say anything to her. After all, she had her own problems to worry about. Arthur soon joined her in sleep, and neither awoke until shortly after nine.

Jan was having some tea by herself in the Main Lounge around ten when Kinley came over and sat down with her.

"It's so sad about your fellow American. He seemed like a very nice man."

"Yes, we're all still in shock over his death, and there's talk over whether he might have committed suicide – that it wasn't an accident. His wife had died two years ago, almost to the day."

"Oh, I don't think he jumped," replied Kinley.

"You don't?"

"Well, Inga doesn't anyway. She told me this morning that she'd heard people talking about him maybe killing himself, but she doesn't believe it. He's been having massages with her and he'd talked about how he'd been so depressed for almost two years, but how he'd decided recently that it was time to move on with his life. That's why he'd been in London just before joining the cruise and had had a confidential meeting with the president of an important investment firm. He was getting ready to move to England in just a few months."

Jan was a bit astounded. "And why would Fred have told this to Inga?"

Kinley giggled. "Oh, Inga has told me many times that it's amazing what people tell her when they're laying naked on her table, getting a massage."

"I suppose so," replied Jan with a smile. "Well, thank you for telling me that."

Captain Ornsdorfer, Arthur and Mary Beth all arrived at Jan's table just a minute later and they chatted about the upcoming portion of the cruise, which would take them to Vienna.

"Travelling on the Danube is always exciting," began

the Captain. "I think of the hundreds of thousands of people who have traveled up and down it over the centuries. Their lives often being changed by such trips — maybe not even knowing what awaited them at the end of their journey. Sometimes such river journeys go pleasantly, other times there are adversities to be faced that challenge and change a person. I started going up and down this river when I was Hanna's age, as a deck hand on a cargo barge. I've grown old, but this ancient river itself never changes; she just keeps flowing."

"My, you're in a philosophical mood today, Captain," commented Mary Beth with a smile.

He chuckled. "I guess the older I get, the more I realize how nothing really changes." The Captain then pulled out his pocket watch and checked the time. "Well, it's time for me and Kinley to go get some work done."

Kinley grabbed hold of her father's hand before he could put the watch away. "Look at his beautiful maritime watch. Someday I'll have a pocket watch like that."

The Captain laughed and patted her on the head. "Go help in the kitchen, young lady. I'll see all of you later."

Once the Captain and Kinley had departed, Jan repeated Kinley's story to Arthur and Mary Beth.

They both thought Inga's opinion was quite interesting. "Funny how Blickensdorfer has told everyone how Fred had seemed very depressed, but Inga told Kinley that Fred was ready to move on with his life," mused Arthur.

"Funny indeed," replied Mary Beth.

Arthur said nothing of his earlier conversation with

the Captain, but in light of it, he was definitely more inclined to accept Inga's story over Blickensdorfer's.

After another delicious lunch, Jan went to their cabin to read and Arthur was just wandering about the ship when he encountered Miles at the far end of the Lounge. It was cold out, but the sun was shining brightly through the window. He was reading, but looked up as Smith approached.

"Good afternoon, Arthur."

"Miles, may I join you, or are you deep in your book?"

Miles laughed and closed the book. "Just reading an old book of mine to pass the time. Please, sit down."

Arthur saw the title embossed in gold lettering of a strange alphabet on a quality leather cover. "Is that Greek?"

"Why, yes it is. Only the oldest son got the money, but the rest of us children were well-educated, and learning Greek and Latin was expected for my generation. Do you read Greek as well?"

Arthur laughed. "No, I went to some fraternity parties back at the university and I remember some of the funny letters that made up their names – but that is the extent of my knowledge. You know, a couple of years back, I'd thought about actually learning the language so as to be able to read some of the famous literary and philosophical works of Ancient Greece. But that idea lasted only three weeks!" They both laughed.

Miles leaned forward and said to Arthur, "I'll let you in on a little secret. I've read a number of such books in modern-day English and in the original Greek or Latin, and I didn't get a thing more out of them in the original!"

"Well, thanks for sharing that. I know now not to waste my time learning ancient Greek."

"Now there is one useful thing to being able to read them in Greek, though since you appear a very happily married man, still of no value to you personally."

Arthur gave him a puzzled look.

Miles smiled and said, "I've noticed that women seem intrigued when they come across an older man reading a book in Greek. And at my age, I need any advantage I can find in courting women!" He winked at Arthur and waved at a waiter. "I think we could both use an afternoon brandy."

"I agree."

When the brandies arrived, Miles asked of Arthur, "Were you in the war? I mean, actually off where the fighting went on?"

"Indeed I was. Horrible memories I'll never forget. And you?"

"Yes. I went up to the Front in a unit of 140 men with whom I'd be training for many months and by the end of the war I learned that I was the only one still alive." He raised his glass, "Well, to fallen comrades."

"To fallen comrades."

After they'd finished their drinks and had discussed what Miles considered to be his most favorite tourist locations around Europe, Arthur decided to raise the topic of Werner Blickensdorfer. Arthur presumed that a British national on board would have to be a prime suspect for the Germans. Given Captain Ornsdorfer's warning that morning of how the Colonel would stop at nothing to prevent certain information from getting back to England,

Arthur felt he should give Miles a warning – in case he was the secret agent being sought. "What do you think Blickensdorfer and Hinz are really up to on this cruise?"

"What do you mean?"

"I mean they've been asking questions about a number of us Americans on board – our backgrounds and political leanings. And then there is their fascination with what we thought of Munich and did we get out and see a lot of it, particularly on Christmas Eve. I understand that they're from Munich and proud of their city, but such curiosity about where we went and what we saw on that particular evening — it's strange. Plus, I'm a banker and I don't believe at all his story about him being a banker taking a needed holiday!"

"You are a keen observer of your fellow man, Arthur. Well, now that you mention it, Werner was quite curious as to whether I'd gone out on Christmas Eve and walked in the beautiful snow fall. As you say, a bit odd."

"Indeed. It's almost as though they are two policemen looking for someone in particular." Arthur just left it at that. He thought that if Miles was the sought after British agent, he should understand perfectly at what Arthur had been hinting.

They sipped their brandies in silence for a minute or so, before Arthur spoke again. "Different topic. I imagine you get tired of being asked this question, but is there going to be another European war? I seek your opinion in particular, given your profession."

Miles seemed a bit startled. "My profession?"

"I mean that of world traveler. It appears as though

you and your daughter have traveled extensively around Europe and even further, so you have collected the views of not only fellow Brits, but of other nationalities as well."

"Ah, of course, of course. Well, I'd say for the Brits and any others who were heavily involved in the Great War, there is no desire for another one. I don't know what was the final tally of dead and wounded for those four years, but every family in the United Kingdom lost either a relative or a close friend, or even several people. I've heard lots of negative talk about Prime Minister Chamberlain, including by myself, but the truth is that no Brit or Frenchmen is willing to die over a dispute between Germany and Czechoslovakia." There was a pause, then Miles asked Arthur, "And what about you Yanks?"

"Oh, there is definitely no desire for participation in another major war. Not that we Americans lost anywhere the numbers of men as did you Europeans, but President Wilson sold American involvement back in 1917 as 'the war to end all wars' – so the American attitude in general now is to simply let all of you fight it out among yourselves, if another war comes."

"And is that your opinion as well, Arthur?"

"Well, my view is a bit more complicated. I look back at the Great War and I wonder what good did it do, aside from getting a million or two people killed? Germany now has Hitler running the country, another dictator, Mussolini, is in charge of Italy and it looks like Stalin is the most brutal thug of the three. How is this any better than if we'd simply let Kaiser Bill have the Balkans back in 1914? So, when it comes to the question of risking another big war just to stop

Hitler from taking Czechoslovakia, I'm inclined to say, let him have it. Life may not be too sweet under Hitler and the Nazis, but the Germans voted him into office, let them get rid of him. I know that sounds quite cynical, but one has to carefully choose your battles – and best to choose to fight when the odds are in your favor."

Miles sighed. "It's a bad business, all around. You know, it some ways the Great War never really ended. Yes, the actually shooting stopped, but many of the territorial issues that had brought on warfare in 1914 are still with us today. And of course, the Germans think that the provisions of that Peace Treaty of 1918 were much too harsh and unfair to them – and it pretty much guaranteed a return to fighting as soon as the German side was again ready for war.

"That's a pretty grim view of the future," replied Arthur.

"I'm afraid it is. I think we better have another brandy," and he signaled once again to the waiter.

"Well, if another war should come, at least you and I are too old this time around to play an active part, sitting in some damned trench," remarked Arthur.

"True, quite true, though I suppose there are still a few patriotic activities us old fogies can perform, if called on by King and Country," said Miles with a little smile.

Arthur laughed. "Well, it would have to be an activity that I could conduct while sitting down, if anybody called on me again!"

Miles took out a Dunhill from his engraved, gold cigarette case, and lighted it. "You know, sometimes people feel sorry for me because I'm nearing the end of my life...

but there are times when I'm glad that I won't have to watch too many more years of man's folly. I'm not planning on dying tomorrow, but should it happen, well, I've had a darn good run. I had a good marriage. I've made love to a number of beautiful women. I've watched the sun set into the South Pacific Ocean from a beach on Bali. I've had exquisite dinners and drank excellent champagnes. As a boy, I actually saw the historic volcanic eruption of Krakatoa from a passenger ship in 1883. How much pleasure am I entitled to in one lifetime?" He shrugged his shoulders.

"You might have a point there, old chap. Maybe any one man is only entitled to so much happiness? Perhaps life should be gauged by quality of living, not quantity of years."

The two men then lapsed into silence as they finished their brandies.

When the lunch gong sounded, Arthur went off to fetch Jan from their cabin, while Miles waited for his daughter to find him in the Lounge. When Elizabeth arrived, he invited her to sit down with him before going down to lunch.

"I just had an interesting and slightly strange conversation with Arthur Smith, the American banker."

"How so?"

"Well, he started talking about two of the Germans on board – Werner Blickensdorfer and Holger Hinz. He likened them to two policemen, with all their questions about what passengers from this ship had seen and done on Christmas Eve in Munich."

"Do you think that means trouble for us?" she asked.

"I don't know yet." He gave her a smile. "We know what we were out doing to a few rich Germans on Christmas Eve in Munich, but as long as no one finds the false bottom in my suitcase, we should be fine. Still, it might be best if you dropped showing interest in the jewelry of the other ladies. We have our target in Vienna already set. We can reassess what jewelry might be worth the risk here on the ship as we get closer to the end of the cruise."

"Fine. Now can we go to lunch?" She gave him a thin smile. "I'm hungry!"

CHAPTER 11
Vienna

The *Danube Princessa* arrived in Vienna on schedule at noon on December 31st. It was quite cool, but with clear blue skies and bright sunshine. The view of the magnificent old city from the ship was just as spectacular as everyone had seen in photographs. Arthur and Mike headed immediately for the American Embassy to report Fred's death and were lucky enough to catch the last junior diplomat about to leave for his multi-day New Year's break. Once he'd heard the reason for their visit, he kindly stayed, made a few phone calls and said that he would personally deal with the police and make arrangements for the burial after the holiday break.

"Unfortunately, with the scheduled departure of our ship in two days' time, none of us will be here for the graveside service."

"I understand completely. I will advise the Military Attaché after the break of Mr. Hendricks' death. Given his naval background, I'm certain that he and some of his staff will be happy to attend the services under these circumstances. And I can arrange for someone to play taps at the grave, if you think that your friend would like that."

"I'm sure that Fred would appreciate the presence of some fellow military officers and the playing of taps."

Once all arrangements had been made, Arthur and Mike hailed a taxi to take them to the Hotel Sacher to rejoin their wives. They'd actually collected several hundred dollars more than needed.

"I think that we should send the rest of the money we collected to some naval charity in Fred's name," suggested Mike. "I'd heard there's one that the Navy runs for widows and orphans of the Service."

"Let's put it to a vote of everyone who donated, but I think they'll all agree to that gesture," replied Arthur.

While riding in the back, separated from the taxi driver by a glass panel, Arthur decided to raise with Mike a slightly delicate issue. He'd passed along to Miles the "warning" that he'd received from Captain Ornsdorfer about who Werner Blickensdorfer really was and thought perhaps he should do the same for Mike, based on the fact that he was carrying a gun on the ship.

"Mike, when you and Jan danced on Christmas Eve back in Munich, she felt a gun under your left arm pit – at least she thought she did. Was she imagining that or were you carrying a gun?"

Mike smiled. "Yes I was. I have one on me now."

"Having grown up and lived in Chicago, you're of course not the first fellow I've known who carries a gun, but I am a little curious as to why a New York financier and accountant does?"

The smile disappeared from Mike's face. "You remember that I grew up in Boston in the Irish neighborhood?"

Arthur nodded in the affirmative.

"Well, I had a number of friends and even a few relatives who were a part of what is glamorously called the 'Irish mob', even though it's not nearly as organized a group as is the Italian Mafia. Once I'd gotten well established down in New York City as an accountant and doing investments, I had an old friend from Boston come to me asking a favor. I'd known Shaun since grade school and he'd become fairly high ranking in the Irish mob. He wanted me to discreetly spread some of his money around in different accounts and investments, and for which I'd be paid a fee for my services. The same as if I was working for the Morgans or Rockefellers."

Arthur smiled. "Accept, Shaun's money probably came from more questionable sources."

"True, but I'm kept quite isolated from that side of his business and simply occasionally receive briefcases of cash to invest for him. I'm not a total innocent, but on the other hand, nobody ever asked the Carnegies and Kennedys exactly where their money came from either and I suspect your bank back there in Chicago doesn't want to know the origins of the cash of some of its depositors either."

Arthur smiled. "We don't ask. And I'm not interested in where your investment money comes from; I'm only interested in why you're carrying a gun?"

"Ah, the gun, well, let's just say there's been a little friction in New York City in recent months with those fellows who dine down in Little Italy. Shaun told me that my name had foolishly gotten mentioned at one point and that I should be careful. For Shaun, 'being careful' generally means to be ready to shoot back in case someone is shooting at you. Besides, Candy thinks my carrying a .45 is rather sexy. We were going to take this cruise anyway, but as it turned out, the date of the departure couldn't have been better in terms of getting out of the city when the situation with the Italians was turning ugly."

"And you think you're actually in danger over here in Europe?"

"Hey, there are more Sicilians here in Europe than there are in Manhattan."

Arthur laughed. "You want to know why I was interested in your gun?"

"I can't resist, tell me."

"Well, I was told recently that Werner Blickensdorfer isn't a banker. That wasn't much of a surprise, since he knows nothing about banking. He's actually a colonel in the German Gestapo on a hunt for some spy on our ship." He went ahead and repeated the entire story that Captain Ornsdorfer had shared with him, but without mentioning the Captain's name as the source of the information.

"Very interesting and flattering that you thought I might be the secret agent the Germans are searching for among the passengers. When we get back to New York, I'll have to tell Candy about this. She'll be very impressed with me!"

"Well, there might be a very serious side to this. I'm wondering if Fred's fall really was an accident, since Blickensdorfer was nearby when it happened. Fred had been in Navy Intelligence. Maybe to Blickensdorfer's mind that meant more than it did, given who he's looking for – and for that matter, Fred might actually have been doing a little espionage work while in Munich for all we know."

"Say, you've got a point there."

"Maybe, but my point for you is that while you know and I know you're not a secret agent, the good Colonel might reach a different conclusion, particularly if he notices you're carrying a gun."

"I see what you're saying, but now I'm wondering whether I should get rid of the gun to avoid suspicion, or whether I'm even gladder that I have it for protection."

"Well, I'd certainly not go walking by yourself on any cliffs or down dark alleys at night, just in case."

They both laughed. "Guess I better just stay at the bar tonight in the hotel ballroom and you can watch my back?"

"Deal," replied Arthur and they shook hands.

"Have you got any other suspects out of the passengers, in addition to me?"

"Not really, though I did drop a hint to Miles Pembroke about Blickensdorfer not being who he claims to be."

"You think Miles is a secret agent?"

"Probably not, for the odd reasoning that he looks and acts so much like a British secret agent, he couldn't really be one."

"Well, he may not be a secret agent, but I'm not sure he isn't something more than the penniless, minor aristocrat he claims to be."

"Could be we're both getting a little paranoid," joked Arthur.

"Perhaps, but my old friend Shaun says that paranoid people live longer."

Just then the taxi pulled up to their hotel, bringing to an end their speculation on what Miles might really be.

The hotel was having a special party in the ballroom that night to ring in 1939, starting at ten-thirty, with a full orchestra. Everyone went their own way for dinner. Weeks earlier, Karen had cabled the hotel and instructed it to make dinner reservations for groups of six people at six different quality restaurants in the city. Whichever of her passengers got to the hotel front desk first, got their choice of restaurant. However, some travelers decided to go out and explore the city and just find a restaurant on their own. Karen knew that was a mistake, as they'd simply find that every restaurant in the city was completely booked, but she'd learned years earlier that she couldn't tell some tourists what was the best thing to do – especially Americans! As night fell, passengers went off in all directions.

Blickensdorfer and Hinz realized it was hopeless to try to keep track of everyone on their suspects list, so they just picked out the remaining top four: Bob Hall, Tom Bishop, Ivan Bogatyr and Miles Pembroke. Blickensdorfer thought it had been Fred Hendricks, but if not, they had to continue their investigation of other possibilities just in case. Arthur Smith was a close fifth, but they had to narrow it down to just four given their limited manpower. Pembroke was on the list in part because he was British and seemed rather secretive, but also because of his association with Princess Landschknect. Aside from meals together, Blickensdorfer had by chance seen him leaving her cabin late one night. The Colonel had received a response to his query about her that afternoon via the local Gestapo office at the German Embassy. She was considered mildly anti-Nazi Party, but mostly because of her typical upper-class arrogance and sense of superiority, not that she was particularly politically active. Holger had observed her several times from behind, but said that he could make no definitive conclusion about whether it had been her silhouette he'd seen that night in Munich or not.

The hotel's New Year's Eve party was quite festive, with excellent champagne, delicious finger foods and a good orchestra. Most of the attendees were in tuxedos and elegant cocktail dresses. Jan was getting all the dances she wanted with Arthur, as he'd promised. She'd gone off to the ladies room at one point and he was alone for several minutes. His mood suddenly saddened as he sat among all the laughter and frivolity. It just wasn't fair. He had the strange thought of whether God was punishing him through Jan's illness for all the pain he'd caused small businessman and home owners back during the Great Depression. His foreclosure actions had been sound business practice for the bank and its stock holders, but many people had suffered. He finally decided that God couldn't be that petty and vengeful; the bank decisions hadn't been Jan's. Why would God punish her in this way for his actions? He also came to a definitive decision at that moment on another matter.

Bob Hall surprised a few people by showing up with Inga as his date. Her dress was quite simple, but on as great a body as Inga had, she could have been wearing old potato sacks stitched together and she still would have turned heads. Jan nudged Arthur and nodded towards Bob and Inga on the dance floor. "I told you Bob looked very happy the last few days."

"Maybe he's happy because he's found a good ending for his movie," replied Arthur, tongue in cheek.

"Yeah, right. Come and dance with me."

"Your wish is my command, darling. You know, you look just as lovely tonight as the first time we were in Vienna shortly after the war on our honeymoon."

"What a lovely lie. Feel free to keep on telling them all night long."

He pulled her close to his chest as they danced.

At the stroke of midnight, balloons were released from the ceiling and much kissing occurred among the guests as the orchestra played Auld Lang Syne. Arthur and Jan indulged in a long kiss at the center of the dance floor. "Thank you for all these great years," he whispered in her ear. She just nuzzled her head close to his neck. A few minutes after midnight, they noticed Tom Bishop and Simone indulging in a rather passionate kiss off in a corner of the ball room. "Must be the champagne," remarked Arthur.

"Must be," she replied with a knowing smile. "We seem to be missing several of our fellow passengers tonight that I expected to be here."

"Who?"

"Ivan Bogatyr for one. When I spoke to him this morning, he told me how much he was looking forward to tonight's affair. And then there's that charming, elderly

British gentleman, Miles, and his daughter. I haven't seen them all evening either."

"You think she's really his daughter?" asked Arthur.

"My, aren't you the suspicious one! What makes you think she's not?"

"Oh, just the way he's watched her as she walked away from him in the Lounge of the ship on a couple of occasions."

"And what were you watching as she walked away?"

"I was watching Mr. Pembroke, of course," he replied with a perfectly straight face.

She slapped his shoulder as she grinned. "Nor have I seen the Princess tonight. I thought for certain that she'd be here in some spectacular gown and dripping with diamonds."

"No mystery there darling. Bob Hall told me this afternoon that she'd been invited to a party given by the Mayor of Vienna."

"I guess his party might rate a point or two above ours on the Viennese social scale," Jan replied with a laugh and then put her head back on her husband's shoulder. "But I'm quite happy here."

Around 12:30, the maître d' and a uniformed police officer were frantically searching for Karen. Once they found her, there ensued a brief, but very serious conversation in German, then Karen's face turned ghastly white. She left immediately with the police officer. Whispers quickly spread around the ball room that Ivan Bogatyr had been hit and killed by a taxi earlier in the evening. Fortunately, he had his hotel room key in his pocket, which is how the police had managed to so quickly learn his name and find his traveling associates.

"My god," remarked Mike Taffe to his companions at his table. "We're dropping like flies on this trip!"

Simone was seated next to Mike. "This is unbelievable. I saw him walking near St. Stephen's Cathedral earlier in the evening."

"Was he with anyone?"

"I don't think so, but it was rather crowded, so I couldn't be sure."

Yet another death out of the tour group definitely put a chill over the celebrating and within a half hour, the entire river cruise group had called it a night and gone to their rooms, leaving the ball room to the local attendees.

At breakfast the next morning, everyone was still discussing Ivan's death when Karen arrived and made an announcement to those who were present.

"As many of your already know, Ivan Bogatyr died last night when he was hit by a taxi around 9:00 p.m. The police captain has told me that according to the driver, it appears that Ivan had suddenly stepped into the street and there was no way for the taxi driver to avoid him. There were also several witnesses who remembered seeing him just moments before his death and all said that he'd appeared drunk. Current thinking by the police is that he'd been drinking, had staggered or tripped on something, fell into the street and had then been hit by the taxi. It appears to have been an unavoidable accident. However, the police will be here at 11:00 a.m. and would like to speak briefly with everyone from the cruise to see if anybody can shed any further light on what he was doing last evening. Was he just out at bars, or was he meeting someone? At the moment, they have no idea of exactly where he'd been all evening or what he'd been doing. I've also sent a telegram to his father back in Paris."

Karen had scheduled a walking tour around old Vienna at 11:00 a.m., but it was canceled as no one was in the mood to go play tourist after Ivan's death. By the time it was Simone's turn to be interviewed by the police, they'd already learned that she and Ivan had exchanged unpleasant words early in the cruise and that she'd claimed to another passenger to have seen Ivan near St. Stephen's, apparently at a time just shortly before the accident had occurred.

"Frau Chevrolet, I am Chief Inspector Schmidt of the Viennese Police. I believe that you speak English, yes?"

"Not as well as when I was a student in America long ago, but yes, I can still speak and understand it fairly well. How can I help you?"

"When I have asked other passengers earlier today whether Mister Bogatyr had any enemies, several people mentioned that you and he had exchanged, shall we say, 'harsh' words earlier in the trip. Would you agree that is an accurate description?"

"Since English is not your or my native language, it might depend on what we both understand the word 'harsh' to mean?" She smiled.

"In German, I would say 'hart' or 'ungnadig', if that helps."

"I don't speak German, so no, that doesn't help much. How about I simply tell you that Ivan Bogatyr said some things in front of my old university friends that were untrue and implied that I had been involved in my ex-husband's illegal activities as a burglar. I resented that and so in response, I suggested that perhaps the police were still looking at him as an accomplice to those robberies, since he and my husband had been such good friends."

Chief Inspector Schmidt smiled. "Would you say that you and Mister Bogatyr had previously been friends?"

"No, I wouldn't say that. Of course I knew him, but it was my husband who had been his friend. They would go to horse races, gamble together and visit brothels together.

"Ah, so would you say that you hated the Russian for his leading your husband astray?"

"If I'd ever given Ivan any thought, I might have disliked him, but I really never thought often enough about him to really care one way or the other."

Making no headway on that front, Schmidt turned to the previous night. You told someone late last night that you'd seen Ivan walking near St. Stephen's Cathedral earlier in the evening. According to the taxi driver, it was 8:55 p.m. when Mister Bogatyr stepped in front of his taxi and he ran over him. That is quite a coincidence that someone who didn't like him just happened to be nearby when he stepped, or was pushed, into the path of an automobile, is it not?"

"Well, first of all, what I said to Mr. Taffe last night was that I'd seen Bogatyr walking 'just a couple of hours ago.' I'm not sure how you've concluded that it was near 9:00 p.m. when I'd seen him. Second, you've gone from the fact that he and I had exchanged 'harsh' words to you now saying that I 'didn't like him.' Do you actually 'dislike' everyone with whom you've exchanged 'harsh' words, Chief Inspector?"

Schmidt did not smile. "Do you know of anyone who might have wanted to kill Ivan Bogatyr?"

"No one in particular, no. Do you have any other questions?"

"That will be all for now, though I may want to speak with you again later, Madame."

"I'll be here all day, but I, along with the other sixty passengers, will be sailing tomorrow morning for Bratislava." She smiled once more and stood to leave. "Oh, I just remembered that I'd also seen Herr Werner Blickensdorfer down around St. Stephens last night. Perhaps you will want to talk with him as well."

"I shall be speaking today with all the passengers. Good day, Madame Chevrolet."

Later in the afternoon, Simone was seated with the Smiths, the Taffes and Mary Beth Long in the hotel restaurant, having afternoon tea. They were all recounting their interviews with the police. Simone gave a very detailed account of her exchange with Chief Inspector Schmidt.

"You actually saw Blickensdorfer around St. Stephen's Cathedral at about the same time as you'd seen Ivan?" asked Arthur.

"Yes, why?"

"Quite a coincidence that that German was nearby when both Fred and Ivan had deadly accidents," observed Mike as he cast a glance over at Arthur.

Smith interrupted that line of speculation. "Maybe, but Karen told me not thirty minutes ago that the police have thought all along that Ivan had been drunk, had inadvertently stepped off the curb and accidently fell in front of the cab. The locals who saw it happen have all said that it looked as though Ivan had just tripped – bad luck for Ivan, but there was no sinister plot by Blickensdorfer or Simone or anyone else."

"I suppose not," conceded Mike, "but I'm getting to the point where I'll be glad to see this cruise end – before there are any more accidents!" They all gave nervous laughs at his black humor.

Simone then added, "And chalk up another one for Miss LeBlanc. She told me that 'death would soon be very near me.' Did she perhaps mean Bogatyr?"

Across the dining room, Bob Hall was hosting Inga and Kinley for tea and cake. Arthur observed that the three were laughing and appeared to be greatly enjoying each other's company. He leaned over and whispered to his wife, nodding with his head towards Bob's table, "Isn't that a happy group over there?"

Jan looked over at Bob, Inga and Kinley. "Kinley told me the other day that she and Inga are very good friends, given that they're the only two women among the crew. So, unless you know something that I don't know about Swedish sexual practices, I'd say that they look like three people who simply enjoy each other's company. So put your mind to rest, you dirty old man."

Finally, only Arthur and Mary Beth were left at the table. He'd continued to ponder the fact that Blickensdorfer had been nearby when both "accidents" had occurred. He'd decided that he didn't want to burden Jan with the subject, but he really wanted to discuss with someone what Captain Ornsdorfer had shared with him about why the Gestapo was on the ship. The restaurant had emptied out and the two were quite alone.

"Mary Beth, I'd like your opinion on something, and not to sound too mysterious, but this must remain between only us two."

"Alright." She thought he was about to tell her something about Jan's health condition.

"I've been informed that Werner Blickensdorfer is a colonel in the Gestapo and that he, Holger Hinz and those two other, younger Germans are on board investigating a case of possible espionage involving a German Army general. They think for some reason that this general secretly met on Christmas Eve with someone traveling on this ship. That's why there have been so many questions by them about what all of us were doing on the evening of the 24th back in Munich."

"Oh my god," she uttered. "How did you learn this?"

"I'd rather not answer that, as I don't think it really matters. The person who told me thought that either I was the secret agent being sought, or I might know who out of the Hoosier group was, and could warn him about Blickensdorfer. I needed someone to talk with about this very strange allegation. Given your comment earlier today about how Blickensdorfer was nearby when both Fred and Ivan had accidental deaths, I thought you were a good choice. It seemed as though you might already have your own suspicions about him."

"I know nothing about him, but it does seem quite a

coincidence that he has been close by when two passengers from the ship have died under suspicious circumstances – whether the police declared them accidental deaths or not. I admit that I don't like the man, which perhaps colors my thoughts about him. He's always asking questions. Now that you say he's a colonel in the Gestapo, that would explain his curiosity."

"Do you remember where Fred and Ivan were on Christmas Eve? Since this alleged meeting with the German general took place that evening, do they fit the picture of being out and alone that evening? And therefore, Blickensdorfer might have thought one of them was this secret agent."

"Hmm, yes, I believe Ivan was out and I don't think ever showed up at the Christmas party that night."

"I recall Fred saying he'd gone to a service at some nearby church, before coming to the party later. So, I suppose either of them could have made a secret meeting." Arthur laughed. "I too went out for a little stroll that evening around 7:30, so I guess I might be on the Colonel's suspect list as well."

Mary Beth smiled. "I was also out for a little bit, but then I think so were a dozen or more from our group. Surely, he isn't just going around bumping off everyone who went out on the streets of Munich on that evening!"

"Let's hope not! But in any case, you don't think this story of a traitorous German general and of German and British spies being on board sounds ridiculous? Like one of Bob's movie plots?"

"Well, it doesn't happen much back in Portsmouth,

New Hampshire, but on the Danube River in Central Europe – who knows?"

"Alright, thanks for talking this over with me. Keep your eyes open when Blickensdorfer is around."

"And don't you go walking alone near the deck railing late at night when we get back on the ship!" She gave him a teasing smile. "I'll see you and Jan at dinner."

Slightly before dinner, Smith had come down to the hotel lobby to enjoy a cigar. He'd quit smoking them near Jan as they aggravated her headaches. He saw Miss LeBlanc checking out of the hotel. He waved and she came over to him.

"You're leaving us? I thought you were going all the way to Budapest on the ship?"

They went over to an empty sofa and sat down together for a few minutes. "I've decided to take the train to reach Athens. There's a sleeper express that leaves Vienna tonight in about an hour. The hotel was able to secure a first class sleeping compartment for me on that train."

"Well, it was certainly a pleasure having you join our group, if only for a few days. We shall miss you."

"That's very kind of you to say." She hesitated for a moment, then said, "Mr. Smith, you are aware of how ill your wife is, yes?"

His smile disappeared. "Yes, we are aware of her condition. Why do you ask?"

She looked down at the floor. "I saw a very black aura around her while doing the card reading of you two. I fear she is not long for our world."

He stared down at the floor. "We were aware of her medical problem before we started this journey."

"Good, as I watched you two together, I assumed that you were. Frankly, I'm leaving your group because I saw many signs of possible death yet to come on that ship and it depressed me. My gift is not something I can just totally turn on or off at my will and the vibrations I've felt over these last few days have disturbed me greatly. It's better that I go my separate way."

"I'm not sure how to respond to that news, other than to say that I hope you're wrong, but thank you for sharing that with me."

"There is also one more 'feeling' that I want to share with you. I saw a tremendous aura of love around you and your wife. It will surely endure into the next plane of existence."

"I hope you're correct about me and my wife. A different topic if I may before you leave. Rumors on the ship are that you've done readings for some very senior Nazi officials, including Heinrich Himmler. I suppose there's sort of a privacy ethic, like a doctor-patient relationship, but can you tell me – do you think there is a war coming?"

"You are correct, I do not share the secrets of my clients, but let me just say, I fear there is a terrible catastrophe coming. There is a cloud blacker on the horizon than any I've ever seen. All men have some evil in them, but these Nazis – I will not come back to Germany again. After Delphi, I'm going back to Louisiana and staying there until the coming storm passes."

"Well, thank you again, Miss LeBlanc. I hope you have an uneventful trip down to Greece and then home to America. Goodbye."

They shook hands. "Farewell, Mr. Smith."

The following morning, January 2nd, they set sail at 10:00 a.m. from Vienna and would arrive at Bratislava in two hours. The sunshine and blue skies had returned, which helped put the passengers in a slightly better mood. Having been together for better than a week, the Indiana reunion crowd had pretty well caught up on news about each other and gossiped about those who weren't there. Many had settled into little cliques based on friendships of old, or in some cases, based on new impressions. Miles and Elizabeth continued to be popular with everyone. Arthur and Mike again had a brief conversation about whether Miles Pembroke was actually who he claimed to be, but concluded that he was such a charming and interesting fellow, who cared. Mike noted that he even steadily and graciously lost money at cards and didn't seem to care.

The landscape along the river remained about the same, though the river itself had broadened. Even though it was winter and nothing was growing, it was obvious that it was all agricultural land on the gentle slopes that ran up from the river. Many of the fields were grape vineyards. Most everyone was in a very relaxed mood of idle contentment, rising a little later each morning. Each day brought forth more good food and drink, along with good music by the "Algerians" and good conversation. Even afternoon naps seemed more relaxing with the gentle vibrations running through the ship as they sailed further south and east every day.

The exception to this scene of everyone appearing more relaxed each day was Blickensdorfer. With each passing day, he seemed more anxious and more inquisitive about his fellow passengers' political views and careers. The other passengers didn't realize that with every hour the ship got closer to Budapest, Blickensdorfer feared the illusive secret agent he sought was getting closer to an escape – and with escape, there would probably go his only chance at promotion and transfer to Berlin.

About an hour into the journey to Bratislava, Werner Blickensdorfer and two of the German ladies on the cruise had gone out onto a small seating area on the stern of the ship. It was sheltered from the wind. If sitting in the sunshine, it was fairly pleasant, even with the temperature just a few degrees above freezing. They were passing a young boy of about ten who was out fishing in a small row boat. He stood up in his boat to wave at people on board the *Danube Princessa*, just as the wake of the ship reached his boat and it dumped him into the water. The strong current was pushing him away from his boat and given the way he was thrashing about it was clear that he could not swim.

While kicking off his shoes and removing his sport coat, he shouted at the ladies to go inside and inform a crew member of what had happened and to stop the ship. A few seconds later, he dove into the frigid, swirling waters. The boy was some forty meters away. Fortunately, he was a strong swimmer and was making quick progress towards the child as the two ladies went back inside, shouting in search of a crewman.

"Hilfe, hilfe!" they shouted loudly in German. "A man is overboard and a boy is drowning!" Within a few seconds, two crewmen had come up to them.

"Herr Blickensdorfer dove into the river, trying to save a young boy who capsized from his small boat. Stop the ship!"

One crewman headed up to the pilot house and the other ran for the stern. Once outside, the latter saw that Blickensdorfer had reached the boy and was keeping him afloat, but he was making little headway in trying to head for the shoreline. Within less than a minute, the ship had reversed its engines and other crewman were lowering a small boat from the *Princessa* to go rescue their passenger and the young boy. By this time, many of the passengers had gone outside or had their faces pressed up to the ship's windows.

Within just a matter of a few minutes, the crewmen had Blickensdorfer and the boy into their craft and they were rowing as fast as possible back to the ship. Both Werner and the boy were shaking from the cold.

In another five minutes, the crew had both wet and cold victims on the ship and were wrapping them in blankets. Captain Ornsdorfer was giving both of them a little brandy and then ordered that both be taken to the small medical cabin. He also ordered the First Mate to head the ship to the first dock that he saw ahead.

Within a half hour, they had delivered the boy to two fishermen at a small dock who knew the boy's family and who would see that he was safely delivered home. Blickensdorfer went to his cabin to take a warm shower and to then put on dry clothes. While he was off changing, the two German ladies had continued to tell of his selfless bravery to one and all.

"He didn't hesitate for a moment. Soon as we three saw the child in distress, he immediately took off his shoes and coat and dove into the water!"

The second lady slightly embellished the event. "And as he dove in, his final words to us were to tell his wife he loved her."

A short while later, Blickensdorfer entered the Dining Room for lunch and all the passengers rose from their tables and applauded him for his heroic efforts at saving the child. Werner humbly acknowledged their applause and repeatedly commented that "it was nothing."

Mary Beth was standing next to Arthur. She leaned closer to him and said softly, "He may be a nasty Gestapo officer, but I guess even a Nazi can have a good point about him."

Arthur nodded in agreement. "At least when it comes to small children." They both continued clapping along with everyone else until Werner took a seat at the Captain's table.

After lunch, Arthur and Bob Hall went up to the Main Lounge for coffee and cigars. They had the front of the Lounge to themselves, which was good as Arthur had a question for Bob.

"As a screen writer, I presume you've often considered the good and bad of some of the characters that you've written about – 'good' vs 'evil' if you will?

"Certainly, that's a favorite theme in dramatic movies. What's on your mind?"

"Well, not that it necessarily has anything to do with events on this ship, but I've been thinking about this question of good vs evil, particularly when it comes to the Nazis and some of the nasty things they've been doing over the last few years. I mean, the treatment of their own citizens."

"Yeah, Hitler's treatment of Jews and Gypsies has gotten pretty nasty," replied Bob.

"Right. So it's easy to chalk off Blickensdorfer, a colonel in the Gestapo, as an evil man, but then he goes and risks his own life to save a completely unknown child who's drowning. Most of us I think would call that a good deed, even a heroic one. How can the same man be capable of such evil and good?" And what exactly is 'evil' anyway?"

Bob smiled. "My friend, mankind has been wrestling with those kind of questions going all the way back to Socrates and Plato. I took a couple of Philosophy classes in college. I only got Cs in them, but let me give you a short answer to your hard questions."

"Excellent, a college drop-out who only got Cs in Philosophy classes is going to advise me on ethical dilemmas!"

"Hey, you get what you pay for my friend," replied Bob with a grin.

"Just answer me this. If smart people have been

debating these issues for two thousand years, how is it that we can still have such evil as the Nazis well into the 20th century?"

"OK, listen, first you have to decide what causes evil actions, before you can think about how to do away with them."

"OK," replied Arthur as he blew a big puff of smoke up into the air and leaned back in his chair to listen to Bob's lecture.

There are two main, contrasting schools of thought. First, there's a big, nasty figure called the Devil, who's always in competition with God and that he lures people off to do evil actions. The second says that there is a desire for good and bad within every man and therefore, it's pretty much your own doing which one you choose. And at times, the same person might choose bad or good. In other words, you have free will and you make your own choices. That's how Blickensdorfer can send innocent gypsies or Jews to jail one week and then save a drowning child the next. Which path you choose most probably comes with your upbringing and education. And I think the circumstances in which you've been living may have a lot to do with it. Most of the German population was living under really tough circumstances from 1919 till say 1935. Just to survive, a lot of them had to resort to measures that under better circumstances they wouldn't have. Then there's always a desire to find somebody to blame for your troubles – for many Germans that's been the gypsies and Jews. Once you start down a slippery slope of doing "bad" things yourself, I guess it's easier to go along with even worse things by your political leaders. I'm not trying to excuse what the Nazis are doing, just to explain them. Maybe had there never been a Great War, we wouldn't be seeing some of the "unfair" things we've been seeing around Germany. Bottom line is that under the right circumstances, most all of us are capable of some pretty nasty actions. If you and Jan were starving, I bet you could steal, lie and cheat with the best of them. And so could I."

"Well, that's all interesting and plausible, but not much help in knowing how do you do away with evil?"

Bob laughed. "That's why people are still asking that question four thousand years after it first came up. It may be that we simply can't do away with evil because the capacity for it is in all of us. Maybe the best we can do is minimize how often it happens through education, be it civics teaching in schools, religious training or just familial instruction to small children."

"I suppose, but what about police and punishment?"

"Great idea, but how do you have police everywhere for all the petty instances of bad actions that occur. And then there's the question of what is a bad action? Hitting someone might be a bad action, but what if I'm hitting someone who has just raped a girl? Is it still a bad action?"

Arthur shook his head and waved for a waiter. "Sorry I asked the question. Let's have some Scotch and maybe an answer will come to us."

"I doubt it, but let's still have the Scotch." They both laughed.

CHAPTER 12
Bratislava

Late that afternoon, the ship pulled up to the dock in the historical city of Bratislava, Czechoslovakia. The excitement over the rescue of the boy had subsided and Blickensdorfer had gone to his cabin for a much needed rest. He had learned to swim as a young boy in Munich and had once been very proficient at swimming, but he'd not done much for many years – and certainly not in frigid waters. He was quite exhausted. Captain Ornsdorfer warned him that there could be delayed reactions to his dip in the cold waters and ordered that someone stay with him in his cabin that afternoon. Holger volunteered for that job and sat reading magazines for several hours while Werner slept. The search for a foreign spy was put on hold for the afternoon. Werner had downplayed in public his efforts, but he realized how close he'd come to himself drowning that morning in the river. He would forevermore have a different perception of the beautiful, blue Danube – now that he'd swallowed a good bit of it in a wintertime bath!

As they were only spending one night in Bratislava, the passengers would simply sleep on the ship that night, rather than transfer to a hotel. Professor Langweilig gave another lecture after lunch, focusing particularly on the castle, then in ruins, that dated back to the 12th century. There had been Roman, Celtic and even older cultures going back another thousand years that had resided there. They had all found that hill overlooking the Danube River to be an excellent, strategic location to occupy.

After the lecture, Karen then led a walking tour through the oldest part of the city. For the Americans, for whom anything over a hundred years was considered "historical", the idea that people would still be living in buildings which were six or seven hundred years old was quite amazing. During the day, there was some discussion of Miss LeBlanc's sudden decision to leave the river cruise and take a train to Greece. Smith didn't share her full story with anyone else. He simply told others that she'd decided that she could reach Delphi quicker if she caught the night train to Athens.

Shortly before dinner, Captain Ornsdorfer came across Smith sitting and reading in the Lounge and greeted him.

"Hello Captain. Do you have time to stop and join me for a schnapps?"

He pulled out his pocket watch to check the time, then agreed. "Yes, gladly, but no more than two or three," he said with a jovial laugh.

"You probably know best what is a good brand that you have on the ship. I suggest that you order for both of us."

"Very well. He waved for one of the waiters and ordered the drinks, then sat down with Smith.

"We had a pretty exciting morning, didn't we! How has the rest of your day been going Mr. Smith? Did you enjoy walking around the old part of Bratislava?"

"Yes, it's indeed a lovely city."

"It's one of my favorite stops. I've been here over a hundred times, but every time I'm here, I see something new."

"I think you're a very lucky man, Captain, to have the job you do – just sailing up and down the Danube with all the beautiful sights and enjoying the excellent food. Many men must envy you!"

"Yes, I am lucky in many ways, but I have worries as well. This is the last voyage of the season. We dock for the winter as soon as we're back to Regensburg until April, and next season will depend on..." His voice trailed off. He debated whether to say more.

Arthur noticed his hesitancy and said, "Anything you say to me, Captain, goes no further."

Ornsdorfer smiled, glad to see that Smith was a man of discretion. "I worry about the future. Not so much for myself, but for Kinley. We have a good life now together, but I haven't been able to save much and there will be little I can give her when I die."

"You're still a relatively young man. I would think you have many years yet ahead of you."

He looked around to make sure no one was close enough in the Lounge so as to overhear him. "May I call you, Arthur?"

"Certainly, please do."

"There is a war coming, Arthur. Who knows if there will even be any tourist cruises next spring? And things happen to ships and their crews in wartime, so I may not see all the years ahead of me that should be expected. I may not be here to look after Kinley as she grows into a woman, and I'm worried what will become of her. This ship is the only world she's really known – and if it were to suddenly disappear…" He shrugged his shoulders. "I saw after the last war what many young girls had to do to put food in their mouths. I don't want Kinley to face such a situation if she winds up on her own during this coming war."

"I can understand your concerns. They are those of any father. Kinley is a very mature young lady, but she is only fifteen years old, correct?"

"Yes, fifteen. Sometimes she acts like she's twenty-five, but legally, she is a minor. I just don't know how to make plans for her, in case of war. A chance which I fear is growing monthly under Hitler and the Nazis. She wouldn't want to leave me now and go to some neutral country, but if I wait till war actually starts, she might not be able to get out of Austria or Germany."

Arthur could see the genuine distress in the Captain's face. "I wish I could help you and Kinley, but for reasons I can't really go in to, Jan and I are not a solution."

"I wasn't trying to hint at anything," replied Johan. "Just a concerned father rambling out loud."

"I know, I know, but I might have an idea. Let me do some checking and we can talk again soon about Kinley's future."

"I don't know if I could even convince her to part from me, but I'd like to have an emergency plan in place, should the situation start looking very dark."

"I understand. Now, let me ask you a related question if I may. It's connected with the possibility of a war coming. Namely, why doesn't anyone oppose Hitler? Has the Nazi Party got everyone so terrified that no one wants to stand up against him?"

The Captain smiled. "Arthur, I'm afraid that you don't understand the Germans and Austrians very well. Perhaps ten percent of the people are simply so afraid of the Nazis that they won't speak out against Hitler, but he's actually very popular. My numbers may not be totally accurate, but I'd say that thirty percent of the people truly don't like Jews, or gypsies and other such minority groups. That anti-Semitism comes from many reasons, but regardless of the reasons, those people support Hitler because of his stand on Jews. Twenty percent more think that Germany lost the Great War because of a *dolchstoss*, a stab-in-back, which ties in with the anti-Semitism and dislike of Communists. The final forty percent feel that the peace treaty unfairly put all the blame for the war on Germany and that the reparations were so harsh that they caused the horrible economic conditions of the 1920s and early 1930s. Hitler has come along and told the people that he is going to again make Germany a strong and proud country with *ordnung* – and the economic situation of the country truly is much better now. That's why he's so popular and if he says there must be war, then the people will support war."

"That's very interesting. You're right, apparently I hadn't accurately understood the political situation in Germany or Austria. Thank you." Arthur rose. "I'll be back in touch about Kinley before we reach Budapest."

They shook hands and Arthur headed to his cabin to talk with Jan.

At the end of their delicious dinner that evening, a local group of folk dancers came on board to entertain the passengers. Towards the finish, they encouraged the more adventurous to come out of their chairs and join them in dancing. It was just the lighthearted and entertaining evening that the group needed to get them out of their depression over the deaths of two of their members.

Arthur saw Bob and Inga up in the Main Lounge later that night, sitting very close and talking very seriously.

The following afternoon, the men went to visit a local brewery that had been in business in Bratislava since 1752, and to sample its product. The ladies visited a number of stores featuring jewelry and local folk craft products typical of the region.

Arthur grabbed Bob as the group headed back to the ship.

"Bob, how about we stop off at that coffee shop over there. I've got something I want to discuss with you. I need your opinion on something."

"Sure, after all that beer, I won't be doing any writing this afternoon anyway!"

Once the waiter had delivered their coffees and apfel strudels, Arthur came quickly to the point. "I hate to be nosy, but you and Inga are looking very serious in each other's company. Anything might be coming of that relationship after the cruise ends?"

Bob laughed. "Aren't you the perceptive banker! I'm actually glad you brought up the subject. I've been needing somebody to talk with about Inga. To answer your question, I don't know what's going to happen after Budapest. There's obviously a special spark between us, besides the great sex." He grinned like an eighteen-year-old college freshman. "But we've only known each other for a few days."

"Well, let me tell you about me and Jan. I met her at an Army camp dance in 1917 and I knew by the end of that very same evening that she was the woman I wanted to marry."

Bob grinned. "Wow, you are a fast mover!"

"I'm just saying, when it's right, you know immediately it's right."

"I think we both feel there's something special between us, but I guess I'm a coward."

"You know, Bob, in some of those Hollywood movies, couples make up their minds about each other in a matter of days. Now, if you both lived in the same city, or hell, if even in the same country, it would be different, but you don't. So maybe you're going to have to make an executive decision here and now. And while I'm no Mikaela LeBlanc, I think there's going to be a terrible war in Europe in the coming year – another reason why it's fish or cut bait time."

Bob smiled. "I know this will sound a bit silly, but you know what really got me to thinking about marriage and Inga in the last few days?"

"I'm listening."

"It's this movie script I'm working on. While this old school teacher does have the pleasant memories of all his students over the decades, he's a widower. He's lived alone for many years and dies alone. I'm thirty-six, and I've been thinking that I don't want to spend my next twenty or thirty years alone. And besides this movie plot, I've also been looking at you and Jan and what a great marriage you two have. I'd like that same happiness."

"I think that's a pretty natural human emotion you're feeling and I'm flattered that we've been a positive role model for you. It has been a great marriage for us. Of course, it's fun having someone with you when you're taking a cruise or going to a show, but what Jan and I also have is that it's great even when we're just sitting at home doing nothing. It may sound odd, but we do 'nothing' together really well."

Bob nodded that he agreed with that statement, but then sat and stared at the bottom of his empty coffee cup. "Listen Arthur, I have one more issue." Then he went silent.

"Yes?"

"My family name isn't Hall. It's Holtzberg, or it was. The summer before I started college, I shortened it down to just Hall, so my Jewish background wouldn't be so obvious. There hadn't really been a problem in the town I was from, but I'd heard stories about how Jews sometimes were treated in big cities and maybe even at college, so I just changed my name. My dad was Jewish, but mom wasn't really anything. I'd never been particularly religious anyway, so I figured why take the risk of being discriminated against when I didn't even think of myself as Jewish."

"Good point. I'm curious, if not against you in particular, did you see much anti-Semitism while you were in Bloomington?"

"Oh, I'd hear some comments at times about some

Jewish student, but usually just from some local bonehead who also didn't like blacks, Poles, Mexicans or about anybody who wasn't a relative of his."

Arthur laughed. "I think I knew that guy. He worked at the grocery down on First Street. But what has any of that got to do with asking Inga to marry you?"

"I'm not even sure. I've refrained from commenting much about Hitler and the Nazis as I didn't want it to seem as if it was a Jewish thing for me. I've never even owned up to being Jewish out in Hollywood even though there are lots of Jews in the movie business. So, do I tell Inga or not about my true background?"

"Hmm, has Inga ever given any indication that she has a feeling one way or the other about Jews?"

"No, not really. She doesn't seem to think about people in those terms. She simply likes or dislikes somebody for the way they personally act."

"Then I guess it really wouldn't matter to her, but if you truly have no inclination at being a practicing Jew and no real interest in that part of your heritage, then maybe just leave it alone. I confess, I'm sort of like you are. I come from English and Dutch ancestry, but have never cared in the least about my past. People are just people. America would probably be a better place, if people just forgot about their past once they landed in North America. I've always thought that what was so good about America was this tradition of it being the great 'melting pot.' You gave up those past prides and prejudices and everybody was simply an American. I don't care what your ancestors did to my ancestors, or vice versa. How people treat me now is all I care about."

"I agree with you on that score, though I have an uncle who judges everything from the perspective of being Jewish. He drives me crazy."

Arthur laughed. "Yeah, I have a few relatives on the Dutch side of the family tree who are the same way. They always want to know if somebody they're doing business with is of Belgian heritage and then they spend five minutes talking about how you can't trust a Belgian."

"Well, like I said I don't give a fig about my background, but I must say that Blickensdorfer made me feel uneasy when he was sniffing around and asking where I'd been on Christmas Eve and what did I think of Hitler."

"Maybe when we leave the ship in Budapest, you should tell him how he's been eating and drinking with a Jew, and see if he has a stroke!"

Bob grinned. "I never knew until now what a mean streak you have hidden under those banker clothes. Up until yesterday, I might have done that, but after his rescuing that drowning boy, my opinion of Blickensdorfer has gone up a few notches."

"Yeah, I guess there's a little good in most all of us, though funny what it takes for some to reveal that goodness."

The two then fell silent for a minute. "I much appreciate your thoughts, Arthur. You've helped a lot in my making up my mind, but just out of curiosity, why is my love life of such interest to you? You have an interest in Inga's future?" He gave Arthur a big smile.

"Say, you're pretty sharp for a guy who doesn't even have a college diploma. Yes, I do have a hidden agenda with you, if it did look like you might be taking a Swedish souvenir back to England with you."

"I'm listening."

Arthur told Bob of his recent conversation with Captain Ornsdorfer and his concern about how to protect Kinley, should war come to Central Europe.

Bob listened in silence and asked no questions.

"We'd offer to take Kinley to Chicago, but well, that's just not a possibility." Arthur stared down at the floor.

"I take it Jan's frequent headaches are more than just headaches?"

"Yes, but let's just leave it at that, and please keep that to yourself."

"I will. So, your idea is that I not only leave this cruise with a wife, but we instantly have a teenage daughter?"

Arthur smiled, "Well, if you put it like that, yes, that is my suggestion. I know this all sounds crazy and we're not yet in a war, but I believe we almost have to start thinking and planning as if a war had already started. You seem to like the kid and Kinley has told Jan that she and Inga are best friends. Think of all the awkward childhood years you'd be cutting out. You and Inga can instantly have a bright, young daughter you're proud of and like having around."

Bob finished off his strudel and just sat thinking. "You're a pretty good salesman. Do you already have this worked out with Inga and Kinley, or are you leaving those two minor details for me to handle?"

Arthur smiled. "Well, I figured I'd better approach you first. You can handle the two ladies anyway you prefer."

"Well, I know it will have to be me who raises the topic of both marriage and Kinley with Inga. I just wish I knew exactly how I should do that."

"Hey, you're a screen writer aren't you? How hard can that be?" he jokingly asked. "Oh, and one more thing."

"Good god, what more can there be?"

"Well, I think you make more money than you've been letting on, but you should know that Kinley comes with a $10,000 endowment, shall we call it. I will write you a check the day we leave the ship, if this is all settled."

"Mercy, ten grand, just how much money do you Chicago bankers make?"

"Let's just say I'll soon have money to spare and I want to do my fair part in looking out for the future of Kinley. She's a good kid who could use a break in life. I don't know quite what to call my feelings, but since being on this river I've come to think that we ought to extend a helping hand, if we can, to people who need it. She may not need help right today, but if a major war does come to Europe, it's innocent people like her who will suffer the most."

"Well said. I'll have to work those lines into a movie script someday. By the way, what does Jan think of all this? I presume you've discussed this with her?"

"Indeed I have and she thinks it's one of the best ideas I've ever had."

"OK, it's sounding less crazy than it did when you first brought it up, but give me till tomorrow morning to give you an answer. I'll probably bring it up with Inga tonight, but if she says it's the craziest thing she's ever heard of, then I'm going to tell her it was your idea!"

"Fair enough. If she goes for the idea about Kinley, then I suggest that you, Inga and I go have a chat first with Captain Ornsdorfer. If he agrees, then we'll bring in Kinley."

"And what do you see as the time line for this insane arrangement?"

"Well, if it was me. I'd take Inga and Kinley straight from the ship in Budapest and get married, then adopt Kinley. Soon as those two steps are accomplished, go to the American Embassy to request passports for them right there in Budapest. It will make it much easier taking them back to London, and in a few months, back to America."

"So, you think war is coming that soon?"

"I don't know an exact date, but we're headed towards war and you know us cautious bankers. I just don't think you'll want to let Inga and Kinley go back up the Danube, and then suddenly find in a few weeks' time, that you can't get them out."

"Good point. Although you know, that would make a hell of a movie plot – my sneaking back to Regensburg in wartime to retrieve the woman I love."

"And who would play you in that movie?"

"I can see Errol Flynn playing me, but you'll be a lot harder to cast." They both laughed.

"All joking aside Bob, I know that this is asking a lot of you on very short notice, but I guess there are occasions in life when we all have to just stand up and do a good deed for other people. Though in this case, it'll be good for you as well. You'll ask Inga to marry you because you've fallen in love with her and know that's a good step, for both of you. Taking Kinley with you isn't as obvious as a good idea, but I still think it would be good for all three of you."

"Hey, I'm sold. Damn, you must be a hell of a banker, the way you can make somebody see the facts."

Arthur grinned. "Alright, we better get back to the ship. You let me know either tonight or first thing in the morning if Inga said yes, and also if it's a 'go' for Kinley as well with her."

"Fair enough."

Once back to the ship, Arthur told Jan of his conversation with Bob.

"And what was his reaction?" she asked anxiously.

"Sounded as if he's going to propose to Inga, but as for Kinley, that's still undecided. He said he'd discuss it with Inga and get back to me."

"I guess you've done all you can do. It's now up to Bob and Inga."

About an hour later, Arthur and Jan were up in the Lounge having tea, when Bob approached them. The wide smile on his face told them what had been Inga's response to his marriage proposal before he ever said a word.

"Looks like congratulations are in order," said Jan.

"Indeed, they are."

"So, she's willing to marry a guy like you?" teased Arthur.

"Yep, she's a little worried about how we'll make a go of it on my sad salary, but she's willing to take a chance."

"That's great news, Bob. I'm sure you've made a wise move." Arthur grabbed a waiter passing by. "A bottle of champagne and three glasses, please."

"Yes, sir."

Arthur turned to Bob. "Or shall we need a fourth glass in a minute or two? Where is Inga?"

"She'll be along later. She went to have a conversation with Kinley."

"So she agreed to taking Kinley with you?" asked Jan.

"Yes, she thought it was a wonderful idea as she would then have a friend with her off in strange America."

"A very good point. And who gets to raise this with Papa?" asked Arthur with a smile.

"Well, Inga and I thought that all of us should approach Captain Ornsdorfer, as a united front, presuming Kinley agreed to the idea."

"Not a bad plan. I know he was the one to first raise the question of Kinley's future, but telling him that his daughter will be gone in a matter of just days is going to be a rude shock!"

Bob was still beaming. "What a day this has been. I don't know if I could have ever brought myself to ask Inga to marry me if it wasn't for our conversation earlier. Thank you both."

"Oh, you knew what you wanted to do. You just needed someone to chat with about it, to get up a little courage."

"And there's one more thing. I thought a long while after our chat earlier today about the Jewish thing and I've decided to quit hiding my background. I'm not a practicing

Jew, but I've decided that it's silly to hide my heritage. If some people don't like it, screw them, particularly the Nazis."

"Well said."

Bob grinned. "Of course, announcing you're a Jew in Hollywood isn't exactly front page news, but it will make my uncle happy."

"Did you bring this up with Inga?"

"Yes, and I was right. She could care less."

The champagne arrived and they started toasting Bob. The waiter brought extra glasses. He'd delivered enough celebratory bottles of bubbly over the years to know that a crowd would soon be gathering at that table.

A few minutes later, Mary Beth came by. "What's all this? Drinking champagne in the middle of the afternoon, and you didn't invite me to the party!"

Bob immediately poured her a glass and quickly shared his exciting news.

"Congratulations! That's wonderful."

"Perhaps we can find someone yet for you on this trip and have a double wedding," responded Bob.

"I haven't gotten an offer yet and the cruise ends tomorrow in Budapest. If I have some secret admirer on board, he better make himself known pretty quick!"

They all laughed then settled down to discussing the many things that Bob would have to get arranged in the coming days. He'd also have to get bigger accommodations back in England and then they'd need to find a place for three back in Hollywood instead of his small bachelor apartment.

About a half hour later, Inga and Kinley came toward them. Both of them had big smiles on their faces. There were hugs and kisses all around and another bottle of champagne ordered.

"So, when do we have our chat with the Captain?" somberly asked Bob. "Arthur, you still think that a group approach is the best way to go?"

Kinley spoke up. "Actually, I think it best if I go alone and speak with Papa. I know my future has been on his mind, and Inga told me that he spoke with you Mr. Smith, but this must be between just him and me."

Bob spoke. "You don't want me to come with you? Inga and I are willing to help explain all of this to your father, if you want."

"No, I appreciate the offer, but he'll want to speak alone with me. In fact, I'd best go do that now, but first I want to thank all of you for making this happen. I'm very grateful to Bob and Inga for this chance to go with them to America, but I suspect that all of you 'Hoosiers' have played a part in it. That's what an Indiana person is called, right, a Hoosier?"

They all laughed. "Yes, Kinley, a Hoosier. Alright, you go talk to Papa and we'll all wait here for you to return." Bob then gave her a hug and off she went to find her father.

Word began to spread around the ship about the coming marriage of Bob and Inga and more people joined the champagne fest in the Lounge.

About thirty minutes later, a crewman came and asked if Bob, Inga and Arthur would please come to the Captain's quarters.

Upon entering, the Captain asked all of them to be seated. Kinley was already there. He had a very somber look on his face.

"Kinley has told me of this proposal for Bob and Inga to take Kinley to America." He nodded at Arthur. "And, yes, I myself raised the idea of some such arrangement to get my daughter to a safe country before a war starts. I have known Inga for several years and I know that she and Kinley are good friends. Inga has only known Bob for a few days, but I think she's a good judge of character. I have only spoken a few times myself with Mr. Hall, but apparently Arthur, you think this a good idea, and I'm inclined to trust your judgement."

The other four people in the room just remained silent in anticipation. It wasn't clear yet just where the Captain was headed with his comments.

"Against those facts are simply the feelings of a father who does not want to see his daughter move far away from him, but all papas feel that way – even though I know that in a few years, even if there wouldn't be a war, Kinley would meet a nice young man, marry and move away. So, that loneliness that will come to my heart when she does move on will eventually come sooner or later. At least this way, I'll know that she'll be safe in the coming years. So, I give my blessing to this idea and also my best wishes to Inga and Bob for their upcoming wedding."

Everyone broke out into broad smiles and began hugging everyone else.

"I told several of you a few days ago that amazing things sometimes happen to people as they travel this magical Danube River, often quite unexpected things, and now you see that I was correct." They all nodded in agreement.

"Let's all go back downstairs to the Lounge and rejoin the party," suggested Bob.

The crowd in the Lounge had grown even larger than before the three had left, with everyone anxiously awaiting word of whether Captain Ornsdorfer would give his blessing for Kinley to go to America. A large cheer rose, when they heard that his answer had been yes.

Tom Bishop had been present for most of the celebrating, but mostly sat off to a side by himself. He was drinking champagne, but had a very serious look on his face. He admired what a chance Bob was willing to take in such short a time frame in order to achieve happiness. A few crazy thoughts of his own started taking shape in his mind.

As the champagne flowed and everyone cheered and hugged, Arthur and Jan sat together a little ways off from the crowd. Smiles on both their faces. She took his hand. "You know, dear, that's one of the nicest things you've ever done. Helping to give a young girl with her whole life ahead of her such an opportunity."

"It's going to be the start of new and exciting lives for all three of them. Some things end, new adventures begin." He leaned over and gave her a kiss. "Have I told you today how much I love you?"

"Perhaps, but feel free to do it again. Say it as often as you like in these remaining days."

To celebrate the last night on the ship, Captain Ornsdorfer had arranged a spectacular dinner for his guests. A local restaurant, which had been serving meals for three hundred years, provided the main dishes. This freed up the ship's chef and small staff to spend the day preparing wonderful desserts. All the guests put on their finest attire. The entire Dining Room was lighted only by hundreds of long taper candles. The Captain put on his full dress uniform and greatly enjoyed wandering about and sharing toasts at all the tables. Hanna had opted for a Slovakian peasant skirt and blouse she'd bought that afternoon. She did give the ensemble a slightly different look by wearing no bra and leaving the top four buttons undone. Fortunately for her, she was not at the table with the Smiths, or Jan would have given both her and her mother a critique of the outfit!

Despite his brief glory of the previous day for saving the young boy, by this stage of the trip, all the Americans, Brits and French had had enough of Blickensdorfer asking so many questions. He, along with Holger, Hans and Manfred, were shunned off to a table with four other German tourists. Werner was looking in a particularly foul mood. The cruise would be at an end in less than 24 hours and whoever was the secret agent was perhaps going to escape his grasp – and there would go his chance for a promotion to the rank of general.

The Smiths were joined at their table by Mike and Candy Taffe, Bob, Simone, Mary Beth and Elizabeth Pembroke. As Inga was part of the crew, she told Bob that she could not be his guest at the farewell dinner – that they'd meet up in the Main Lounge immediately after dinner had finished. Kinley had duties to perform as well and also rejected an invitation to join Bob at his table. Arthur and Jan seemed to be in a very sentimental mood. Much of the table talk was of course about the upcoming wedding and of taking Kinley to America.

"Yes, Arthur has convinced me to get the necessary paper work done right here in Budapest — that avoids any issues of Inga and Kinley travelling with me to England and then on to America. The American Embassy can issue Inga and Kinley American passports as soon as we show the consular officer our marriage certificate and the adoption papers issued by a Hungarian government official." He then lowered his voice and added, "Also, Captain Ornsdorfer has told me that we can get the adoption process carried out in Budapest very quickly, as he knows a particular judge in the city – especially if an envelope with a few hundred Hungarian pengoes accompanies the legal documents." Everyone laughed.

"What about their clothes and other possessions that are back in Regensburg?" asked Mary Beth.

"The Captain has told me that he can arrange for everything that's wanted to be shipped by train from Regensburg to London, but I think my two new ladies might want to do a lot of shopping in London!"

More old stories of hijinks back in Bloomington were exchanged around the table that evening. Bob had a few more scandalous stories from Hollywood parties to share, particularly by a group known as the Uplifters – a group of actors and the rich that had suffered no shortage of alcohol all through Prohibition on their private grounds in the Pacific Palisades area of greater Los Angeles.

"Elizabeth, where is your father tonight? Is he not feeling well?" asked Arthur.

"Well, he may think he's still twenty-one and tries to act like he is, but the cruise and all the land tours have worn him out. I suspect he's already sound asleep."

While they all laughed, Miles was down in his cabin, putting on the attire of a ship's waiter, complete with a white coat and cap. If any passenger happened to see just his back or profile from down the corridor as he was entering one of the cabins, they would not think it odd that a crewman was doing so. Miles knew that the ladies would be wearing their finest pieces of jewelry at the farewell dinner, but he preferred to steal lesser pieces anyway – items that the owners might not immediately notice were missing. At least not until Miles and Elizabeth were off the ship early the next morning and were well gone from Budapest.

Towards the end of the dinner, Arthur stood and called the group to attention.

"My apologies to our other passengers, but I'd like to offer a special toast to my old classmates of Indiana University. It's been great seeing old friends, reliving memories and seeing how everyone's life has progressed over the last fifteen years. It has meant a lot to Jan and me that so many of you were able to join us as we took this 'second' honeymoon journey. My sincerest hope is that 1939 will be a good one for all of us, and a peaceful one for the entire world. Will you all please now join me in a toast to my beautiful and charming wife, without whom I would be nothing."

Arthur had arranged in advance that full champagne flutes had been passed out to all the tables as he had started his comments. All the guests stood. Bob raised his voice, "To Arthur and Jan!" All joined in. At that moment, Simone went over and joined the Jeffersonians.

"We have prepared a small gift for you Arthur, for all the work you put into arranging this wonderful gathering of old friends. A couple of months ago on Broadway, Mary Martin had a tremendous hit with a new Cole Porter song, *My Heart Belongs to Daddy.* This is a love song from Jan to you, Arthur." She gave Joe a nod and they started playing.

When she'd finished the slightly suggestive song, the crowd stood and applauded loudly for Simone, and for Arthur and Jan. Mary Beth thought Jan looked happy, but very tired.

As the dinner party in the Dining Room was starting to break up, some passengers headed for their cabins and others headed for the Main Lounge and bar to continue partying. Herr Blickensdorfer stopped Mary Beth as she neared the stairway to go down to her cabin.

"Frau Long, may I have a word with you, please?"

"Yes, what can I do for you?"

"Let's go down to the Small Lounge at the back of the ship. It will be more private." He took hold of her arm, making it clear that his statement had been a command, not a request.

Holger saw the two leaving together and wondered what was going on, as the Colonel had said nothing in particular to him about Mary Beth at a meeting they'd had only an hour before the dinner had started. He slowly followed and saw them go into the Small Lounge. Holger passed on by the closed door and went out onto the deck and stood quietly near the porthole of the room. It was cracked slightly open, and thus he could hear their conversation.

"Frau Long, I am a Colonel of the German Gestapo and I am on board this ship investigating serious crimes which have been committed recently against the Third Reich."

She tried to maintain a calm demeanor, but if the German was trying to scare her, he was doing a good job at it. "And what does any of that have to do with me?"

"There was a clandestine meeting the night of December 24th, in Munich, between a traitorous Wehrmacht General named Fritz von Breithaupt and a foreign agent. I believe that agent was you." He stared hard at her.

"I've never even heard the name of Breithaupt, much less secretly met with him on any day or night." She thought to herself that what she'd just said was absolutely true.

"Tell me please, where were you on the evening of Christmas Eve in Munich?"

"We had a nice party at our hotel as I recall," she replied.

"Before that party, at say seven o'clock."

"Let's see. I believe I'd gone out to take a walk in the lovely snow fall and I'd stopped in at one of the churches in the old city, before coming back to the hotel to get ready for the party that night."

"So, you have no witnesses who can vouch for where you were for several hours?"

"I don't know why I need any witnesses."

"You have been heard making anti-Hitler comments during the cruise and I myself have heard you speaking German to several of the ship's crew. Your whereabouts are unaccounted for when the General was having his secret meeting." He pulled a telegram out of his pocket. "And just this afternoon, I've received a telegram informing me that your father-in-law is a senior officer in the British MI-6 organization." The Colonel paused and simply stared at Mary Beth. She remained silent. "If you will only confirm for me with whom you met that night in Munich, perhaps I could allow you to travel on with your friends. We have no interest in you personally."

"I met with no one that night."

"Very well, if that is your response, we will continue this discussion at the local Gestapo office at Kittsee, just across the Danube, in Austria."

"You have a vivid imagination, Colonel, but what are the facts? On what charges are you detaining me?" she asked indignantly.

"You have been found to be in possession of pornographic literature, in violation of German laws. That will be enough to arrest and hold you for several weeks, while we discuss further just what you were doing on the night of December 24th in Munich.

"We're in Czechoslovakia, you have no authority here."

He began to pull a Lugar pistol from his side coat

pocket, as he started to say, "In the name of the Third Reich, I am…" Mary Beth had been holding her sequined, clutch bag in both hands in front of her. She managed to pull out Joe's Baby Browning faster than the Colonel's hand moved and put a shot in his chest. He pulled the trigger, but he only put a hole in the wooden floor before he collapsed.

Upon the sound of gunfire, Holger rushed into the cabin to see what had happened. He found Mary Beth frozen in shock, still holding her gun. Holger quickly took it from her hand. He leaned over and checked Werner's pulse, observing the spreading red spot on his shirt, directly above his heart. He was dead. Whether skill or luck, it was a perfect shot. "Go immediately next door to the Letter Writing Room and start writing a letter. If anybody asks you later, claim that you had been in there 15-20 minutes before you heard two shots and then the sound of someone running in the corridor and out the door onto the deck. We'll talk later tonight, when we can be alone."

She still seemed quite dazed, but nodded her head in agreement and did as he'd told her. He took the Colonel's wrist watch and his wallet from his back pocket. He took the money out and put it into his own wallet. He then went out onto the deck and after checking that no one could see him, he dropped her Browning and the watch down into the river. He pulled his own Lugar from his pocket and shot twice into the river, while loudly shouting "halt" several times. He then ran to the gangplank and down it to the dock. He continued to shout "halt" as he ran several blocks away from the ship. Once he'd reached a small side street, he tossed the Colonel's empty wallet into the shadows, then returned to the ship.

Many people, including Captain Ornsdorfer, had come out onto the upper deck, after hearing his shots and his shouting. Upon his return, he quickly informed the Captain and the other two Gestapo men, "Herr Blickensdorfer has been shot. I saw a man run down the gangplank. I fired several shots at him, but I don't think I hit him. I chased him for several blocks, but lost him in the dark."

Captain Ornsdorfer ordered one of his men to run to the Port Office and alert the local police, while he proceeded with Holger to the Small Lounge at the rear of the ship. They found Mary Beth standing in the doorway of the adjacent Writing Room, looking quite stunned and bewildered. In truth, she was. She'd never killed a man before. Nor could she comprehend why this Gestapo officer was protecting her, having just seen her kill his colleague.

Captain Ornsdorfer had said in his comments at the start of the dinner that they were going to have a memorable last night on the ship. He had no idea of how prophetic his toast would be.

CHAPTER 13
The Investigation

While waiting for the police to arrive, Holger and Mary Beth managed to slip away from the others and meet up on the deserted top deck for a private conversation.

"What caused the two of you to draw your weapons and fire at each other?" asked Holger.

She wasn't sure whether she could totally trust the German, but he'd lied on her behalf about the shooting and felt that she had to continue cooperating with him.

"He was about to arrest me and take me across the river into Austria. He accused me of being a foreign agent and having met with some German Army general back in Munich, on the night of Christmas Eve."

"And had you?"

She hesitated in answering. "No, I met with no German officer that night."

He sensed she was definitely hiding something. "But, were you supposed to have met with someone that night?"

Again, she hesitated. "Yes, I was, but I didn't know with whom. I was simply to be in a certain courtyard at a specific time, and carrying a book, but I arrived late as I had gotten lost. When I arrived, there was no one there. But how do you know about that scheduled meeting?"

"Because I had been following General Breithaupt for several weeks and I found him in that courtyard that night, acting suspiciously. But..."

"But what?" she asked.

"Well, I'd been having doubts recently about some of the things I've been doing for the Gestapo anyway, even before we began investigating the General. And everything I learned about him showed me that he was a good and honorable man, and that he couldn't betray the Germany he loved."

"And you didn't arrest him?"

"No, he and I talked and then he told me what he was trying to do to bring an end to Hitler's leadership – but that no one from the British Army had appeared that night. He showed me the letter that he was prepared to pass to this contact – you, I guess?"

"Yes, I was to be his contact with British Intelligence."

"You are a British intelligence officer?" asked Holger, somewhat confused.

"No, my father-in-law is. He asked me to do this 'small' favor for him."

"Strange. Anyway, the General and I worked out this plan whereby I was to claim that I'd very briefly seen someone meeting with him that night and to link the suspect somehow to a group of tourists who were leaving Germany in the next day or so. Later that evening, I selected your cruise group, as it included a large number of Americans and they were about to depart on the trip to Budapest. The idea was that by putting suspicion on that group, it would give me an excuse to travel with them to Budapest. Once in a country outside of German control, I could then pass his letter to someone at a British Embassy."

"Ah, I couldn't understand why there were Gestapo officers on our ship, since there'd been no meeting with the German volunteer, but now I see." She saw no reason to tell him what Arthur Smith had shared with her about why Blickensdorfer was on the ship. "Do you want to give me the letter now?" she asked, and held out her hand.

"I think that until the investigation of the shooting of Colonel Blickensdorfer is resolved, it would be better for me to keep it in my possession."

He saw several police vehicles nearing the ship. "We should get back downstairs now. We can talk again later, once the ship has been cleared to sail for Budapest. Stick with your story that you were simply writing a letter when you heard the two shots, and then heard someone running."

"Very well."

"You go on back down first and I'll follow in a few minutes."

Mary Beth had begun to shiver from the cold and happily departed first. Holger remained on the top deck for several more minutes, staring out at the lights of Bratislava. He lighted a cigarette and began reflecting on the crazy game that he and Breithaupt had begun on Christmas Eve. He had rationalized to himself since that evening that he could always change his mind about what he'd started. Simply tear up the letter and throw it in the river, if the risk got too great. He realized that having helped Mary Beth cover up the murder of the Colonel, he had now crossed the point of no return. He would either have to successfully make it to a British Embassy and receive political asylum, or it was just a matter of time before he himself was dead. He tossed his cigarette into the Danube and went back down to the Main Lounge.

A few minutes later, Captain Brunner, the Chief of the Homicide Department of the Bratislava City Police came onboard the ship. He was a no-nonsense, career policeman, who was within one year of being able to retire and receive his pension. While still wanting to solve murders committed in his city, his main goal was to do nothing that jeopardized his pension. He immediately met with Captain Ornsdorfer and Lt. Hinz to discuss what had happened. Holger repeated his story of having heard two shots, then seen a man running down the gangplank, and finally of his own shots and unsuccessful pursuit of this suspect in the narrow streets near the dock.

Captain Brunner had simply listened and nodded till the finish of Holger's story. "And why were Colonel Blickensdorfer and yourself on board this ship in the first place?" he asked.

"The Colonel, myself and two enlisted men joined this group of tourists at Regensburg as part of a counterintelligence investigation. I can't go into specifics of that investigation, but unofficially between you and me, I don't think that investigation had much merit. I believe the Colonel was mostly indulging in wishful thinking, in hopes of getting promoted should he catch some foreign spy."

"So you don't think the shooting of the Colonel had

anything to do with your investigation?" asked the police Captain.

"I do not. I believe that Colonel Blickensdorfer bravely gave his life in preventing a common robbery of the passengers of this ship."

At that moment, the Gestapo Chief Schulz from Kittsee arrived. As a matter of courtesy, he'd been informed by the Czech Police of the shooting of a fellow Gestapo officer, even though he had no official jurisdiction on the Czechoslovakian side of the river. Holger then repeated his entire story for Schulz.

Captain Brunner ordered a dozen men of the Bratislava City Police force to start a search of the nearby streets for this alleged murderer or any signs of evidence related to the onboard killing. He didn't particularly care that a Gestapo colonel had been killed, but he did resent murders of any kind being committed in his city. He also knew that his political masters would want to be able to tell the German Embassy that all steps possible had been taken to find the killer. Pressure was thus on him to at least make a good show of the investigation.

"Captain Ornsdorfer, would you please assemble all of the passengers in the Main Lounge so that I can question them. Perhaps one of them might have seen or heard something related to the shooting. And as I don't speak English, if you would please serve as my interpreter?"

"Of course, Captain Brunner."

"I will also want my men to search all of the cabins, both passengers and crew."

"Our men have discreetly searched all the passenger

cabins just within the last few days and found no weapons," replied Holger.

"And I can vouch for my crew. They have all been with me for several years," added Captain Ornsdorfer.

"Yes, I'm sure your crew is very loyal and I'm sure that the search of all the passenger cabins was thorough, but my men will make our own search for a weapon."

Eventually, all of the passengers were present in the Main Lounge; several of them none too happy at having been awakened and forced to dress. Captain Ornsdorfer got their attention.

"Ladies and gentlemen, as some of you have heard, Mr. Werner Blickensdorfer was shot and killed earlier this evening down in the Small Lounge by an as-yet-unknown assailant. The Bratislava City Police have been called in and Captain Brunner, the Chief of their Homicide Department, needs to ask all of you some questions. I will serve as his interpreter."

After introducing himself and explaining the necessity of a thorough investigation, Captain Brunner got to his actual questions. "How many of you heard the gun shots earlier this evening?"

Approximately twenty people raised their hands. He then had them move to one side of the Lounge and he began asking each person where he or she was when they heard the shots. This made several passengers regret that they'd raised their hands. He finally got to Mary Beth.

"And where were you when you heard the shots?"

"I was in the Letter Writing Room, which is next to the Small Lounge."

"Ah, very good. And had you heard any arguing or shouting before the shots were fired?"

"No, I don't believe so, but then the door to my room was closed."

"And what did you do, when you heard the shots?"

"Well, for several seconds I don't think I did anything. I guess I was frightened by the sound and wasn't initially quite sure what I'd heard. Finally, I stood, opened the door and looked out into the corridor."

"Very good. And did you see anything?"

"Just as I opened the door I heard some running footsteps and then as I looked out, I saw just a glimpse of the back of a man going out the door and onto the deck."

"Did you recognize this man?" eagerly asked Captain Brunner.

"No."

"Please describe him."

"Well, I guess he was about your height and build, with brown hair. He had on dark pants and some sort of lightweight jacket. I think it was also brown in color. I only saw him for a second."

The policeman then continued his questioning of the remaining passengers who'd heard the shots, but with little results.

By then, his men had finished their search of all the cabins, without finding any weapons, though they had "confiscated" from crew cabins several French magazines with pictures of naked women.

After consulting with his Sergeant about the results of the cabin searches, Captain Brunner turned back to the passengers, and again using Captain Ornsdorfer as interpreter, announced his decision to everyone.

"Ladies and gentlemen, while I am inclined to believe Lt. Hinz's interpretation of the shooting of Herr Blickensdorfer by a burglar, I am going to hold the ship here in port for another day or two. I need time to thoroughly investigate this shooting further and to question each of you about your whereabouts at the time of the shooting." He then turned back to several of his men and started giving orders to them in Czech.

This caused a great deal of murmuring among the passengers, but no one moved or spoke out. Arthur was having a quick internal discussion with himself. He recalled his recent "best not to get involved in other people's business" speech to Miles, but this was a much more personal situation. He wondered how long a person should put up with being pushed around before acting. He thought that at times perhaps one individual had to step forward and do something for the good of all, regardless of the personal risk. There was no reason to detain the ship. Police Captain Brunner was just being an unreasonable bully. People's onward travels would be disrupted. He also thought about the alleged secret agent onboard. He assumed that that person would certainly like to get to Budapest and leave the ship as soon as possible. Arthur had never been one to contradict police actions prior to this point of his life, but he recalled telling Jan when they'd decided to take this trip that it was time to be more adventurous. Now seemed to be that time. He didn't know how his upcoming action would end, but he had to try to do something. He rose from his chair and stepped to the center of the room as he began to speak.

"Captain Brunner, a moment of your time before you issue any more orders."

Brunner, Ornsdorfer and everyone else in the room fell silent as they turned to look at Mr. Smith. As Arthur spoke, he paused every couple of sentences to give Ornsdorfer time to translate.

"Sir, this is an outrageous interference in the free travel of American, British and French citizens, over whom you have no authority. If there are any Czechoslovakian citizens on board that you wish to detain, that is an issue you can take up with your government, but if you detain American citizens, I shall immediately report your action to the American Embassy in Prague."

Captain Brunner was growing redder with every translated sentence.

"And I wish to add, that Lt. Hinz has given you his testimony that he saw a man running down the gangplank. We're not missing any passengers or crew members, so obviously it was someone who had boarded the ship from the dock who committed this crime. Therefore, I suggest that you go conduct your investigation on shore and let our ship sail as scheduled."

Captain Brunner finally spoke. "Who are you?"

"I am Arthur Smith of Chicago."

"Well, Mr. Smith, you are interfering in an official police investigation and if you continue to do so, I shall have you arrested."

"Do as you think best Captain, but I shall simply add

that to my complaint to the American Ambassador, who will take it up with your Foreign Minister and probably directly with your Prime Minister."

The two men then stood there in silence, staring at each other.

Maurice Garnier suddenly spoke up. "I also saw a man running down the gangplank while Lt. Hinz was shooting at him." And before Brunner could ask, he quickly added, "No, I didn't get much of a look at him, other than it was a man in a dark pants and a brown jacket, as Mrs. Long has already told you."

Miles Pembroke then also stepped forward. "I also saw a man in a brown jacket running down the gangplank, just shortly after hearing the two gunshots. I was sitting over there by a window and had an excellent view of the gangplank." Pembroke certainly did not care to have the ship detained and a more thorough search of the cabins conducted. The false bottom in his suitcase was quality made, but no sense in tempting fate by having it repeatedly checked. Plus, he felt a sense of solidarity with a fellow war veteran and wished to assist Arthur as best he could.

Lt. Hinz remained silent, but since he knew that there hadn't been any man running down the gangplank, he was secretly amused that two others were now stating that they had also seen such a man. He was, however, very grateful to Mr. Smith for speaking up, as he absolutely wanted to get moving on schedule for Budapest and safety. He wasn't sure if Mary Beth could stand up to hard questioning over several days, should Captain Brunner detain the ship.

Mary Beth was also wondering what was going on, but refrained from looking over at Hinz.

Captain Brunner's position was getting weaker by the moment, when in came one of his men, who'd been involved in the search on shore. He was holding a brown leather wallet.

"Sir, one of our men just found this on a side street, five blocks from the ship. It's empty."

Without being asked, Holger spoke up. "That is Colonel Blickensdorfer's wallet. I recognize it."

Captain Brunner's resolve seemed to be cracking and then the very unhappy Princess came forward from the back of the crowd.

"I am Princess Caroline Landschkneckt. Who is in charge here?" she asked in German with her most imperious tone of voice.

Captain Brunner stepped forward and bowed slightly to her. "I am Captain Brunner, the Chief of the Homicide Department of the Bratislava City Police, at your service."

"I wish to speak with you in private," she stated and then without even waiting for his reply, turned and walked to the far end of the Main Lounge.

Once she, Captain Brunner, Captain Ornsdorfer, Lt. Hinz and Gestapo Chief Schulz had all gathered away from the rest of the passengers, Princess Landschkneckt coldly stated to him, "Captain Brunner, if this ship does not sail as scheduled I will immediately phone the German Ambassador to your country and then German Foreign Minister von Ribbentrop, a personal friend of mine, with a complaint personally about you." She then simply turned and headed for her cabin.

Brunner saw no reason to put his career in jeopardy over the death of a German Gestapo officer, whom he hadn't even personally known. He stated to the others, "Finding of the empty wallet on shore would seem to confirm Lt. Hinz's impression that this was a simple robbery gone bad. The search of the cabins has produced nothing." He shrugged his shoulders. "Perhaps we should let the ship sail as scheduled."

"I agree with you Captain Brunner. This is simply a tragic robbery incident and delaying the departure of the ship serves no purpose," stated Lt. Hinz.

Gestapo Chief Schulz from Kitt, however, disagreed. "We have had a colonel of the Gestapo murdered. There needs to be a thorough investigation, which will take several days."

This unfortunately put the decision back on Captain Brunner's shoulders, which he didn't like at all.

Captain Ornsdorfer had not offered an opinion all evening, but he admired Smith for having spoken out and decided that he too should show a little personal courage and weighed in on the discussion. "If you are going to detain the ship, then I must immediately inform the company headquarters in Vienna. We will be put off our schedule and there are likely additional expenses that will be incurred. Will the Bratislava Police Department be responsible for those costs? There are also likely to be complaints that will come in from many of the foreign passengers and possibly financial claims by some of them for missing their onward ship or plane reservations."

This gave police Captain Brunner a way not to appear as though he was simply buckling under the threat of the Princess and he offered a compromise solution. "A very good point Captain Ornsdorfer. We found nothing in the cabins, but we will now conduct a search of all passengers, and if still nothing turns up, the ship may sail at midnight as scheduled. I will send immediately for several female police matrons to come to the ship to search the ladies." He started to walk back to the passengers, but then stopped and added, "And I see no reason to inconvenience the Princess further tonight."

Gestapo Chief Schulz was not pleased, but he silently agreed to that compromise. Upon hearing Captain Brunner's announcement that all were to be searched, some passengers were still outraged, but at least Mr. Smith had won his fight for letting the ship depart as scheduled. Mary Beth was very glad that Holger had kept the letter from the General on him, rather than giving it to her as she'd suggested. The ladies were escorted to the Dining Room, to await the arrival of the female police matrons. The men stayed in the Lounge and the searches began on them. Captain Brunner instructed all of his police officers that they were looking for guns, nothing else. Arthur was wondering if Mike was still carrying his .45 that night and how that would look during the upcoming body search. He looked over at Mike, but he appeared quite calm and bored with the entire evening.

By 11:15 p.m., the searches were finished, without

the tiniest Derringer being found on anyone. "Ladies and gentlemen, thank you for your cooperation. You are free to depart as planned." Captain Brunner bowed slightly to the passengers, turned and shook Captain Ornsdorfer's hand. He and all his men then departed the ship. An unhappy Lt. Schulz also left. Holger presumed that he was heading directly to his office back across the river to send a report to Gestapo Headquarters in Berlin. He didn't really care, because he would be in Budapest by tomorrow morning and beyond the Gestapo's reach, at least legally. Colonel Blickensdorfer's body had already been removed to the morgue and the ship was preparing for its scheduled midnight departure for Budapest.

Many of the passengers were crowding around Arthur Smith, congratulating him on standing up so firmly to the police. Bob Hall commented that Arthur had tread a thin line. "That was a great job you did, standing up to the Police Captain, but you came close to getting yourself arrested, or even worse!"

Arthur laughed, looked over at this wife, and gave her a wink before replying. "Oh, it was no big deal. Besides, do I want to live forever?" Everyone laughed. He hadn't communicated to her yet that just before taking his dramatic stand with the Czech Police, he'd also reached a final decision on an action he'd been considering the entire journey.

Maurice Garnier came up to Arthur to shake his hand.

"Thank you, Maurice, your statement certainly strengthened my position."

Maurice shook his head in modesty. "It was nothing. I was simply showing you international solidarity."

Arthur smiled. "And had Captain Brunner arrested me, would you have gone to jail with me in solidarity?"

"No, but I would have sent you a cake with a file in it," he replied with a straight face.

Arthur smiled. "Good enough!" And he patted Maurice on the back.

Arthur went over to Mike and discretely inquired in a lowered voice, "I thought you never went anywhere without your little 'toy'?"

Mike smiled. "Hey, I'm from New York City. Soon as I heard that someone had been shot and the police were coming, I put baby in a safe place." He nodded towards the artificial fern plant in a large brass floor pot, sitting by the mahogany bar. "My .45 has been guarding that fern plant all evening. Hell of a search the local Keystone Cops performed tonight! I'll retrieve it later once the place empties out."

"Well done," replied Arthur with a smile and moved on.

As the crowd in the Lounge began to thin out, Smith and Captain Ornsdorfer came across each other. Jan was at a table talking with a couple of ladies.

"A very exciting evening, Captain," remarked Smith with a slight smile.

"Yes, too exciting. You know, you took a real chance with Captain Brunner. He might have thrown you in jail for a day or two, even if he did let the ship sail as planned. He doesn't like to be challenged."

"I'm too old to be bullied. And after I saw the Princess involve herself, I knew I had nothing to worry about. She has real influence. What is her story anyway? I heard she takes this cruise every New Year's."

The Captain smiled and led Arthur over to the bar and ordered up two brandies. Once they had their drinks, he took Smith over to a quiet table in the corner. "She has no real influence even though her title is real, but she puts on a good performance and can bluff her way past a police captain of Bratislava." They both laughed. "Her husband died almost five years ago. This is the third year she comes on this cruise at the holiday time, basically to have sex, as often as she can over the ten days journey. Back home, she has to be respectable, but she gets lonely I guess, so once a year she travels down here and makes love as often as she can with as many men as she can!"

Smith looked skeptical. "And you know this, personally?"

The Captain smiled. "Yes, I know this is true, first hand. And if she will have sex with a broken down old man like me, you can judge that she will have sex with any man!"

Smith returned the smile. "Well, I guess that sex is more interesting than Professor Langweilig's lectures." He finished his brandy, bid the Captain goodnight and went to find his wife to suggest they go listen one last time to Joe play the piano.

With all the excitement and discussion among the passengers about the dramatic events of the previous few hours, no one noticed that Mary Beth had quietly left the

Main Lounge and went up on the top deck. The cold air actually felt good on her face. Holger arrived a few minutes later.

"I guess it's a good thing that you kept the letter on you," was her opening remark.

He grinned. "Yes, I believe so." He didn't tell her that he would be asking for asylum from England and figured that the General's letter was his best bargaining chip. He didn't really know Mary Beth. The shooting of Blickensdorfer had thrown their paths and interests together, but he didn't know whether he could totally trust her with the letter. For all he knew, she might get to London and "forget" entirely about his role in getting the letter out of Germany.

"Do you have a specific plan for getting whatever you were expecting to receive on Christmas Eve in Munich into the hands of the British?"

"Yes, I'm to report to a person at the British Embassy in Athens about what happened with the 'volunteer' and pass to him anything that I received from the anonymous volunteer. However, given the two 'accidental' deaths we've had of members of my tour group and now the shooting of Blickensdorfer, I'm thinking that perhaps it would be better if I go the British Embassy in Budapest, soon as we arrive there. I presume that the British have an embassy in Budapest."

"I believe there is and perhaps that would be the safest maneuver. And I imagine there's an MI-6 representative in their Budapest Embassy. But let's discuss that once we arrive in Budapest. It's been a trying evening and we might think better in the morning."

"Perhaps you're right, I am exhausted."

"I do have one last question for you tonight. You told me earlier that your father-in-law asked you to make the meeting in Munich. How did that come about?"

"He's a fairly senior official with MI-6 and he's assigned to the British Embassy in Washington DC. I told you how he's made a great effort at staying in touch with me since the death of his son. We've discussed several times the problem of the Nazis and what an evil man Hitler is. He came to see me back in early December and simply asked if I'd be willing to help in the fight against Hitler? When I agreed, he requested that I travel to Munich later in the month and meet with some German military officer who wanted to pass information to the British Army. I remembered the notice about the alumni cruise being planned and that seemed like the easiest and most low profile way to travel to Munich at the right time."

"That was very clever and very brave of you," admiringly replied Holger.

She laughed nervously. "I didn't feel very brave when your Colonel started to pull out his pistol. And I don't feel very well right now, knowing that I killed a man."

"You reacted in a perfectly normal way. No one could have done better even if they'd had months of training. You acted in an extraordinary manner."

"Thank you, but I don't feel special. My father-in-law once told me that there are no extraordinary men – only extraordinary challenges that ordinary people must deal with."

"Perhaps that's true, but in any case, you dealt with

your challenge magnificently. Now, we'd best get back down with the others and as I said earlier, we can talk further once we've checked into the hotel in Budapest. You go down first. I'll follow in a few minutes."

"Very well." She returned to the Main Lounge and was going to go to the bar to have a drink.

As she was crossing the room, Karen came up to her. "What a frightening night it's been."

"Indeed. I'm glad it's over and tomorrow this cruise will be at an end. Three men dead, for whatever reasons."

"Could I speak with you in private, my dear? I need your advice on something."

"Yes, of course."

Karen linked their arms together and led her out of the Main Lounge. "Let's find a place where we can talk privately."

Holger had just reentered the Lounge himself and saw Mary Beth and Karen departing, arm in arm. He was curious as to where they were headed, but just then Arthur Smith came up to him.

"I'm sorry about Herr Blickensdorfer, Lieutenant. Did he have a family?"

"Yes, there is a wife back in Munich and a son. Like most men, he had his good and bad points, but he will be missed by his wife and colleagues."

"Well, that could probably be said about most of us when our time comes. Do you think the local police will find the man who shot him?"

"One hopes, but Bratislava is a good-sized city and there are many criminals. Plus, without any witnesses, it would be hard to prove him guilty, unless he is stupid enough to keep his gun."

"Ah, good point."

"And frankly, with all the problems going on in the world at the moment, I doubt if one dead German will remain at the top of Captain Brunner's to-do list for more than a few days."

"Sadly, I fear you're right. Neither of us are politicians, but I don't like the way the world is headed and we may all soon face a situation where just one dead German or American won't be of any great consequence."

Holger said nothing, but did nod his head slowly in agreement with Arthur's pessimistic view of the future.

"Anyway, as I said, I'm very sorry for the loss of your colleague."

"Forgive me for saying this Mr. Smith, but I find it curious that you seem so moved by his death, when clearly most of the Americans on board saw his death only as a possible inconvenient interruption of their cruise."

"Perhaps because we both had fought in the trenches of the Great War. When he and I were chatting a few days ago, I'd asked him if he'd been in the war, given that he and I seemed to be of about the same age. He told me that he'd been in the infantry of the Imperial Army, a mere enlisted man as I was. While on opposite sides, I guess that I felt a certain kinship with a man who had endured the difficult and dangerous life in the trenches as I had. It seems ironic that he survived four years of war and then is killed on a luxury cruise liner by a petty thief."

"Yes, that is an ironic ending to his life. By the way,

did he tell you that he was a recipient of the Iron Cross, for bravery at Passchendaele?"

"No, he made no mention of it. Our conversation was simply along the lines of what we shared in common – survival under horrible conditions while men all around us were dying."

"Yes, indeed, that would have given you two a special link that civilians can never really understand."

They both stood in silence for several more seconds till Arthur spoke. "Well, I'll see you in the morning when we dock in Budapest."

"Yes, I'll see you in the morning."

Arthur headed off to find his wife. Holger looked around to see where Mary Beth and Karen had gone off to on the ship.

Karen had directed Mary Beth to the small Writing Room. Once they'd entered, Mary Beth sat at the writing desk, but Karen remained standing, her back to the door.

"When Captain Brunner was questioning all of us, you said that you'd been sitting in here, writing a letter for some fifteen to twenty minutes before you heard the gun shots from next door."

Mary Beth hesitated, but finally said, "Yes, I'm not certain about the precise number of minutes, but I was in here something like fifteen or twenty minutes before I heard two shots fired."

Karen maintained her sweet smile and gentle voice, but replied, "My dear, I think you're lying. You see, I was at that very desk until perhaps just five minutes before all the commotion started and Lt. Hinz began shouting for someone to stop and he was firing at a person running down the gangplank."

Mary Beth remained silent, not knowing quite how to reply to Karen.

"I don't want to get you in trouble, but why don't you tell me the truth about what happened down here earlier this evening. I only want to help you if I can." She gave Mary Beth a sweet and understanding smile.

Mary Beth hesitated, but decided to trust a fellow American. Holger had lied for her so far, but she wasn't sure just how much she could trust him. "Well," she hesitatingly began. "Herr Blickensdorfer had asked to speak with me and had led me into the small room next door. He then accused me of having secretly met with some German Army general back in Munich on Christmas Eve. I told him that I had done no such thing, but he started to tell me that he was arresting me and began taking a gun out of his coat pocket. I pulled a gun out of my purse and, well, we both fired, but I fired a little quicker. I didn't even mean to shoot him, much less kill him, but he'd frightened me and so I pulled out the gun."

"Oh my poor dear, you must have been terrified. And then what happened?"

"Lt. Hinz entered the room just a few seconds later. He took my gun, told me to go into this room and say that I'd been here for twenty minutes. He then ran out on to the deck and he was shouting at someone to stop, and I heard more shots." She didn't tell Karen about talking with Holger later in the evening.

Suddenly, Karen pulled a small gun from her own

purse and pointed it at Mary Beth. The tone of her voice changed from her normally sweet and gentle sound to a very authoritative one and the smile disappeared from her face. "I am arresting you in the name of the Bavarian State Police, for whom I work."

Mary Beth was in a state of shock and for several seconds just stared at Karen in silence. Finally, she managed to say, "You're with the Bavarian Police? Are you even an American?"

"Oh yes, I'm an American, but after my husband died, there were legal questions about my German citizenship and also a need to pay the rent. The Bavarian Police made me a simple offer that solved both of those problems. If I would work some of the time for them, there would be no questioning of my legal right to continue to live in Bavaria and I would receive two hundred marks per month for my assistance. So you see my dear, it's nothing personal, but I fear that you will be going to prison for killing Colonel Blickensdorfer."

Mary Beth was so focused on Karen's words, her eyes didn't even shift as Holger quietly entered the room and picked up a foot tall, bronze bust of Adolf Hitler from a small table by the door. A second later, he swung it with all his strength into the side of Karen's head.

CHAPTER 14
Preparing to Sail for Budapest

After the blow by Holger to her head, Karen slumped immediately to the floor. The gun still clutched in her hand, but motionless. Perhaps she was still alive, but definitely unconscious and bleeding from her head. He took out his handkerchief and wiped the blood and his fingerprints from the bust of Hitler and sat it back on the table. He then pressed the handkerchief against the wound on her head in an attempt to stop the flow of blood.

"We must quickly move her to her cabin. Pick up her feet." Holger reached under her shoulders and they were able to move her fairly easily down the corridor, as she was not a large woman. Fortunately, her cabin was only four doors down the passageway. They put her on the floor of her bathroom.

Holger gave Mary Beth a hand towel. "Go back to the Writing Room, wipe up any blood on the floor, and get her purse and the gun, using this towel."

While she went to do that, Holger began to remove her shoes and outer garments, careful not to get any blood on them. He then lifted her up and slammed her head where the wound already was, against the edge of the porcelain sink. If she was not already dead, she certainly was then and now there was a nice bloody smear on the sink. He hoped it would look as though the cause of her death had been the sink. Mary Beth returned with the purse and gun and gave them to Holger. He used the towel to put the gun back in the purse at which time he found her police credentials. He removed that ID card and would later toss it into the river.

"Now, take this towel and fill two glasses there on the table with some of that brandy. I want to make it look as if she'd had a lover in here tonight."

He started to remove Karen's underwear, but Mary Beth stopped him. "No, leave her underwear on. If she and her 'lover' had just been at the stage of drinking, she would not have been naked."

Holger shrugged his shoulders. "Alright, I guess you should know these things better than me."

Mary Beth thought to herself that writing those porno novels had given her useful knowledge!

Holger then used a bathroom glass to pour some water on the bathroom floor. When the body was finally discovered the next day in Budapest, he wanted to leave for the police several options to explain her death. Perhaps, she'd slipped on a wet floor and accidently hit her head on the sink. Perhaps, she'd had a fight with her lover and he'd shoved her and she hit her head. And finally, they could wonder why she had a small pistol in her purse.

"By the time she's found in the morning, we shall have already left the ship. It's only about five hours sailing time from here to Budapest. Be packed and ready to disembark in Budapest as soon as any others are starting to leave the ship. We will want to be gone before the police are called in the morning, but not look as though we alone left early."

"Very well. Where and when shall we meet on shore?"

"At what hotel are you staying?" he asked.

"I have a reservation at the Hotel Gellert, as do most all of my group."

"Good, go there as if everything is normal. I shall wait for you in their lobby. Once you've checked in, simply follow me outside and we'll find a café where we can talk and plan our next move. Given what's just happened, I think you should definitely go to the British Embassy in Budapest."

"Agreed." She knew it was in poor taste, but she couldn't resist the black humor of it all. "You know, Holger, we've got to quit meeting over dead bodies like this."

He smiled. "Well, that's one a piece. Shall we just leave it as a tie?"

She returned his smile and then silently left the cabin.

Holger hung the Do Not Disturb sign on the door knob outside her cabin. He went back to the Writing Lounge to check to make sure that they'd left nothing there and that there were no signs of a struggle. He saw a small amount of blood on the wooden floor and used a cloth doily from under a table lamp to wipe up the blood. He went out on the deck and in the darkness dropped the doily, his handkerchief, the hand towel and her credentials into the Danube River as the ship sailed quietly southward. He then went to his cabin, set his alarm clock for 6:00 a.m. and laid down on his bed.

He'd beaten up a number of people over the years with the Gestapo, but Karen was the first person he'd actually killed and sleep did not come easily.

Mary Beth couldn't face going to her cabin and being alone, so she decided to go up to the bar. She wanted a drink. It was almost deserted, but she found Arthur and Jan listening to Joe play the piano. She sat down on a stool at the bar. Stefan served her a large brandy and then he closed up for the night. Mary Beth thought the usually calm and charming bartender seemed nervous, but then, so was she.

Arthur and Jan were talking to one another.

"I'm very proud of you dear for standing up to Police Captain Brunner earlier this evening, but you took quite a risk with him."

"Oh, I don't think it was as big a deal as some people are making it out, but I will share a small secret with you."

"Yes."

"My adrenalin was really flowing when I started talking to Captain Brunner. I've closed some major business deals in my life, but I've never felt a rush before as I did when I confronted Brunner – and especially when he backed down. I liked that feeling." He gave her a big smile.

"She patted his arm. "You were very courageous dear... just don't make a habit of it! Don't go thinking you're Sam Spade or Nick Charles."

He laughed. "Alright, dear, I'll just remain mild mannered Arthur Smith." He leaned over the table and kissed her cheek.

Joe stopped his playing for a moment, to talk with the Smiths.

"Mr. and Mrs. Smith, it's been real nice having you folks to play for every night on this cruise."

"Well, it's been a real treat for us to hear your beautiful playing," replied Jan. Joe hadn't found it yet, but earlier, when Joe had gone out of the room for a few minutes, Arthur had slipped an envelope into his musical bag. It contained a nice note from him and Jan saying how Joe had helped make it a memorable trip, and included a US$100 bill.

"That's very kind of you Mrs. Smith. You know, I can see how much love there is between you two and I been saving a special song for our last night together. It's a little something that Irving Berlin wrote back in 1925 as a wedding present for his bride. I think you'll like it."

He then began to play and sing the old song, *I'll be loving you, Always.*

Jan and Arthur just sat there, tightly holding hands. Tears began to roll down both their faces as they listened to the sentimental verses. When Joe finished the piece, he stood and said, "I'm going out for a smoke. I'll see you all on the next cruise." He then strolled out and gave them some privacy.

Mary Beth's eyes had also watered up and she simply sat in silence for a full minute looking at the charming couple. Arthur finally cleared his throat and called over for Mary Beth to join them. As she sat down, he commented, "What a beautiful song. That Joe has real talent."

"Indeed, he has. This has been a great trip. Thank you for putting it together and getting us back in touch. Funny how once we all left the University, we just sort of drifted apart, even though we'd been good friends while in Bloomington."

"Well, people get busy with jobs and families. We all got on with our lives in different parts of the country."

"I hope it won't be another fifteen years before we do this again," she replied softly.

Arthur thought that Mary Beth seemed rather distraught and decided to simply ask her, "Is everything OK with you? You seem upset tonight?"

"Oh, I guess the death of Herr Blickensdorfer has me a little on edge," she replied and took a long sip of her brandy. "What time do you think people will start leaving the ship in the morning?" she asked.

"Well, I believe they start serving breakfast at 7:00 a.m., but I don't think most people will come to the dining room until 8:30 or so, and then it would be 9:30 or later before many passengers actually disembark and head for the hotel. I don't recall that Karen has anything special planned for the morning, so there's no reason to rush. When were you thinking of leaving the ship?"

"I'd like to be gone as early as possible, but I don't want to seem unusual. I mean, I don't want to bother the crew with a very early departure just for me."

Arthur found her answer a bit odd. He was a fairly sharp fellow and wondered if her wanting to leave early, but not to appear "unusual", just might have something to do with the two accidental deaths they'd had on the cruise and now the murder of Gestapo Colonel Blickensdorfer.

"When you say, you don't want to appear unusual,

do you mean you don't want to leave earlier than other passengers?"

She simply nodded in agreement with his question.

"So, it would help if others from our group also left early?"

"Yes."

"And might I assume that whatever is afoot here is in the interest of the common good, as professor Thaddeus Long used to lecture about in that class we both took from him on Ancient Roman Society? Something that Cicero had written about as I vaguely recall."

She'd mistakenly trusted Karen, but she knew that Arthur certainly could be. "Yes, it would be in the interest of the common good, but I really can't go into details," was her reply.

"Your word that it's important is enough for me." Smith checked his watch. It was close to 1:00 a.m. "You'd best go to your cabin now and get packed. Be in the dining room promptly at 7:00 and be ready to depart the ship at 7:30 with some others of the I.U. crowd."

"But how...?"

"Leave that part to me."

Arthur and Jan rose to go to their cabin. "We'll see you in the morning."

"Goodnight. I'll just finish my brandy then I'll head for my cabin."

Joe came back a minute after the Smiths had departed and started playing again. In another five minutes, Mary Beth stood to leave and went over to him to say farewell. "Joe, I've loved your music."

"Thank you Miss Mary Beth." He gave her a wide smile.

"Joe, have you ever thought about coming back to America?"

"No, I'm happy here in Europe."

"You know, the situation for blacks is getting better and better back home, if perhaps that had anything to do with you moving to France in the first place?"

"No, that was never much of a problem for me in Chicago." He kept playing a gentle version of *Sleepy Lagoon* as they continued to talk. "You see Miss Mary Beth, I killed a man back in Chicago over a woman, so it wouldn't be such a good idea for me to go back to America."

"Oh, so that's why you carry a gun?"

He smiled. "Well, that's one reason, but Paris late at night can be tough in my neighborhood. By the way, if you're done needing my Baby Browning, I'll get that back from you before you leave the ship in the morning."

Mary Beth had somehow forgotten all about his gun until that moment. She hadn't thought about it since Holger had tossed it into the river. "Well, you see... I lost it somewhere back in Bratislava when I was out walking around yesterday afternoon. Just tell me how much it cost and I'll give you the money for you to buy a new one back in Paris."

"I see," was all that Joe said out loud, but he knew a lie when he heard one.

"I'm curious, Joe, if you don't mind my asking, how did you feel after you killed that man back in Chicago?

I mean, did you keep thinking about it for a long time afterwards?"

Joe had been rather skeptical all evening about the story of how Blickensdorfer had been shot by a mysterious burglar who'd then run away. Now he had a good idea who'd really shot that German. His attitude was simply that the world was a better place with one less Nazi in it.

"Well, for the first few weeks, I thought about it, but then it passed. He was a bad man and the world was better off without him. Since a few months passed, I've rarely ever thought about him at all." He hoped she believed his lie. He saw no reason in making her feel any worse than she probably already was.

"OK, I was just curious. So, what do I owe you for the gun?"

"Well, I got that gun for free, so I don't reckon you owe me anything. You just go on and have a good time on the rest of your vacation."

Now it was her turn to know that she'd just heard a lie.

She went over and gave him a hug. "You ever find yourself up in New Hampshire, you look me up."

"I'll do that for sure, Miss Mary Beth. Yes, sir, I'll do that for sure."

Mary Beth headed for her cabin and Joe started playing *Stormy Weather,* a song that matched the mood for both of them.

Arthur left Jan in their room to start packing, while he started making his way around to knock on the doors of his fellow alumni. He started with Mike Taffe, who eventually opened the door with a sleepy "Good god, Arthur, is the ship sinking?"

"Nothing as trivial as that, old friend. Listen, you've known me since 1921, and if I tell you that it's very important that we all leave the ship in the morning by 7:30, will you and your wife simply take my word for it? Just do it with no questions asked – at least for a day or two?"

He stared at Smith for several seconds to make sure he wasn't the victim of some sort of practical joke. Arthur wasn't grinning. "By god, you're serious, aren't you?"

"Deadly serious, I'm afraid."

"Of course we'll do it, if you say it's important."

"Thank you. Have your bags all packed when you come to breakfast at 7:00 a.m. sharp, and tell the porter you'll be wanting to leave the ship at 7:30."

They shook hands and Smith moved on to the next cabin door. A similar conversation occurred at each stop. A few thought he must be crazy, but they all agreed to do as he asked. Nobody said anything, but several people presumed that his odd request had something to do with Jan's health

Promptly at 7:00 a.m., twenty I.U. alumni and spouses, most all of the group, entered the dining room and all told the First Mate that they wanted to leave the ship at 7:30 a.m. He was surprised by the mass exodus at such an early hour, but he promised that there would be taxis standing by to take all of them to the Hotel Gellert. Mary Beth was present at breakfast, but she seemed to Arthur to be in a very somber mood and did not speak with him.

Holger and the Pembrokes were the only non-I.U. passengers to be up so early. Holger left a note with Captain

Ornsdorfer for his two Gestapo colleagues explaining that he'd left the ship so early so as to get to the German Embassy and report what had been happening during the cruise. Miles and Elizabeth wanted to be gone early as well, before any of their fellow passengers might notice they were missing bits of jewelry. They were surprised by so many other passengers already being in the Dining Room as they reached the entranceway and decided to skip breakfast and just immediately get away from the ship.

Just as they started to turn around to leave, they bumped into Mike and Candy.

"Good morning, Miles, Elizabeth. How are you two today?"

"Very well, thank you, Mike. There's quite a crowd in there for breakfast. Something special happening this morning?"

Mike lowered his voice. "Well, Arthur came around late last night and asked us to be here for breakfast promptly at 7:00, without any real explanation. I think it has something to do with Jan's health. They're leaving the ship, as are we, at 7:30."

"Ah, I see," replied Miles. "I'd noticed that she hadn't looked well the last few days, but I didn't want to say anything to Arthur."

"Well, a number of us have been thinking the whole cruise that she's seriously ill and I think that perhaps she took a turn for the worse last evening – and that Arthur just wanted to give her a chance to see everyone this morning before they headed off to a hospital."

"Oh, we are so sorry to hear that," replied Elizabeth. "They are such a lovely couple."

"Are you two going into have breakfast?" asked Mike.

"No, unfortunately we don't have time. We're headed off to the train station to take the 7:45 a.m. express train to Belgrade."

"Well, have a safe journey. It's been very nice meeting you and your daughter. If you two are ever in New York City, do look us up. You have my card."

"Yes, it's been a delight getting to know you and Candy. Do pass along our farewells to Arthur and Jan. Well, we must be going."

Mike and Candy headed in for breakfast and the British couple arranged with a crewman to take their bags down the dock.

There was in fact such an early morning train to Belgrade, but the two of them would actually be on the noon day flight to Athens. Once on shore, they quickly found a cab to take them directly to the airport. "Such a shame about Mrs. Smith," commented Miles. "She's such a charming lady."

As it neared 7:25 a.m., Arthur Smith rose to his feet and called everyone to attention. "I want to thank all of you for joining us on this cruise and making it a memorable one for Jan and me. We sadly lost our old friend Fred, but it was great to have had this time together."

He received a round of applause. Jan looked very pale and many concluded that this peculiar early morning departure did indeed have something to do with her health. Someone shouted out, "God bless you and Jan."

Arthur and Jan were both almost in tears when Simone stood and asked everyone to join her, as she started singing their old alumni song "Gloriana, Frangipani." They all stood and joined her in singing, their arms interlinked, many in tears. They had been youthful friends, when they all believed that they were invincible and had nothing but good years ahead of them. Now, they were approaching middle age. Some had not been all that successful in life, and for the first time, one of their gang had even died. It was a very happy and very sad occasion all at the same time.

When they finished the song, everyone then quickly headed for their cabins to fetch their hats and hand luggage. Captain Ornsdorfer and his daughter Kinley arrived in the Dining Room just as the group was exiting. The Captain and Kinley came over to Mr. and Mrs. Smith to bid them farewell. Kinley and Inga would simply remain on the ship until it sailed northward in three days. If all the legal paperwork could not be done that quickly, then the two of them would move into a modest hotel in the city, until they could all fly to Athens, and then on to London. Bob still had to finish the current movie, before he and his new "family" could head off for California.

"Well, Arthur and Jan, I hope it's been a memorable reliving of your honeymoon journey."

"You have been a perfect host, Captain. We've had a wonderful time," replied Jan.

Arthur took from his vest pocket his gold pocket watch, unhooked it from his vest and handed it to Kinley.

"I don't think you should wait any longer to have a beautiful watch like your father's. I want you to wear this one in the coming years, as you become a successful woman, and it will always remind you of us. You'll need a good watch when you get to California." He'd been given the watch by his bank when he'd become a vice-president.

Kinley was speechless. It nearly rivaled her father's in beauty. She gave Arthur and Jan big hugs.

Kinley was out on the deck five minutes later, waving goodbye as the couple headed down the gangplank and entered their taxi.

Captain Ornsdorfer, Bob, Inga and Kinley would head off later that morning to get the bureaucratic wheels of the Budapest city government rolling for a marriage and an adoption. However, Hungarian bureaucrats never came to work until 10:00 a.m., so they had time for a leisurely breakfast.

When the Captain finally went up to the bridge, he found a brief note waiting for him from Stefan. It simply read that he had received an outstanding job offer that he could not turn down, and wished the Captain well. Crewmen had occasionally suddenly left the ship over the years, but he was surprised at Stefan's action as he thought the young man had seemed quite happy with his position.

Stefan's action became clearer to him when an hour later, Mr. and Mrs. Bishop came frantically to his door.

"I just knocked on our daughter's cabin door, to make sure Hanna was awake and getting her suitcases packed. She was not there, nor her luggage, but I found this note in an envelope on the bed addressed to us." Tom started to hand the letter to the Captain, but then decided it would be better to read it to him, as Hanna's handwriting was not very good.

"Dear Mom and Dad,

I have decided to go off and start my own life. Please do not come looking for me, or get the police involved, as I will be well gone from Budapest by the time you read this. I simply cannot face going back to Cincinnati. Thank you for everything. I will be in touch once I'm settled.

Love, Hanna."

Captain Ornsdorfer didn't know quite what to say.

Lenora spoke up. "Surely, someone must have seen her leave the ship with her luggage during the night, or even helped her. Did any of your crew see her leave?" Don't you have a duty officer or someone awake on the ship all night long?"

"Yes, there is an officer on duty throughout the night, but when we're docked at a port, frankly, I don't think the watch officer is really watching much of anything, if he's even awake. By the way, what is it that your daughter cannot face back in Cincinnati?"

Lenora had no intention of sharing with the Captain the details of how Hanna was about to be named as the "other woman" in a scandalous divorce case of a prominent citizen just starting back home. She simply continued on, "Never mind Cincinnati. Are any of your crew missing? I find it hard to believe that she left on her own. If one of your men has taken away my teenage daughter, I'll be contacting the local police and the American Embassy!"

The Captain fingered Stefan's note in his pocket, debating how to handle this. He'd taken a great dislike to Mrs. Bishop during the cruise, and had felt sorry for both the daughter and the husband.

"As far as I know, all the crew who have assigned duties are on board, but this is the end of the cruise and a number of my men have been given shore leave, since we will be docked here for the next three days. It will probably be late tonight before I could say for certain whether any crew member is not here." He shrugged his shoulders, indicating he didn't know what he could do for the Bishops.

"Well, what are you going to do about my missing daughter?"

"I'm not going to do anything. Your family paid for a cruise from Regensburg to Budapest. The cruise ended at 8:00 a.m. this morning and I safely delivered the three of you to Budapest." He checked his pocket watch. "It is now almost nine. There is no evidence of a crime against Hanna having occurred on the ship. At this time, the location of your daughter is your concern, Mrs. Smith. Feel free to go to the Hungarian police, the American Ambassador or the King of Siam – that is entirely up to you. And now if you will excuse me, I have a ship to run. Good day." He tipped his hat and walked away. He too had enjoyed standing up to Captain Brunner the previous night, in his own small way – and if he could do so with a local police captain, he figured he could certainly do so with an annoying woman from Cincinnati, wherever exactly that was.

"Well, I never."

Tom interceded. "Come on, Lenora, let's get our luggage over to the hotel, and then we can go to the police.

Captain Ornsdorfer would have to go to the cruise line's representative in Budapest at some point, in order to request a new bartender and a masseuse, and he'd mention Hanna's running away while there as well. However, first he had much more important business to attend to — accompanying Bob, Inga and Kinley to see a local judge.

A stream of taxis arrived at the Hotel Gellert with all the Americans and their luggage. The hotel had not expected the arrival of so many guests so early in the morning, but the Management did its best to arrange for coffee and pastries for the group in a private dining room while they waited for rooms. They even offered a guided walking tour of the downtown area of the city at 9:00 a.m. While the American group was sitting about at the hotel, Candy Taffe mentioned to her husband that she hadn't been able to find several pieces of her jewelry that morning when they'd been in such a rush to pack and depart the ship. Mike assured her that they would no doubt show up when they unpacked later in their room. Another wife heard Candy talking of this and commented that she too had not been able to find her diamond earrings that morning while packing.

Lt. Hinz arrived at the hotel shortly after the alumni group and was able to easily secure a reservation, although he too was told that no room would actually be available until perhaps noon.

Once Mary Beth saw Holger in the grand lobby of

the hotel, she did as instructed and followed him as he left the hotel. She followed him to a nearby café and once they'd ordered coffees and rolls, they turned to the topic of what to do next. They couldn't be sure at what time Karen's body would be found on the ship, but probably the local police would soon thereafter come to the hotel to talk to the passengers who'd departed so early.

"A number of your group will spend most of today out and about exploring Budapest. You should definitely be one of them, just to minimize the possibility that if the police come around, you won't be available to question."

"Very well, and what about going to the British Embassy here?" she asked.

"I still think that would be the smart move, rather than waiting until Athens. I asked at the hotel front desk and they told me that the British Embassy is but a ten minute walk from the hotel. However, they also told me that their understanding was that it did not open to the public until 10:00 a.m., so we have almost an hour to wait."

"You think there will be an MI-6 officer at this British Embassy?"

"I would think that there would be one at every embassy, but I don't know for sure. If there is not, I wouldn't go into much detail with just some ordinary diplomat."

"And where will you be?"

"I'll simply wait here until you return, hopefully with an MI-6 officer with you. I can give him directly the letter from the General." Holger was coming to trust Mary Beth more, but still not enough to part yet with the valuable letter. That letter was his only bargaining chip to get himself to England, where he would be safe.

At 10:00 a.m., Mary Beth walked to the British Embassy. Her first unpleasant surprise was to see a heavy Hungarian police presence around the Embassy, and an officer was seated at a table to question anyone who wished to reach the front entrance.

As she approached the table, she held out her American passport and said in English, "I wish to visit the British Embassy."

The police officer smiled at her, but did not speak English. She repeated her statement in pretend "beginners German" and again waved her passport at him.

In German this time, he inquired, "Why do you want to enter the British Embassy? Your American Embassy is nearby."

She stuck with her "pidgin-German." "I'm traveling soon to England and have questions about whether I need a visa." She actually found it rather hard to sound as if she didn't know German well, yet still make herself understood to the Hungarian officer. Finally, the officer gave up and simply waved her forward.

Once she passed through the front door of the lovely old building, she encountered a Hungarian employee of the Embassy at the reception desk, but at least he spoke English.

"How may I help you?" he inquired with a British accent.

"I need to speak with the Principal Secretary." Father-in-law Nigel had briefed her that if she encountered difficulty on her journey and needed assistance at any British Embassy, to always ask for the Principal Secretary, not the Ambassador. A Principal Secretary was important and had power, but did still have to work and see people who came to the Embassy without an appointment.

"And what is your business with the Principal Secretary, Miss?"

He spoke with a very officious tone. She'd run into such lowly people in the publishing business in New York City, who always wanted to make themselves appear more important than they really were.

"My business is with the Principal Secretary, not some local clerk. Please notify him immediately that Mrs. Mary Beth Long, a British citizen, is waiting to speak with him." Mary Beth herself knew how to sound "official" when needed and she hoped the clerk would think that Mrs. Long might be someone important and not to be trifled with.

The clerk turned to his phone. He made her wait some ten minutes, before escorting her up the main staircase, just to show her that he was important, but she was finally taken into the office of Principal Secretary Reginald Parker.

He was most gracious and oh so British. He offered her a chair in front of his large wooden desk, which was completely clear of a single piece of paper.

"How may I be of assistance, Mrs. Long?"

"I need to pass a report I recently obtained in Germany to the MI-6 representative here at the embassy. Could you please have that man come here immediately and meet with me?"

Mr. Parker looked as if Mary Beth had just asked to have King George stop by. "My dear young lady, I can assure you that there is no one of that organization here at my Embassy."

"Yes, yes I know that 'officially' no one of MI-6 is here, but I still need to pass that person something very important, regardless of what position he's pretending to hold."

"I fear Mrs. Long that you have been reading too many spy novels and I resent your implication that anyone at my Embassy is engaged in anything so tawdry as espionage!"

"But, I must ..."

Secretary Parker held up his hand in protest and shook his head.

Mary Beth realized that she would be wasting her time in pursuing the issue any further with Parker. "Very well, Principal Secretary Parker. I shall not waste any further of my time. Good day!"

He started to phone down to the local receptionist, to escort her out, but she stood and headed for the door. The imperious receptionist met her halfway down the staircase and escorted her to the front door. He now had a smug look upon his face, as if to say, "I knew you were no one of real importance."

Ten minutes later, she met with Holger at the same coffee shop where they'd so optimistically planned her visit to the embassy earlier that morning.

"How did it go?" asked Holger.

She took off her coat and sat down before answering,

but he could tell by her somber face that she'd not brought good news.

"I'm afraid that it didn't go well at all."

She gave him a quick recount of her conversation with pompous Parker and how he'd denied there even being an MI-6 officer in the Budapest Embassy. Holger looked very disappointed.

"I guess, we'll just have to go on to Athens where I can contact this Tristan Kensington-Smyth, as I had originally been instructed to do."

"Yes, I suppose that's all that you can do. I, however, have a problem. I'm not sure how I can get permission to travel on to Greece. The reason for traveling on the ship to Budapest was to find some mysterious spy who may have met with General Breithaupt in Munich. Colonel Blickensdorfer is now dead and the cruise has ended, with no evidence of a foreign spy being among the passengers. How can I explain why I need to travel on to Athens?"

They both sat in silence with somber faces for several long minutes, sipping their coffee.

Finally, Mary Beth spoke. "Were you and the Colonel close? Or, at least did it appear to the other Gestapo men on the ship that you were?"

"Well, he was a colonel and I am only a lieutenant, so we would not have been expected to be close friends, but he could have been a mentor. Why?"

"Who could give you permission on short notice to travel to Athens? Could someone at the German Embassy here in Budapest do that?"

"Yes, I suppose so. There is a Gestapo officer here in Budapest, of that I'm sure."

"Could you claim to that local Gestapo officer that you feel that Colonel Blickensdorfer's death was somehow a failure on your part — that as a matter of loyalty to him, you want to continue your investigation of the passengers in Greece — just in case it wasn't a common criminal who killed your mentor and friend on the ship in Bratislava?"

"Yes, that might work," he replied slowly as he gave her suggestion further thought. "In any case, you must proceed tomorrow to Athens and deliver the letter to your British contact at the embassy." He pulled Blickensdorfer's letter from an inner pocket and passed it to her under the table.

"OK, I will do that, but I still think it's very important that you go to Athens as well, so as to explain the background about the General and how the letter first came into your possession and then mine. The background to the letter will give it much more credibility in London."

Holger agreed with her point, and he also knew that the prospect of him being given permission to move to England would be much greater if he was personally there to explain his role in obtaining the letter. Given all that had occurred, he definitely could not return to Germany.

"Alright, I'll go immediately to the German Embassy and see if I can obtain permission to travel onto Athens with the group, so as to continue my investigation. You may see me at the Budapest airport tomorrow. If you do not, proceed onto Athens as planned and perhaps I'll arrive there in a day or two. If I am at the airport tomorrow, pay no particular attention to me. Simply stay close to the other Americans. Go out now and play tourist around Budapest and don't return to the hotel until dinner time. I'm sure the Hungarian police will come to the hotel to ask questions of the passengers from the ship, once Karen's body is found this morning in her cabin."

"One more thing. Why do you think that Karen didn't speak up with her suspicions about me when Captain Brunner was still on the ship?"

Holger smiled slightly. "I can't be sure, but I suspect it's the usual jealousy that exists between different police organizations. There's definitely a rivalry between the Bavarian State Police and the Gestapo and probably with the Bratislava City Police as well. She wanted the prestige of the arrest all for herself and her organization."

Mary Beth shook her head and slightly raised her eyebrows in amazement. "I don't really understand it, but thank goodness for me there's such rivalry, or I'd be in a jail cell today!"

"Yes, sometimes being lucky is better than being skilled."

"Very well. Good luck with your visit to your Embassy." She reached across the table and gave his hand a firm squeeze. "I'll see you tomorrow at the airport." They both then went off on their separate missions.

Upon reaching the German Embassy, Lieutenant Hinz requested to meet with the local Gestapo officer, to whom he then gave a lengthy oral report of all that had happened since Munich. He requested that he be allowed to write up a report and that it immediately be sent to Munich and Berlin. Local Gestapo Chief Becker naturally gave his immediate concurrence to that request.

During their conversation, the two junior Gestapo men who'd been on the ship arrived at the embassy with news of the death of the tour guide Karen Connor. They said that the matter had been turned over to the Budapest police authorities for investigation. After hearing about the death of the tour guide, Becker dismissed the two enlisted men.

"My god, you've had four deaths during a one-week cruise!" said Becker. "Lieutenant, you're lucky to have arrived at Budapest alive," he added with a smile. "Is there anything that I can do at this point to be of assistance to your investigation?"

"Well, Captain Becker. I would like to raise a personal matter with you, in connection with Colonel Blickensdorfer's death."

"Please."

"Werner was very much my mentor and I owed him a great deal. I feel as if I have personally let him down with his being murdered on the ship. Perhaps it was a common criminal who did it, but as I have been thinking about the matter over the last day, I think there's also a good possibility that his death is connected with the suspected spy among the passengers. We had narrowed the list down to just three or four serious suspects. They'll all be flying tomorrow to Athens, ostensibly to continue their holiday travels. If it's one of them who killed my Colonel, he will no doubt be feeling a sense of victory and safety, having reached Greece and might perhaps let his guard down. I'm not quite sure exactly what I will do in Athens, but I request permission to be allowed to travel there tomorrow with these foreigners to see what I might possibly learn. I feel it's my duty to Colonel Blickensdorfer."

Captain Becker was very touched by Holger's attitude and loyalty to his dead superior. "Yes, I agree with you completely that you should continue your mission to the finish. I will send a message immediately to Gestapo headquarters in Berlin requesting the authorization for your onward travel. In expectation of a positive response, we will proceed today with acquiring for you a German passport, a visa from the Greek Embassy here in Budapest and an airline reservation for you on tomorrow's noon flight to Athens."

"Thank you very much, Captain."

"I do have one question for you Lieutenant, just unofficially between you and me."

Holger nodded his assent. "Anything."

"Gestapo Headquarters never tells me what's going on. I learn more from reading the local newspapers than I do in messages from Berlin." He paused for a second. "Is there a war coming? Just what the hell is going on?"

Holger's face turned very somber. "I believe war is coming. Perhaps in just a few months. Perhaps not until the fall, but one is definitely coming."

"Thank you for sharing that with me. At last, we will be able to correct the wrongs that have been done to Germany since 1918 and expand the borders of a superior race to where they should be."

"Yes, there are glorious days ahead for the German people," replied Holger.

Becker gave a broad smile. "I'll get the request for

your travel to Greece immediately off to Berlin, with my positive concurrence included. And now a word of advice to you."

"Yes?"

"As soon as you've finished writing up your report, I suggest you go to your hotel and get yourself some sleep." The Captain laughed. "No offense, Lieutenant, but you look like hell and clearly you need some rest! I shall send word to you at the hotel as soon we receive concurrence from Berlin."

Upon Holger's return to the hotel, he immediately encountered several of the American cruise passengers in the lobby, all of whom asked him if he'd heard of Karen's death. He acted quite surprised for their benefit and said that he'd been busy the last several hours at his Embassy. He asked if the local police had been by yet to question everyone that had been on the ship. Arthur Smith informed him that no one from the Hungarian Police had come yet to the hotel to question anyone. What they did know was simply from a few passengers who'd departed the ship late in the morning, after Karen's body had been found. Mike Taffe began to wonder if Arthur's request for an early departure by the Indiana group from the ship had any connection with Karen's death, but he said nothing to Arthur. The rest of the gang still speculated that it had to do with Jan's health, particularly after the hotel manager magically found a room for the Smiths alone very shortly after arrival at the Gellert.

As Holger chatted with different passengers in the lobby and then in the dining room for lunch, he was rather amused by how the rumors about her death had grown. A French couple at his luncheon table told everyone that according to a ship's crewman with whom they'd spoken just before leaving the ship at 11:00 a.m., there were four or five glasses on the table in Karen's cabin and several empty champagne bottles on the floor. The crewman claimed that a policeman had told him that there had obviously been some sort of sexual orgy going on in her cabin. As lunch ended, all the people at his table hurried over to speak with other passengers from the cruise. Each one stated that they didn't believe for one moment that sweet Karen had been killed during an orgy, but repeated every detail that the French couple had provided.

Holger saw Captain Ornsdorfer passing through the ornately decorated lobby of the hotel and asked him if he had a moment.

"Captain, I've heard that cruise director Karen Conner has been found dead on the ship, but everyone I speak with here at the hotel has a wilder story than the last as to what exactly happened. Can you tell me what did happen and whether the local police have been brought in to investigate?"

"The crewman who went in to clean her cabin found her dead on the bathroom floor at about ten this morning. She was wearing only her under garments. She may have simply slipped and hit her head on the porcelain sink, although there is some evidence that perhaps she had been entertaining a guest in her cabin last night. I sent for the

Hungarian city police and they have been there looking around her room for the last several hours."

"Will they be coming here to the hotel to question the passengers?"

Ornsdorfer smiled. "No, I don't think they will. They saw that she has a German passport, she was on an Austrian-registered ship and according to a quick examination by the police doctor, she's been dead since about midnight. That means she was killed while we were still within the territory of Czechoslovakia. The Hungarians are notifying the Czech police at Bratislava and the Bavarian police in Munich, inviting them to come to Budapest if they wish. It will be tomorrow afternoon at the earliest before either country can get someone here."

"Thank you Captain, that is quite interesting."

"Oh, and the young Bishop girl, Hanna, has apparently run away from her parents. Don't suppose you have any information related to her disappearance?"

"No, none at all, sorry," Holger replied with a genuine look of surprise on his face.

"Well, it's not really my problem. I just thought I'd ask. By the way, my ship will begin its return journey to Germany in three days. Will you be booking passage with us again for the return to Regensburg?"

"I'm not sure yet. I may be staying on here in Budapest for some time."

"In that case, I will say farewell now and wish you well."

Holger extended his hand and shook the Captain's.

"It was a pleasurable voyage, except for the four deaths." He gave a wry smile.

The Captain smiled back. "Four is a record. One was the most for any previous trip. Well, I must be getting on with my duties."

"Oh, just one more thing. I heard how your daughter will be going to America with Mr. Hall and Inga. Please give my congratulations to the wedding couple and I think that is wonderful that Kinley will have a chance to grow up in America."

"I shall pass along your sentiments to the couple. And may you stay safe in the coming months. Auf Wiedersehen."

Holger gave a quick wave and then he was gone.

Once Mr. and Mrs. Bishop arrived at the hotel, Karen's death was quickly forgotten and discussion began about the disappearance of Hanna. Within an hour, speculation began as to whether Hanna's middle-of-the-night disappearance had anything to do with Karen's death.

At four o'clock, Captain Becker phoned Lt. Hinz at his hotel room. "Lieutenant, I have received authorization from Gestapo Headquarters in Berlin for you to proceed on to Athens to continue your investigation for one week. I have spoken with the Greek Consul-General and he has promised to have your visa ready at 9:00 a.m. tomorrow morning. I've also made you a reservation on the noon flight tomorrow to Athens."

"That is good news, Captain. Thank you for your efforts."

"Oh, and you shall be happy to know Gestapo Headquarters sent word after reading your report that

Blickensdorfer has been posthumously promoted to the rank of general and will be given a general's funeral once his body is returned to Munich."

"That is most gratifying to know. Werner will be very pleased, achieving the rank of general had been one of his major goals."

"I'm sure his widow will be gratified to know that he died a hero for the Third Reich. As for your travel, if you will please come by the Embassy in the morning, at 10:00, I will give you your passport, the visa and also money to cover your expenses for one week in Greece. You're to check in with the German Embassy once you have reached Athens."

"Very good. I'll see you tomorrow morning. Good evening."

Holger replaced the phone on its apparatus and smiled. Mary Beth's idea had worked. He and she would both be in Greece before any investigation of Karen's death would get underway in Budapest. He stayed in his room and had food delivered for dinner. He simply wasn't in the mood to have any more conversations with his fellow passengers about Karen's death.

ATHENS, GREECE

Holger and Mary Beth saw each other at the Budapest airport, but didn't speak until after the plane arrived in Athens. He gave her the name of a restaurant on the Syntagma Square where they would meet at eight o'clock for dinner. She and several other Americans proceeded to the Hotel Grande Bretagne, where they already had reservations. Captain Becker had given Holger the name of a much more modest and reasonably priced hotel near the docks.

Holger was already seated when Mary Beth arrived promptly at 8:00 p.m. at the restaurant.

"I was very relieved when I saw you at the airport this morning," began Mary Beth. "I presume your Embassy gave you the needed permission to fly here to continue your investigation."

"Yes, I was authorized to come here for a week. I'm to check in with the local German Embassy each day, beginning tomorrow. So, I suggest you go to the British Embassy first thing tomorrow morning and find this contact of yours. It would be best for us to leave for England as soon as possible."

"Yes, I'll go to the Embassy promptly at 10:00 a.m. and ask for Mr. Kensington-Smyth and explain to him what all has happened so far. I will insist that he come with me to meet you and hear your story. I will also strongly suggest to him that you be brought to England, to tell of your conversation with General Breithaupt and hopefully they will offer you political asylum."

"I hope so too, as I learned this morning at my Embassy in Budapest that General Breithaupt is dead. There were no further details. Obviously, he never said anything about me, or I wouldn't have been given permission to fly to Greece. Still, I cannot return to Germany. Someone is eventually going to come to the correct conclusion about the deaths of Colonel Blickensdorfer and Karen Connor."

"I will do my very best with Kensington-Smyth in the morning."

"There is a small outdoor café connected with this restaurant. I will be waiting in it from 10:30 a.m. onward until you arrive tomorrow."

"Very well. Let's order, I'm starving. I'm afraid all of this intrigue has built up a tremendous appetite in me." They both laughed. The first time in several days for either that they'd found anything even mildly humorous.

CHAPTER 15
Athens

Mary Beth arrived at the British Embassy promptly at 10:00 a.m. and asked for Mr. Tristan Kensington-Smyth of the Passport Control Office. A minute later, a tall, very good-looking man in his mid-thirties, wearing a well-tailored, gray suit arrived at the Reception Desk. His short, dark-brown hair was perfectly coifed. Not that she personally knew any British spies other than her father-in-law, but she had the thought that Tristan certainly looked like an MI-6 officer should. She then had the odd thought that wouldn't it better if a spy didn't look like a spy? In any case, at long last, she was in contact with the man she needed. He escorted her to his private office and inquired if she'd like some tea.

After he'd served her tea, he began by inquiring, "Do you prefer Miss or Mrs. Long. I'm afraid that London was a bit vague on that point." He offered a lovely smile.

"I generally go by Miss Long, because of my writing, but why don't you simply call me, Mary Beth."

"Splendid, Mary Beth. London informed me of your task and to expect you this week, but other than that, I'm not really up to speed. What has been happening with you since Paris and your brief meeting there with my colleague, Mr. Philby? How is Kim, by the way? I haven't seen him for several years."

"He seemed just fine. Well, nothing went as planned in Munich, but before I get into details, here is the letter that German General Fritz von Breithaupt wished to pass to the British Government." She took it from her purse and handed it to Tristan. "I do hope it's of value, as four people have died during the river voyage to get it to you."

Tristan's demeanor turned somber at that news as he quickly glanced at it. "I must confess that I don't read German, but I have a man here who knows German quite well. He pressed a buzzer on his desk and a moment later a young man entered his office. "Take this around to Clarke and tell him I need a rough translation as quickly as possible. After that he should start on a high-quality translation that we'll be sending off to London yet today."

"Yes, sir, right away, sir." He took the letter from his superior's hand and started to leave.

"And bring the rough translation into me as soon as it's ready."

The assistant nodded, then continued on out the door, quietly shutting it behind him.

"While that's being worked on, why don't you simply tell me what happened on Christmas Eve in Munich, and subsequently."

Mary Beth began her tale. Being a writer, she did have a skill at organizing facts in a logical manner. She spoke for almost twenty minutes, without Tristan interrupting her with any questions. She decided at the last minute not to share the most recent news of General Breithaupt's death. She feared that if MI-6 knew of his death, they would have less incentive to bring Holger to England. She really didn't know how his death might affect their thinking, but decided not to take any risk.

When she finished, he simply replied, "Good show."

She thought that rather an understatement. "Lieutenant Holger Hinz is waiting at a nearby café to meet with us at 11:30. I believe you'll find his story of his conversation with the General on Christmas Eve quite valuable in assessing how credible is his letter."

"Yes, quite so." He looked at his watch. "I suppose we should leave in a few minutes to go meet Lt. Hinz, but are there any other major points you want to tell me now?"

"Well, yes, there is one more thing. Holger would like to be allowed to come to England. Given all that happened on the cruise, he cannot safely return home. Nor, with his change of political views, does he want to return to Nazi Germany."

"I'm not in a position to make such a promise on my own, but I'll be happy to pass along his request to London. We should be able to get an answer in just a day or so."

"Very well, but please make it clear in your telegram to London that this is my request as well. I believe that he's performed a great service on my behalf and for England, and he should not simply be cast adrift here in Greece. Without him, that letter would not be in your hands now and I would probably be in a jail cell."

"I shall make your very valid points in my report.

Now, I think it's time we headed for this café. I'm sure he's very anxious to see you."

She smiled. "I'm sure he is."

"One last question before we go. I'm afraid it's a rather cheeky one, but I'm sure London will want to know. Has any sort of personal relationship developed between you two? I mean, is there more to your request for him to accompany you to England than simply as a reward to him for a job well done?"

Mary Beth laughed. "No, Tristan, there is no love interest in my advocating for him. But to be frank about it. I think after a man saves my life, he and I are much closer than I ever would be simply with a lover."

"Quite so, quite so." He looked at his watch. "I was hoping to have a quick read through the letter before going to meet this Holger fellow. You've read the letter I presume. Perhaps you could just give me the highlights of the contents."

"Certainly. I'm sure London will be quite interested to know the date that Hitler plans to send his Army in to conquer the rest of Czechoslovakia. It also shows the different points of attack along the border and by what units of the Wehrmacht."

Upon hearing that, even Tristan, who until that moment had seemed unflappable, went silent for several seconds. "Yes, I'm sure they'll find that date quite useful to know." If she'd intended with that comment to tweak his interest in the contents of the General's letter, she had succeeded. Just then there was a knock on the door and the young assistant entered carrying a brown leather folder.

"Here is Clarke's rough translation, sir. He said he should have a more precise translation done in about an hour."

"Excellent. I'm about to go out with Miss Long to meet someone. We should be back in one hour. I'd like you and Clarke to be standing by as we'll be cracking busy getting messages off to London as soon as I return."

"Yes, sir."

Tristan opened the folder. "And go tell Timmons we shall proceed as usual."

The assistant nodded and immediately left the room.

Tristan did not wish to cause affront to Miss Long by suggesting that her story was anything other than she had told him, but his phrase to the assistant was the discreet indicator that his bodyguard, Timmons, was to follow and make sure he came back safely. Timmons had been an amateur boxer in his younger days and was also an excellent shot with the Webley revolver he always carried about Athens. Tristan had no particular reason to doubt anything Miss Long had told him so far, but taking along Timmons to meet a Gestapo officer seemed the prudent thing to do.

Tristan gave a quick read through the translation and looked up, smiling at Mary Beth. "Yes, I agree with you. I do believe London will be quite interested in this letter."

He then locked the folder in his desk. "Shall we be on our way, Mary Beth?"

Holger was indeed a happy man when he saw Mary Beth and an obviously British-looking fellow approaching him at the appointed café. Mary Beth made the introductions.

"Holger, this is Tristan. Tristan, my friend Holger."

The two men shook hands and then all sat down. They ordered three cups of the strong, black Greek coffee for which the country was famous. Timmons leaned up against the wall of a building across the street, enjoyed a cigarette and kept an eye out for anyone looking suspicious who was approaching Tristan.

"Mary Beth has been telling me the extraordinary story of what's been happening on the ship. Needless to say, I'm quite pleased that you both made it to Athens alive."

Holger simply nodded in agreement, but remained silent, preferring that Tristan continued with whatever he'd come to say.

"She told me that it would be best if I heard directly from you what you and the General discussed on Christmas Eve in Munich, as it would put his letter into context."

"Certainly. I'd been instructed to conduct surveillance on the General and also gather reporting on him from our informants. There'd been negative reports on him for several weeks for his making critical remarks about the Fuhrer. These were always done in a joking manner, but caused enough of a worry that the Gestapo Chief in Munich, Colonel Werner Blickensdorfer, decided to investigate him."

"And on Christmas Eve you had followed him to this courtyard, where he was expecting to meet someone from England?"

"Correct." Holger proceeded to tell Tristan about his conversation that night with the General, as he'd previously related it to Mary Beth. "He was disappointed that no one had showed up to meet with him as he'd requested, and not sure what to do next to get his letter into the proper hands in England. After I'd told him that I'd had a change of heart about the Nazis myself, he and I came up with the idea to use me to get his letter out of Germany. I was to claim the next morning to my superior that I'd seen just the end of perhaps a clandestine meeting between the General and a fleetingly-seen stranger. Also, that when I searched the area later, I'd found a clue possibly linking the mysterious second person to a group of foreign tourists about to sail down the Danube River to Budapest. We hoped that would make Colonel Blickensdorfer think that he and I should accompany that group on its trip so as to investigate them. It did and thus I was able to bring the letter out of Germany."

"A very clever plan, which has succeeded. I'm having it translated right now, and as soon as I return to my Embassy, it will be coded and sent off to London. By the way, is there any way that we can get back in touch with the General?"

"I'm afraid not. I learned at the German Embassy in Budapest yesterday morning that General Breithaupt is dead. There were no specific details, but I presume that he died during interrogation. Gestapo techniques can become very harsh."

"That is a shame," replied Tristan solemnly. "Thank goodness you arrived here safely with his letter."

Mary Beth wished that Holger hadn't said anything about the death of the General, but there'd been no way to warn him. She hoped that he hadn't been too honest for his own good.

"Did Mary Beth mention to you that I would like

political asylum in England? It would not be safe for me to return to Germany after all that happened on the cruise, regardless of whether the General talked about me before he died or not."

"I don't have the authority to personally agree to such a request, but I will immediately raise that question with London. I'm optimistic that MI-6 Headquarters will concur, but we'll have to wait till probably tomorrow morning to have an answer. Are you set for a place to stay tonight?"

"Yes, I am. I'm supposed to check in each day with the German Embassy here in Athens, though I would prefer not to go there even once. If London agrees with my request, could Mary Beth and I begin our journey to England as early as tomorrow?"

"There is in fact an early afternoon flight tomorrow to Lisbon, Portugal, which is the usual route to reach London. Anticipating a positive response from my Headquarters, let's plan on putting the two of you on that flight. I'll go ahead and make plane reservations for 'Mr. and Mrs. Smythe.' I suggest that we three meet tomorrow at 11:00 a.m. at that small café just across the Square, called Aristotle's." He pointed across the street. "Mary Beth, just leave your luggage at the hotel with the porter and instructions that a Mr. Timmons will be calling for them to take to the airport. Holger, I'd suggest you leave most of your belongings at the hotel where you are staying and bring only a few essentials you will need for the onward journey. We can get you new kit and clothing once you reach London. Your belongings still being in your room might make your German colleagues wonder whether you simply got mugged and murdered in Athens."

The two novices to the world of espionage nodded in agreement with Tristan's clever instructions.

Tristan took out a camera. "Oh, just one more thing. Let me get a nice photo of each of you for your new passports."

After Tristan left, Holger asked Mary Beth, "Do you think I can trust this Tristan?"

"I've only known him for an hour or so, but he does come across as a competent and trustworthy person. We'll find out tomorrow. What are your plans for tonight?"

"I'm simply going to stay in my room, and also tomorrow morning till it's time to come to the meeting at 11:00. If Tristan has an answer from London and we're leaving in the afternoon, great. If not, I'll go to the German Embassy and report in as directed, and hope he has a response by the following day."

"Very well. I'm going to go back to my hotel now and stay there until tomorrow's meeting. I must say I'm very relieved to have delivered that letter to the Embassy today. The General may be dead, but at least his letter has reached the British Government as he wished. I, however, will be nervous until we're on a plane out of Athens. The Nazis have too much influence in Greece for me to feel comfortable here."

"We're agreed then. Bis morgen!" He stood and slowly disappeared into the crowd on the Square. She found herself praying that that would not be the last time she saw him. It would be so unfair if he'd gotten this far on the journey and then have something go wrong. She walked slowly back to the Grand Bretagne Hotel, reflecting on all that had happened on the journey. She didn't notice that Timmons was now following her – in part to make sure that she remained safe, but Tristan was a cynical fellow and also wanted to make sure that she wasn't going to report to anyone else after her meeting with him.

Mary Beth was mentally and physically exhausted from the morning's meetings and wanted a nap. She ran into Arthur and Jan in the lobby. They were just going out to find a bit of lunch. Mary Beth thought that Jan looked very weak, and like many of the other passengers, was beginning to wonder if Jan was not suffering from something far more serious than a lingering cold and headaches. Mary Beth declined to go with them for lunch, but agreed to join them for dinner at seven o'clock in the hotel dining room.

Arthur and Jan had only gotten a couple of blocks when she told her husband that she wasn't up for going any further and they went into the very next Greek taverna. It didn't look like much from the outside, or even the inside, but the food turned out to be delicious.

"You don't look well. How are you feeling?"

Jan put on a smile for her solicitous husband, but decided it was time for honesty. "I haven't been feeling very well since Vienna. I just didn't want to make a big deal of it, until I had to say something."

Arthur fought back his emotions. "I don't know what a local doctor could do, but should we go to the hospital or at least get the name of a good doctor from the hotel?"

"I don't know what any doctor is going to do beyond

what Dr. Henke did for me back in Chicago." She hesitated for several seconds. "You brought those pills he gave you, didn't you?"

"Yes, are we at that stage?"

"No, not quite, but I don't think there's any point in our getting on a ship in two days' time as originally planned."

"OK, do you want to stay at the hotel or should we perhaps see if we can rent a house with a view of the bay or something like that?"

"Oh, that would be so nice. Something close enough to the water so that we could hear the waves roll in and out."

"I'll inquire of the concierge about such a place as soon as we get back to the hotel."

"It would be great if we could have several days together near the beach, in the warm Mediterranean sun… before you would need to find a ship to take you back to America."

"I won't be sailing back to America either," he replied slowly and softly. "Dr. Henke gave me enough pills for both of us."

"Oh, no dear. You have years ahead of you yet."

"There's nothing back in Chicago that interests me if you're not part of it."

She reached across the red and white checkered table cloth and squeezed his hand and gave him one of her great smiles that he'd loved seeing since the first day they'd met.

The silence was broken when their waiter approached with menus and a plate of olives. The menu was only in Greek and the waiter knew only a few words of English, but they recognized one food item as he read off for them what they had to offer – gyros. They'd gone to an ethnic food festival the previous summer in Chicago. The city was full of different ethnic groups and they'd tried a gyros at a Greek stand, and had liked it. They ordered two gyros and also a bottle of white wine.

The sliced lamb meat with onions and tzatziki sauce laced with garlic, wrapped up in warm pita bread was messy, but tasty. When the bottle of wine arrived, Arthur poured them each a glass and offered a toast. "To all of our good years together."

"Yes, to us," she replied and then both took a sip of their wine.

They almost spit it out on the floor. It was terrible. "Oh, well dear, it was an excellent toast!" They both laughed.

Once back at the Grand Bretagne, Jan went up to her room to rest before dinner and Arthur went to speak to the Concierge about beach front rentals. Being January, there were all sorts of cottages available. After arranging for a cottage, Arthur bumped into Mike Taffe in the lobby. He led him off to a quiet corner of the bar for a frank conversation.

Once settled at a table with drinks in hand, Arthur began, "Mike, I know you're not a lawyer, but I believe you've dealt with a lot of legal issues in your financial business back in New York, and I need a favor."

"Sure, anything, if I can." Mike suspected from the look on Arthur's face that this wasn't going to be a pleasant favor.

"I understand that you and Fanny are staying around

Greece for a week or so, before sailing back to America. Is that correct?"

"Yes, we're staying here in Athens for about ten days, just making a few day trips out to historical places, typical tourist stuff."

"This is in strictest confidence."

"Of course."

"Jan is terminally ill and the end is very near. We're not sailing back to America in two days with the others."

"I understand. What will you need my help in doing?"

"Well, her doctor back in Chicago sent along with her pills that will bring it all to a peaceful end – so she needn't suffer in the final days."

"That's good." Mike couldn't think of anything else more appropriate to say.

"And we have enough pills for both of us. I won't be going back as a passenger either. But we need someone who can handle arrangements here in Athens for our bodies to be shipped back to Chicago and the usual wrapping up of affairs. Can you handle that for us?"

Mike cleared his throat. He'd had to tell veteran actors that they were being cut from shows and a few other unpleasant tasks over the years, but he'd never faced a situation like this one.

"I will take care of everything needed. Don't worry about a thing. I assume you have a will back in Chicago, so all that sort of stuff will be taken care of on that end?"

"Yes, you just need to get us on our way home and settle any accounts here in Athens." He handed Mike an envelope. "In here are all the names, addresses, etc. that you will need. Plus a signed check made out to you. You just fill in the amount that is needed to cover all our expenses. And you may find with us at the seaside cottage where we'll be staying, a few last letters. I'd appreciate it if you'll please see that those get mailed once you're back in America. I'll phone and leave a message for you here at the hotel the morning of when you'll need to come to the cottage."

"Of course, of course – just leave everything to me. I'll keep this a secret as you've requested Arthur, but do let me say you are one hell of a guy and it's been a privilege to call you and Jan my friends."

"Thank you, my sentiments about you as well, old friend."

They stood and firmly shook hands. Mike then quickly turned and walked away, not wanting to show how devastated he really was.

While Arthur and Mike were having their private conversation in the bar, Tom and Lenora Bishop were just starting an equally somber discussion up in their hotel room as Tom finished packing his bags. His face was taut, knowing they were about to have a necessary, but unpleasant conversation as she entered their room.

"Why are you already packing, Tom? We don't sail for another two days. You have plenty of time."

"You're sailing on Thursday, I'm leaving by train this afternoon." He continued to neatly place his socks and underwear in one of his cases.

Lenora was dumbfounded. "Why would you leave by train? How are you getting back to Cincinnati?"

"I'm not going back to Ohio. I'm staying in Europe.

I'll be filing for divorce shortly. Eventually, some lawyer back in Cincinnati will be getting in touch with you. You're welcome to the house and everything else, though I suspect most everything will wind up being confiscated by the court once my company figures out about the missing funds."

"You've stolen money from the insurance company?" She acted quite shocked.

"How do you think I've been paying for all those fancy clothes of yours, the second car and this trip?"

"You can't just run away and leave me facing all of those problems." Lenora was quite adamant.

"Hanna is gone, so there's no further need for me to be around to help care for her, and you and I have been washed up for several years, except as your meal ticket."

"You're running away with that French hussy, Simone, aren't you? I've seen the way you two have been behaving. Look, once we get back home, you'll forget all about her."

"Believe whatever you like Lenora, but in fact I'm headed for Rome, alone." He doubted that she believed that lie, but at least it might throw off the Cincinnati police should they ever actually make an effort to find him in Europe. He'd finished packing both suitcases and was fastening the second one. "Look on the bright side. This story will give your friends something to talk about besides the divorce case involving Hanna."

Lenora remained silent.

He stopped briefly at the room door before exiting. "I wish you well my dear. Perhaps your jewelry will tide you over for a while, but you're no longer my problem."

Several other cruise passengers saw Tom pass through the lobby with two suitcases, though he didn't stop to speak to anyone. Simone was already outside in a taxi, waiting for him. The driver took his bags. He entered the back seat and in a moment, they were gone.

She was the first to speak. "I know this is difficult, but you'll be much happier once we arrive in Paris in a few days."

He took her hand. "I know this is best, but it's hard being so unsure about the future. The last time I spoke French was my freshman year in Bloomington."

"It will come quickly to you and you'll make an excellent greeter and manager at my nightclub. And most importantly, we shall be together. We both made a mistake back in 1924 by going our separate ways without telling the other how we really felt. I'm not going to make that mistake again."

"What you just said about 1924, and now, is absolutely true. I'm simply not as sure as you are about my being a great asset for your club, but I do agree with you about the importance of our being together. I just hope the French police don't come to arrest me someday and ship me back to Ohio to stand trial for embezzlement."

She smiled. "I think the French police have better things to do than look for Tom Bishop of Cincinnati. Not that there will be any Tom Bishop in Paris. We'll get you a new passport once we're back in Paris. Be thinking about what name you'd like to use in the future."

Maurice Garnier had just been getting out of a taxi as Tom with suitcases was getting into the one with Simone.

He smiled and mentally wished them well. He decided that he wouldn't even mention that intriguing, but minor event in his final report to the Soviet Security Service when he got back to France. He'd learned nothing specific about who might have been a British agent among the passengers, but he'd had a very pleasant vacation at the NKVD's expense. Building a new world socialist order cost money.

When Arthur and Jan entered the dining room at 7:00 p.m. most all of the Indiana crowd were there for dinner as well. Arthur couldn't decide whether Mike had blabbed to others and everybody wanted to see him and Jan one last time, or people just didn't want to go out anywhere for dinner at the end of a long journey. He noticed that they were missing Lenora and Tom Bishop and also Simone.

In fact, Mike had not told anyone of his conversation earlier that day with Arthur, but many had concluded on their own that Jan was seriously ill, though much of the conversation at the dinner tables was about the Bishops. Word had spread quickly about people seeing first Simone, then shortly thereafter, Tom, passing through the lobby with their suitcases. Maurice confirmed everyone's speculation once he'd told the others about seeing the two of them depart in the same taxi cab.

Simone had left a note at the front desk for Jan, telling her how much she'd enjoyed seeing her and Arthur after all those years. Simone also believed that Jan was quite ill, but stuck with the pretense of "just a cold" and told Jan that she hoped to see the two of them in Paris in the future. She also told Jan about Tom going with her to France, but Jan and

Arthur kept that secret to themselves – not that it was much of a secret by halfway through the dinner.

Towards the end of dinner, two others of the Indiana crowd, Alex and Kate, stopped by Arthur's table and Alex brought up the question of the cruise home in two days' time. "What time do you think we should head down to the pier on Thursday?" he casually inquired of Arthur.

"I haven't really given it much thought, Alex. Jan and I have decided to stay on here in Greece for a few weeks and catch a later ship for America."

Jan chimed in, "No reason to rush back to the cold and snow of a Chicago winter."

"No, certainly not," he mumbled. "You two should stay here and soak up the sun on a Greek beach. I wish I could do that, but I have to be back at work in Virginia in ten days' time. Well, if I don't see you two before we depart, I just want to say what a great trip this has been. You did a wonderful job organizing this reunion."

Arthur smiled. "Yes, it's been a memorable trip."

Alex and Kate moved on. Jan reached over and gave her husband's hand a quick squeeze. She turned to Mary Beth. "What about you, Mary Beth? When are you headed for home?"

"Actually, I have to fly out tomorrow. I received a telegram from my publisher today. There's a great opportunity for me and I need to get to London immediately to discuss it with a British publishing firm." She hoped her little white lie sounded convincing.

There was also conversation during dinner among some of the ladies as to how five of them had not been able to find certain rings, earrings and necklaces after their last night on the ship. Several possibilities had been discussed, but the Pembroke pair was at the top of the list, as all the ladies remembered how interested young Elizabeth had been in everyone's jewelry. Then Mike Taffe commented about the father-daughter pair's very early departure from the ship in Budapest. Most all agreed that whomever had been the thief, there was little chance of recovering any pieces now that they were all off in Greece and the culprit could be almost anywhere in Europe.

As the gang was finishing their desserts, Taffe tapped on his crystal water glass to get the attention of his old classmates and their spouses. "Old friends, despite a few setbacks, this has been a tremendous journey together. Arthur has done an outstanding job arranging this and I'll let you all in on a little secret. Arthur has already started planning a similar cruise for all of us for New Year's Eve of 1939 – down to Rio de Janeiro! So start practicing your Portuguese." Everyone cheered and applauded, pretending that they believed that such a trip with Jan Smith would actually occur. The dinner gathering went on quite late. The Indiana alumni crowd consumed many bottles of champagne. With each glass, they came closer and closer to it once again being 1924. No one wanted to be the first to leave and end the magic spell that had settled upon them. They were all twenty-one again and had nothing but good years ahead of them.

Arthur and Jan slept late the following morning. After they awoke, they laid there talking. "Do you think things will work out for Tom and Simone?" asked Jan.

"I hope so," replied her yawning and still half asleep husband. "They're both very nice people and deserve to be happy."

"Yes they do." Jan forced herself to look at the clock and when seeing that it was almost ten, decided it was time to rise and start the day. Arthur was perfectly happy remaining horizontal. After washing her face, Jan walked over to her dressing table.

"Oh my god," she exclaimed. "I don't believe it."

Arthur sat up quickly "What is it? What's wrong?"

She came over to the bed and held up the emerald earrings and matching pendant that she hadn't been able to find since Budapest. "There's a note with them. 'I couldn't remove this jewelry from such a charming woman.' The thief on the ship has returned my jewelry!"

Arthur smiled. "That clinches it for me. It had to be that British fellow, Miles. You remember he wasn't at the farewell dinner the last night on the ship. And he's also the only person among the passengers or crew who's that gallant."

She put on the jewelry, then crawled back into bed and snuggled up next to her husband. "Oh, I don't know. You're handsome and dashing enough to be an international jewel thief."

Tristan met Mary Beth and Holger at Aristotle's as planned at eleven o'clock. Tristan simply pulled up in his Embassy vehicle, waved for the two to join him and off they drove. There was a second British car right behind them. During the drive to the airport, he handed them British passports in the names of Jane and Nigel Smythe, airline tickets in those names and an envelope containing two hundred English Pound Sterling notes. The tickets would take them to Lisbon via Rome, from which on the following day, they would fly directly to London.

"Give me your current passports. I'll send them along in the diplomatic pouch tomorrow to London. My colleague, a Mr. Winslow, will meet you at the airport in Lisbon and take care of everything for you."

"So, your Government has agreed to my political asylum in England?" asked Holger.

"Well, they've agreed for the moment to bring you to London, with the assurance that you will be well taken care of in the future. The decision on exactly where that will be is still being sorted out."

That wasn't quite the firm answer Holger had hoped for, but at least he would soon be on the soil of the United Kingdom. He looked at his new passport and noticed that it expired in ten days' time. He smiled and concluded that the MI-6 people only trusted him so far.

Once at the airport, six rough-looking, Greek longshoremen were waiting for Tristan's arrival. Tristan, Mr. and Mrs. Smythe and the six Greeks headed for the check-in counter. The passports and tickets were handed over to the clerk, along with Holger's one small bag. Timmons had already delivered Mary Beth's two suitcases.

Boarding passes in hand, they had just started for Gate No. 3 when two uniformed German Army officers came up to Holger and started speaking to him in German. Tristan didn't understand German, but he could see that there was clearly a question as to exactly where Holger thought he was going. Tristan waved his hand in the air and the six burly longshoreman stepped forward to surround the two German officers. Accompanied by much shouting and pushing, they were quickly shoved into a nearby Men's lavatory, in a scene reminiscent of a Marx Brother's movie.

"Let's continue on to your Boarding Gate, shall we," said Tristan in a calm voice. "Oh, don't worry, the two Germans will be released in a few hours down by the docks, outside one of the more tawdry brothels for seamen. They will be drunk and their uniforms doused in alcohol and cheap perfume. They can choose to explain to their superiors or the Greek police whatever story they like."

Mary Beth smiled. She liked Tristan more and more. Timmons remained close by the three until it was time to walk out to the plane. Mary Beth leaned in and gave Tristan a big kiss just before departing, which actually made him blush. He was glad that Holger settled for a formal handshake to make his farewell. Tristan and Timmons remained at the gate until the plane was well into the air and safely on its way to Rome.

Late that same day, the two landed in Lisbon and were met at the Arrival's Gate by Mr. Winslow. He also had several tough-looking "friends" with him, just in case. Officially, Portugal was claiming to be neutral in the growing European controversy, but Germany had many friends in the country, so Winslow was taking no chances.

"Welcome to Lisbon, Mr. and Mrs. Smythe."

CHAPTER 16
Lisbon

Winslow put Mary Beth and Holger in a very nice pousada several miles outside of Lisbon, in the direction of the small, historical town of Sintra, rather than in a downtown hotel. The inn, with its traditional red tile roof was nearly two hundred years old, but in excellent condition. Winslow knew that no German diplomats resided out that way, plus he had the owner on MI-6's payroll to make sure that "guests" he placed there remained safe and undisturbed. The next flight to England would not be for about 36 hours, so the two weary travelers would have a chance to relax a bit after the stresses of the last several days.

Mama Maria, the middle-aged wife of the owner, looked as if she'd been plucked off a tourist poster as to how a Portuguese peasant woman should look and dress. Between her hundred words of English and her multi-lingual hand gestures, she could communicate with her two special guests just fine. Most importantly, she was a wonderful cook and the two had her full attention as they were the only residents — January being well outside of the normal tourist season. The main dish on their first evening there was frango piri piri, a traditional fare of roasted chicken coated with the zesty African spice of piri piri. They both thought it was delicious, especially when washed down with a good Portuguese white wine. The two weary travelers suspected this might be the last opportunity they would have for a private dinner and conversation and they lingered late into the evening over their coffees.

"Well, Holger, this has been quite a journey. I'm not sure that just saying 'thank you' is adequate for a man who literally saved my life."

Holger was embarrassed. "I only did what needed to be done. You have been very brave all through your journey. Let's hope that General Breithaupt's death will have been worthwhile. Surely, being forewarned, the British Government will now be able to prevent Hitler's conquest of Czechoslovakia, which will hopefully start the collapse of Hitler's rule. The German people suffered enough in the Great War and we don't need another one."

"I don't think anybody in Europe wants another war. Hopefully, what the General, you, me and Arthur Smith have done to make this operation a success will be able to preserve the peace."

"General Breithaupt and I are soldiers. What we did was a professional duty. You are a civilian and yet you were very brave and carried out your assignment as well as any professionally trained British or German spy could have done."

Mary Beth almost blushed. "Well, thank you. While I have a chance, I would like to ask you, what made you change your mind that night in Munich? You were investigating him and had you found me meeting him, you would have simply arrested us both wouldn't you?"

"Probably. As for changing my mind while talking with the General that night, it's rather complicated. My mother had always told me as a young boy that you can't be called 'good' if you just sit by and do nothing while others are doing evil around you. So my measuring stick for what was the right thing to do had always been — what if I had to explain my actions to my mother? I'd forgotten that rule for many years when I'd been very hungry back in the 1920s. Getting to know about the General and then actually talking with him that night brought it back to mind. I'd been growing evermore upset at what the Gestapo had been doing to innocent German citizens, but it was that twenty-minute conversation with Breithaupt in the snow on Christmas Eve that really changed my mind. The General told me he didn't know if only one man could make a difference, but he felt that he had to try."

Mary Beth nodded that she understood what he meant.

"Now my turn," began Holger. "Why did you undertake this dangerous mission?"

"When the British MI-6 first proposed the operation, I took several days to think it over. While I was considering what to do, I recalled something I'd learned back at the University, in a class on Roman history. There'd been a Roman leader who'd said that one should always act in the interest of the common good. I guess that Cicero fellow and your mother had pretty much the same idea."

Holger laughed at the thought of his mother being

compared to an ancient Roman philosopher. "I'm not sure if we'll see each other much, if ever again, once we reach London, but I wish you a successful and peaceful life." He then fell into silence for several long seconds as he stared at her. "I must get hold of your books and read about this remarkable Riley the Rabbit."

Mary Beth laughed. "I'll see if I can find a few of my books in London, autograph them and get MI-6 to deliver them to you, as a fond remembrance of our days together. In fact, I'll do better than that. In my next novel, I'm going to introduce a new character named Holger. He will be a good friend of Riley's."

Now it was Holger's turn to blush, hearing of such an honor to be bestowed upon him.

Mary Beth picked up her wine glass, as did Holger. "To us, to rabbits and a peaceful 1939."

There was a long goodnight embrace between them – a farewell gesture between two people who'd played a dangerous game of international espionage, in which losers lost their lives. Only a handful of people ever played that game. They would have that special bond between them forever.

As she lay in her bed that night, she began thinking again about her completed mission. One of the hardest things of the whole trip had been not being able to talk to anyone about it, until that night on the top deck with Holger after she'd shot Blickensdorfer. When there was no one at the meeting location on Christmas Eve, she didn't know what to do next and would have loved to have been able to discuss her dilemma with someone, but she couldn't. She was confused by the presence of Gestapo officers on the ship, since to her knowledge, nothing had happened. What were they investigating? Again, there had been no one to whom she could turn and discuss the situation. She decided that she wasn't really cut out for the espionage game and she was glad that her first and last mission was nearly to an end. She did feel proud of her small role in getting such important information to London – and helping prevent a war. She'd always have that pride, but she would never be able to discuss her mission with anyone. Once she'd been debriefed in London and returned to America, it would be her secret alone for the rest of her life.

She concluded that the ability to feel satisfaction for a successful espionage job simply from within was the most important personal trait required of a good spy. As she thought back through history, "heroes" generally got public accolade. But clearly there was another category of hero – the spy who achieved his task and only a handful of people would ever know what he or she had even done. She was truly looking forward to getting back to her simpler world of writing children's books!

They had the entire next day to relax. Winslow picked them up mid-morning on the following day and took them to the airport. It was a B.O.A.C flight and as a British diplomat he was allowed to drive them directly to plane side where they boarded the plane.

The engines roared and the wheels of the plane turned. A minute later, they were airborne and headed for London. They were on the last leg of their long journey. Mary Beth felt as if she was finally nearing the end of a long, dark tunnel.

London

Upon arrival in London at Croydon Airport, two cars and four men from MI-6 awaited them. As soon as they came down the ramp, they were separated from the other passengers and were immediately whisked away to separate safe houses. The two would never see each other again.

Mary Beth's "handler" was Ian, a charming gentleman from Edinburgh in his early fifties who spoke with a thick Scottish accent. He drove her to the nondescript, but nice flat somewhere in central London to which she'd been assigned. The flat had two bedrooms; one for her and one for the housekeeper who was always available. Ian gave her a few hours to unpack and rest and then they dined alone on an excellent meal prepared by the housekeeper.

He began with questions about her own background, but soon worked his way onto the topic of the cruise. She noticed that he made no notes, so she assumed that there was a hidden microphone and some sort of recording device, or others were listening elsewhere in the dwelling. She went into great detail for Ian about all the events from the time she first got to Paris and joined up with the tour group, until the plane door closed in Lisbon. She particularly emphasized the steps Holger had taken to save her life, in hopes of assuring that he would be treated well by MI-6. She mentioned twice how valuable it would be for Ian to speak directly with Holger, so as to get the background on the General, in case there were any doubts about Breithaupt's motivations or his information. He told her that colleagues were debriefing Holger at another location.

It was almost ten o'clock before Ian brought the session to a close. He looked at his watch, then said, "Well, it's been a long day for you and I'm sure you'd like to get some sleep."

She'd been yawning for the last half hour. "Yes, I think I could use some rest."

"You go to bed and get some sleep. I'll get my notes prepared and in the morning we'll chat further. Perhaps, during the night, some other details will come to your mind."

She doubted if there could possibly be a single fact she hadn't already mentioned, but quickly agreed with him so she could get off to bed and sleep.

It took several firm knocks on her bedroom door by the housekeeper to get Mary Beth awake in the morning. She had fallen asleep almost as soon as her head had touched the pillow the night before. She hadn't realized just how physically and mentally tired she really was after the several days of stress she'd experienced since leaving the ship early that morning in Budapest. While showering, she was glad that Ian had pushed her so hard the first evening to tell her entire story. Already, parts of it were beginning to seem like a dream, which couldn't have happened to her. Had she really killed Colonel Blickensdorfer, seen the death of Karen before her eyes, and finally reached London safely with a secret letter?

Once out to the breakfast table and having drank several cups of strong, black coffee she was starting to feel awake. Ian arrived just after 9:00 a.m.

"Good morning, Mary Beth. Did you sleep well?" he asked with cheerful smile and his lovely accent.

"Yes, I definitely needed a long sleep."

"I thought you might. I would have let you sleep longer, but you have a visitor arriving here shortly to speak with you and I needed you bright eyes and bushy tail, as you would say in one of your children's books."

"More questions?"

"In a way, but also to thank you. It's the Director of MI-6 who's coming to see you in about fifteen minutes. A chap we generally just refer to as 'C'; a bit silly as everyone knows his real name, but upon rising to that position, a person becomes a letter of the alphabet." He laughed and Mary Beth smiled. "It all started back with the first director, Captain Sir Mansfield Smith-Cummings, who would always sign correspondence with just a large C, and it became a tradition that our director is simply referred to as C. And you know how the English love their traditions. Anyway, he's quite a pleasant chap and he wanted to drop by and thank you personally for all you've done for us."

For one of the few times in her life, Mary Beth was speechless.

Ian checked his watch. "He'll be here in just a few minutes, if you'd like to check your make-up or whatever it is you ladies like to do." Again, his lovely smile.

"Yes, I would." As she rose to leave the room, she found herself thinking about how each MI-6 officer she'd met so far had a lovely smile and decided that it must be a requirement for the job.

Ian and Mary Beth were still drinking coffee at the dining table when C arrived a few minutes later.

"Good morning, Mary Beth. I hope my people are taking good care of you?"

"Oh, yes, everything is first-rate." She couldn't bring herself to call him by a letter of the alphabet, so she opted for not calling him anything.

Ian poured C a cup of coffee and he joined them at the table.

"Well, I just wanted to swing by and thank you personally for all you've done for us over the past couple of weeks. I've read Ian's report and I know what a challenging ordeal you've had. You performed magnificently."

"Thank you, but I wouldn't be here today and you wouldn't have General Breithaupt's report if it wasn't for the assistance that Lt. Hinz provided me." She thought she'd make one last plug for her anxious partner in espionage.

C smiled. "Don't worry, my dear. We appreciate his role and we're going to take care of Holger. As I said, I've read the General's letter and Ian's report and I have but one question of my own for you, if I may."

"Certainly, ask anything you wish."

"My question is about your impression of Holger Hinz, you're feminine intuition if I may call it that. You never personally met General Breithaupt, but you spent many days around Holger. In my business, sometimes one country will try to deceive another with some fanciful story. Is there any doubt at all in your mind that Hinz is exactly who he claims to be and that his story about the

General and his letter are exactly as he described them to you?"

"None whatsoever. As you possibly know, I write children's stories and his interactions with me, never mind his killing a woman on my behalf, were genuine. No one is that good an actor."

C smiled. "Excellent, that's as good an answer as there could be. I'm seeing our Prime Minister this afternoon about all of this and I just wanted to be able to tell him that I'd met you myself and asked you face-to-face if you had any reservations whatsoever about this amazing story."

They both just sat and stared at each other in silence. Mary Beth could think of nothing to say to further express her confidence in Holger or the General's letter.

C finished the last of his coffee. "Very good. I'll be off then, but I believe that Ian here has some good news for you concerning your father-in-law."

He stood, shook her hand, and he was gone. He'd simply wanted to see for himself that Mary Beth wasn't some flighty female given to a vivid imagination.

Mary Beth turned to Ian for her news.

"Yes, Nigel arrived by steamer yesterday at Southampton in anticipation of your safe arrival to London about this time. He'll be coming here to have lunch with you today."

Mary Beth smiled brightly. "That is good news. As you know, he's the one who talked me into this journey, so I can understand that he wanted to be here to welcome me back. We've stayed quite close since my husband's death."

"Yes, I know. You might also like to know how long

we're going to hold you prisoner in this horrible dungeon…"
He laughed. "I believe that once C has his meeting with
Prime Minister Chamberlain this afternoon, if there aren't
any follow-up questions that you could assist with, you'll
be free to be on your way. Do you have any specific plans
while here in London or will you be returning immediately
to America?

"You know, I hadn't really planned that far ahead.
I know my publisher would like me back quite soon, as I
have my latest book to put the finishing touches on, but I'll
see what Nigel might have in mind. Perhaps he and I could
sail back together to America."

"Very well. I know you've been to London before,
but if there's anything in particular that you'd like to see
while you're here, do let us know. We have some influence
about the city," he added with a perfectly straight face.

"There is one thing you might be able to assist me
with – I need to find a bookstore and pick up a few of my
children's books with Riley the Rabbit. I promised Holger
that if I could find any here in London, I would sign them for
him. I presume you can handle getting them to him wherever
he's staying."

"I can take care of both of those tasks for you. My
granddaughter is a big fan of Riley and your stories, so I
know where I can get at least a couple of them. You can sign
them this evening and Holger will get them by tomorrow
morning. Oh, don't address them to 'Holger', as he may not
be using that name in the future."

"That would be wonderful." A smile came to her

face as she remembered Mikaela LeBlanc's tarot reading and bringing up the importance of a rabbit in her life.

Ian wondered what she was thinking about that had produced her slight smile, but he left her to her private thoughts.

C entered Prime Minister Neville Chamberlain's office promptly at two o'clock. C didn't think much of the man as a politician, but did concede that he was always punctual.

"Good afternoon, Prime Minister."

They shook hands. Chamberlain pointed at a chair.

"I've read your overall report and the translation of this General Breithaupt's letter – quite a story."

"Yes, it is and I've also met this morning with the extraordinary American woman, who managed to bring the letter out. I wanted to personally ask her if she had any doubts, any 'feminine intuition', that any of this story is anything other than as reported. She told me that she has no doubts whatsoever."

"I must say that I was quite shocked by your report. The man just gave me his word barely two months ago that the Sudetenland was his last territorial demand." The P.M. sat in silence staring at the report. "Any chance that this is the work of a rival faction to Hitler, trying to discredit him?"

"I suppose that's a possibility, but I don't see how this would gain anything for a rival group."

"And we've heard of this General Breithaupt?"

"Yes, sir. He's a well-known career officer and comes

from a family that has provided senior military personnel to Germany for generations. There was a German newspaper report in Munich last week that he'd just died in a tragic training accident. That would seem to support Lt. Hinz' story as well."

"Yes, it could. Don't suppose you've gotten a collaborating report from anywhere else about this alleged invasion of Czechoslovakia? I know you intelligence chaps are always looking for a second source."

"No, sir, this is the only report we have, though coming as it does from one of the German Army's senior generals, we are inclined to give it a lot of weight."

"Of course, of course." There was another long silence. "Do you think that Hitler is now aware of the actions that General Breithaupt has taken?"

"Yes, between the news of the General's 'accidental' death and the disappearance of Lt. Hinz, after the two deaths on the cruise ship, I think the Germans would have to at least seriously suspect that the news has reached us."

A brighter face came to Chamberlain. "Well, in that case, surely Hitler would postpone any planned invasion by many months, or drop the plan entirely – knowing that we are now aware of his plans."

"I suppose that is a possibility Prime Minister."

"Well, thank you very much for this interesting report. Do let me know immediately if you receive any corroborating intelligence to support this allegation."

"Yes, sir."

"I don't doubt the American woman is reporting truthfully what she knows, but I was just wondering whether this whole story might just be a clever ploy by this Lt. Hinz to get himself out of Germany and acquire a packet of money to start a new life elsewhere?"

C simply remained silent as it was generally considered bad form to tell a Prime Minister his statement was ridiculous.

"Well, thank you for personally stopping by, C. We'll be in touch if anything else develops."

"Thank you for your time, Prime Minister." As C left the room, he concluded that the gutless wonder leading the country had no intention of doing anything whatsoever with the intelligence. A second corroborating source? Perhaps when 50,000 German soldiers march across the bloody border, he'll consider that a corroborating source for the "allegation!"

C's senior staff was anxiously awaiting him upon his return to MI-6 Headquarters to hear of the Prime Minister's reaction. He called together all who had played some role in the operation and gave them the bad news.

"Prime Minister Chamberlain intends to do absolutely nothing with our report. He inquired if we had a corroborating second source, wondered if this was a ploy by a rival faction to discredit Hitler, and asked if perhaps Lt. Hinz had simply made up the whole story just to get out of Germany with some money. And he was shocked, shocked mind you, at the idea of an alleged invasion plan, seeing as how Hitler had personally given him his word that Sudetenland was his last territorial demand! The bloody fool."

The six others in the room remained silent while shaking their heads in disbelief.

"Oh, and his final bit of logic was that if the allegation of a planned attack for March had even been true, now that Hitler knows that perhaps we've learned the date, he'll postpone or cancel the attack entirely."

C's deputy finally spoke. "Well, this isn't the first time in history that a political leader has ignored unpleasant intelligence, is it sir?"

"No, sadly it isn't. Well, there isn't much we can do about Chamberlain's lack of a spine, but we can start preparing for a war, and war it shall soon be, as sure as we're sitting here. Churchill's comment three months ago to Chamberlain was spot on when he told him, 'You were given the choice between war and dishonour. You chose dishonour, and you will have war.' So, let's start preparing for war."

Mary Beth had a wonderful afternoon with Nigel, retelling him in detail about her adventure. They dined that evening at one of the finest restaurants in London. When she returned to the safehouse, she found two of her books laying on the dining table, waiting for her to autograph. As she drifted off to sleep that night she had a dream of being awarded an OBE, or whatever medal can be given to a foreigner. The following evening, they went to the West End to see a hit comedy titled *Spring Meeting* and the following day she received a private guided tour of the British Museum. However, after the fourth day of playing tourist, she asked if Ian could come round to see her.

"I trust you're enjoying London, Miss Long," began

Ian after they'd both been served tea and scones by the house keeper.

"I've had a wonderful time, but I was wondering what was happening with General Breithaupt's report. I believe C was to have met with the Prime Minister four days ago. I know I'm not entitled to state secrets, but I am naturally curious as what actions will be taken with this news that I brought out of Germany."

"Rest assured Miss Long that the Prime Minister took your warning quite seriously and MI-6 is diligently at work trying to confirm General Breithaupt's information." He continued for over a minute with further blah, blah, blah. Mary Beth knew BS when she heard it.

"I presume that no one at MI-6 has any further questions for me?"

"Nothing at this time, no, Miss Long. You have been quite thorough in your retelling of events on your journey."

"Good, as I would like to sail for New York City as soon as possible. I need to get on with my life. Should I contact the shipping lines myself, or would MI-6 possibly have some influence, given such short notice?"

Ian smiled politely. "Why don't you let me take care of those arrangements for you. I'm sure we can arrange a very nice accommodation, and at the British Government's expense – it's the least we can do for you after your excellent service for England. I'll phone you this afternoon with specifics."

"Thank you Ian. You have been most kind. Oh, one last question, if I may. What has happened with Holger?"

"He's still undergoing debriefing, which will continue

for another few days, but don't worry, he will be well taken care of once his debriefing is completed."

Now it was Mary Beth's turn to smile. "Ian, you have the wonderful ability to speak at length, but not actually say anything. What decision has been reached on his request for political asylum here in England?"

He finished his last sip of tea. "Well, you didn't hear this from me, but he's being given a new name and a new passport. However, the upper levels have decided that they didn't really want a former Gestapo man wandering around England. He will be given two thousand pounds and a ticket to sail to Rio de Janeiro in about a week or so, so as to start a new life in South America. He should do just fine to start a new life with that much money in his pocket."

Mary Beth wasn't sure whether to even believe Ian's story, but it certainly wasn't what Holger had requested. "Well, thank you for sharing that with me. I don't know if we'll see each other again, but thank you for your kindness while I've been your guest."

"And all the best to you Miss Long." Again, that great smile.

Mary Beth and Nigel had a farewell dinner that evening. She informed him of her decision to return immediately to America and that Ian had even managed to arrange a small suite for her on the Queen Mary, which was sailing the following afternoon. He needed to stay on in London for several more days and so, unfortunately, he couldn't sail with her back to America.

"I asked Ian this morning what's happening with the intelligence that Holger and I brought back from General

Breithaupt. He gave me a lot of words, but it sounded like a classic run-around when in fact, nothing at all is being done with it. Do you know anything I don't?"

Nigel smiled. "I've known you too long and too well to bother trying to deceive you." He paused for several long seconds. "No, Prime Minister Chamberlain has no intention of doing anything with your intelligence. Our Service is gearing up for war with Germany, so in that sense Breithaupt's report served some function – but as for his desire to prevent a war, I'm afraid not."

"General Breithaupt is dead, two innocent people on the cruise were probably murdered, I had to kill a man and Holger killed a woman, and nothing is to be done! What was the point?" She shook her head in disgust.

"Intelligence is intelligence and politics is politics," he vaguely replied.

"What the devil does that mean?"

"It means that sometimes what should be done, doesn't get done, regardless of what good information has been gathered. Chamberlain is a coward, but frankly the British people don't want another war. They don't care what Hitler does in places like Czechoslovakia, as long as they don't get dragged into fighting. I know that seems short-sighted, but there is hardly a person on this island who didn't lose a family member or friend in the Great War. The people just don't want to face the reality that another great war is coming."

Mary Beth shook her head in amazement. "Let's just change subjects. It's been wonderful spending time with you."

"Indeed, it has. Shall we have some dessert?"

Athens

Arthur and Jan were having wonderful days at their secluded bungalow, which sat on a rock precipice a mere fifty feet from the beach and about twenty feet above sea level. They could indeed hear the tide rolling in and out and the sound of seagulls circling above. The weather had been perfect, warm and sunny during the day and then a few lazy, white clouds drifting in around dusk. They'd sit out on the deck of their bungalow and watch the sun slowly sink into the ocean. They had two local ladies who would prepare breakfast and dinner for them. They would go away for the middle of the day, so that the two had all the privacy they wanted. Both had written several letters to old friends and relatives back in America, and they'd spent many hours recounting previous pleasurable events in their lives. The greatest had been finding each other at that Army dance many years earlier, which had led to all else. Arthur brought up the theme that he and Miles had discussed back on the ship – that one's life should be measured in the quality of good times, not simply the number of years passed. Jan agreed totally.

Jan was clearly experiencing more pain each day. At the end of a lovely breakfast on the fifth morning, she took Arthur's hand on the table and gave it a weak squeeze. "I think today is the day, dear."

Arthur simply nodded. He rose and went to the kitchen, just in time to catch Cassia before she left.

"We won't need you and Anna until tomorrow morning. I'm going to cook dinner this evening."

"Very well, we'll see you tomorrow." She gave Arthur a wide smile, a wave and then she was off.

He went over to the telephone and placed a call to the Hotel Grand Bretagne and left a simple message for Mr. Taffe. "Today is the day." Arthur took care of leaving two envelopes full of money on the kitchen table for Cassia and Anna, who'd been wonderful cooks and shoppers for them over the past five days.

Per their prior agreement, there was to be no big ceremony. Once she'd told him that it was time, he was to just quietly put their pills in their drinks at some point that day. The two of them took a nice walk down along the beach in late morning and after showering, Arthur even did his best to give Jan a massage. She'd truly been missing Inga's massages.

Arthur fixed them a little snack for a late lunch and then they settled into two comfortable chairs side-by-side out on the balcony. Arthur had brought with them three very good and very expensive French white wines, which they sat and drank slowly through the afternoon.

"How do you think Bob, Inga and Kinley are doing in England?" asked Jan. "That was such a whirlwind romance!"

"I suspect they're doing just fine. From my chat with Bob that afternoon after the visit to the old brewery, I could tell he was truly in love with her. He was just afraid to take action."

Jan grinned. "Yes, when you know it's right, you know pretty quick don't you?"

"We certainly did." He reached over and took her hand.

"And what about Tom and Simone up in Paris?"

"Well, that one I'm not as sure about, but I think he definitely needed to move on from Lenora. Hopefully, their love will also blossom. It's a shame they lost fifteen years after the last year at school simply because neither could bring themselves to tell the other how much they loved the other."

"And what happened with Hanna? Do you think she really just ran off on her own?"

"Nonsense. You don't have to be a clever detective to figure out that Stefan leaving the ship in Budapest and Hanna running away the same day wasn't a coincidence!"

"How do you know that?" she asked.

"The Captain told me that when I bumped into him at our hotel that last morning in Budapest."

"Alright, clever man, just what was going on during that whole cruise? We had four deaths. Two supposedly accidents, but the last two clearly murders. And several people wanting to know who'd been doing what on Christmas Eve in Munich. Then that strange incident when Mary Beth wanted to leave the ship the last morning as early as possible. Half of our friends still think you were drunk or crazy, going around at one in the morning, waking them up and telling them to be at breakfast at 7:00 a.m."

Arthur laughed. "Yes, I suppose that was a little odd. Clearly, Mary Beth was tied in somehow with the Gestapo fellow, but god knows how. Hard to think of a writer of children's books as a spy, but who knows. No longer our concern, dear."

"No, not our concern."

"And despite all of the problems, I'd still say it was a pretty good last voyage."

"Yes dear, a pretty good voyage."

As the sun was dropping nearer the sea, Jan started to feel a little drowsy, though whether it was the wine or the pills, she wasn't sure. "Any last minute regrets?" she asked.

"None at all. If you were going to be around, it would be a different situation, but to tell you the truth there's a new era coming, and I don't think I'll like it. First, barring some miracle, there's a major war coming and all the death, pain and destruction that will come with it. And after this next war, I fear the new world will be a very different place. There will be no more elegant, leisurely Danube cruises for men in tuxedos and ladies in gowns. Our era is simply ending and a new one is soon coming, a faster-paced one, wherein there will be continual struggling and fighting around the world. I'm a slow-paced fellow." He looked directly at her and smiled.

"I thought you were the new Sam Spade?"

"Oh, that was just for one evening. What about you? Care to offer any sort of overall assessment of our lives?"

"Oh, there's such a long list of your shortcomings, but I don't want to get in to those issues now." They both laughed. "But seriously, other than losing our daughter, I think we've had a life that most people would envy."

"Yes, I'd say we've done alright."

"Kelsey is going to be livid with you when she hears what's happened."

Arthur smiled. "I know, but I did send her a post card from every city we visited on the trip as I promised, even from Athens. Besides, she'll have Nick there to console her."

Jan's turn to smile, at his matchmaking efforts on Kelsey's behalf. "She is a beautiful girl. At the bank's 4th of July picnic last summer, several of the other wives asked me if I wasn't a little worried about you having the loveliest secretary on the entire fifth floor!"

Arthur laughed out loud. "And what did you tell them, my dear?"

"I told them I wished you would have a wild affair with a young girl, then you wouldn't be so amorous all the time at home – that it was wearing me out."

He started to say, "You told them what!", but then he realized that she was just teasing him and he laughed.

The sun touched the sea shortly after five o'clock, just as it had each previous day and the water glistened like diamonds. Both of them were feeling drowsier as they listened to the waves roll gently in and out. They were just sitting silently, still holding hands, as the last glimmer of the sun sank beneath the water. There was really nothing significant left to say between them; the last thing Jan heard was Arthur saying, "I love you."

CHAPTER 17
America

Within a week of sailing from England, Mary Beth was back home in Portsmouth, New Hampshire. By the end of January, she'd finished the current porno novel and hand delivered it to her publisher down in New York City. She wouldn't trust the Postal Service with such sordid material. She'd rewritten the novel a bit and made all the events happen on a ship. She titled it *Lust on the High Seas,* as an odd sort of tribute to all her fellow passengers on the *Danube Princessa.* She spent half of the money she received for the story on a few new clothes and a couple of days of fun in Manhattan.

She managed to track down Mike Taffe and had lunch with him one afternoon at the famous Sardi's restaurant, where actors, celebrities and celebrity-watchers dined.

"Nice to see you again, Mike."

"And you as well. Have you ever been here before?" he asked as the head waiter showed them to a table towards the back.

"No, I've heard of it of course, but never been here."

After they were seated, he continued, "You'll notice that we're seated at a table fairly towards the back."

She nodded in agreement. "Yes, a very nice table."

He laughed. "Well, they do vaguely know me, but I'm not considered famous in any sense and that's why we're back here."

"I don't understand. It's a nice table, back here where it's quiet."

"Ah, well, you see, celebrities come here to be seen and thus are given prominent places at tables in the center towards the front, depending on their ranking. The tourists are sat at those tables with their backs to the walls on the sides."

She laughed. "Oh, I see." She looked around. She lowered her voice. "I hate to sound like a tourist, but is that Eddie Cantor over there?"

"Yes, I believe it is. And up there on the right is Robert Taylor."

"My, don't you dine with the upper class!"

"Well, I'm not an A-list customer, but the waiters have seen me in here enough with various Broadway stage stars that they figure I must be somebody."

They brought each other up to date on what they'd been up to since the cruise ended, at least the part Mary Beth could talk about.

"Hey, I got a letter from Bob Hall last week. He, Inga and Kinley are settled into England, at least for a few more weeks, then they head to California."

"So, they got all the needed paperwork done in Budapest?" asked Mary Beth.

"Apparently so. Bob said that all three are happy and

that the Director of the film even liked the new ending he came up with while on the cruise."

"Did he say what that was?"

"No, guess we'll just have to go see the movie this summer."

"Any word about Simone and Tom?"

"Yes, I had a musician friend of mine reach out to an acquaintance of his in Paris, who went round to Simone's nightclub, and he wrote me that all seemed fine. He said that Simone was singing and sounding great, but that there was no Tom Bishop around as far as he could tell."

Mary Beth's smile disappeared. "Oh, that's too bad. I thought that those two would be together forever."

Mike grinned. "Well, he did write that there's some middle-aged American named Charlie Earle, who's the new manager at her place and dating Simone, and whose physical description sounded a lot like Tom's."

Simone laughed. "Wasn't Charlie Earle the head bartender at that English pub on Kirkwood when we were students in Bloomington? I hadn't heard that he'd moved to Paris!"

Mike smiled. "Well, I doubt if the Cincinnati Police are searching for Charlie Earle."

"Probably not. I'm just glad that it's working out for Simone."

They put in their food order and then Mike turned to a sadder subject.

"I suspect you heard about Arthur and Jan?" he asked.

"Yes, I heard second hand that they'd both died on some beach near Athens, but no specifics."

"Well, Fanny and I were still in Athens when it happened. In fact, Arthur had spoken to me about what was coming when we were all still at the Grand Bretagne – and arranged with me that I'd take care of a few things for them after they were dead."

"Oh my god, so it was planned? I mean, I suspected that Jan was very ill, but you mean it was suicide by both of them?"

Mike nodded yes and paused for a moment. "Jan was in fact terminally ill and I guess Arthur just had no desire to go on without her." There was a long silence between them. "Well, there are worse ways to go than drinking fine wine with the one you love on a Mediterranean beach."

Mary Beth raised her wine glass, as did Mike. "To Arthur and Jan!"

"Yeah, chalk up another one to Miss LeBlanc."

"Well, your news is a shock, but not a surprise. You could tell that those two were just so devoted to each other."

Mary Beth started to laugh. Mike gave her a strange look, wondering what was so funny about two people's deaths.

"Sorry, I was just thinking about that police captain's face when Arthur stood up to him in Bratislava. I thought the man was going to have a stroke right there in the Lounge!"

They both laughed.

"Well, he was a real classy guy. Just between you and me, I know that he sent Kinley off with Bob and Inga with a $10,000 'endowment' as he called it.

"Wow, nice gesture. That trip turned out to be a pretty memorable reunion cruise, even though Fred, Arthur and Jan all died. But then Simone and Tom got started on a new life, as did Bob, Inga and Kinley. I recall Captain Ornsdorfer waxing eloquent one day about how the lives of people over the centuries had changed as they sailed down the Danube into the unknown. And I remember his toast that first day on the ship about how it would be the last voyage of 1938. How prophetic – for six people it really was their last voyage."

"A strange trip indeed, but I wouldn't have missed it for the world. Listen, am I the only person who thinks that something very odd was happening on that ship?"

"What do you mean?"

"I mean, Fred fell off a cliff, Ivan got hit by a taxi, Blickensdorfer got shot by a burglar and Karen died mysteriously in her cabin on the last night of the cruise. That's four dead people in the course of a week! I'm not an insurance agent, but the actuarial statistics for that happening out of a group of only sixty people must be unbelievable."

"Well, when you put it like that, it does sound pretty weird, but are you suggesting that those deaths were somehow linked?"

"I don't know what I'm suggesting. I just think that something was afoot on that cruise that most of us didn't know about – and maybe I don't want to know about even at this late date, but there was definitely something secretive going on I'm sure."

Mary Beth shrugged her shoulders. "Who knows? Too complicated for me. I'm just the writer of children's books!" She gave him a smile.

"But didn't you sense there was something going on? Besides the deaths, in the end we learned there were four Gestapo officers on board, supposedly just taking a holiday river cruise! I don't believe it."

"You know Bob also mentioned a similar feeling to me the last day I saw him at the hotel in Budapest. You guys in the entertainment business all have such imaginative minds!" She gave him a big smile and hoped he'd move on to a different subject.

He smiled as well. "Well, I'll be out in Los Angeles in April on business and I'm going to look up Bob and discuss this with him."

Mary Beth ran a finger around the top of her wine glass. "It was interesting to see how all our lives have progressed since 1924. Some have made more money than others, but I guess we've all done reasonably well in that regard. As for 'romance', I guess the record there is a little less clear."

"True, I guess for every Arthur and Jan, there's a Tom and Lenora, but then there's also just bad luck. You lost your husband to a medical problem and Fred lost his wife to a car accident. Nothing's guaranteed in life, is it?"

"No, no guarantees come with that birth certificate." She continued to play with her glass.

"And I hate to sound too pessimistic, but I still think that mess in Europe with Hitler is going to turn real ugly one of these days – and in the end, America will get dragged into another war whether we want to or not."

"I try not to even think about such things. I'm going back to New Hampshire and write another Riley the Rabbit book!"

"That's good. The world will always need such books to talk about the good things in life."

"I suppose. Say, did anybody ever learn anything about who stole the jewelry on the last night on the ship?"

"Nothing official, but my money's on that phony English nobleman, Miles."

Mary Beth smiled. "Well phony and jewel thief or not, he was awfully charming."

"You women! That's exactly what Fanny said about him!"

Mary Beth checked her watch. "I better head on over to the train station. I'm on the 3:20 to Boston this afternoon."

"Hey, whatever happened with that great publishing opportunity that you had in England that you flew off to when we were all leaving Greece?"

"Oh that, well, it turned out to be just big talk. I'm afraid those London-based chaps talked a good game, but they didn't have the you-know-whats when it came to taking action."

He grinned. "Yeah, we have some guys around Broadway who suffer from that same birth defect!"

"It's been wonderful seeing you, Mike. Let me know if you and Fanny would like to come up sometime this winter. We have some decent ski slopes not too far away from my home."

"We just might do that. You have a safe trip back up to Portsmouth."

As the first days of March rolled in, Mary Beth started tuning into the international news in the evenings on her radio. Her house was on a hill and on most days she could get several Boston stations. On the morning of March 16, there was an unconfirmed report that German troops had invaded Czechoslovakia the day before. The British Government announced that it had been taken totally by surprise by this action, in gross violation of the Munich Pact of the previous September.

She made some tea. She was not sure against whom she was the maddest – Hitler and the Nazis, or the British Government, which had been given the date and the plan of the invasion two months earlier and had done nothing. She wondered what Holger was thinking down in Brazil? He'd given up everything – his life, his friends and family in Munich. He even gave up his name and had to move to South America – all to try to prevent the invasion of Czechoslovakia, and it had all been for nothing. She feared that worse things were coming.

That evening, Nigel phoned her from Washington. "I presume you heard the news today about the invasion of Czechoslovakia yesterday. A sad business."

"Yes, very sad indeed."

"Details are very sparse at the moment, but it doesn't look good for the Czech Army."

"I'm sure it doesn't. Too bad they didn't have advance warning of the German attack," she snidely added.

"We both know that we're now one step closer to a

European-wide war, which will involve England. I'm sure my friends back there in London are going to need the aid of clever people like you in the near future. I hope…"

Mary Beth silently shook her head and put down the receiver. She went back into her study and returned to work on her next children's story. Riley had just met a new friend in the garden – a very good man named Holger.

Printed in the United States
By Bookmasters